By Peter Abrahams

Novels

The Fan
Lights Out
Revolution # 9
Pressure Drop
Hard Rain
Red Message
Tongues of Fire
The Fury of Rachel Monette

Nonfiction

Turning the Tide:
One Man Against The Medellin Cartel
(with Sidney Kirkpatrick)

THE FAN

PETER ABRAHAMS

WARNER BOOKS

A Time Warner Company

WARNER BOOKS EDITION

Warner Books, Inc.
1271 Avenue of the Americas
New York, NY 10020

Visit our web site at
http://pathfinder.com/twep

 A Time Warner Company

Printed in the United States of America

Originally published in hardcover by Warner Books.
First Paperback Printing: May, 1996
Reissued: August, 1996
10 9 8 7 6 5 4 3

To Di, Rosie, Lily, Ben, and Seth

Acknowledgments

I am grateful to Keith Bartling, Ky Dewan, and Mike de Punte for technical advice; and many, many thanks to Molly Friedrich, Bill Malloy, and Joel Gotler.

The beast won't go to sleep.
—"I'm Your Man," Leonard Cohen

1

"Who's next? Gil on the car phone? What's shakin', Gil?"

Dead air.

"Speak, Gil."

"Is this . . ."

"Go on."

"Hello?"

"You're on the JOC."

"Am I on?"

"Not for long, Gil, the way we're going. This is supposed to be entertainment."

Dead air.

"Got a question or a comment for us, Gil?"

"First-time caller."

"Fantabulous. What's on your mind?"

"I'm a little nervous.

"What's to be nervous? Just three million pairs of ears out there, hanging on your every word. What's the topic?"

"The Sox."

"I like the way you say that."

"How do I say it?"

"Like—what *else* could it be?"

Dead air.

"What about the Sox, Gil?"

"Just that I'm psyched, Bernie."

"Bernie's off today. This is Norm. Everybody gets psyched in the spring. That's a given in this game. Like ballpark mustard."

"This is different."

"How?"

Dead air.

"Gil?"

"I've been waiting a long time."

"For what?"

"This year.

"What's special about it?"

"It's their year."

"Why so tentative?"

"Tentative?"

"Just pulling your leg. The way you sound so sure. Like it's a lead-pipe cinch. The mark of the true-blue fan."

Dead air.

"Gil?"

"Yeah?"

"The Vegas odds are—what are they, Fred? Fred in the control room there, doing something repulsive with a pastrami on rye—ten to one on the Sox for the pennant, twenty, what is it, twenty-five to one on the whole shebang. Just to give us some perspective on this, Gil, what would you wager at those odds, if you were a wagering man?"

"Everything I owe."

"Owe? Hey. I like this guy. He's got a sense of humor

after all. But, Gil—you're setting yourself up for a season of disillusion, my friend."

"Disillusion?"

"Yeah, like—"

"I know what *disillusion* means.

"Do you? Then you must—"

"They went down to the wire last year, didn't they?"

"Ancient history, Gil."

"And now they've got Rayburn on top of it."

"Rayburn, Rayburn. Sheesh. Everybody wants to talk about the Rayburn signing. He's not the Messiah, good people. He's not coming down from heaven with a Louisville Slugger raised on high. On Opening Day, he's flying in on the team charter from Orlando, plugged into his Walkman. Puts on his pants one leg at a time, just like you and—"

"For Christ's sake, he—"

"Can't say that on the air, Gil. And I can cut you off by pressing this little button right here."

"Don't. The kid's—"

"What kid? He turns thirty-two in July. That's middle-aged in this—"

"—averaging a hundred and twenty-three RBIs for the past three years playing on that piece of—"

"Watch it—"

"—dung outfit—can I say *dung*?"

"*Dung's* okay."

"—they've got out there. What kind of numbers is he going to put up in the bandbox, and with that sweet swing of his?"

"Who knows? Check out the record on free agents, my friend, especially the happy-go-lucky ones taking home the cabbage he signed for. Not so sweet, honeylike swing or not."

"Why are you so g—"

"Don't get ugly, Gil. Come on now. 'Fess up. You honestly in the bottom of your heart believe he's worth what they shelled out? Answer me that."

Dead air.

"Hello? Hello? Lost Gil. Let's go to Donnie, downtown. You're on JOC-Radio, Donnie, WJOC, fifty thousand non-stop watts of clear-channel sports talk, twenty-four hours a day, seven days a week, fifty-two weeks a year. What's shakin'?"

2

Gil parked his 325i a block from the office, thinking too late of things he could have said to Bernie, or Norm, or whoever the hell it was. Order book and sample case in hand, he stepped out onto the icy sidewalk as the first snowflakes drifted down around him, hardly bigger than dust motes. It didn't look like the start of a major storm, didn't feel like the beginning of a bad day. Two teenaged boys slouched by, caps pulled low over their eyes. They noticed his license plate—WNSOX—and he heard one say, "Yeah, right."

Gil bought a Lottabucks Kwikpik and the *Sporting News* at the ground-floor newsstand and skimmed the training-camp reports on the elevator. There was a photograph of Rayburn smiling beside the batting cage. The caption read, "Banking all those RBI'$." Gil folded the paper and slid it into his coat pocket.

Ding. Five. Gil walked down the hall, the floor sticky under his feet. The company's office was next to Prime National

Mortgage, which had been vacant all winter, and another suite, without lettering on the door, tenantless much longer. He went in. Bridgid was at her desk, unwrapping a bouquet of roses. She pricked her finger, said, "Ow," and sucked on it.

"Hi," Gil said. "Tickets in yet?"

The company had season tickets, two box seats halfway down the first baseline, eighteen rows back. The reps divided them according to a complicated formula that was revised every season and this year had alloted Opening Day to Gil.

"Have to ask Garrity," said Bridgid. Was there something funny about the way she said it? Funny enough, anyway, to register with Gil in passing.

Gil entered the conference room. Sales meetings began at eight sharp, second Wednesday of the month. They were all sitting around the table—the eleven other Northeast reps, and Garrity, regional sales manager. The room smelled of aftershave. Garrity's eyes went from Gil to the wall clock, as though he were willing him to look at it too. Gil looked. 8:04.

He sat down. Figuerido, area six, just west of his, rolled a tube of Lifesavers across the table; the kind with all the flavors. Gil took one—cherry—and rolled them back to Figgy. Breakfast.

"How's the Beamer?" Figgy asked in a loud whisper; Figgy was stoked on Gil's wheels.

Gil made a hand movement like a car speeding down a winding road and sucked on the Lifesaver, waiting for Garrity to get on with it. Garrity always began with a gloomy summation of how they were doing, followed by an uplifting anecdote from his past about how he'd come up off the canvas when all hope was gone and fought his way to victory, hawking vacuum cleaners in Southie or some shit. That was to inspire them before he handed out the new quotas. But Garrity wasn't on commission now, he was management, and management had no idea what it was like out there. That was fact one.

Garrity's phone buzzed. He picked it up, listened, said

"Yup." He turned to the door. O'Meara walked in. O'Meara was the national sales manager. He flew in from Cincinnati once a year, took them all to dinner. But a year wasn't up since his last visit; and it wasn't dinnertime.

"Welcome, Keith," Garrity said, rising.

O'Meara ignored him. He made a little beckoning motion with his finger—at Waxman, at Larsen, at Figuerido. They followed him from the room. Figgy forgot his Lifesavers on the table.

"Bonus time already?" someone said. No one laughed. December was bonus time; besides, you had to make quota first, and who was doing that?

Silence until O'Meara returned, followed by three people—white males, like Waxman, Larsen, and Figuerido, dressed in $150 suits like Waxman, Larsen, and Figuerido, but not Waxman, Larsen, and Figuerido. O'Meara introduced them. They took their places in the empty chairs. The one who sat in Figgy's glanced at the Lifesavers but didn't touch them.

O'Meara moved to the head of the table. Garrity slid out of his seat. O'Meara could have been Garrity's upwardly mobile son, better fed and better educated. He put his foot on Garrity's chair and leaned over the table. "Guys," he said. "I've seen the figures." He paused. Gil smelled someone's sweat. Not his: he was cool and dry, not sweating at all. In fact, Gil's mind wasn't even on whatever was about to go down. He was remembering an at bat he'd had against the Yankees, one he hadn't thought of in years. Man on second—must have been Claymore, Gil could still see him, red hair, freckles—last ups, two strikes, two out, one run down, pitch on the way. He almost felt the sunshine.

O'Meara had brightened suddenly, as though struck by an idea. "Unless it's a misprint," he was saying. He turned to Garrity. "Any chance it's a misprint?"

"Wish it was.

"Me too," said O'Meara. "Because these numbers suck." He

sat down; Garrity drew up another chair beside him. O'Meara paused again, and in that pause met their gazes one by one. He had small green eyes, set deep in crowfooted pink pouches. "Oh, I know what you're thinking—what a prick, expecting us to sell into this manure-pile economy, expecting us to compete with those Japs gobbling up the whole fucking business. Am I right?"

Nods from the three new men, various facial expressions from the others, nothing from Gil.

"Hit it on the head or what?" said Garrity.

O'Meara didn't respond. He held up his index finger. His hands were small and plump, not even big enough to grip a baseball properly, Gil thought with contempt. "Let's take the economy first. Does the expression *self-fulfilling prophecy* mean anything to anybody?" His eyes fastened on Gil. "Renard?"

"Nope," Gil said, almost adding, Maybe it means something to Figgy.

"You were going to say?"

"Nothing."

O'Meara didn't take his eyes off him. "The thing is, Renard, all the pissing and moaning about the economy swells up into one big pig of an excuse. *Self. Fulfilling. Prophecy.* If the economy sucks, well, hell, how can I be expected to beat my quota, or even meet it, for Christ's sake? Not my fault, right? So you don't even try anymore, and then the economy really is in the toilet. Like lemmings, right? Whoosh. Boom." He gestured out the window. It needed washing. Beyond it gray flakes, fatter now, swirled out of a dark sky. "That's the beauty of our system, curse and beauty at the same time. We control it. Us. Guys like you and me, the folks in this room, up to our elbows in the machinery. We're the ones who can make the economy whatever we want."

Gil watched the snowflakes. A fastball, it had been, low and away, but too close to take. He'd slapped it to right, past the diving second baseman, whose name he couldn't recall. He remembered the pitcher though: Bouchard, the Yankee ace. And he remembered the roar of the crowd as Claymore scored the tying run and he himself went all the way to third when they overthrew the cutoff.

"Let me give you an example," O'Meara said. "Would you stand up, Verrucci?"

The man who now presided over Figgy's Lifesavers rose.

"Verrucci's come up from Texas to lend a hand for a while in area six. Mind telling us your take for the month of Feb?"

"Feb just passed, Mr. O'Meara?"

"That's right, Verrucci."

Verrucci named a figure Gil had never touched, not even when things were steaming during the Reagan years.

"Pay much attention to the state of the economy, Verrucci?"

"Don't have the time, Mr. O'Meara."

O'Meara laughed. "Ignorance is bliss." He studied his audience. "Still with us, Renard?"

Gil nodded, thinking, Texas, that explained everything.

Verrucci was still standing. "Thank you, Verrucci. Sit down." Verrucci sat, picked up the Lifesavers, peeled back the wrapper, and popped one in his mouth.

"Enough philosophy," O'Meara said. He raised a second finger. "Which brings us to the Japs." He smiled. "I think we've finally got something that'll help you with them." He reached inside his jacket and pulled out a knife. It was a tanto, about eleven inches, with a six-inch blade and a red-white-and-blue-checkered polymer handle. He held it high, like a king leading his men into battle, then nodded to Verrucci.

Verrucci left the room. O'Meara took off his jacket, rolled up his sleeve, and passed the blade lightly down his forearm, shaving off an inch-wide strip of wiry, rust-colored hair. It fell on the open pages of Garrity's appointment book.

Verrucci returned with a car door. Japanese?—Gil wondered. Verrucci laid it on the table. O'Meara opened his briefcase, took out a claw hammer, positioned the knife a few inches below the door handle, and began pounding on the pommel. Pounding hard; a sweat stain spread over his right armpit, and his face pinkened in pleasure. Ten blows—Gil counted them, too many—and the blade sank down to the choil. With a grunt, Verrucci stood the door on end, showing the tip of the blade protruding through a speaker grille inside. O'Meara jerked the knife free, extended his forearm, cut another swath. Garrity watched the wiry hairs falling on his appointment book.

O'Meara passed the knife around the table. "Say hello to the Survivor," he said. "State-of-the-art workhorse of our new state-of-the-art line."

"A new line?" someone said.

"The Iwo Jima Experience," O'Meara replied. "Doesn't that say it all?"

The reps hefted the Survivor, ran their thumbs across its edge, balanced it on their index fingers. All but Gil: he just handed it on to the next man. But that was enough to tell him that the Survivor wasn't state of the art, or even an improvement on the rest of their product: two or three grades below that. Blade too thin—quarter inch, when similar Japanese models were all five-sixteenths; pommel too small; light in the handle, indicating a half tang hidden in there. The spec sheet followed: 440 steel, acceptable, if inferior to the Japanese, and hardened to 61 on the Rockwell scale, an impressive number, but much too hard for a survival knife. Better, though, than junk; and maybe some buyers would go for that flashy handle.

The Survivor came back around to O'Meara. "Who thinks they can sell this baby?"

"Banzai," said Verrucci.

"That's the ticket," O'Meara said. "Renard?"

"Depends on the price," Gil answered, thinking: why me today?

"Thirty-seven seventy-five."

Wholesale. That kicked retail to $70, $75, even $80. Would the Survivor sell at that kind of price? Gil had no idea. He didn't know why any of their stuff sold at any price.

"What's the commission?" Gil said.

O'Meara made a face, as though he didn't like talking about money. "Twelve and a half."

"For a new line?"

"Cincinnati thinks it's more than fair. Any objections?"

There were none.

"Then let's get it done."

O'Meara packed up his claw hammer and left for the airport. Garrity handed out new catalogues that included the Iwo Jima line, gave them each a Survivor for their sample cases, and wished them luck. The reps filed out, all except Gil.

Garrity blew O'Meara's hairs off his appointment book.

"Tickets in yet?" Gil said.

"Tickets?"

"Sox."

Garrity studied the ruined car door, still lying on the conference table. "What am I going to do with this fucking thing?"

"Bridgid said to ask you."

Garrity looked up. "No tickets this year, boyo."

"They didn't come in?"

"They came in, all right. And we sold them off—to Marriott, Gillette, couple others."

"Sold them?"

"At cost."

"Why?"

"Orders."

"Whose orders?"

"Cincinnati. Who else gives orders?"

"But I already promised all mine to clients." Not entirely true, but he had promised some. "You're making us look like assholes."

"Boyo. You got other things to worry about."

"Like?"

"I'll let you in on a secret—you came this close." Garrity held up his hand, thumb and index finger almost touching. "This close. To being out on the street. O'Meara had you on the list with the rest of them when he flew in last night. I talked him out of it. Don't make me regret it."

"Thanks, massa."

"Fuck off."

They glared at each other. Gil picked up the Survivor lying on the table in front of him, flipped it in his sample case, and walked out. Bridgid was crying at her desk. Right. She had a thing with Figgy. Saving for a down payment, or fertility treatments, or something.

"I got you one month," Garrity called after him. Gil kept going. Garrity raised his voice. "He had your replacement on the plane with the others. Flew him back this morning. At company expense. Hear what I'm saying to you?"

Gil didn't answer.

"Make your quota, you son of a bitch."

Gil rode alone in the elevator. When was the last time he'd made quota? He couldn't remember. But no one else was making it either. Maybe down in Texas, blade heaven, but not here. The reps saw each other's numbers every month in *The Cutting Edge,* the company fact sheet. It never mentioned two facts: the product and the job—they both sucked. Gil slapped at the elevator buttons, as though he were slapping O'Meara's face, lighting every floor. That got rid of some of what was building inside, made him wonder if he should feel grateful to Garrity. Garrity had saved his job, hell, given it to him in the first place. But that was all because of the old man, and what they'd done to him. He didn't feel grateful.

Outside the snow was falling harder, hard enough now to accumulate, rounding edges, muffling city sound. Gil brushed off the windshield of the 325i with his bare hand—left hand, not pitching hand, by long habit—got in, drove off. Car time. Was it Figgy who said he got his best ideas on the road? What was Figgy thinking now? Gil knew he should be thinking too, specifically about how to find another job. What were the jobs again?

The amazing thing—like a magic trick—was that he'd stolen home on the very next pitch. No signal from the dugout, no sign from the third-base coach, no forethought at all, not even in his own mind. Just—zoom. Like that. Now he could scarcely believe it.

Someone honked. Gil honked back, checked the time. 10:45. He always made an eleven o'clock call on Everest and Co. after sales meeting. Everest and Co. was his biggest client: twenty-five outlets, eighty million in sales, excluding the catalogue. "Hit them while you're still hyped from the meeting," Garrity had advised long ago.

"I'm hyped," Gil said aloud. If he was going to make quota, Everest and Co. was where to start. Traffic wasn't bad and Gil was making good time—he'd grown up driving in snow— so good he decided to swing by the ballpark on his way. The problem was that he'd promised Opening Day to Richie.

Gil stopped in front of the box office, jumped out, left the car running. Only one ticket booth was open. An old man with watery eyes and a runny nose sat in it, staring into space. Gil knocked on the glass.

"Two grandstand seats for the opener," he said. "Reds if you got 'em."

The old man grinned savagely. "Reds if I got 'em? Opening Day?"

"Anything in the grandstand, then."

"Grandstand? I got nuttin' in the grandstand. Nuttin' in the bleachers. Nuttin' in the obstructed views. Nuttin'." He leaned a little closer. "What's more, I got nuttin' in the grandstand till the twenty-first. Of August. And that's last row."

"What about the bleachers?"

The old man looked furious. "Opening Day?"

Gil nodded.

"Cripes. What did I just finish tellin' you? Nuttin'. Can't know much about baseball think you can just swan in here 'n get seats for Opening Day."

"I know baseball," Gil said, maybe louder than he'd intended. The old man yanked down the shade.

Gil turned away. A man in a watch cap was leaning against the brick wall near the Gate B sign.

"Lookin' for tickets?" he said.

"Opening Day."

The man came forward. His nose was runny too; a silver drop of phlegm quivered from the tip. "How many?"

"Two."

He pulled a fistful from his pocket, leafed through them. Snowflakes melted on his fingers. "Got a pair right behind home plate, three rows back."

"How much?"

"One-fifty."

Gil thought: about his bank balance, near zero; his plastic, maxed out; his child-support and car payments, due; then realized he probably didn't even have one-fifty on him. While he was thinking, the man added:

"Each."

Gil walked away. "Two seventy-five for the pair," the man called after him. Gil got in his car, but slowly, giving the man time to lower the price again. The man didn't say another word; he returned to his post near the Gate B sign, wiping his nose on the back of his sleeve.

Gil took out his wallet and counted the money inside. One twenty-three. Problem was he'd promised Richie. He slid down the window. "Take a check?"

"You nuts?"

Traffic thickened, and Gil didn't arrive at Everest and Co. until 11:25. Took the sample case, the order book, the Iwo

Jima catalogue, the Survivor, rode the elevator, said, "Hi, Angie," to the purchasing VP's secretary—know the names of the secretaries, that was basic—and handed her his card.

Angie handed it back. "He's gone."

"When'll he be back?"

"For the day."

"That's funny. We had an appointment."

"At eleven."

Don't ever fight with a client, Gil told himself. But he couldn't stop himself from saying, "Looked out the window today?"

"I suggest you call to reschedule."

Gil sat in the 325i, parked outside Everest and Co. He liked sitting in his car, liked the smell, no longer a new smell, but a nice one of leather and wax. He liked the sound system, the phone, the light that came through the moon roof, now covered in snow. He just sat there, running the engine, staying warm, not thinking about where the next car payment was coming from—he already knew what the answer to that had to be—or about O'Meara, or Richie, or Opening Day. After a while a plow came up behind him, and he slipped the Beamer into gear. He didn't have another call till three—The Cutler's Corner, downtown. Only a few blocks from Cleats. He was hungry.

Gil had lunch at Cleats: potato skins and a draft. Leon was behind the bar and "Sportswrap" on the big screen. The commentator was going over Rayburn's contract: $2.5 million signing bonus, half this year, half next, $5.05 million the first year, $5.45 million the next, $5.85 million the year after that, with an option year of $6.05 million if he reached five hundred at bats in the last year. There were also incentive bonuses, based on winning the MVP or any parts of the Triple Crown, and a separate $1 million fund to provide deferred payments starting in 2007.

Leon shook his head.

"Why not?" Gil said. "He's going to take them all the way."

Leon kept shaking his head. "What's that oh-five million shit, anyway?"

"Fifty grand."

Leon laughed. "I don't even make that. Not close. Not close to his piddly little tacked-on oh-five. And I'm working three jobs, if you count that sanitation scam."

Gil had another draft, then one more. He walked into The Cutler's Corner at three on the dot. There was no one inside except the owner, smoking a cigarette at the back. He started to put it out, recognized Gil, kept smoking. Just one more thing Gil hated about his job.

The Cutler's Corner wasn't a big client, usually good for a two- or three-hundred-dollar order. Gil took out the sample case, showed the owner everything, including the Iwo Jima catalogue. The owner examined the Survivor. "Not a bad handle." He ordered one.

"What else can I do for you?"

"Nothing else."

"That's it?"

"This time."

"But what about reorders on our other lines? The Clip-its—you've always done well with them."

"Not lately." The owner waved at the display cases. "Nothing's moving except the Jap stuff, and not enough of that."

Gil wrote the order: one Survivor, gross $37.75, commission $4.72.

Four dollars and seventy-two cents. A day's work. Less what he'd spent at Cleats, on parking, lottery ticket, *Sporting News*, gas. But you couldn't think like that, couldn't think minus, not in his business. You got in the car. You kept plugging.

Gil got in the car. He drove home. Snow was still falling, the roads jammed. It took him an hour.

Home was a studio at the back of the second floor of a peeling three-decker west of the ring road. He had a bed, a floor lamp, a chest of drawers with a photograph of Richie on top. He opened the bottom drawer, felt under the clothing, took out what was left of his inheritance.

Two knives, both from his father's forge. The first was a Damascus-steel bowie, with a foot-long blade and an ivory handle, probably dating from the forties. The second, not quite as old, was a heavy, soft-steel thrower, almost as big as the bowie, with a double-edged blade and a leather leg sheath. Gil held them under the lamp. He hadn't looked at them in a long time, had forgotten their beauty, especially the beauty of that Damascus steel: its patterns like waves on a shining sea. A work of art. But it would have to be the bowie. The thrower wasn't worth much more than a few hundred; barely enough for the tickets.

Gil switched off the lamp and lay on the bed with the knives beside him. He gazed at his view, an alley backed by a brick wall. The light began to fail. He heard the front door open, heard footsteps on the stairs. Lenore. Would she come down the hall, knock on the door? She didn't. The footsteps kept going, up the next flight, then overhead. Her shoes thumped on the floor above, one, two.

He'd stolen home, just like that. Hard to believe, but he could summon memories: the catcher, lunging at him through the dust raised by his slide, too late; the umpire, bent so close to the ground he brushed his leg making the safe sign; the batter, just standing there, mouth open. The game was over. They carried him off the field on their shoulders. The sun shone down from a clear blue sky. Absolute fact.

Or was that the game where he'd still had to come back and pitch the bottom of the last inning? He wasn't sure. His mind flashed an image of himself on the mound, of the ball tracing a blurred path toward Boucicaut's black mitt. He'd been able to put it anywhere he wanted, and he'd had a gun for an arm, especially when it wasn't sore. But it had been sore almost all the time.

Gil was close to sleep when he heard a noise in the far corner of the room, near the dresser; so close that he almost incorporated it in his dream and did nothing. But he sat up, and saw something moving in the shadows. He switched the floor lamp back on.

A mouse. Scared by the light, or the sound of the switch, it ran toward the dresser, toward the darkness underneath, and safety. Distance fifteen feet, turning cycle about twice that: the thrower was in Gil's hand. He hadn't thrown a knife in a long time, but it all came back—the bent-back angle of the wrist, the acceleration, the snapless release. The knife made half a revolution as it flashed across the room and stuck deep in the floor, cutting the mouse in half. The tail end twitched for a moment, then went still.

Gil had a funny thought: there's nothing wrong with my arm now. He turned off the light.

3

" . . . by Bud and Bud Lite."

"Hey. We're back. We'll have the scores, but first let's take a call from Manny in—"

Bobby Rayburn rolled over, hit the slumber button, and tried to go back to sleep. Normally he couldn't; when he was up he was up, end of story, but this morning he awoke still tired from yesterday's cross-country trip and probably could have eased back into sleep, if he hadn't had to piss so bad. After a minute or two he gave up, got out of bed. The curtains in his room at the Flamingo Bay Motor Inn and Spa were drawn, but not completely: a shaft of light penetrated the darkness, falling across the shoulder and face of the girl sleeping in the bed. Bobby tried to remember her name.

He went into the bathroom and pissed. He felt good. A little hung over, but good. The rib-cage thing was all better, or just about. He saw his reflection in the mirror: he was in shape, in great shape considering it was only March.

Back in the bedroom, the phone was ringing. He answered it. "Yeah?"

"Morning, big guy." It was Wald. "How was the flight?"

"Fine."

"How's that rib cage?"

"Fine."

"Hungry?"

"Starving."

"Pick you up in fifteen minutes, if that's okay."

"Yeah."

"Got a little surprise for you."

"What?"

"You'll see."

The girl opened her eyes. They were on him right away. She gave him a long look. Oh, Christ.

"Good morning, Bobby," she said.

"Morning, babe."

She sat up, exposing her breasts. Nice ones.

"Last night was fantastic, Bobby."

"Yeah." Or *thanks;* should he have said thanks? Or that it was fantastic for him too? Yeah. That was probably it. Too late. He recalled how she'd come over to him in the bar, while the front-desk people took care of his bags; or maybe that was another time, another girl, and this one had been waiting by the pool when he'd left the bar and walked across the inner court to his room.

Under the sheets, her lower body made a grinding motion. "Feels early," she said. "Coming back to bed?" Her nipples hardened, just like that.

"Sorry," he told her. "Got to run."

"When'll you be back?"

"Late." She didn't take the hint. "Maybe you better get going too."

She bit her lip. "How about a little kiss good-bye?"

Bobby leaned over and gave her a little kiss. She smelled

of sex. He considered and rejected a peck on the forehead, went with a lip kiss, but closemouthed and quick. She had other ideas; turning his kiss into something else, and taking hold of his dick.

"Mmm," she said.

They left the room together. Wald was parked outside in his Targa with the 6 PRCNT vanity plate.

"Bye, Bobby," she said. "See you sometime."

"Bye."

He got into the car. Wald was smiling. "Nice," he said, watching the girl hurry off, tossing her hair in the sunshine. "Does she have a sister?"

"I don't know."

"Even the mother would probably do."

Bobby was tired of the subject. "Where're we going?"

"Pancake Palace?"

"Sure."

"And then I'll run you over to the facility. They're expecting you at ten-thirty. Photos, handshakes, all that, but no inter-views. BP at eleven. Okay?"

"Sure."

"And last but not least." Wald reached inside his linen jacket, handed Bobby an envelope.

Bobby opened it. Inside was a check in his name, drawn on the Chase Manhattan Bank for $1,175,000. "This is? . . ."

"First half of the signing bonus," Wald said. "Minus the agency fee."

"Oh."

He started to put it in his pocket, but Wald said, "Want me to bank it this afternoon? Shame to lose out on a day's interest."

"What's a day's interest?"

"On this? Hundred and fifty, two hundred bucks, at current rates. Something like that. Maybe we can make a deal."

"You can make a deal on interest rates?"

"It's like Archimedes, Bobby. Get me a lever long enough and I can move the earth. Your job is to—"

"Get you the lever." Bobby handed him the check.

Wald laughed. "No flies on you." The breeze blew through the open roof of the Targa, heavy, hot, humid.

They sat at a booth along the back wall of Pancake Palace. Bobby had blueberry pancakes with maple syrup, OJ, coffee.

"Get ready," Wald said.

A father at a nearby table was nudging his son. The son didn't want to do it. "He won't bite," said the father in a stage whisper, maybe hoping Bobby would look up, smile at the boy, seem approachable, nonbiting. Bobby kept eating, head down.

But still the boy came, holding out a baseball and a pen. Didn't say anything, just laid them by the pancakes. Bobby wrote his name on the ball. Didn't say anything either. Then the father came over, big smile, hitching up his pants, toast crumbs on his lips.

"Gonna hit one out for us this year, Bobby?"

"I'm eating breakfast," Bobby said.

The father, still smiling, laid four or five more balls in front of him. This was a money-making operation. Bobby started to repeat what he'd just said, but Wald, glancing around the room, said, *"Globe's* watching," so Bobby signed the balls.

"All *right,"* said the father, as though about to high-five somebody. Not "thanks." He dropped the balls in a plastic bag.

Wald picked up the check. They got in the Targa, drove south past fast-food places, an alligator farm, a fireworks stand. Wald switched on the radio.

". . . shoulda been running on the play, situation like that. What I can't understand is—"

Bobby switched it off.

"When's Valerie coming?" Wald asked.

Bobby's wife didn't like to be called Val anymore. Bobby kept forgetting, but Wald never did. "School vacation," Bobby said.

"When's that?"

"Don't know. She's supposed to call." Bobby saw a man in rags doing a stiff-legged dance by the side of the road. "What's the surprise?" he asked.

"Surprise?"

"You were talking about on the phone."

"I gave it to you already. The check, Bobby. The bonus."

"Oh."

Wald pulled into the training complex, parked in front of a palm tree with Bobby's name posted on it. Bobby slipped on his headphones, pressed PLAY. They got out. Wald popped the trunk, took out the equipment bag. Bobby looked around. He didn't like Florida, didn't like the heavy air. He liked the air in Arizona, where he'd trained for the last ten years. They walked toward the clubhouse.

"I'll take that," Bobby said. He carried his equipment bag inside.

They were waiting: Mr. Hakimora, the new owner; Thorpe, the GM; Burrows, the manager. Bobby pressed STOP. He shook hands with them, faced the cameras when voices called, "Over here, Bobby," and said, "I'm looking forward to the season," when they asked him how he felt, and, "One-hundred percent," when they asked him about the rib cage, even though there were supposed to be no interviews. Then he went into the clubhouse.

"A little glitch I forgot to mention," Wald said in Bobby's ear as he stood before his stall. Mail was already stacked on the shelf. A dozen bats still taped together for shipping—thirty-two-ounce, thirty-four-and-a-half-inch Adirondack 433B's, unfinished because of Bobby's belief that laquer took English off the ball—leaned in one corner. His spring-training uniform waited on a hanger, white pants and a red-mesh shirt with black-and-white trim. No names were stitched on the backs of the spring shirts because of all the extra players in camp, but there were numbers. They'd given him number twenty-eight.

"No problem," Bobby said. He had worn number eleven ever since freshman year in high school, but they were paying him the big money and he didn't want to make trouble. "I'll just wear sweats today while they get it switched."

Pause. "Regrettably," said Wald, "it's not that simple."

"Why not?"

A sweating man with a sunburned bald head hurried toward them, wiping his hand on his pant leg, then offering it to Bobby.

"Stook," he said. "Equipment manager.

Bobby remembered him from the All-Star locker room in Chicago, a few years before. They shook hands.

"Anything I can do for you, just holler," Stook said.

"As a matter of fact," Bobby said, eyeing the shirt.

"Oh, that's for practice. Your name'll be on the game shirts, home and away, in four-inch letters. Rayburn. We can stretch it out on that back of yours real nice."

"It's not the name," Bobby said. "It's the number."

"The number?"

"I wear eleven."

Stook looked at Wald.

Wald put his hand on Bobby's shoulder. "See, Bobby, there's been a little screwup. Nobody's fault, really. Just one of those things—permutations, if you like—that can happen in complex, drawn-out negotiations. Maybe it should have been brought to the table at the time, but with the kind of numbers—money numbers, I'm talking about—being discussed, it seemed like such an insig—make that lesser—"

"I wear eleven." Bobby shook Wald's hand off his shoulder.

"Thirty-three's available, Bobby," Stook said. "That's three times eleven. And so's forty-one. That's got a one in it."

"Is there some problem with eleven?" Bobby said.

Again Stook looked at Wald. "A bit of one, " Wald said, glancing at a lean man sitting naked on a stool across the room, playing Nintendo. "Primo's already got it."

Primo was the shortstop. Four- or five-year veteran, mediocre stick, magician with the glove: Bobby didn't really know him, but didn't like him much anyway. Once, after Bobby'd doubled against someone in spring training—couldn't remember the pitcher, or even the season—Primo had made a remark in Spanish to the second baseman. Bobby didn't understand Spanish, but he hadn't liked the sound of it all the same, or the arrogant expression in Primo's eyes; like some conquistador, although there was more Indian and black than Spaniard in Primo.

"Better talk to him," Bobby said. "I'll wear sweats for today."

"Who's his agent?" Wald said.

"I can find out," Stook replied.

"Never mind," Wald told him. "I'll take care of it."

Bobby hung his clothes in the stall, getting a whiff of the girl as he did so, then opened his equipment bag and dressed: sleeves first, then jock, sanitaries, stirrups, the white uniform pants, cleats, and finally, just for today, a USA sweat shirt he still had from a Japan winter tour a few seasons before. His gear always went on in that precise order.

Bobby cut the tape from the bats, hefted a few, chose the one his hands liked the best, then walked onto the field and stood by the batting cage. Burrows himself was behind the screen in front of the mound, throwing BP. Bobby watched some big kid take his cuts. At first he looked good, driving a few sharply to left. Then Bobby noticed that it was all arms; his feet were too quick, taking his body right out of the swing.

"Bobby?" said someone behind him.

Bobby turned, saw a woman with a tape recorder.

"Jewel Stern from JOC-Radio," she said. "Got time for a few questions?"

"Okay," Bobby said, forgetting for a moment—was it because he'd noticed flaws in the big kid's swing, or because the reporter was good-looking, even if a little older than his usual type?—that there weren't supposed to be interviews.

"Right here's fine," the reporter said. "Get that thwack of bat on ball. One of my favorite ambient sounds."

"Mine too."

"Yeah?" She gave him a quick glance. He said nothing.

The reporter—he'd forgotten her name—started adjusting her equipment. "What do you think of the phenom?" she asked, checking her levels.

"What phenom?"

She jerked her head at the kid in the batting cage. "Simkins. They thought he was a year or two away, now it's even money he'll go north."

"Yeah?" Bobby said.

The kid skyed one to right and stepped out of the cage. Burrows motioned at Bobby.

"Try your luck, Mr. Rayburn?" he said.

"There," said the reporter. "All set."

"Got to go," Bobby told her.

"One quick question." She spoke into her mike: "Do you feel under any special pressure because of the big contract this year, Bobby?" She thrust the mike at him.

"No," he said, walking toward the cage with his bat on his shoulder.

She followed him. "But what about the fans?"

"What about them?"

"Won't the money raise their expectations?"

"The fans," said Bobby, "are what it's all about."

"What do you mean by that?"

Bobby, stepping into the cage, didn't reply.

He stood in the batter's box, touched the middle of the

plate with the bat, took his stance, looked out. All at once, as though he were waking from a nap, everything was defined with exaggerated clarity, like objects in a coffee table book: the silvery whiskers on Burrows's face, the loping and shagging shadows of the outfielders on the deep-green grass, the glints of sunshine on the chain-link fence, the waxy leaves of the fake-looking palm trees beyond.

"Not going to hurt me now, are you, Bobby?" said Burrows. Had he been a pitcher, long ago? Bobby wasn't sure. Burrows fed him a fat one. First pitch of the season—so clear—and Bobby was surprised by a sudden physical tingling, not unlike the feeling when you know you're going to get laid, just a little higher up inside him. Bobby waited on that coffee table pitch, maybe a hair too long, and smashed it off the screen right in front of Burrows's chest.

"Jesus Christ," said Burrows.

Bobby smiled.

Burrows dipped into the ball basket, put a little more on the next one. This time Bobby didn't wait long enough, but got a good piece, one-hopping the fence in left center. Then he found his timing, or it found him; he felt that almost imperceptible tightening along the outside of his left leg and around the left side of his torso that always meant his swing was right. Down the left-field line. Off the top of the fence in left center. Over the fence in center. Over the fence in right center. Over the fence in left. Over the phony palm trees in center. Off the screen in front of Burrows, who flinched, after the fact.

"Jesus Christ."

Bobby stepped out. The phenom stepped in, trying not to see him. Jesus Christ. Bobby almost spoke the words aloud. Day one, and he was there already. He felt absurdly strong, as though he could do a thousand pushups, or hop the ten-foot fence himself. They got him cheap.

The phenom took his cuts. Not so good this time. Bobby

saw that Burrows wasn't throwing any harder, probably couldn't, but that he was moving the ball around, up and in, down and out; looking for weaknesses, and finding some. The phenom bounced a few through the unmanned infield, fouled one off, and another, and another, then nubbed one that rolled weakly to the foot of Burrows's screen.

" 'Kay," Burrows said.

Phenom out, Bobby in.

"Outside," Bobby said. Burrows sent one over the outside half. Bobby drilled it down the right-field line. He drove the next one between first and second, lined the one after that over Burrow's head, pulled the last two, one to straight-away left, one down the line.

"Inside," Bobby said, and he worked his way back around, lining the last one, the toughest one, inside-out over first base.

"Gonna have us a little fun this year," Burrows said.

Bobby stepped out. Contract pressure? They got him cheap.

He ran for a while in the outfield, stretched, ran some more, shagged. After an hour or so, he went into the clubhouse, showered, changed. The number twenty-eight shirt was gone from his stall, but nothing hung in its place.

Bobby went to the buffet, made himself a sandwich, took a beer. Primo, wearing a towel, came to the other side of the table, made a sandwich, took a beer, didn't look at him. Bobby was trying to decide whether he should say something and, if so, what, when someone behind him said:

"Bobby?"

Bobby turned, saw a skinny little guy with glasses and frizzy hair.

"Hi," he said and spoke his name, which Bobby didn't catch. "I'm the DCR—director of community relations."

Bobby shook hands; was doing a lot of handshaking today, now that he thought about it, and getting tired of it. He tried to remember if Wald had his clubs in the trunk.

"Wonder if you could do me a very special favor, Bobby," the skinny guy said.

"What's that?"

"We got a call about this kid. They've got a thing at the hospital here, what's it called?" He took a notebook from his blazer pocket. " 'The Wish Upon a Star Benefit Program,' " he read. "It's for sick kids, really sick—terminal, that type of situation." Bobby looked over the skinny guy's shoulder; Wald had come in, speaking on a portable phone. The DCR talked faster. "Anyway, the idea is these kids get to make a kind of last wish, and the folks in the program try to make it come true. Within reason. The thing is this kid wants to see you."

Wald was laughing into his portable phone. "What kid?" Bobby said.

The DCR checked his notebook. "Looks like john something. Can't read my own writing."

Bobby started to walk away. "Sure," he said. "Maybe. Sometime."

The DCR followed him. "Don't mean to be a pest, Bobby, but the problem is, if you're going to do it, it's going to have to be soon. Very soon. Like tonight."

"Tonight?"

"The nurse or whoever it was said he might not be strong enough later."

Wald clicked off his phone, stuck it in his monogrammed shirt pocket. "All set?" he said.

"I don't know," Bobby answered.

"You don't know?"

"It's about this kid," the DCR said and explained it all over again.

Bobby and the DCR waited for Wald's reaction. "It's up to you, Bobby," he said.

"Up to me?"

"If you want to do it or not."

Bobby turned to the DCR. "What is it, exactly?"

"Just a hospital visit. It's about fifteen minutes away. I can run you over right now, if you want."

Did Bobby want to do it? No. But he found himself saying, "All right." He knew why, too: because he'd been seeing the ball so well, made such a good beginning, didn't want to screw it up. Made no sense, but that was the reason.

"Fantastic," said the DCR, and Bobby realized he'd just earned the DCR some points with his boss, whoever that was.

Wald checked his watch. "This'll work okay, actually. I've got a meeting, the bank, make a few calls—we'll still have time to play nine." He turned to the DCR. "You know the Three Pines C.C.? Drop him there by three."

"Got my clubs?" Bobby said.

"I'm your man," said Wald. He hurried out.

The DCR rubbed his hands. "Fantastic," he said again.

"Should we take some balls?" Bobby asked. "For the kid?"

The DCR thought about it. "Maybe a bat would be nicer, for something like this."

"One of my bats?"

"Oh, I'm sure any bat'll be fine."

But why not one of his own? He had an unlimited free supply. Bobby went to his stall, glanced at the bats, selected one he knew his hands wouldn't like, just by the pattern of the grain on the handle. "We'll give him this," Bobby said.

"That's awfully nice of you, Bobby."

The DCR drove Bobby to the hospital. "Great to have you here, Bobby," he said on the way. "It's my first year with the organization too."

"Where were you before?"

"Wharton."

Bobby hadn't played a day in the minors. He couldn't place it.

* * *

A nurse met them at the front door. "So nice of you to come, Mr. Rayburn," she said, offering her hand and holding onto Bobby's for an extra moment. Not a fox like the girl from last night, but not bad looking at all.

The nurse led Bobby and the DCR, who carried the bat, into an elevator. They rode up a few floors, people getting in and out, shooting glances at Bobby from the sides of their eyes; then walked down a brightly lit, airless corridor and into a room. The DCR gave the bat to Bobby.

A heavy woman sat in a chair, fingering the crucifix that hung around her neck. She got to her feet. "Oh, thank God you've come," she said, "thank you, thank you." She seized Bobby's free hand in both of hers; for a second he thought she was about to kiss it.

The woman drew Bobby to the bed. "Look, baby," she said, almost cooing, "look who's come to see you."

The boy in the bed opened his eyes. He seemed small, but not necessarily young. His head was bald, his face hollow and lemon-colored. The boy's eyes, feverish and muddy, fastened on Bobby. He spoke, but too softly for Bobby to hear.

"Pardon?" said Bobby.

The boy took a deep breath; it made him wince. He tried again. This time Bobby heard. "You're my hero."

Bobby didn't know what to say. The feverish, muddy eyes were locked on his.

"Why don't you shake hands with him, baby?" the mother said.

The boy's hand rose an inch or two off the sheets, subsided. Bobby laid his own hand on top. The boy's hand felt hot; Bobby's looked like a work by Michelangelo. "Hi, John," he said.

"It's Sean," the mother said.

"Sorry," said the DCR and muttered, "my goddamn handwriting."

"Sean," Bobby said. It was his own boy's name; he almost winced himself. "I've brought you something." He raised the bat to where the boy could see. Bobby felt the boy's hand straining beneath his. He let go. The boy's hand rose again, an inch or two. Bobby slid the bat underneath.

"Would you sign it for him?" asked the mother.

The DCR gave Bobby a felt pen. Bobby wrote on the barrel, "To Sean"—then what? The pen kept moving, ahead of his thoughts: "a brave kid," and he signed his name. The mother made a sobbing sound, clamped her hand over her face and turned away, but the boy heard. He sighed. The mother grew quiet. The room went silent. Bobby heard breaking glass, far away.

The boy licked his lips. They were cracked and dry, as was his tongue. He took a deep breath and spoke again. "Did you play today?" he said.

"Just practice. We've got a game tomorrow."

"Against who?"

Bobby didn't know.

"The Tigers," said the DCR.

All at once, the boy tried to raise his head, tried to sit up. The cords in his shrunken neck rose, but he got nowhere. He stopped trying, lay panting for a moment or two.

"Bobby?" he said when he recovered his breath.

"Yeah?"

His eyes, muddier, hotter, found Bobby's again. "Hit a home run for me."

Bobby said nothing.

"Please," said the boy.

"I'll try."

"You'll do it," the boy said. "I know you will. You're a superstar."

"I'll try."

The boy smiled a little smile. Then his eyes closed. Was he dead? Bobby almost blurted the thought before the nurse stepped forward, saying, "We'd better let him rest."

They went out into the corridor, leaving the boy lying quietly on the bed, the bat beside him. The mother embraced Bobby, dampening his polo shirt with her face. "Bless you, Mr. Rayburn," she said. "You're like a god to him."

The nurse walked Bobby and the DCR to the elevator. She slipped Bobby a note. He read it on the way down: "I'm off at eight," she'd written over her name and number.

Bobby crumpled it. "Mind if I have that?" said the DCR. Bobby gave it to him, then put on his headphones and pressed PLAY.

Bobby got to the first tee at 2:55. Wald was taking practice swings. "How'd it go?" he asked.

"Okay," said Bobby. "I promised the kid I'd hit one out tomorrow. Like Babe Ruth."

Wald teed up, waggled his driver. "That wasn't the Babe, Bobby. It was William Bendix." He hooked the ball into a grove of scrub pine, not far away.

4

"... and so in a Freudian sense, Bernie, the catcher is the father, and the son is the pitcher. It couldn't be more obvious, once you know the psychoanalytical lay of the land."

"Fascinating, Doc. Running out of time here, absolutely fascinating, I love this stuff, but if what you're saying is true, what's the bat and ball represent?"

"The bat I don't think I need to spell out. The ball symbolizes the family gene pool."

"Gene pool?"

"In the form of ejaculate."

"Meaning?"

"Semen, Bernie. The male fluid."

"Wow. Wish we had more time. Thanks for being on the JOC."

"You're—"

"That was Dr. Helmut Behr, author of *Three Dreams and You're Out: Freud, Jung, Baseball.* We'll be back with all the scores from last night, and the morning spring-training roundup. Don't go away.

Gil, waiting at a red light, turned down the radio, dialed Everest and Co. on the car phone, got through to the purchasing VP.

"Sorry about that screwup yesterday, Chuck," he said. "The weather . . ."

The VP was silent.

"So when can we get together? Can't wait to show you our new Iwo Jima line. Heard about it?"

"No."

Gil glanced down at the catalogue, lying on the seat. "Iwo Jima Experience, the full name. We're taking on the Japanese head to head." Gil waited for the VP to say something. When he didn't, Gil said, "Any chance you're free this afternoon?"

He heard pages riffling. "Tied up until the eighth," said the VP. "Two-thirty."

"The eighteenth, you mean? The eighth was last week."

"Eighth of April."

"Next month?"

"Got it."

"But we always—"

"Taking another call. Bye."

"—meet monthly," Gil said to a dial tone.

Someone honked at him. Green light. He drove through the intersection, fishtailing on an icy patch. The asshole honked again, or maybe another asshole, and Gil honked back.

Make your quota, you son of a bitch. How was he supposed to do that without the monthly order from Everest and Co.? In his anger, Gil pictured himself doing all sorts of things— banging the steering wheel, yelling at the top of his lungs, sideswiping the car in the next lane. He turned up the radio.

"What have you got for us this morning, Jewel, besides a nice suntan?"

"No suntan, Bernie. Do you find melanoma attractive? The

big news down here was the arrival in camp yesterday of high-priced free agent Bobby Rayburn—"

"Norm says the phones were lit up all day."

"As well they might be. It was only batting-practice pitching, but let me tell you something, he looked prodigious. He's got that textbook swing everybody talks about, but what you really don't appreciate until you're up close is the tremendous power he generates. The ball comes off his bat like a firecracker. Sid Burrows was positively beaming, and beaming is not the natural state of Sid's face."

"And that's an understatement. Did you get a chance to talk to him?"

"Rayburn? Briefly, Bernie. Contrary to some reports, he seems very approachable."

"What did he say?"

"I can play that interview if you like."

"Okay. Before we open up the lines."

Gil dialed FANLINE.

"Do you feel under any special pressure because of the big contract this year, Bobby?"

"No."

"But what about the fans?"

"What about them?"

Gil got a dial tone. Someone picked up. "Fanline," he said. "Hold the—" He shouted: "Fifteen seconds." He lowered his voice slightly: "Name?"

"Gil."

"Calling from?"

"Car phone."

"About?"

"Rayburn."

"Know the format? Bernie'll intro you and—hang on. Just a—putting you through . . ."

"Let's take a few calls. Gil on the car phone."

". . . now."

"Hi, Gil."

"Am I on?"

"You're on the JOC."

"Can you hear me?"

"I can hear you fine, Gil. Mind turning down your radio?" Gil turned it down.

"Much better. What's on your mind?"

"Bet you guys are eating crow today."

"How's that, Gil?"

"Based on the way you were running down Rayburn yesterday."

"Easy now. I was in Atlantic City yesterday."

"Your pal Norm, then."

"What's your point? . . . Hello? You still there?"

"Why are you guys so negative all the time? I guess that's my point."

"Negative? I'm a well-known Pollyanna in this business. The thing is, good people—"

"Then why get on Rayburn before the season's even started?" Gil began a second sentence, "If you were as good at your job as he is at his, you'd be—" but stopped when realized he was listening once more to a dial tone. He turned the radio back up.

"—isn't a religion, for God's sake. It's not the Catholic church. Or the Protestant church, for that matter, or the Jewish synagogue, or the Muslim mosque. What am I leaving out? The Buddhist shrine? Temple? Baseball's none of that. It's just—"

The car phone buzzed, and Gil missed whatever baseball was.

"Yeah?" he said.

"Gil?"

"Who's this?"

"Figgy."

"Oh."

"Was that you? On the JOC?"

Gil laughed, embarrassed.

"You shit disturber," Figgy said. Then came a long pause that cost them both money—Gil could hear that Figgy was on his car phone too. "What're you doing right now?" Figgy said.

"Working."

"Oh," said Figgy. Pause. "Thought we might meet somewhere."

"Can't."

"How about tonight? At Cleats."

"I'll try," Gil said.

He swung onto a ramp, walled in on both sides by snow crusted like burned marshmallow skins. Expressway traffic was heavy. Gil didn't mind. He liked challenging the 325i. He stepped on the gas and headed south, changing lanes frequently to pass, being passed by no one, listening to the JOC. Twenty or thirty miles past the city, beyond the suburbs, traffic thinned. Fog flowed in from the sea, first in little tongues through the bare trees, then in high-banked tides. The 325i took over; Gil slumped a little behind the wheel.

Hanging onto a one-run lead against the Tigers. Bases loaded. Two out. Bottom of the twelfth. Pease, the cleanup hitter, at the plate, waggling his huge black bat. Boucicaut comes out for a conference, pushing up his mask; sweat streaks make war-paint patterns on his dusty face. There's a dusky hint of mustache over his upper lip.

"Just throw strikes," he says, handing Gil the ball.

"What do you think I'm trying to do, you idiot?"

Boucicaut stares at him. "Got any gum?"

"No."

Boucicaut pulls down his mask, trudges back behind the plate, squats. Gil glances into the dugout. No one is moving, no one is coming to get him, although that would be fine with him. Gil takes a deep breath, looks at nothing but the round shadow in the center of Boucicaut's black Rawlings, tries to ignore his elbow, sore inside and out. "Just imagine a pipe from you to the catcher," his father always said, "and fling the ball down that pipe. It's simple."

Gil flings the ball down the imaginary pipe. Pease turns on it, catches it square, rockets it down the third-base line, foul. Gil's next two pitches are in the dirt, both blocked by Boucicaut. He takes another deep breath, thinks he hears his father calling from the stands, "C'mon, Gil," but that isn't possible, since his father's in the hospital.

The next pitch just misses the outside corner.

"What's the count?" Gil calls.

The umpire holds up his fingers. Three and one.

Gil stares into the shadow in Boucicaut's mitt, goes into his windup, comes over the top with all his strength. As he lets go, he hears the sound of paper tearing, feels pain like hot barbed wire being drawn through his elbow. Pease hits this one over the fence, foul.

The umpire tosses Gil a new ball, holds up his fingers. Three and two.

Gil rubs the ball in his hands, checks the still dugout. Waiting for his elbow to settle down, he walks around the mound. He knows he can't throw the ball past Pease. He considers his curve. Can't trust it, not on a full count; can't even throw it, not with his arm like this, not with the prospect of what he would feel the instant after. That leaves the change-up, which he doesn't have, and the knuckler he fools around with on the side and has never thrown in a game.

He plants his foot on the rubber, grips the ball with the tips of all four fingers and his thumb. The knuckler. Pease waggles his bat. Gil winds up, puffing out his chest as though he were reaching back for a little extra, and fires.

In the movies, everything happens in slow motion after that. In life, it happens so fast, the swing, the miss, that Gil isn't sure it's all over until Boucicaut, charging out with his arms open wide, knocks him on his back and jumps on him.

Absolute fact; except perhaps for the part about believing he'd heard his father's voice.

The wind had risen, driving away the fog. Gil checked the speedometer, saw he was doing ninety, eased off. Boucicaut. A rock. He'd had his best years with Boucicaut.

Gil crossed the bridge onto the Mid-Cape. He had it almost to himself. The wind blew across the highway but didn't bother the 325i at all. Gil loved the way it handled, loved its smell. He remembered the car payment, due tomorrow, and the years of car payments still to come. He was adding his debts in his mind when he came to the exit, circled off the ramp, and headed for the shore. Couldn't give up the wheels; without wheels, you were dead.

Gil drove past a village green, a stone church, and a seafood restaurant, boarded up, and onto a road with a PRIVATE sign posted at the entrance. He stopped at the gatehouse.

An old man came out, dressed in a pea-green army coat too big for him.

"Renard," Gil said. "To see Mr. Hale."

The old man ran his finger down the page on his clipboard, nodded, raised the barrier. Gil went through.

The road cut across a golf course to the sea, followed it for a few hundred yards, past three or four big houses and up a bluff Another big house stood on top of the bluff, its windows beaten gold in the sunlight. Gil parked in the driveway, took the bowie and the thrower from the glove compartment, wrapped them in a chamois cloth, and walked to the door, the wind snapping at his pant legs. He rang the bell.

The door opened. A uniformed maid looked out. Her black eyes went to the point of the bowie, sticking out of the chamois.

"Renard," Gil said again. "To see Mr. Hale."

She led him across the marble floor of the entrance hall, along a corridor lined with oil paintings of lighthouses, sailing ships, whaling, and into a library. It overlooked a gazebo, where Mrs. Hale stood at an easel, and the sea, breaking on the rocks below.

Mr. Hale was sitting by the fire, oiling a basket-hilt rapier. He rose, holding up glistening hands. "I won't shake," he said, "but how about a pick-me-up?"

It was early for that. "Only if you are," Gil replied.

"Why not?" Mr. Hale gestured out the window, where the wind was whipping the tops off the whitecaps. "Need something warming on a day like this." Mr. Hale shivered. He wore thick gray-flannel pants and a wool sweater with an embroidered golfer on the front; the fire crackled behind him.

Hanging the rapier on the wall, he went to the drinks table and returned with two heavy crystal glasses, half filled with Scotch. "You take it neat, if I remember?"

The truth was Gil didn't drink Scotch, preferred tequila if it came to hard liquor. While Gil was wondering whether to request it, or perhaps a beer, Mr. Hale added, "Meaning no ice.

"I know that," Gil said, taking the glass; it felt oily in his hand.

"Of course you do." Mr. Hale raised his glass. "Here's to cold steel." They drank. Mr. Hale watched Gil's face. "That's more like it, n'est-ce pas?"

"Yeah."

Gil expected that Mr. Hale would now invite him to sit. Instead he asked, "How's business?"

"Up and down."

Mr. Hale, sipping his drink, peered over the top of his glass. "How do you like the work, Gil?"

"Fine."

"You know the product," said Mr. Hale. "That's your strength."

Gil waited for Mr. Hale to say what his weakness was. While he was waiting, he drank some more. Mr. Hale didn't reveal Gil's weakness. Looking down at the bundle in Gil's hand, he said, "What have you got for me?"

Gil laid the chamois on the drinks table, unwrapped it. Mr. Hale went for the bowie at once. He picked it up, one hand on the pommel, one on the point, held it to the light. The damascene whorls shimmered on the blade.

"My God," he said, "he was an artist." He gulped down half his drink, then plucked a book from the shelves, leafed through, read. After a minute or two, he looked up and said: "Fifteen hundred."

"It's worth a lot more than that, Mr. Hale."

"Gil. You're in sales. There's what it's worth, and what it's worth to me. You must have learned that by now." His bleached-out eyes met Gil's. "Seventeen hundred."

"Two G's."

"Seventeen fifty, Gil. Don't push it."

"Eighteen."

Mr. Hale drained his glass. "Nice seeing you," he said.

"All right," Gil said. "Seventeen fifty. What about the thrower?"

"Not interested in throwers, not even his," said Mr. Hale. "Ugly little buggers. No character."

He picked up the bowie, moved to the wall opposite the fireplace. It was lined with built-in drawers. He took out a key, unlocked one, opened it. Bowie knives, but not his father's, gleamed on blue velvet. They were Randalls, Gil decided, just as Mr. Hale said, "Oops," locked the drawer, unlocked another. In this one lay a dozen of his father's bowies, all tagged with dates purchased and amounts paid. Gil recognized three he had sold himself. Mr. Hale laid the new one on the velvet, then took out his checkbook.

"Would cash be a possibility?"

Mr. Hale stared at him for a moment before saying, "If

you like." He took down a framed photograph of a long-ago Radcliffe fencing team with an unsmiling and very young-looking Mrs. Hale in the center, and exposed a wall safe. Then, hunching over, he spun the dial and opened it. Gil saw a stack of bills inside, two or three inches high. Mr. Hale glanced back over his shoulder. Gil turned away.

He gazed down into the drawer at his father's knives. He recognized one, a classic bowie with a curving stag handle, even remembered some hunter's pickup bumping up their dirt road, and his father hurrying from the forge in his leather apron to examine the deer in the back. Gil picked up the knife, studied the tag. Mr. Hale had bought it from a doctor in Oregon five years before, paying $4,500.

Mr. Hale came forward with a wad of bills in his hand. He smiled at Gil, took the knife. "A beauty, isn't it?"

"His first one-hundred-dollar knife," Gil said. His father had drunk a sixpack or two in celebration, while Gil did his homework at the kitchen table in the trailer and a blizzard blew outside.

"You don't say." Mr. Hale laid the knife in the drawer, closed it, turned the key. He held out the money.

Gil didn't take it. "Big spread between forty-five hundred and seventeen fifty," he said.

Mr. Hale said nothing.

"They're both mint."

"There are other factors, as well you know," said Mr. Hale "Are you welshing on me, Gil?"

Gil wasn't in a position to. He took the money, and since he had to do something to get back, counted it out in front of Mr. Hale. Seventeen hundred-dollar bills and one fifty.

"All there?" asked Mr. Hale.

Gil nodded.

Mr. Hale moved him toward the door. "Decide to part with something else, you just give me a call."

Gil stopped, his back to a huge painting of a naval battle.

He had nothing left to part with. "Tell me something," he said.

"If I can."

"What do people like you make a year?"

"What a question."

"Millions?"

"People like me? Millions?"

"Five or six million."

Mr. Hale laughed. "Don't be silly. Nobody honest makes that kind of money."

"Bobby Rayburn does."

"Who's he?" Beyond Mr. Hale's picture window, the wind caught a scrap of paper and carried it up, up, and out of sight.

Gil drove back off the Cape and over the bridge. After forty or fifty miles, he stopped by the side of the road for a piss. He was just unzipping when a cop pulled up behind him, got out of his car.

"Some problem?" the cop said.

"No," Gil told him, trying to remember if Mr. Hale had freshened his drink and, if so, how many times. All the cop had to do was ask for his license, get a whiff of his breath, and then hours of bullshit would follow.

"You'll find sanitary facilities at the next exit," the cop said.

Gil got back in the car. The cop glanced inside. The thrower lay on the passenger seat, wrapped in the chamois cloth. Gil drove off at a moderate pace, took the next exit, stopped at a gas station. Inside the men's room, he strapped the thrower to his right leg.

Just outside the city limits, Gil remembered the ball game. He turned on the radio in time to catch the bottom of the first. Primo singled up the middle and Lanz grounded into a fielder's choice. Rayburn was stepping into the batter's box when Gil dipped into the tunnel, losing reception. Traffic in the tunnel was stop and go; when Gil reached daylight, the inning was over.

Gil drove to the box office. The man in the watch cap was at his post, leaning against the brick wall under the Gate B sign. Gil got out of the car.

"Lookin' for tickets?" the man said, not appearing to recognize him.

"The two behind home plate, Opening Day."

"One fifty," said the man. "Each."

"You were down to two seventy-five for the pair yesterday."

"I wasn't even here yesterday."

They looked at each other. Gil realized he was tired of everyone else having the whip hand—O'Meara, Garrity, the VP at Everest, pink-faced patricians like Hale, blotch-faced scum like this scalper: they all knew how to cut a piece off him. Gil felt the weight of the thrower on his leg. It was comforting.

"A'right, a'right," said the scalper. "You got the two seventy-five?"

"I've got two fifty," Gil said. "That's what I'll pay."

"You jerkin' me around? Two seventy-five, and it's your lucky day."

They looked at each other some more. Gil remembered a little of what he knew about knife fighting. The thrower could be used for stabbing, but stabbing wasn't so easy if an opponent knew what he was doing. Slashing was better. Even a piece of junk like the Iwo Jima Survivor would do: hit the pavement, roll, come up slashing through the sinews at the back of the knees. Never done it for real, although he'd practiced for years with his father, using rubber knives in the clearing behind the forge, and his father had done it for real, more than once, with the Rangers.

"You in a coma, buddy, or what?" said the scalper.

"Let's see the tickets." Gil examined them. Right section—BB, seats 3 and 4; right game—Game 1, Opening Day, April

8, 1:00 P.M. He handed over the $275 and walked away, checking the tickets once more. The printed price was $18.50 each.

Gil had a baconburger and fries at Cleats. Figgy was already there. He'd had a few. Gil had a few with him. They watched a spring-training game from Arizona on the big screen.

"Gil?"

"Yeah?"

"Do me a favor?"

"Like what?"

"I could use a couple hundred, tide me over. Going out to Connecticut this weekend to check things out."

"What things?"

"Friend of a friend of mine makes fishing rods out there. Looking for a rep. I'll be able to pay you back in a week, two weeks tops."

"You're a city boy. What do you know about fishing rods?"

"I'll know enough by the weekend. I've been reading up. Besides, selling is selling."

They ordered another round. Gil watched some kid stretch a single into a double, slanting into the bag with a perfect hook slide. A memory came to him, of a game long ago, maybe against the Indians. He'd been on first base, taking his lead, when—

"So how about it?" said Figgy.

"How about what?"

"Couple hundred."

On the screen the pitcher spun around and fired to the shortstop, sneaking in behind the kid at second base. The umpire made a hammering motion with his fist. The kid jogged off the field, head down.

"It's not like I've got any job security myself," Gil said.

"You kidding? Your name's on the catalogue. They'll never can you."

"My father's name," Gil said. "And don't be so sure."

Figgy took a deep breath, blew it out. "How about a hundred and fifty?"

Gil realized that for once he had the whip hand.

"What are you smiling about?" Figgy asked.

"Nothing." Gil was all set to say no to Figgy when he remembered the Lifesavers. "I can spare fifty. That's it."

Figgy took it, and left soon after. Gil stayed until the game was over, then watched "Baseball Tonight" and "SportsCenter" before driving home.

Gil lay naked on his bed, except for the thrower, still strapped to his leg. He listened for Lenore upstairs. Once he thought he heard her moan. It gave him an erection. He wondered if she was up there with another man, then decided he had imagined the whole thing. She was sleeping, or working the late shift, or at her sister's. He considered a quiet trip upstairs, a quiet knock on her door. He stayed where he was. He didn't like to go to her.

Gil turned off the light. The last thing he saw was Richie's picture, on the dresser.

Time passed. He drifted in a dark and pleasant fog, close to sleep, playing a little catch with Bobby Rayburn. Bobby was impressed; he could tell.

All at once, Gil sat up, snapped on the light. He got out of bed, picked his jacket off the floor, fumbled for the tickets.

Game 1. April 8. 1:00 P.M. His appointment with the VP at Everest and Co. was for two-thirty, the same day.

5

This one's name was Dawna. Bobby didn't have to remember because she wore a necklace with the word spelled out in fourteen-carat-gold letters, like a name tag. When he awoke in his room at the Flamingo Bay Motor Inn and Spa, she was lying on her side, gazing at him.

"You look so peaceful when you're sleeping," she said. "And you've got the most beautiful hands."

Bobby had heard that before: both parts, especially the second. The kind of woman who noticed hands always noticed his. Val was that kind of woman too: she'd said exactly the same words when he'd picked up his fork on their first date, dinner at Longhorn Subs and Pizza, two blocks from the athletic dorm. Years later, having gone back to college for her master's, she put a new twist on it. Now his hands reminded her of something Aristotle Onassis had told Maria Callas: "You'd be nothing without that bird in your throat." He hadn't known who Maria Callas was. Wald had explained it to him, explained it was a putdown. But, after some thought, Bobby had decided to take it as a compliment. His hands, his eyes, his body: they were a gift, like Einstein's brain.

"Thanks," he said to Dawna.

"And the rest of you's not so bad, either." Bobby had heard that segue before as well. Dawna felt for him under the sheets and soon rolled on top, her hands on his shoulders and her necklace swinging lightly against his chin as she began to move. Bobby moved too, although he had intended to sleep alone, had in fact gone to bed alone. But keyed up by the way he'd hit in BP and unable to sleep, he'd gotten out of bed, dressed, and gone to the bar. There she'd been.

The phone rang. Bobby picked it up. "Hello." Dawna slid under the sheets, went down on him.

"Did I wake you?" Wald said.

"No."

"Good. Sorry to call so early, but I wanted to get this cleared up before game time. How're the ribs, by the way?"

"Fine. Get what cleared up?"

"They want fifty grand."

"Stop it," Bobby said.

"Huh?"

"I wasn't talking to you. Who wants fifty grand? For what?"

"Primo's people. Or else he won't give up the number."

"Goddamn it."

"Right. Your decision. Is it worth fifty G's?"

"Goddamn it."

"I know."

"Can't you talk them down?"

"They started at a hundred, Bobby."

Bobby sat up. The girl didn't stop what she was doing. "Who's behind it—him or them?"

"Very astute, Bobby. I thought of that—whether they were shaking you down, all on their own—so I spoke to Primo himself. It's him."

"Why?"

"He says it's his lucky number. He speaks good English, incidentally."

"It's my lucky number too."

"Then it's going to cost."

Bobby couldn't think. He pushed the girl away with his foot.

"Bobby?"

"Yeah?"

"You thinking?"

"Yeah." He thought *fifty grand* and *that asshole Primo*, but didn't get further than that.

"Thirty-three and forty-one are still available," Wald said. "So's fifty-one, according to Stook. That's got a one in it too."

"You told Stook about this?"

"The money? Nobody knows about the money, except Primo, his people, you and me."

"But word'll get out, won't it, especially if I pay? And I'll look dumb."

"Could be, Bobby. Astute of you—again. You should be doing my job."

Bobby had never considered doing anyone else's job. The idea appalled him. "Do I have to decide now?"

"Soon," Wald said. "Game's at two-oh-five."

The girl came up from under the covers, looking hurt. Bobby patted her on the leg. "I've decided," he told Wald.

"Yeah?"

"The hell with it." Allowing himself to get jerked around by a Jheri-curled punk like Primo was no way to start off with a new team. The number on his back didn't matter; all that mattered was to keep swinging the bat the way he had yesterday, to keep seeing the ball with coffee table book clarity.

Bobby hung up. The girl said, "What's wrong?"

Bobby reached for her. "Just business."

"Business?" the girl replied, as though struck by the possibility she'd made a horrid mistake. "Aren't you a ball player?"

Bobby left in a taxi for Soxtown. Halfway there he spotted a car dealer's. "Pull in," he said. He was tired of the driver's glances in the rearview mirror, didn't want to take taxis for the next three weeks, getting glanced at. Besides, he was going to need a car on the east coast, probably two, maybe three. Bobby went inside.

"I don't want anything flashy," he said. "Just a solid, family vehicle."

He chose a Jeep Grand Cherokee Limited. V8, ABS, 4WD, AM-FM CD, $35,991, with the gold hubcaps. Bobby wrote a check. An insurance agent arrived, called Bobby's insurance company in California, collected another check. Someone else took the papers to the registry, returned with the license plate: 983 KRZ. Bobby didn't want a K on his plate. They went back and got him another one. It all took about an hour. Bobby signed a few autographs and drove off

Nice car. He had nicer ones, but Bobby liked riding up high, liked the sound system, liked the power and heft. He drove along happily for a while, testing the features. Then, just before the turnoff to Soxtown, Bobby realized he was bored with it. He'd give it to Val, get something else for himself after she came. He parked in his reserved place by the palm tree. The odometer read 000018.

Stook met him in the clubhouse. "What's it gonna be?" he said. The three shirts—33, 41, 51—were hanging in his stall. Thirty-three was out—wasn't that Jesus' age when he died? Bobby tested the divisibility of the remaining numbers. Three went into 51, but nothing went into 41. He saw Primo watching from across the room.

"Hey, Primo," he called. "You'd know this."

"Know what?"

"If forty-one's a prime number."

Primo frowned. "I don't get it."

Bobby laughed. He took 41.

Bobby dressed: sleeves, jock, sanitaries, stirrups, pants, cleats, shirt. He had fried chicken and iced tea from the buffet, then went outside for BP. The pitching coach was throwing, harder than Burrows and with more stuff, but the ball was still out of a coffee table book, even bigger, slower, clearer than yesterday. Bobby banged it around the yard, then shagged flies until the Tigers came on.

He returned to the clubhouse, drank more iced tea, checked his mail. The usual: requests for autographed pictures, most from preteen boys and slightly older girls; phone numbers from girls a little older than that, some accompanied by bathing-suit pictures of the writers; a letter from a man who wanted to know why Bobby never bunted; and a fourleaf clover in a plastic locket on a chain, sent by a granny in Texas. Bobby hung the locket around his neck.

Burrows came in, lit a cigarette, and took out the lineup card. Bobby, who had hit third since freshman year in high school, bent down and retied his shoelaces; casual.

"Primo at short, bats one," read Burrows. "Lanz in left, bats two. Rayburn in center, bats three. Washington at first, bats—" Bobby slipped on his headphones, pressed PLAY.

A few minutes later, they took the field. Boyle started. He struck out the first two batters, walked the next. The runner stole second; Odell's throw was perfect, but Primo dropped the ball.

"Tut-tut," Bobby said, quietly, all by himself in center field.

Twenty or thirty feet behind him a voice spoke: "You said it."

Bobby glanced around and saw a sunburned old man sitting in a wheelchair just beyond the chain-link fence, binoculars hanging on his white-haired chest.

"He's such a fucking showboat," the old man said. "They're all like that, the spics."

Bobby turned back to the field, saying nothing.

Boyle walked another batter. When the next one came up, Burrows motioned Bobby toward right. Bobby changed his position. Then Odell flashed the sign: curve. Bobby was astonished: he'd never been able to read the catcher's sign from center field, not even as a kid.

"Jesus," he said. *I'm going to fucking hit .400 this year*.

"Tell me about it," said the old man with binoculars, as Boyle went into his motion and threw. "Burrows. Shit. Moves you over and then calls for the deuce. They shoulda fired him years—"

The batter swung, connected. A screamer, into the gap in left between Bobby and Lanz. Bobby took off. He might have had a play if Burrows hadn't shifted him. That thought was obliterated by the realization that he just might have a play anyway. Bobby dove, weightless for a long moment, fully stretched out in the air. First the ball was a hissing white blur; then it disappeared and went silent, leaving its sting on the palm of his glove hand. Bobby fell hard on his chest, rolled over, stayed down.

Lanz was kneeling beside him. "You okay?"

Bobby struggled for breath. "Ball in my glove?"

"Hell of a catch," Lanz said. "But let's not get crazy in spring training."

Bobby heard a boat whistle, far away; smelled the grass; felt a tiny insect walking across the back of his neck. "Three outs?"

"Yeah."

Bobby rose just as the trainer jogged up, breathing hard.

"You okay?"

Lightheaded, then fine. "Yeah."

"Rib cage?"

"No problem."

Bobby ran off. Cheers from the little crowd. He sat down in the dugout, drank water. Something tickled his chest. Had he landed on an ant hill? Bobby peered down his shirt. No ants. He'd smashed the plastic locket. The fourleaf clover was gone.

Burrows was standing over him, his cigarette cupped in his hand in case a camera was pointed his way. "You all right?"

"Yeah."

"How's that rib cage?"

"Fine."

"Wanna come out?"

"No." Bobby didn't want to sit. He'd been sitting all winter. He wanted to play.

Burrows went back to his seat in the corner, took a deep drag. "Bibbity bobbity," he said, rubbing his hands together.

First pitch. Slider; Bobby could tell from the dugout, before the ball was halfway to the plate. It came in just above the belt, and Primo slapped it over second base.

"Bibbity bobbity," Burrows said.

"Knock off that bibbity-bobbity shit," someone said.

"I can say what I like," Burrows said. "Even the poor got rights in this country."

Bobby pulled his bat from the rack and walked to the on-deck circle. "What'd he hit last year?" he asked Lanz.

"Primo? I don't know. Two-fifty, two-sixty?"

Bobby nodded. He himself had hit .319.

Lanz stepped in. Bobby slid the donut down the barrel. Sky blue, sun warm, his body loose and strong. He timed the pitcher's first pitch to Lanz, swinging as it crossed the plate. Fastball, low and away. Lanz swung and missed. Now comes that chickenshit slider. Just wait on it and unload. But Lanz couldn't make himself wait long enough. He topped the ball, sending a slow roller to the shortstop, who threw to second, forcing Primo.

Bobby went to the plate. The catcher, who'd been with him in California five or six years before, said, "Welcome to the bullshit league."

"You can say that again," the umpire said.

"Don't spoil it for me," Bobby said.

The pitcher stared down for the sign. Bobby waited in his stance, completely still, but loose, all the way to his fingertips. Show me that chickenshit slider, you asshole.

It came. Fat, clear, spinning sideways. Bobby got it all, hitting it so squarely he didn't even feel the impact. It cleared the fence still rising, and disappeared. Foul by fifteen feet.

"Ooo-wee," said the catcher.

Bobby took a few swings, stepped back in, looked for the fastball inside, and got it: fat, clear, spinning backwards. Bobby hit it as far as the first one, maybe farther, and not quite as foul.

"Oh and two," said the ump.

Bobby took a few more swings, resumed his stance. Now would come the slider, but down and away, out of the strike zone. The pitcher checked Lanz, kicked. Bobby heard a voice from the stands: "Straighten it out, Bobby Rayburn, straighten it out." He recognized that voice: the skinny little community-relations guy. He'd forgotten all about him, forgotten about the boy, forgotten all that home-run shit. John? Sean.

Pitch on the way. Fat and clear, but not the slider; back-spinning, but not the fastball: a change-up. An 0-and-2 change-up, so slow Bobby thought he could see the diagonal pattern of the stitches on the ball. He watched it all the way.

"Strike three."

"Lucky son of a bitch," said the catcher. He snapped a throw down to first, in case Lanz was napping.

A perfect afternoon for baseball. Bright sun, no wind, eighty degrees. Bobby struck out in the fourth, struck out in the seventh. Burrows substituted for everyone after that. Bobby walked to the end of the bench. "I'd like to stay in," he said.

"Yeah?" said Burrows.

"Yeah."

"Thought you got a little shook up making that catch. Outstanding."

"I'm fine."

"Okay." Burrows rose and scratched the name of some rookie off the lineup card taped to the dugout wall and inked Bobby back in.

Bobby batted again in the bottom of the ninth, two out, no one on, thunderheads rolling in now, maybe a hundred people left in the stands, game meaningless. He heard the community-relations guy calling, "Come on, Bobby Rayburn." He had one of those high, carrying voices that separated itself from the crowd noise.

"Shut the fuck up," Bobby said.

"I didn't say shit," the catcher said.

Bobby struck out on three pitches. A cold raindrop landed on his nose as he went back to the dugout.

Bobby showered and changed. The community-relations guy approached his stall, talking on a cellular phone. He handed it to Bobby. "Call for you.

"Yeah?" Bobby said.

"Mr. Rayburn?" said a woman. "I just want to thank you so much."

"For what?"

"For trying."

"Who's this?" Bobby asked.

The woman spoke her name. It meant nothing to Bobby. "Sean's mother," she explained.

"Oh, yeah," said Bobby. "Don't worry. I'll get hold of one for him, sooner or later."

The woman made a strange sound, high-pitched, ragged. "He passed away, Mr. Rayburn. I'm sorry."

"Passed away?"

"Right after the game. The doctor said by all rights he

should have died last night. He just willed himself to stay alive. Because of you. Thank you for that extra day, Mr. Rayburn." Her voice broke. The line went dead.

Bobby handed the phone back to the community-relations guy. "Screen my calls from now on," he said.

Bobby took a taxi to a restaurant, remembering his new car only when he got there. The restaurant was dark inside, which suited him fine. Bobby sat by himself at a back table, watching the thunderheads through the window, waiting for the rain to fall. It never did. Just that one stupid drop. At sunset the sky cleared and then went dark. The moon came out. Bobby had a few beers, then a New York cut with salad and baked potato, then a few more beers. He called home on his way out. No answer.

Bobby took a cab back to Soxtown, stopping to buy a flashlight on the way. The complex was dark, Bobby's car alone in the parking lot. Bobby walked all the way around, until he stood outside the center-field fence of the game field. He climbed over.

Beaming the flashlight a few feet ahead, Bobby moved back and forth across the grass in left center. After a while he got down on his hands and knees, combed the grass with his fingers. He found a divot, lifted by the impact of his diving catch, found the bared spot it had come from, even found a tiny plastic chip from the locket, buried in the skid mark. But he didn't find the four-leaf clover.

Bobby drove back to the Flamingo Bay Motor Inn and Spa, let himself into his room, switched on the light. A woman was in his bed, sleeping on her stomach.

"Christ," Bobby said.

The woman rolled over. "Disappointed?" she said. It was his wife.

"You said you were going to call."

"I'm sure you meant that to sound more welcoming."

Bobby saw she hadn't been sleeping at all; she still wore lipstick, eye shadow, earrings. "Where's Sean?" he asked.

"At my mother's."

"You should have brought him."

Val looked at him in surprise.

His ribs hurt. And he'd stopped seeing the ball.

6

Edge geometry," Gil's father would say. "That's what it's all about." He'd tap the steel with the tuning hammer, indicating the spot. Gil would strike with the twelve-pounder. Tap, strike, tap, strike: the steel cherry-red from the forge; the anvil live and quiet; Gil still a boy, but big and strong; his father the master.

They lived in the trailer. The forge was out back, in the barn. RENARD STEEL FORGE, read the sign over the door. Winters were best, when the coke in the forge glowed hot, and the wind whined and moaned through cracks in the old walls. In airless summers, nothing came through the wide-open door but black flies, and Gil's sweat ran down his bare arms, down the twelve-pounder, sizzling on the steel with every stroke. He got stronger and stronger, became the finest striker his father had ever had. But by then it was an anachronism. Every smith who could afford one had a power hammer; and Gil never mastered edge geometry, or any of the other precision skills. He just liked to swing the big hammer.

Gil awoke from a forge dream in sheets damp with sweat. Edge geometry; precision skills: none of it mattered anyway. His father got sick, and soon after the moneymen came and took their name away. Gil's eyes went to the picture of Richie; his father had been called Richie too. There was no resemblance. Gil turned on the radio.

"—may have reinjured those ribs making a sensational diving catch in the first inning. Certainly there was a lot of comment in the press box about Burrows leaving him in."

"Why take chances with the big-ticket guys, Jewel, especially in the month of March?"

"That's it exactly, Norm. And the thing is he didn't look like himself up there at the plate yesterday. Sid Burrows may have a lot to answer for."

"Thanks, Jewel. See you at the top of the hour. We'll go to the phones after this brief—"

In a bad mood now, Gil put on his robe, picked up his toilet kit, and walked down the hall to the bathroom. Lenore had already been there. The mirror was steamed, except for a cleared circle in the center where his own face now appeared, sniffing. He smelled her perfume, a dense, rich smell of tropical flowers, a smell that gave him a headache, or made him aware of the headache he already had. Gil shaved, showered, went back to his room.

"—Ron in Brighton. What've you got for us, Ron?"

"Can we talk hockey for a sec?"

"Anything you want."

Gil dressed: white shirt, blue suit, yellow tie. He had five or six yellow ties, left over from the days when they were in. This one, with a pattern of tiny mauve discs, was his lucky tie, worn the day he earned his highest single commission, $3,740, from a sporting-goods chain that went bankrupt not long after. Gil was knotting his lucky tie when someone knocked on his door.

"It's open."

Lenore walked in, wearing her kimono, the one that came halfway to her knees. Gil's headache, confined until then in a narrow wedge behind his right eye, began to spread.

"Nice tie," Lenore said.

"Thanks."

"Guess what the temperature is."

Gil glanced out his window, saw no clues in the brick wall.

"Fourteen degrees," Lenore told him. "And they're calling for snow."

That wasn't cold to Gil, and snow didn't bother him.

"It's my day off, thank God," said Lenore. "I'm going to spend it in bed." The kimono opened a little, revealing more of her leg. Lenore had well-shaped, muscular legs; she'd run track in high school, had trophies on the cracked bureau in her room to prove it. Now she sold jewelry in a mall off the ring road.

Gil switched off the radio, took his coat from the wall hook.

Lenore toyed with a lock of her hair. "I wouldn't mind a little company," she said.

"Got to work." Gil moved toward the door. Lenore stepped aside, but not enough to keep him from bumping against her hip.

"Sorry," he said.

"Don't be." Lenore pressed against him, pressed hard with her soft breasts, backing him against the bed.

Gil had work to do: he could see the day's schedule in his head, laid out in neat boxes, ready to be checked off. He put his hands on her shoulders, almost pushed her away. But Lenore's hips made a comma-shaped motion, like a preview of what could be happening in the next minute, and the neat boxes in his head collapsed.

The blue suit, the yellow tie, the white shirt, the kimono,

all came off. "I'm so pent-up," said Lenore, as they moved onto the bed, their bare skins, warm and soft from the shower, prickling up in goosebumps.

Gil was pent-up too. He was inside her in moments, her buttocks cupped in his hands.

"Gentle."

But what good would *gentle* do? Not with this headache, not in this mood. His body took over. Her mouth was at his ear and he heard her suck in her breath, heard every nuance and texture of the sound. It was basic, animal, a world in itself. He came.

"Gil?"

He lay on her, the boxes rebuilding themselves in his head.

"You didn't wait for me?"

First: call Everest. Second: bank what was left of Hale's money, pay the car bill and something on the credit cards. Third: hit Bluewater Fishing and Tackle. Fourth: try a cold call at the new Great Outdoors on the north shore. That would leave just enough time to drive down for Richie at five.

"Gil?"

"Yeah?

"You can't just leave me like this."

"Like what?"

"Pent-up, Gil. I'm still pent-up."

"What do you want me to do?"

"Something."

He stuck his hand down there.

Her mouth was at his ear again. "Lick me, baby." He still heard every nuance and texture of the sound, but now it didn't have the same effect. She would have to settle for his finger. He moved it in circles, mentally putting on his white shirt, blue suit, yellow tie, unlocking the 325i, driving off, punching in Everest and Co. on the car phone.

* * *

You got in the car, you kept plugging. Gil told himself that a few times, until he was hyped enough to call Everest. He had to rehype twice before he got past the purchasing VP's secretary.

"Hi, Chuck. Gil Renard here."

"What is it?"

"Our meeting on the eighth. Two-thirty's tough for me, Chuck. How's the morning?"

"Full up."

"Maybe late afternoon, then."

"Flying to Chicago."

"Any chance we could make it earlier?"

"Earlier?"

"A day or two earlier. The sixth? The seventh?"

"Didn't we go through this already?"

"I just thought maybe you'd had a cancellation or something, could squeeze me in." Shit. First rule of the commission rep: Look and sound successful.

"No."

"What about later that week?"

"In Chicago. Didn't I say that?"

"When are you coming back?"

"End of the month."

"End of the month?"

"I'm in Chicago till the twelfth. Then we're taking two weeks in Maui."

Rule two: take the offensive. Gil tried to think of a line that would do that, and failed.

"Hello?" said the VP. "You still there?"

"Yeah."

"So what is it? Scratch you for the eighth?"

"No," Gil said. "I'll be there." He thought of a line. "Have that checkbook ready."

"We'll see," said the VP, and hung up.

Rule three: ignore rejection. He called Garrity. "Good news," he said. "Everest loves the Iwo Jima stuff. Going to build their whole approach around it. Thing is, they're asking for a few weeks to solidify their plans. Should I give it to them?"

"You mean they're not going to order this month?"

"They need time to retool, like I said."

Silence. "Give it to them," Garrity said at last. "But it better be a whopper, Gil."

"What?"

"Their order, I'm talking about."

"Count on it," Gil said.

"We are," said Garrity. "See you on the ninth."

"The ninth?"

"Sales meeting."

"Right," said Gil. "Got to go. I'm on a call." Look and sound successful.

Gil stopped at Cleats for a quick one, then got back in the car, kept plugging. First, the bank. After making the car payment and the interest payments on his cards, he had $693.20 in his checking account and three or four hundred in his pocket. Plus the tickets. Free and clear, big boy, free and clear.

He hit Bluewater Fishing and Tackle. The owner's son was out front. Gil showed him the Iwo Jima catalogue, got him excited. Then the owner, a fat old guy in a plaid shirt, walked in from the back room. He checked out the catalogue, asked if Gil had any samples. Gil handed him the Survivor.

"Great handle," said the owner's son.

The owner turned the Survivor over in his hands a few times, then looked up at Gil. "This is shit, Gil. You know that."

Gil wanted to say, "Shit sells." Especially if it's got a fancy handle. But: don't argue with a customer. He put the Survivor away. "What about the regular stuff?" His headache, which had shrunk back to the wedge behind his right eye, now expanded again.

"I'll take three-dozen Clipits," the owner said. "And a dozen of those folding hunters with big bolsters."

"Eight-inch?"

"Five and a quarter. A dozen skinners, two boxes of pocket-knives—"

"Red?"

"Blue. Dozen fillet knives, and maybe two of those birders.

"And?"

"That'll do it."

"That'll do it?" March was supposed to be a big month. Bluewater had ordered three or four times as much the year before.

"Blame the economy," the owner said.

Gil wrote up the order. Commission: $187.63. He faxed it in from the car, then stopped at Cleats and checked the box scores over a hamburger and a beer. Rayburn: 0 for 4, 4 K's.

"Burrows is an asshole," Gil said.

"Just because he wants them to work for their money?" Leon said, drawing a pint of Harpoon.

"Use your head, Leon. Rayburn's an investment. Like an oil well. Got to protect your investments."

"I feel like shit today," Leon replied, "and I'm in here busting my ass. No one said, 'You're our oil well, Leon. Take the day off.'"

"You're replaceable. That's the difference."

"And you're not?" Leon said, before he remembered they stood on opposite sides of the bar, or noticed the expression on Gil's face. "Hey, no offense." Leon drew another pint. "On me."

Gil drank up, went outside. Snow was falling, just as Lenore had forecast. He realized he had to piss, didn't want to go back inside. He stepped into an alley, pissed a yellow circle in the fresh snow, added crescent seams inside its borders: a baseball. And had plenty left inside him to melt it all away.

North of the city, snow fell harder. It took Gil an hour to reach Great Outdoors, a big well-stocked store with a waterfall and a wall for rock climbing. Gil walked around until a woman with a name tag on her down vest approached and said, "May I help you, sir?"

Look and sound successful. "I'd like to see the owner."

"The owner?"

"Or the manager."

"May I ask what it's about?"

"Business," Gil said. Tell nothing to underlings. That was another rule.

The woman looked him over, then led him to the manager's office, went in by herself, came out a moment later. "He'll see you."

Gil walked in, pulling out his card. The first thirty seconds were everything on a cold call. Hype, hype. "Gil Renard," Gil said, laying the card on the desk: R.G. RENARD FINE KNIVES. He smiled a confident smile. The man at the desk didn't look at the card. He sat behind a computer, fingers poised over the keys.

"You're a rep?"

"Right. And I couldn't help noticing that in this big beautiful store devoted to the outdoors, there isn't a single knife." He opened his briefcase.

"We'll have scads of them in a few days," said the manager.

"Excuse me?"

"The ship docked in San Francisco last night."

"You've got a supplier?"

"Exactly." The manager named a Japanese company, one of the best.

Gil smiled his confident smile. "If you'll give me three minutes"—he'd stolen that line from Figgy—"I can prove to you that we're competitive with them in quality, and better in price. In fact, we've got a new—"

"Not possible," said the manager. "We've signed a three-year exclusive."

There was no line to counter that. "Maybe I could leave our catalogue."

"Just lay it there." The manager's fingers fluttered down to the keys.

Outside the snowflakes had grown fat, moist, silvery; almost rain. Gil walked around the Great Outdoors building and pissed against a packing case. Then he got in the car and drove south.

The phone buzzed.

"I'm looking at the Bluewater order." Garrity. "What the hell's going on?"

"He says it's the economy."

"I'm not talking about the size of the order, although that stinks too. I'm talking about why aren't you pushing the goddamn Iwo Jima line?"

"I'm pushing it. The old guy knows his stuff, that's all."

"What's that supposed to mean?"

"That it's shit and he knows it." Was he yelling? The woman in the next car was watching him.

There was a pause before Garrity spoke again. "You'd better do some thinking, Gil."

"About what?"

"I don't have to spell it out, boyo." Click. Hum.

Gil tried to do some thinking. The first thought he had was about the time Boucicaut knocked himself out against the backstop, chasing a pop foul. Boucicaut. A rock. Odell, for all his strength and skill, wasn't a rock like Boucicaut.

Gil turned on the radio.

Bottom of the fourth at Soxtown. Primo tripled. Lanz struck out. Washington came to the plate. Gil dialed FANLINE.

"Where's Rayburn hitting?"

"FANLINE's closed," a woman said. "We're not taking calls till after the game."

"I don't care about that. Just where's he hitting?"

"I wouldn't know."

Washington flied out, ending the inning. Gil listened hard, waiting for an explanation. None came. He called Cleats. Leon answered.

"Leon. This is Gil. Got the game on?"

"Gil?"

"Renard. You know."

"Oh, yeah."

"Where's Rayburn batting?"

"Huh?"

"In the order. Where's he batting?"

Gil heard Leon call, "Any of you guys watching this?" Pause. Voices. "Where's Rayburn batting?" More voices. Gil strained to hear what they were saying. Leon came back on. "He's not in the lineup."

"How come?"

"You're asking me?"

"I just meant—"

"Kind of busy in here. Got to go."

Goddamn rib cage. Those things took forever to heal, and by then you'd lost your timing. He could have killed Burrows.

Gil changed the station, tried to get into the music, think about something else. But he couldn't. After a while, he called information, got the press-box number at Soxtown. He entered it on his speed dialer, then rang it.

"Yeah," said a man at the other end.

What was her name? "Jewel," Gil said. "Jewel Stern."

Background noise. Gil thought he heard the crack of a bat. A woman was saying, ". . . bored out of my mind." Then the same woman was on the phone. "Yeah?"

"Jewel Stern?" Gil said.

"Speaking."

"What's wrong with Rayburn?"

"Who's this?"

Gil thought of giving his name, but what was the point? "Just a fan."

"Listen, fan. This is a working press box, not twenty questions."

"What's your problem, lady? I'm asking one simple—"

Jewel Stern hung up the phone. "Getting crazy out there," she said.

The *Herald* guy said, *"Prodigious* isn't in my goddamn spellcheck."

"Or in your readers' vocabulary," Jewel said, before spelling it for him.

By five o'clock, the snow had turned to rain. It soaked Gil's hair as he stood outside the middle door of the rented South Shore triplex, waiting for someone to answer his knock. After a minute or two, Ellen opened the door. She was still in her office clothes, wore her hair in a new cut, had lost weight.

"You don't have to pound like that," she said. "I was in the john."

"Where's Richie?"

"With Tim."

"What do you mean—with Tim?" Tim was the boyfriend. "I told you I was taking him to the movies."

"Please don't raise your voice in public."

Gil lowered it. "What do you mean with Tim?"

"Little League tryouts are tonight. I couldn't reach you."

"They won't have tryouts in this."

"Wrong. It's indoors, at the high school."

"When did it start?"

"Don't ask me."

"Why didn't you tell me?"

"Please don't raise your voice."

"Why didn't you tell me?"

"I tried. Didn't I say that already?"

"The office can always get me. You know that."

Ellen didn't reply. She stared at him, eyes made small by the lenses of her glasses. He noticed she had new red frames, the kind that made a statement, although he didn't know what it was. He didn't say anything either, just walked back to his car and drove off.

The high school was three blocks away. Gil hurried into the gym, rain dripping down his face. A man with a whistle around his neck hit a ground ball to a boy standing at center court, the number twenty pinned to his chest. The ball bounced off the boy's glove. He chased it down and threw a two-hopper to a teenager standing by the man with the whistle. "That's the way," said the man with the whistle. He tossed the boy three fly balls, two of which he caught. "Nice job. Off you go." The boy ran off, joining a woman in the stands. The men on the sideline wrote on their clipboards.

"Twenty-one," said the man with the whistle. Twenty-one emerged from a group of fifty or sixty kids waiting at the far end of the court.

"Hustle."

Gil moved down the near side, his eyes on the numbered kids. He spotted Richie: 26. He was chewing on the rawhide lace of his glove. Gil took a seat in the stands.

The drill: three grounders, three flies, six throws. Twenty-one missed them all, and threw poorly, but 22 fielded every ball cleanly and had a strong arm. Twenty-three's arm was even stronger, and this time when the man with the whistle said, "Nice job," his tone said it too. Twenty-three was a big kid, not possibly the same age as Richie.

Gil was aware of a man stepping down through the stands, sitting beside him. "Hi, Gil," he said. "Aren't they cute?"

Gil turned. Tim.

"Who?" Gil said.

"The kids. It's the best age." Tim held out his hand. "How're you doing?"

Gil shook hands. "They're not all nine, are they?"

"Supposed to be," Tim said. "The tens are next, then the elevens and the twelves. The draft's in a couple weeks, not that it matters where Richie's concerned."

"What do you mean?"

"Only a handful of nines make the majors. The rest play in the minors. No pressure."

But Richie was good. Gil remembered how they'd rolled a tennis ball back and forth across the floor while Richie was still in diapers. "He'll be right up there," Gil said.

"Sure." Tim opened a file. Inside were sheets of paper with five or six lines of handwritten *W*'s on the top half and crayon drawings of wigwams, willows, and winter below. Tim made a red check mark on the first sheet and wrote, "Wonderful!" underlining the *W*, then turned to the next one.

"Twenty-six," called the man with the whistle. Richie came forward, chewing on his glove.

Hustle, thought Gil.

"Hustle," said the man with the whistle.

Richie jogged to center court, his right foot glancing out to the side slightly on every stride. "Does he always run like that?" Gil said.

"Like what?" asked Tim, looking up from his papers.

The man with the whistle hit the first ground ball, right at Richie, but much harder than any of the other ground balls yet hit, Gil thought, and picking up topspin on the composite floor.

Glove down, glove down.

Richie stuck his glove down, but too late, and the ball went through his legs.

"Oops," said Tim.

"No problem," said the man with the whistle, and hit Richie another. Again: harder than the balls he'd hit the other kids.

"Glove down." This time Gil said it aloud, but quietly, he was sure of that.

Richie got his glove down a little faster, deflecting the ball to the side. He ran after it, bobbled it, scooped it up, threw a sidearm rainbow that bounced a few times and finally rolled to the feet of the teenager.

"Much better," said Tim.

"How long have you known about this?" Gil said.

"About what?"

"This tryout."

"A few weeks?"

"Have you been practicing with him?"

"In this weather?"

The third grounder was on its way. "Look how hard the asshole's hitting it," Gil said, not loudly, and, not much louder, "Butt down, butt down." Get your butt down and the glove comes down automatically. Had Richie heard him? Probably not, but he did get down for this one, and the ball popped into his glove.

"All right, twenty-six," said the man with the whistle. Richie threw the ball in, a little more strongly this time, but still a sidearm toss that didn't come close to reaching in the air.

"Crow-hop, for Christ's sake," Gil said. But quietly.

Richie looked into the stands.

"Here we go," said the man with the whistle, and tossed the first fly ball.

Richie turned from the stands, realized what was happening, tried to find the ball, glancing up wildly at the gym ceiling.

"Get your fucking glove up."

"Hey," said Tim. "Easy."

Richie got his glove up, but never saw the ball. It arced under the gaudy championship banners for basketball, football, wrestling, and hit him on the head.

Richie collapsed screaming on the gym floor, holding his

head, jerking around in agony. The coaches with the clipboards, the man with the whistle, the teenager, all ran to him, but Gil got there first. He knelt, put his hand on Richie's shoulder, felt his boniness under the sweat shirt.

"Richie, it's me. You're all right."

Richie kept screaming and jerking.

"You're all right. Control yourself."

Gil pushed Richie's hands aside, felt his head: a little bump sprouting on the side. Nothing.

"Come on, now," Gil said. He squeezed Richie's shoulder, not too hard.

Richie quieted. "It's your fault," he said, so softly Gil hardly heard. Maybe he'd imagined it.

Gil grew aware of the people standing around. He reached for Richie's hand, helped him up. Applause from the stands.

"He okay?" asked the man with the whistle.

Gil turned on him. "You don't worry about that," he said. "You just worry about hitting them fair to everybody." He walked Richie off the court.

By the second Coke and third slice of pizza, Richie had cheered up. "I did pretty good on that grounder, didn't I?"

"Yeah. Remember to square to the ball and get your butt down."

"I did."

"Well, that's the way to do it. Even more."

"Think I'll make it?"

"Make what?"

"The majors."

Gil looked into his son's eyes, light brown eyes, the same shade as his mother's, watching closely. Richie was probably going to need glasses too, maybe needed them already. Gil was still searching for the right answer when Richie said, "Daddy Tim says it doesn't matter whether I make it this year or not."

That was new, Daddy Tim. Gil swallowed the rest of his beer and said, "He's right."

Richie nodded. He ate more pizza, drank more Coke. "The uniforms are better in the majors. You get button shirts and your name on the back. Rossi Plumbing's the best. Green pin stripes."

Gil ordered another beer.

"Do you think they'll pick me?"

"Who?"

"Rossi Plumbing. That was their coach, hitting the grounders."

"Hard to predict a draft," Gil said.

"Think I'll go in the first round?"

"Hard to say. How about another Coke?"

"I'm not supposed to drink Coke."

"Who says?"

"Mom and Da—and Tim."

"Miss?" said Gil, flagging down the waitress. "Another Coke." He turned to Richie. "Different rules when you're with your father."

Richie chewed on his straw. "Did you see Jason Pellegrini?"

"Who's he?"

"Twenty-three."

"I think so."

"He's pretty good, huh?"

"Not bad. I wasn't really watching."

"Better than me?"

"About the same. All kids are about the same at your age."

Richie gave him a look. "How were you, at my age?"

First pick. First pick, every goddamn time. Would have made that number twenty-three look like . . . like *you*. "About the same," Gil said. He reached into his pocket, laid the tickets on the table. "Speaking of the majors," he said.

Richie picked them up, holding them a little closer to his eyes than Gil thought normal. "Opening Day!"

"Didn't I tell you?"

"Yeah, you told me. Thanks. Dad."

"Pick you up at eleven, sharp."

"How many days away is it?"

They counted them. Then they went to a movie. Something about a pirate who drowns in a shipwreck and returns to a Caribbean resort as a ghost. Gil thought it was a comedy until the ghost-pirate chopped off a croupier's hand with his cutlass. The cutlass didn't look authentic to Gil. Turning to point this out to Richie, he saw that his son had his eyes covered.

Gil drove Richie home, parked outside the triplex. He thought of putting his arm around Richie, giving him a hug good-bye. Then he wondered how Richie would take it, decided it might be better if Richie made the first move. Nothing happened.

Richie opened the car door. "Bye," he said.

"Bye." Richie closed the door, started walking across the narrow lawn.

Gil slid down the window. "Richie?"

Richie stopped and turned. "Yeah?"

"When was the last time you saw the eye doctor?"

"Was I that bad?" Richie went into the house.

7

You know what you can do with spring training."

"What's that, Jewel?"

"Get a grip on that dirty mind of yours, Bernie. What you can do with spring training is what Moby Dick did to Captain Ahab."

"I'm sorry?"

"Deep-six it, Bernie. Spring training doesn't mean—what would be a good word?"

"Squat?"

"Perfect. When are we going to learn? It's the same routine every year. The pitchers always jump ahead of the hitters— that was certainly true this spring, with none of the Sox swinging the bat well, excepting Primo, who's turned into Lou Gehrig, for how long we don't know—and everybody goes to Wallyworld and lowers his handicap. The end."

"Then what's the point?"

"It's the overture, Bernie."

"I like that. And the curtain goes up today?"

"The moment the president of the United States throws that first pitch in the dirt."

"How do you know he's going to do that?"

"Because that's the way things are breaking for him. Check out the front section of the paper, Bernie. It's not just a protective wrapper for the sports."

Opening Day, and a beauty. Snow gone, temperature in the sixties, sky blue. Gil wore his lightweight tan suit, a blue shirt, the lucky yellow tie. He hit Mr. Fixit Hardware at nine on the dot, writing a two-box reorder on Swiss Army knives and selling a dozen Survivors, almost in passing; commission $59.36. Then he went to Cleats, ordered scrambled eggs, bacon, a draft. He took out his Survivor sample, just to assure himself he had really sold some.

"What's that?" said Leon.

"The future of American blade making."

"Cool handle. How much?"

"Retail? Seventy, seventy-five."

Leon reached into his pocket. "How about sixty, for a friend?"

"It's my sample."

"Seventy."

Gil sold the sample for $70. He felt a sudden lightness, as though something inside him had been cut loose from a heavy weight. Luck was in the air; such a rare sensation that at first Gil misidentified it as an alcohol buzz. He ordered another draft, a small one, and studied the Opening Day sports supplements.

The *Globe* had color photos of all the starters, complete with bios and lifetime stats. Rayburn lived in San Diego, with his wife, Valerie, a former cheerleader at the University of Texas, and their son, Sean, age five. He liked golf, country music, and, best of all, just hanging out with his family.

"Three hundred and twenty-seven doubles," said Gil.

"Who?" asked Leon.

"Rayburn. That's averaging better than thirty a year. Averaging." Gil tore out the half column devoted to Rayburn and put it in his pocket.

"Where are your seats?" Leon asked.

"Right behind home plate."

"Wave to the camera," Leon said.

Gil picked Richie up at eleven-thirty. Ellen was waiting at the door, coat on.

"You're late."

"Traffic."

"How original."

Richie stepped forward, wearing a Sox cap, carrying his glove. "Hi, Slugger," Gil said.

"Hi."

"When will you have him back?"

"Hard to say, exactly."

"Approximately."

"Depends on the length of the game, right, Slugger?"

"Yeah, Mom. What if it's thirty-three innings, like Rochester-Pawtucket, 1981?"

Ellen smiled. "Hum-babe," she said, ruffling Richie's hair. The moment she said that, Gil found himself wishing that he could undo some things, too many to count; that he could return to some fork in the road that he hadn't even seen on the way by. Here were all the necessary parts—Richie, Ellen, himself—together in the front hall of Ellen and Tim's triplex, no longer shaped to forge a whole.

"Six at the latest," Gil said.

Ellen gave him a look he hadn't seen in a long time, not completely hostile. Luck was in the air. "Have fun," she said and kissed Richie good-bye.

They got in the car. Gil made sure the tickets were in his

pocket, then flipped on the JOC. "I'm psyched," he said "How about you?"

"What's *psyched?*"

"You know. Looking forward to it. Excited. Optimistic. Positive."

"About the game?"

"Opening Day. The season. Everything." Gil laughed, just for the hell of it.

"Me too," said Richie. "Think we'll snag a foul ball?"

"I don't know. Feeling lucky?"

Richie didn't answer immediately. Gil glanced at him. He was chewing his lip. "I hope so," he said. "Today's the draft."

"The draft?"

"Whether I make the majors. Jason Pellegrini said his dad's going to pick me, if I'm still available."

"If you're still available? That sounds good."

"I thought so too," Richie said.

"You're a smart boy," Gil said. "Take after your mom."

He felt Richie's eyes on him. "Aren't you smart?"

"Naw," Gil said. He turned up the volume. Jewel Stern was on.

"... players can't help but feel jittery. I'm feeling a bit jittery myself."

"An old pro like you?"

"Watch how you say that, Norm."

"Jewel Stern, down at the ball yard. We'll be back."

Gil parked in the closest lot to the ballpark—$15. He handed the attendant an extra five. "Keep it unblocked," he said. "And up front."

The attendant frowned.

Gil gave him five more. His calculations depended on a quick getaway.

The attendant nodded and pocketed the money.

They were in their seats an hour before game time. On the

field, the Sox were still taking BP. Rayburn was in the cage. He topped two pitches toward short, then lofted a fly to medium right. "Close enough for you?" Gil said. Richie looked around. "But how are we going to catch foul balls?" It was true: they were behind the screen and under the net.

"Maybe you could get some autographs instead," Gil said.

"How?"

Gil pointed to the kids packed around the Sox dugout on the first-base side.

"I can go down there?"

"Why not?"

Gil bought Richie a program, gave him a pen, watched him make his way to the dugout. The players began coming off the field. The kids surged forward, hanging over the railing, waving programs, baseball cards, scraps of paper, shouting the players' names. Richie tried to push through, was forced back, sat down hard on the steps.

"Don't cry," Gil said, but Richie was crying, Gil could see that even from where he was, two or three sections away. He hurried through the almost-empty rows of seats and down the aisle to Richie.

"Stop crying," he said, raising Richie to his feet, feeling again how bony the boy was; lifting him was effortless.

Richie wiped his eyes with the back of his hand. "I don't want any autographs."

"Sure you do." Gil took Richie's hand, pushed through the shouting kids to the rail, towing Richie behind him.

And there was Rayburn, so close he could have touched him. He was big, but not as big as Gil. His white home uniform shone in the sun. Rayburn was signing autographs; he looked at no one and didn't say a word, just wrote rapidly, while his body leaned almost imperceptibly toward the dugout, as though drawn by gravity. He had a fresh tan, except for pale semicircles under his eyes; but hadn't shaved that day, and there was a blackhead on the side of his nose. Gil could smell that coconut shampoo he used in the ads, and a faint odor of sweat, although there wasn't a bead of it on his face.

Gil squeezed Richie forward, against the rail. Richie stood there, hands at his sides, eyes open wide. "Ask him," Gil said.

"Autograph," said Richie, the word barely audible even to Gil.

Rayburn signed someone's scorecard, took a step or two toward the dugout.

"Not like that," Gil said. "Louder. 'Can I have your autograph, please?' "

Richie raised his voice. "Can I have your autograph, please?"

" 'Mr. Rayburn.' "

"Mr. Rayburn?"

Rayburn spoke. "That's it," he said, and ignoring the pens, pencils, and programs waving in his face, and the cries of "Please!" began moving away.

Gil leaned over the rail. "Hey, come on, Bobby," he said, perhaps too loudly. "Sign one for the kid."

Rayburn paused on the top step. His eyes met Gil's. "You don't look like a kid to me, Slugger," he said, and ducked into the dugout.

Gil felt his face go hot. At first, he was aware of nothing else. Then he heard the stadium buzzing all around him. And finally felt the damp little hand in his. He looked down.

"Dad?"

"What is it?"

"How come he's so mean?"

He let go of Richie's hand. "When are you going to grow up?"

Richie's eyes filled with tears.

"Don't cry, for Christ's sake," Gil said. "He has to get ready, that's all."

"But he's got all his stuff on."

"Mentally."

"Mentally?"

"The game's ninety-percent mental. Don't you know that yet?"

"Then I'm going to be good," Richie said. "I'm getting straight A's."

They bought food—hot dogs, onion rings, Coke for Richie, beer for Gil—and took their seats. The ballpark, hung with bunting, soon filled to capacity, kept buzzing. The players were introduced one by one. The marine color guard played "The Star-Spangled Banner." Then the president of the United States came out and threw the first ball into the dirt. Odell backhanded it smoothly, ran out to the mound, shook the president's hand. The president laughed at something Odell said, and walked off the field, waving and smiling, to cheers and boos; and all the time that buzz in the background never went away.

The starters ran onto the field; even Boyle, the pitcher, couldn't quite slow himself down to a walk. He took his warm-ups. Odell threw the last one down to Primo, covering second. The umpire called, "Play," in a voice that surprised Gil by how high it was, almost female. The batter stepped in. Socko the mascot danced madly on the home-team dugout. Buzzing turned to roaring.

The first pitch was a ball, low. Gil checked his watch. 1:14. Running late already. He went over the calculations one more time: five minutes to the car, fifteen minutes to Everest and Co., five minutes for parking. It meant leaving at 2:05 at the latest.

Ball two, high and inside.

Then half an hour, tops, with the VP, and twenty-five minutes of driving and parking in order to be back in his seat before 3:30, to catch the last two innings—maybe even more, the way they played these days.

Ball three.

"Did you see that curve?" Richie said.

"Just missed."

"I could really see it."

Gil wasn't sure what Richie meant. Was he referring to his eyesight? He gazed down at the boy.

"These seats are great, Dad."

"Oh," said Gil. He tried putting his arm around Richie. A white-haired woman in the next seat smiled at them. She wore pearls and a Harvard baseball cap. Opening Day, a beauty, and the Sox were back.

Strike one.

It was 1:36 when Primo led off the home half of the first. He lined the first pitch over the second baseman's head; clean single. But Primo took the turn at first and kept going. The crowd rose, Gil and Richie too. The throw from right field was on the money. Primo slid headfirst, reaching for the bag. Cloud of dust. Safe. The crowd roared, Gil and Richie too; Richie even jumped up and down a little. He had mustard on his nose. Gil wiped it off with his hand.

"Don't," Richie said.

Lanz flied to left, not advancing the runner. Rayburn came to the plate. The crowd rose in welcome, Gil too, but not Richie.

"Why are you clapping?" Richie said. "He's mean."

"I explained all that." Gil stayed on his feet, but he stopped clapping. Still, he thought: bang one, Bobby, bang one. He could stop clapping, but he couldn't stop his mind from thinking that. Rayburn took his sweet swing and popped to the catcher in foul territory. 1:47.

At the end of the inning, Richie said, "Where are the souvenirs?"

"Like what?"

"Those little bats."

"Down below."

"Can I go? Mom gave me some money."

"Forget that," said Gil. "You're with me."

He went down the ramp, first to the urinals, then to the souvenir stand for the bat. They sold posters too. Gil put his hand on Odell's, on Boyle's, on Zamora's. Someone in the line behind him grew restless. Gil bought the poster of Bobby Rayburn. Quick stop for beers, and back to his seat. Richie was helping himself to peanuts offered by the woman in the Harvard cap and the Sox were batting again.

"What a nice boy you've got," said the woman.

"What happened?"

"Happened?" said the woman.

Gil gestured toward the field, spilling a little beer.

"Quick inning," she said. She handed the bag of peanuts to Richie. "You keep these," she said, and turned to the diamond.

"Here," said Gil.

"Thanks." Richie put the bat and the poster on the seat beside him. Gil checked the time. 1:59.

"Having fun?"

"Yeah."

"I've got to go for a little while," Gil said.

"Go?"

"Just make some calls. You sit tight. Okay?"

"Okay."

"Do you have to pee or anything?"

"No."

"Good." He patted Richie's shoulder. 2:01. Down on the field, the Sox had something going. First and second, nobody out. A sac bunt. 2:04. He could get to the car in three minutes or less, if he ran. Base on balls to Primo. 2:08. He didn't need five minutes for parking; he could doublepark if necessary. Lanz went to a full count, fouled off the next pitch. Socko raised his huge three-fingered hands to the heavens.

"Come on, come on," Gil shouted.

Lanz fouled off three more before striking out. Socko rolled over and died on the dugout roof. Gil hated mascots.

2:14. Rayburn walked in from the on-deck circle, entered the batter's box. The pitcher toed the rubber. Rayburn stepped out, knocked the dirt from his cleats.

"Jesus Christ, let's go," Gil shouted, barely conscious of the Harvard woman's eyes on him.

Ball one, outside.

Rayburn stepped out again. 2:16.

"Down in front, down in front."

Strike one, swinging. Rayburn glanced back at the umpire.

"Down in front." Gil felt a tug on his jacket, realized he was standing, sat.

Ball two. 2:18. Rayburn tapped his cleats again.

"Let's go, let's go."

"Down in front." Another tug. Gil wheeled around, spilling more beer, this time down his shirt.

"Get your hands off me," he said to the man sitting behind him.

"How am I supposed to see?"

"Just ask politely," Gil said, feeling the weight of the thrower around his leg.

"I did."

"Down in front, down in front," yelled someone else.

Gil heard the ball smack leather, turned to see the catcher throwing back to the pitcher. Strike two. 2:19.

Then came a ball, a foul, another foul. Rayburn stepped out.

"For fuck sake."

"Down in front."

The stadium buzzed, louder and louder, beer seeped down his shirt. 2:23. He gazed at the numbers on his watch, and their meaning penetrated. All at once, his tie felt too tight and his heart began to race. He knew the meaning of 2:23: Move, asshole.

Gil pushed past Richie, past the Harvard woman's stare, into the aisle. By the time he reached the ramp, he was running. He ran through the darkness under the stands, loosening his tie, pumping like a sprinter. A tremendous roar went up from the crowd. The whole stadium shook. The vibration came up from the cement floor, through the soles of Gil's shoes, into his body.

8

Three strikes.

One: the parking lot, 2:34. Gil, breathless, ran up to the ticket booth, loosening his lucky tie, feeling beery dampness on the fabric. He checked for the 325i in the front row—hadn't he said, "Keep it unblocked," and tipped the son of a bitch ten dollars? But the car wasn't there. Gil saw that at once, and then saw it again slowly, scanning the row car by car. His head filled with interrogative noise: was this a different lot? had he left by the wrong gate? had his instructions been somehow unclear? Then he spotted it, in the very last row. The noise level inside his head rose, although outside his head the city seemed uncommonly quiet, as though it were Christmas Day; a bleak Christmas Day, with luck no longer in the air. He pounded on the side of the ticket booth, but the pounding made sounds weak and muffled to his ear, so he pounded harder. The attendant, reading a book in an alphabet Gil didn't know, looked up in surprise through the open door.

"Sir?" he said.

Pakistani or some damned thing. Gil hadn't even noticed before. He couldn't patch together a sentence out of the noisy fragments spinning in his head. All that came out of his mouth was, "My fucking car."

"Sir?" said the attendant, half rising, closing the book but retaining his place in its foreign pages with his foreign finger.

It struck Gil then that the little bastard probably didn't understand English, had taken the ten bucks without grasping a word he'd said. An innocent mistake, maybe, but it maddened him all the same: he had no time for mistakes, no time for translation. He took the attendant by the shoulder and pulled him outside, a little roughly, perhaps. Pointing with his free hand, Gil said, "Is that what they call unblocked where you come from, Slugger?"

"But, sir," said the attendant in English only slightly accented, "it is."

Gil let go. The attendant went to the back of the lot, unlocked a gate that Gil hadn't noticed, swung it open. Then he got into the 325i, backed smoothly into the alley, swung around the lot, and came to a stop on the street, right next to Gil.

He got out. Gil got in, slammed the door.

"Do you wish a receipt?" asked the attendant.

Almost no accent, and he spoke a fancier English than Gil's. Gil didn't reply. He just floored it, glancing back once, to see the attendant's dark and watchful image shrinking in his rearview mirror.

Two: in the tunnel, 2:51. Stop and go.

"Come on, come on."

And without warning, Gil had to piss, bad. He squirmed in his seat, unbuckled his seat belt, looked around for a place to pull over. But there was nowhere: even the breakdown lane was jammed. Gil honked his horn, just like those asshole drivers he couldn't stand; and someone honked back, long and hard, blaring through the normal tunnel din.

"Come on, come on."

Long lines of brake lights flashed on, reddening the gloom. Traffic stopped.

2:51.

2:52.

"Jesus, Jesus, Jesus," Gil said, rocking back and forth. So late; he should have been rehearsing his excuse, but all he could think of was the pressure building in his bladder. He unbuckled his belt. That helped a little.

2:53.

2:54.

2:55.

Still stuck deep inside the tunnel, and rocking again. Frantic to get to Everest and Co., frantic to piss. "Jesus, Jesus, Jesus." Gil put his hand on his crotch, squeezed the end of his cock through his suit pants. A mistake. His bladder, or some muscle or whatever it was, abruptly felt free to just let go, so nothing was holding in all that piss but the clamping of his hand. At that moment, traffic jerked forward and started rolling. But Gil couldn't move before shifting into first, and he needed his hand for that. He let go and piss shot out of him, hot and uncontrollable, was still flowing as he banged through the gears and bumped up out of the tunnel and into bright light, feeling nothing at first except dumb relief. But: leather seat soaked, suit pants soaked, executive-length socks soaked, piss in his shoes, cooling fast. The noise in his head grew louder.

Three: outside Everest and Co., 3:07. Every meter taken, the nearest lot three blocks away. Gil swung the car in a U-turn and braked hard beside a hydrant on the other side of the street. Then he grabbed his sample case and ran: across the street, up the steps, through the door, into the lobby. Elevators all in use. He charged up the stairs, piss-soaked pants clinging to his cold skin, beery tie waving like a flag over his shoulder. Three flights. Down the carpeted, softly lit hall and into the outer office of the purchasing VP, the door banging open against the wall.

"Chuck here?"

"Excuse me?"

"Chuck. Two-thirty." Gil sucked in a lungful of air. "Couldn't be helped."

"Excuse me?"

"Being late. The traffic . . ."

The secretary had a little turned-up nose. Not Angie, Chuck's usual secretary, Gil realized, and let his words trail off. She sniffed the air. "You're?"

"Gil Renard. R. G. Renard Fine Knives. Chuckie and I had a two-thirty meeting, should be there on your schedule, but like I said—"

She held up her hand, a stubby hand with bitten nails. "He's not here."

"Shit."

"Begging your pardon?"

"He's gone already?"

"That's what I said."

"What flight's he on?" Gil said, a backup plan forming in his mind.

"Flight?"

"To Chicago. Unless he's not going anymore?"

"He's going," the secretary said. "But not till tonight."

Gil went closer to her desk, his backup plan already revising itself. "Then maybe I could catch him somewhere before he heads for the airport."

"I don't think so," the secretary said. "He's going straight there from the ball game."

"From where?" He was leaning over her desk now, plan forgotten. His damp socks slipped down around his ankles. "From where did you say?"

She rolled her chair back a little. "The ball game. But he left you this note," she said, holding up a sealed envelope.

He snatched it from her hand, tore it open.

Gil—

A supplier laid a couple of Sox tickets on me this morning. Not a big fan, but it is Opening Day, and why not be a hero to my kid? Tried to get hold of you. Sorry.

But this is probably as good a time as any to inform you that, due to the current economic climate, management has opted for a reconfiguration of our purchasing strategy. One upshot is that we won't be renewing the Renard contract at this time.

Always interested in new product, of course, so keep in touch. Been good doing business with you.

Chuck

Gil read the note twice. The first time the noise in his head made him miss some of the details. Then he balled it in his hand and squeezed hard. The secretary was watching him, eyes narrowing in suspicion. "He didn't draw a smiley face, did he?"

"What?"

"The previous assistant got him in the habit of putting a smiley face instead of *sincerely*. I keep telling him it's not always appropriate."

Gil tried to think of something stinging to say, but couldn't. All he could think of were targets for the tight paper ball in his hand: Chuck's window, the photograph of Chuck and his family on the wall, Chuck's secretary's hard little face. He dropped it on the carpet instead, like dog shit, and walked out.

Out. The irony had already hit him, but it hit him again. It hit him on the elevator, and in the lobby. And again when he got to the street: *he's going straight there from the ball game.* Gil knew about irony; he went to the movies. He almost laughed out loud, might have done so if he hadn't suddenly thought of something, a strange quote that he couldn't place or understand: *They kill us for their sport.* Didn't understand: but knew that only an idiot would laugh.

They kill us for their sport: he could fax that to Garrity, by way of explanation. Gil, standing on the sidewalk outside Everest and Co., was just beginning to think of how he would handle Garrity, when he noticed the tow truck on the other side of the street. It had already hooked a car, and, as he watched, it lifted the front end off the pavement with a jerk. A 325i, just like his. That was Gil's first thought.

Then he was racing across the street, tearing off his tie.

"That's my car," he shouted at the tow-truck driver, through the rolled-up window of the cab. The driver, wearing headphones, didn't hear. Gil banged hard on his door. The driver turned, startled, yanked off the headphones.

"That's my car."

The driver snapped down the door lock with his elbow. The window slid open a couple of inches. "You can pick it up at the pound," he said, closing the window and putting the headphones back on.

"Fuck that." Gil grabbed the handle of the driver's door, struggled with it. The tow truck began rolling. Gil hung on, running alongside, screaming unbidden words through the driver's window until the bumper of a parked car caught his left knee. He went down, lost his grip, looked up in time to see the 325i go by on two wheels, like a hobbled prisoner, and hear his phone buzzing inside.

Gil got to his feet. Suit pants ripped at the knee, blood seeping through the polyblend fabric. There was blood in his mouth too. He spat it out, and maybe a tooth as well. Cars went by. No one seemed to notice him. No one gave a shit. Well, he knew that already, right? A taxi approached. Gil stuck up his hand and it pulled over, proving he wasn't invisible.

"Where to?"

"The pound."

"Dog pound?"

"Car pound, for Christ's sake." As the cab pulled away, Gil saw his lucky tie curled up in the gutter. He opened the window and spat out more blood.

A twelve-dollar ride. At the car pound, he paid $50 for parking by a hydrant, $90 for the tow, and $25 for one day's storage, even though the car hadn't been there for twenty minutes.

Gil unlocked it, got in. He took a deep breath to calm himself. The nice smell of leather and wax was gone. The car smelled of piss.

Gil saw his face in the mirror, scratched and hard. He grinned. One of his lower teeth was chipped. He ran his tongue along the roughened edge, and thought of serrated blades pounding deep. Was he looking and sounding successful? Taking the offensive? Ignoring rejection? He ran the rules of the successful commission salesman through his mind, searching for some clue. No clues; he just knew he wanted a shower. First a shower, then a drink.

"What're you waiting for, bud?"

Gil turned the key. His gaze fell on the dashboard clock: 4:27.

4:27. At that moment, he remembered Richie.

He snapped on JOC-Radio. A voice said: "We'll be right back with the wrap-up and all the scores from around the league."

Gil stomped on the gas. He shot through the gate of the

car pound, fishtailed around a corner, clipping something, he didn't know what; only to brake half a block later into a long line of rush-hour traffic. The phone buzzed. He grabbed it.

"Richie?"

But it wasn't Richie. "Been trying to reach you." Garrity. "How'd it go?"

"How did what go?"

"Everest. What else? Is something wrong?"

"Wrong?"

"You sound funny."

"Nothing's wrong," Gil said. His tongue found the jagged tooth edge and rubbed hard.

"Meaning what, in dollars and cents?"

"Can't go into it now. I'm on a call."

Pause. "See you tomorrow, then."

"Tomorrow?"

"Second Wednesday."

"Sales conference?"

"You got it, boyo."

Clouds rolled in from the north, grew heavier, sank over the downtown buildings. On the road, where the best ideas were supposed to happen, Gil waited for one, about Richie, about the sales conference, his tooth, anything. None came. He listened to something scraping under the car, squeezed the steering wheel until his hands cramped. He didn't reach the ballpark until 5:18.

Gil sprang out of the car, ran to the nearest gate. It was locked. Beyond the chain link, unlit ramps curved away into the shadows. No one was around.

"Hey!" Gil called. "Hey!"

A veiny-faced old man in a red blazer appeared on the other side.

"Yeah?" he said.

"My boy's in there."

"Huh?"

"I was supposed to meet him. He hasn't come out."

"No way," the old man said. "We do a sweep. There's nobody."

Gil glanced around, saw a few people on the street, but no kids. "Then where is he?" The question echoed through the concrete spaces under the stands, and Gil realized he'd been shouting. He lowered his voice. "Let me in."

The old man disappeared. He returned a few minutes later. "Checked security. No lost kids. You must have missed him in the crush."

Gil's voice rose again. "He's in there."

The man went away, came back with a second man, much younger, wearing a suit and the air of authority. "What's the problem?"

Gil explained.

"Let him in," said the man in the suit.

"But there's no kid in here," said the old man.

"He'll see that for himself."

The old man unlocked the gate. Gil went in, walked with them up the ramp and out into the stands. Every seat empty. Fans, players, marine color guard, president of the United States, even the Opening Day bunting—all gone. He made his way down to section BB, seats 3 and 4, just the same, in case Richie had left a note. He hadn't, or if he had it had been swept up with the popcorn, beer cups, scorecards, ice-cream wrappers.

"Richie," Gil called, down the left-field line, out to center, down the right-field line. "Richie, Richie." The ballpark was silent. The first drops of rain made the infield tarp quiver here and there. Gil turned to find the two men watching him from the walkway above. He mounted the steps, felt their eyes on him all the way.

"Maybe he's in the can," Gil said.

"We do a sweep," replied the man in the suit. "Didn't you tell him?"

"Sure I told him," said the oldest man. "You think I don't know my job after fifty-six years?"

Gil just stood there. The man in the suit glanced down at Gil's torn pant leg. "That it, then?" he said.

Gil didn't say anything. The old man said, "That's it," for him.

The man in the suit said, "Then show this gentleman out."

The old man walked Gil to the gate. His mood improved as he swung it open. "Nothing to get stressed about," he said.

"What the hell are you talking about?"

"You know—uptight," said the old man. "Happens all the time. Probably went home on his own."

Would Richie know how? Gil wasn't sure.

"Or he's waiting in a burger joint," the old man said, locking the gate.

That was a thought. Gil stepped quickly into the street, without looking. A big Jeep swerved to avoid him. Gil caught a glimpse of Bobby Rayburn at the wheel, laughing into a car phone.

Gil tried all the restaurants and coffee shops within three blocks of the ballpark. He described Richie to a hot-dog vendor, a street cop, and a woman who might have been a hooker. Then he got into his car and drove up and down the streets around the ballpark. Night fell. *Probably went home on his own.* Gil turned toward the expressway and Ellen's. Something dragging under the car scraped pavement all the way.

It was raining hard by the time Gil pulled up at the South Shore triplex. Light shining over the front door, no anxious faces peering from the windows: Gil saw nothing unusual except the big Mercedes parked behind Ellen's car in the driveway.

He knocked on the door. Footsteps. The door opened. Tim. Gil blurted it out. "Have you got Richie?"

Tim licked his lips. "Ellen?" he called.

Ellen appeared. Her cheeks flushed at the sight of him. That meant she had Richie—thank God, Gil said to himself, he really thanked God—but he asked anyway.

"Richie here?"

"What's it to you?"

"Don't start."

"Don't you start. Or do you think you're the injured party? That would be just your style—feeling sorry for yourself."

"Where is he?"

"Safely asleep in his bed, no thanks to you."

"I can explain, Ellen."

"No one wants to hear it."

"Richie will."

"What makes you think that?"

"I owe it to him anyway."

"No one could repay what you owe. And I said he was asleep."

"Isn't it a little early?"

"Not for an exhausted nine-year-old boy. Physically and emotionally exhausted."

"Then I'll just go up and have a peek at him."

"You will not," Ellen said.

"He's my son."

"That remains to be seen."

"What do you mean by that?" No reply. Gil stepped into the hall. Did Tim really move to block him? Gil brushed past him, brushed past Ellen too.

"Stop," Ellen said.

Did she really grab his arm, dig her fingernails through his jacket? That wasn't her at all. What was going on? He shook her off, kept going toward the stairs. As he went past the entrance to the living room, a woman said, "That's him."

He glanced in, saw an old couple sitting on the couch, cups and saucers on their laps. Gil recognized the woman: she was still wearing her Harvard cap.

"Just a minute," the man said, rising. He was tall, square-shouldered, well but modestly dressed: the picture of all those bullshit Yankee virtues. "I don't believe Ellen wants you in her house."

"I don't believe it's got anything to do with you." Gil faced the man.

Ellen grabbed his arm again, but she didn't use her nails this time. "What is wrong with you? You should be down on your knees thanking these people."

"That's not necessary," said the man.

"On the contrary, Judge," said Tim. "Who knows what could have happened to Richie?"

Gil turned on Tim. Tim had a smile on his face that Gil had never seen before and didn't like at all. Gil shoved him against the wall. "Not another word," he said. Then he climbed the stairs.

There were two bedrooms on the second floor. The first, once his and Ellen's, now Ellen's alone, or Ellen's and Tim's, who cared? the second, Richie's. The door was open a few inches, the way Richie liked, or at least the way he had liked it when they had all still been together; and the room was dark inside. Gil went in. A shaft of hall light fell across the bed. Richie lay with his face toward the wall.

"Richie?"

No answer.

"Sorry, pal, if you can hear me. I screwed up, big time."

No answer. Gil had a strong desire to lay his hand on Richie's shoulder, or rumple his hair, something. But he might wake him, if Richie was indeed sleeping, might even frighten him. Gil shrank from that second thought.

"Richie?"

No answer.

"I . . ."

Gil stood in Richie's room, silent. He could hear the boy's breathing, light and regular; sound asleep. Above him Bobby

Rayburn smiled down from the poster, bat resting easily on his shoulder.

Gil wanted something very simple: to lie down on that bed and fall asleep beside his son. The impossible. He had thanked God for Richie's safety. Gil had never addressed God before, but now that the ice was broken he made a little prayer, or request.

"Give me the whip hand," he said.

Richie moaned in his sleep.

Suddenly Gil wondered whether Richie had made the majors.

"Richie?"

No answer.

"Did you hear from the coach?"

Richie moaned again.

9

The ophthalmologist was an old Jewish guy with one of those pendants shaped like the Greek letter *pi*. They sat in the dark and quiet examination room, the ophthalmologist clicking new lenses through the lens machine, Bobby Rayburn peering through them and reporting what he saw in the illuminated square on the far wall.

"E, W, N, T, R, F."

Click. "And the line that begins with L?"

"L, P, Z, Y, O, A."

Click. "Possibly the one below?"

"U, B, D, F, C, R."

Click. "Better or worse?"

"Worse."

Click. "Better or worse?"

"Better."

Click. "Better or worse?"

"About the same."

The ophthalmologist had bright blue eyes. They came closer, gazed through the pupils of Bobby's eyes and into their depths. A long black hair curled out of the old man's right nostril. He rolled back his stool, switched on a desk lamp, wrote on a chart. Bobby watched the pen wiggling in the pool of light, then examined the other light sources in the room—the letters on the wall, his Rolex.

"So, Doc—do I need glasses?"

"Glasses?" The ophthalmologist stopped writing. "Only to make a fashion statement. Your vision is perfect. More than perfect—twenty-fifteen in the right eye and even better in the left. Even better. Almost twenty-ten. Such acuity I find only in children, and then seldom. Glasses? You could qualify as an astronaut or a jet pilot or something of that nature, Mr.—" He checked the chart. "—Rayburn."

"There's nothing wrong with my eyes?"

The ophthalmologist pursed his lips. "Quite the opposite. That's what I'm trying to tell you." He swung the lens machine out of the way, pointed at the wall. "Read that bottom line, if you please."

"D, Y, X, C, N, R."

"You see? You're the first patient I've had in here since January who could do that, and he was a child, not ten years old. You've been blessed, Mr.—" Another glance at the chart. "—Rayburn."

"Then how come I'm not seeing as well as I used to?"

"What makes you think you're not seeing as well as you used to?"

Bobby didn't want to go into it. The guy didn't know who he was or what he did, probably was one of those people who knew nothing about baseball, not even the basics, like balls and strikes. Bobby liked that in a way but it made going into it too difficult. "I don't know," he said.

The ophthalmologist smiled a little smile. Bobby didn't like that smile; he had seen similar ones on the faces of sportswriters. "It's almost impossible from an optical point of view that you ever saw measurably better than you're seeing now," said the ophthalmologist. "Do you follow me?"

"Yes," Bobby said, although he wasn't sure he did.

"You're so close to the theoretical upper limit, the polar opposite of blindness, if you will," the ophthalmologist continued. "How you interpret visual data, on the other hand, is a different question."

"What's that supposed to mean?"

The ophthalmologist's smile faded. "It means that your physical equipment is fine. Other factors may be influencing the way you see the physical world, or think you are seeing it."

"What other factors?"

"Lack of sleep. Alcohol abuse. Drug abuse."

Bobby shook his head to each of those. "What else?"

"Stress."

"Like?"

"What causes stress?"

Bobby nodded.

"All the usual problems. Money worries, love worries, job worries, sickness in the family, death of someone close. And sometimes good things are stressful too." The bright blue eyes looked deep into Bobby's again, probing this time beyond the retinas. "Have you had a period of stress lately?" The long nostril hair quivered like a tendril.

"What do you mean *good things?*"

"A promotion. Birth of a child. Winning a lottery. Any big change is stressful."

"I did sign a new contract," Bobby said.

"When was that?"

"Last month."

"Well, then."

"So when will I start seeing better?"

The ophthalmologist laughed, although Bobby didn't see what was funny. He looked again at the letters on the bottom line, read them easily. But they were just sitting there on the wall, motionless. What if they were suddenly spinning, and coming toward him fast? Could he identify them then? And how soon?

"It's easy to read them when they're not moving," Bobby said.

"Not moving?" The ophthalmologist fingered his little *pi* pendant.

Bobby thought of his four-leaf clover, lost in center field. "Never mind."

The ophthalmologist laid his hand, light and bony, on Bobby's knee. "Try perhaps to relax," he said.

"Relax?"

"You might consider taking some time off from work, for example."

"I had the whole winter off," Bobby said.

The ophthalmologist removed his hand. A Jewish guy, but not like Wald with his $100 haircuts and his mouth; more like one of those scholars in the movies, with a skull cap and gloves that kept your fingers free for writing in unheated studies.

"Have you ever seen a therapist, Mr. Rayburn?"

"Every day."

"Every day?"

"Sure," said Bobby; because of the rib thing. "Physio."

The old man blinked his blue eyes. "I meant the psychological kind."

"You're talking about a shrink?"

"Not necessarily."

But something like a shrink. Out of the question.

And then he remembered the radio reporter's question: *Do you feel any special pressure because of the big contract?*

* * *

"I take it security's one of your prime considerations," the real-estate agent was saying as Bobby walked into the skylit entrance hall, his footsteps clicking on the terra cotta, echoing through the empty house.

They turned to him, Val with a look on her face that said, *You're late,* the real-estate agent hurrying forward with his hand out: "Mr. Rayburn?" That meant that like the ophthalmologist he wasn't a fan either: fans called him Bobby. "Delighted to meet you."

They shook hands. The real-estate agent was as tall as Bobby but much thinner; he wore the kind of flowing double-breasted suit that Wald always wore, only looked good in it. He gave his name, which Bobby didn't catch, and said: "Just delighted."

Delighted. Oh, Christ, Bobby thought.

Val read his reaction, he could tell from her tone when she said, "Roger was just describing the security system here."

"State of the art, naturally," the real-estate agent said. "The vendor had an important collection of Latin American art. A lovely Rivera used to hang right here." He indicated the blank wall opposite the door, blank except for a small video screen beside the light switch. A message was flashing on it. Roger, following Bobby's gaze, said, "That's just the internal part of the system. The whole network's plugged into the police station, the fire station, and the security company's master control." Roger moved toward the screen. Bobby, with his eyes, could read it from where he was: "Motion in foyer. Motion in foyer."

They toured the house. Saw the kitchen, with its terracotta floor, granite countertops, stained-glass windows in the break-fast bay. "From an old church near Sienna," Roger said. Then the living room with its enormous fieldstone hearth and windows two stories tall. And the indoor pool with the chandelier hanging over it. The master suite with another huge fireplace, a walk-in closet as big as their bedroom in California, a balcony overlooking the terrace, the outdoor pool, and the broad lawn, sloping down to the sea, two hundred feet away.

"I almost forgot," said Roger, turning a knob on the wall. The house filled with music, deep, rich, full—classical shit, but as though the orchestra were all around them. "Wonderful, no?" Roger said.

"Yes," said Val.

Bobby opened a door.

"Half lav," said Roger. "Seven others, not counting the maid's quarters."

Bobby went in, closed the door. The music followed him: strings, woodwinds, brass, swelling all around him. He took his stance in the mirror, swung an invisible bat. Opening Day: one for four. Popped out in foul ground, K'd twice; and the grand slam in the second. Boom. Total luck—he hadn't seen the pitch at all, just flicked the bat through the waist-high plane. The ball hit it on the screws. Total luck, but only Bobby knew. He turned on a gold tap, watched water swirl around a blue-marble sink. He saw everything clearly: the silver-and-black flecks in the marble, the changing colors pulsing through the running water. But was he seeing it with that coffee table book clarity? He didn't know. Relax, that was the key. He concentrated on various parts of his body: shoulders, upper back, neck, hips. He thought he felt relaxed, even in his chest, over the rib cage. The only thing he wasn't relaxed about was not seeing the ball.

Bobby splashed water on his face, went out. The real-estate guy was talking on a cellular phone; Val was fixing her lipstick, making those funny lip shapes women do.

"I'll show you something," she said.

He followed her down a hall, into another room, empty except for a space station in one corner, big enough for a kid to play in. "They had grandchildren," Val said.

"Who?"

"The owners."

"How come they're selling?"

"Died in plane crash," Val said.

Bobby didn't like that.

"Private plane," Val added. "I think on a ski trip."

"What difference does that make?"

"Does what make?"

"Whether it was a private plane or not."

"Let's not fight, Bobby."

Bobby walked over to the space station, sat at the control panel, pressed a button. Words appeared on a screen: "Welcome to Saturn Station U.S. 2, orbiting Titan at an altitude of fifty miles, speed 1,200 miles per hour, distance from earth 887.9 million miles, outside temperature minus 270.4 degrees Celsius, all systems go. Awaiting further instructions."

You could qualify as an astronaut. Was that a sign? Bobby said: "You like this place?"

"I love it."

A cheerleader from Lubbock, and now she loved a place like this. Bobby looked for signs of the cheerleader in her. She still had the great body, the blond hair, except not piled up anymore; she'd had it cut, in the style of a woman lawyer or something, although she hadn't worked a day since they got married. Bobby didn't care about that. Why should she work? She hadn't worked, but was starting to look like she had; and the cheerleader was gone.

"Don't you?" Val said.

"Don't I what?"

"Love it."

"This?" said Bobby. "It's not me."

"Why not?"

"Or you either, Val."

"Valerie. And don't tell me what is or isn't me."

The real-estate guy bounded into the room. "Ah," said, "Sean's room."

Bobby got up from the space-station console. The asshole already knew about Sean, name and everything. The screen flashed: "Unidentified object approaching at 87 degrees, 41 minutes. Approx. speed 16,000 m.p.h. Approx. distance 8,000 miles. Awaiting further instructions." They had half an hour, Bobby thought.

"Want to visit the cellar, Mr. Rayburn? Inspect all the machinery?"

Bobby shook his head.

"State of the art," the real-estate guy added.

"I'm sure it's fine, Roger," Val said. "I wouldn't mind having a look at the outdoor pool, though."

"Sure thing."

He led them out back. Putting green, stone barbecue, cabana, pool.

"Twenty-five meters," said Roger. "By—" He consulted a leatherbound notebook. "Fifteen. Heated, of course."

"It's not fenced in," Val said.

"Not necessary, since the whole property is," Roger replied, quickly adding, "but I'm sure something suitable could be designed, if it's Sean you're thinking about."

The pool was empty. A whiffle-ball bat lay on the bottom. Bobby walked to the shallow end, down the stairs, across the bottom of the pool, picked it up. Roger, looking down at him, laughed and said, "Busman's holiday?"

"Huh?"

Roger stopped laughing. Bobby got out of the pool, carrying the whiffle-ball bat. He saw the back door of the house open and Wald came out, walking fast across the lawn.

Wald handed him the *Herald*. "Nice poke yesterday." The back page was a full shot of Bobby, swinging from the heels; off balance, he could tell just from the still photo. Terrible. The headline read: "Rayburn burns Birds."

Roger, reading over Bobby's shoulder, said: "Wow, isn't that something?"

Wald glanced around. "What's all this?" he said.

"We're just looking," Bobby told him.

"Like it, Chaz?" Val asked.

"How much?" Wald said.

"The owners are asking one point six," Roger said. "That includes appliances, all the built-ins, the security, the sound, the—"

"That's not what I asked," Wald interrupted, "what they're asking. I asked how much."

Roger blinked.

"Who are these owners?" Wald said.

"They died in a private plane crash," Val told him.

"Invitation only?" Wald said.

Val laughed. That surprised Bobby. Wald turned to Roger. "So it's an estate sale."

"Something like that." Roger unfastened one of the buttons on the cuff of his double-breasted jacket, fastened it again.

"Something like that." Wald looked at Bobby and Val standing by the edge of the empty pool. "Well? You like it?"

"I do," said Val.

"We'd have to talk," said Bobby.

"So talk."

Bobby and Val walked down toward the sea. The lawn sloped sharply, then leveled out all the way to the beach, flat as a ball field. It was gray under a gray sky. A red sail cut through the water far away, like a shark fin. "Why not?" Val said. "We have to live somewhere. Unless you want me to stay in California. Me and Sean."

"Why would I want that? I just signed a three-year deal here, for Christ's sake."

Val didn't answer. She and Sean? Bobby tried to picture Sean's face; the only face that appeared belonged to the other Sean, yellow and drawn on the hospital pillow. That was bad

She was watching him. "You like it?" Bobby said.

"Don't you?"

Bobby shrugged. "Isn't it a bit. . . too much?"

"The money?"

"The place."

'Too much in what way?"

Bobby couldn't put it into words.

"It's in the best of taste, Bobby," Val said. "So much . . . tonier than California."

"Tonier?"

"You know what I mean. Roger says *Architectural Digest* did a piece on it a few years ago."

"Who are they?"

Val sighed.

Bobby looked up at the pool. Wald and Roger were both still standing there, talking on cellular phones.

"Why not?" Val said again.

Why not? Bobby had no answer. Besides, there was the whiffle-ball bat: a good sign.

"Okay," Bobby said. Val leaned across the space between them, kissed him on the cheek. Bobby thought of his Aunt Greta. She'd been a cheerleader too, he recalled.

They walked back up to the pool. Wald and Roger said good-bye into their phones and pocketed them.

"I guess we like it," said Bobby.

Wald nodded. "Spill it," he said to Roger.

"Spill it?"

"The number."

"As I mentioned, they're asking—"

Wald held up his hand. "We haven't got time for all the bullshit. Bobby's got to be at BP in less than an hour. What'll they take, absolute bottom figure?"

Roger brushed a hand through his beautifully cut hair. "I couldn't really say with any accuracy. I mean, it's not my—"

"Knock it off. You're in the business. What's your best guess?"

"One three."

"We'll go to nine and a quarter. Period. Finito."

"I don't really think that's a realistic—"

"Offer good until midnight tonight. Subject to inspections, etcetera. You and I'll go draw up the papers, Bobby doesn't have to hang around for that, then I'll drop Valerie at the hotel."

"Chaz?" said Bobby.

"Yes?"

"Can we talk?"

"You're the boss."

Bobby walked down toward the sea again, this time with Wald. He couldn't find the red sail. "Nine and a quarter," he said. "Can I afford that?"

"Had a look at your contract, Bobby? Hell, yes, you can afford it. What's more, anything under one one would be a steal for this spread—checked into it before I came over."

"Yeah?"

"Yeah. I do my job, just like you do yours. If you let me."

"A steal?"

"On the water, Bobby. That's what it's all about for these old-money putzes."

Bobby looked around. He couldn't see any other houses. "That's who lives here—old-money putzes?"

Wald clapped him on the back. "They won't bother you, Bobby. No one's going to bother you in a place like this."

Bobby stared out to sea. Now he spotted the red sail, on the edge of the horizon, a red drop on a gray wall. "Can you see that?"

"See what?"

"The red sail." Bobby pointed.

Wald squinted. "Don't see anything."

"All right," Bobby said. "Do it."

"Jawohl."

Bobby drove himself to the ballpark. It was raining lightly so there was no BP. He sat in the clubhouse, pressed PLAY, read the paper, signed balls; all the while avoiding Primo, who sat on his stool, playing Nintendo.

At 12:50 Bobby put on his game shirt, number forty-one. He wasn't getting used to it. It was like a bad haircut, or too-tight shoes, something that made you look and feel stupid. He shot a glance at Primo, crossing himself in front of his locker, wearing 11.

At 1:05 they took the field. Primo went three for three with a walk. Bobby forced him at second twice, grounding into two double plays. He also flied out and struck out. Ofer. They lost in the rain, three zip.

After, there was a girl waiting outside the players' lot. Bobby didn't catch her name; maybe she didn't mention it. He took her to a hotel, not his, and banged her pitilessly.

"Oh, Bobby, I've never felt like this, ever."

"What do you mean?"

"The orgasm you gave me. It was just so . . ."

Later, he returned alone to his own hotel, entered the suite. Val wasn't there. Bobby lay in the Jacuzzi, drinking a beer. Relaxing. He counted the rings holding up the shower curtain. Eleven. He stopped relaxing.

Bobby got out of the Jacuzzi, went to bed. He awoke in the night, feeling someone beside him. He forgot where he was, thought it was the girl from the players' lot, started getting hard.

"Bobby?"

It was Val.

"What?"

"It's done."

"What is?"

"The house. Nine and a half. Chaz is amazing. We can move in next week."

Bobby didn't say anything. Val reached for him. They hadn't had sex in a long time. They had it now. Nothing special. Val had that great body, much nicer than the parking-lot girl's, but in bed she was nothing special.

After, they lay side by side, not quite touching. "Things are working out, aren't they?" Val said. "Wait till Sean gets a load of that space station."

Bobby wondered what had become of the unidentified object, zooming in at sixteen thousand miles per hour. Then he tried to picture Sean's face, and again got the other Sean, wide-eyed on his pillow. He went back to sleep.

Bobby woke up once during the night. He couldn't remember where he'd put the lucky whiffle-ball bat.

10

"——as in the case of John Paciorek, to give you a for-instance."

"You don't mean Tom?"

"I said what I meant, Bernie. John Paciorek. September 29, 1963. First major-league game. Houston Colt .45's."

"Remember that uniform, Jewel? A collector's item now."

"Before my time, Bernie, as you know. Back to Paciorek, John. First game in the bigs. Goes three for three with three ribbies and four runs scored against the Mets, and never plays again. Never plays again, Bernie. True story. What do you think it means?"

"Beats me, Jewel."

"That baseball's like a European movie, Bernie. That's what it means."

"European movies aren't exactly my forte, Jewel. I can't even think of any off hand, except maybe *The Crying Game.*"

"That's close enough."

* * *

April 9, second Wednesday of the month. 7:59. Ding. Fifth floor: linoleum still sticky, Prime National Mortgage still vacant. Gil: all showered and shaved, decked out in a clean shirt and a sober suit fresh out of dry-cleaner's plastic carrying his order book and sample case and a jumbo takeout black coffee; and on time. He also had a new tie—red and black, nothing like his old lucky one—and a plan for breaking the Everest news gently, even with an optimistic spin. He now knew, at last, that yellow was a lousy color for a tie. Red and black, so much better: stand-up, optimistic, take no prisoners. The face of the rep is an optimistic face—he'd read that in a memo from Cincinnati—and wasn't the tie the face of the suit? He liked that idea, would have to try it out on someone—Lenore? Ellen? Gil couldn't think of the right person. He put on a sunny smile to go with his crisp clean freshness. The thrower felt light and warm against his leg.

"Morning, Bridgid. How's Figgy doing with the fishing rod thing?"

Bridgid didn't look up from her keyboard. "It's over."

"Probably just as well. Once a city boy, always a city boy, right?"

Now she glanced at him, then quickly turned away. "Right."

But if the fishing-rod thing was over, where were the fifty bucks going to come from? Gil, staying optimistic, pushed the thought from his mind and opened the conference-room door. Garrity and the eleven other Northeast reps were already sitting around the table. Twelve, actually: the eight veterans, plus the three brought in by O'Meara last month, plus one more: Figgy. He was passing Lifesavers to Verrucci, the new rep from Texas. Garrity saw Gil, held up his index finger, hurried to the door.

"Got a second?"

"If you do," said Gil. "It's eight o'clock."

Garrity backed him into the hall, closing the door with Gil

halfway through a recount. They went down the hall, into Garrity's office. "Sit down, Gil," Garrity said, indicating the couch that he had brought in after his divorce a few years ago. Much too soft and homey for an office couch: Gil had never seen anyone using it.

He sat, sinking down too deep for comfort. Garrity perched on a corner of his desk. His pant leg slid up, revealing his shiny, pink, hairless shin: an old man's leg. Gil's father wouldn't have been much older than Garrity, if he'd lived.

"Figgy's back?" Gil said.

"Nothing I could do about it," Garrity said. "Cincinnati."

Garrity's attitude surprised him. "Figgy's not so bad."

"Nice of you to say so," Garrity said, "under the circumstances."

Circumstances? Did Garrity somehow know about the fifty? It wasn't that big a deal. "What do you mean?"

Garrity took a deep breath, blew it out through pursed lips. "Gil," he said.

"What?"

"Do I have to spell it out?"

"Spell what out?"

"O'Meara's been on the phone with the Everest people." Garrity waited for Gil to say something. Gil, trying to remember the spin plan, trying to stay optimistic, was quiet. Garrity continued, "The long and the short of it, and I wish to God it wasn't me having to say this, is that you're—"

Gil found his voice. "I can explain all about the Everest thing." But not sitting down on this stupid couch with my knees in the air. Gil rose. He had the order book, sample case, and jumbo black coffee in his hands. Too much: the coffee spilled, mostly on his pants, some on the couch. Scalding pain, but he ignored it. He also ignored the fact that for the second day in a row, he'd ruined his clean crisp freshness, wet himself. This realization was harder to ignore than the pain; it made him want to rip his clothes off, to go into a frenzy. Instead he found himself talking a mile a minute. "I can explain the Everest reconfiguration. First of all, I don't know what you heard from O'Meara, or what Everest told him, except it couldn't have been Chuckie, he's in Chicago, but I can promise you it's not nearly as bad as it—"

Garrity was shaking his head. "Save it, Gil. The word's come down from Cincinnati."

"What word?"

"Aw, Gil, don't make me. The word that you're . . . you know."

"That I'm what?" He took a step closer to Garrity, loomed over him.

Garrity's face hardened. "I'll need your order book, Gil. And your sample case. Outstanding commission checks will be forwarded."

"That I'm what? That I'm what? That I'm what?"

Garrity didn't answer, although Gil's face was now inches from his own.

Gil still had the order book and sample case in his hands. He pictured himself raising them high and bringing them down on Garrity's head, even felt the beginning of the rush of hot pleasure that would accompany the act. But he didn't do it. He just let go, dropping them on the floor.

Garrity didn't move, didn't raise his voice. "You've got to get your life under control, boyo. As an old friend of your father I'm saying that."

Gil glanced down at that pink leg. He could probably snap it in two with his bare hands. Would Garrity raise his voice then? Again he felt an incipient wave of hot pleasure, glimpsed a jumbled future of confused possibilities, disturbing and exciting; and again stifled the act. "As an old friend you keep your mouth shut about my father," he said. "He started this business."

Garrity shook his head. "Your father made beautiful knives. Cincinnati made it a business."

"By ripping him off."

"He was happy with the deal at the time."

"He was dying at the time, you stupid shit."

"He wasn't a businessman, Gil. Bottom line."

It hit Gil then for some reason, the Figgy part. "You gave Figgy my area?"

"Not me personally. O'Meara."

Gil spun away, bursting out of Garrity's office, down the hall, to Bridgid's desk. She was bent over the keyboard, glasses slipped down to the end of her nose.

"How many dicks did you have to suck to get Figgy back on the payroll?" he said.

Her head jerked up, eyes widening.

"Garrity, O'Meara, who else?"

Bridgid's face went red, just like a swelling dick, in fact: guilty as charged, he thought. Then she burst into tears. But he got no pleasure out of that; too easy, like pressing a button. Gil needed action.

He started for the conference room. A man in a windbreaker rose from one of the waiting-room chairs and stepped into his path, not quite blocking it.

"Mr. Renard?" he said with a smile.

"Yeah?"

"Have a nice day." He handed Gil a long white envelope and left the office.

Stuffing it in his pocket, Gil strode to the conference room, banged the door open. In a moment he took in the essentials of a boisterous scene: the reps' mouths open wide in laughter, all eyes on Figgy; Figgy balancing a wavering tower of cherry Lifesavers on his nose.

Then came silence, except for the Lifesavers skittering across the floor, and all eyes were on him. Gil had no plan; he wanted action, that was all. He walked around the table to Figgy. Figgy got out of his chair, backing up a little. Gil smiled—smiling was a simple baring of teeth, right?—and held out his hand. Reluctantly, as though fearing a bone crusher, or some other trick, Figgy extended his; but he couldn't refuse—he was a rep. They shook, Gil hardly squeezing at all, just smiling this new smile he couldn't remember smiling before, but that seemed so right.

"Congratulations, Figgy," he said. "And continued success in your new endeavors."

He released Figgy's damp hand.

"That's really nice of you, Gil," Figgy said. He lower his voice: "Don't think I've forgotten that money."

That's what he'd picked to feel ashamed about. "Money?" said Gil.

Figgy lowered his voice some more. "That money I owe you."

Gil laughed, a new laugh that went nicely with his new smile. "Forget it. What's fifty bucks between amigos? Buy a little something for old Bridgid out there. Be a sport."

Then he turned and walked out, past Garrity who was hovering over Bridgid, still crying at her desk, and down to the street. Out. Free.

He got into the 325i, started it, drove a few blocks before the scraping sound bothered him. He stopped in the middle of the street, walked around to the back of the car. There was a big dent behind the left-rear wheel, and the tailpipe was dragging. He bent down and tore it off. The muffler came with it. Then he overcame an impulse to tear the whole car apart right there, piece by piece; and drove to Cleats.

Gil ordered a draft with a shot of Jose Cuervo Gold on the side.

"Your son enjoy the game?" Leon said, setting the drinks on the bar.

Gil looked at him.

"Richie. That's his name, isn't it?"

"How did you know that?"

"You've mentioned it a few times," said Leon, his voice rising a little in surprise.

Ease up, Gil said to himself Leon was a pal, right? He smiled at Leon, hoping it was his old smile, not the new one, but unsure. "Yeah, he enjoyed it. What kid wouldn't?"

"Opening Day," said Leon. "Some game."

"Yeah."

"Maybe you were right about Rayburn."

"I was?"

"Hard to argue with a poke like that." Leon drew someone a pint.

The *Globe* sports section lay on the bar. Gil picked it up and started reading. He read about the grand slam, hunted up all the details of the game, studied the box score, then all the box scores; downed the beer and the shot, ordered another round. Feeling pretty good now, and, yes, even optimistic. Of course he'd been right about Rayburn. He knew the game, knew the team, knew the man. He checked his red-and-black tie in the mirror behind the bar. Nice.

Then he came to a sidebar on Bobby Rayburn— "Paying Early Dividends"—that included the breakdown of his contract. Gil went over them—$2.5 million signing bonus, $5.05 million the first year, $5.45 million the next, $5.85 million the year after that, $6.05 million in the option year, the separate $1 million deferred-payment fund. The reporter estimated Rayburn's endorsement income at $750,000 a year. Well, why not? One swing of the bat. He was going to take them all the way, as Gil had foreseen. He tore out the article, folded it, and put it in his wallet.

A few minutes later he took it out to read again the part about the deferred payments. They began in 2007, $50,000 a year for as long as he lived. That was the part Gil liked best of all: Rayburn knew right now where his money was coming from in 2007. Gil didn't know where his money was coming from next week. He examined his face in the mirror for signs of optimism. It was dark and swollen, as though gorged with blood.

He had one more round. His pants were almost dry.

"Guess who stopped in last night?" Leon said.

"Figgy."

"Yeah, Figgy was here. With that girlfriend of his. Drinking champagne. But that's not who I meant."

"Who did you mean?"

"Ball players. They usually go to Bluebeard's. Maybe they're going to start coming here—I know they liked the buffalo wings. I brought them two helpings each."

"What ball players?"

"Primo. Sanchez. Zamora. Couple of others."

"Where'd they sit?"

Leon pointed to a table in the back alcove, under the autographed Louisville Sluggers of Aaron and Mays, crossed like a device on a medieval shield.

"What were they talking about?"

Leon shrugged. "They spoke Spanish." He thought. "Is there some guy called Onsay in baseball?"

"Not they I've heard of."

"They kept joking about him."

"What do you mean?"

"Primo'd say *Onsay,* and the others would crack up."

"Got the encyclopedia?"

Leon pulled the *Baseball Encyclopedia* from under the bar. There was no one between Manuel Dominguez "Curly" Onis, who'd gone to the plate once for the 1935 Brooklyn Dodgers and singled, and Edward Joseph Onslow, who'd hit .232 in 207 at bats spread over four years between 1912 and 1927.

Gil returned to Curly Onis's meager line. "What's *The Crying Game?*" he said.

"Some movie."

"About baseball?"

"I don't think so," Leon replied. He ran his finger down the page. "Maybe Onsay's a rookie."

"I'd have heard of him," Gil said. He had a hit of tequila, drained his beer, and was considering another round or two, just to sit at the bar, poring over the small print, when Leon said:

"Day off?"

"Naw." That ruined it. Gil closed the book and asked for his bill.

"That's okay," Leon said.

"What's okay?"

"This one's on the house."

Meaning that Leon knew what Figgy'd been celebrating.

Gil drove north, out of the city, into the mountains. At first the car smelled of the ammonia soap he'd scrubbed it with in the middle of the night; later, with the heat on, he detected pissy smells. Everything was brown, except for the artificial snow on the trails of the ski resorts. Gil listened to the ball game, heard them lose three zip, with Rayburn going oh for four. Meant nothing. After, on the JOC, a caller wondered about Rayburn's rib cage and Bernie said the story had been blown out of proportion, Rayburn was fine, and Burrows had handled it fine.

"Bullshit," Gil said; and then, at the top of his lungs, all alone in the car, "Bullshit." Burrows had jeopardized Rayburn's career and the team's entire season, and the media were covering it up. The rib cage was obviously killing Rayburn—why else would he have been short with him in front of the dugout? He called the JOC to blast Bernie, but couldn't get through.

Gil left the interstate, followed secondary roads. From time to time he stopped for a drink, the last one in a crummy sports bar—nothing like Cleats—in a crummy town.

It was dark, and Gil hadn't eaten. Sitting at the bar, he

drank a beer and a shot while he looked at the menu. Then he ordered another beer and another shot.

"And something to eat?"

Gil shook his head.

Sometime later, he found that this bar too had a copy of the *Baseball Encyclopedia*. Gil, hunched alone in the far corner of the bar, lost himself in it.

Much later, he looked up Onsay again. Then Boucicaut. And Claymore. And himself. Renard, Gilbert Marcel. None of them were there. He left at closing time, walking out to a cold and silent street. Main Street, he saw, in his old hometown.

11

The night was black and full of stars, the air cold and quiet, Gil's breathing and footsteps the only sound. He walked down Main Street to the last arc light, past darkened shops, some boarded up, and took a left on Spring. Drunk, yes, but he'd been drunk in his old hometown before, long ago, as a teenager, when the town was bigger and being drunk on a cold black night like this meant feeling huge and light and full of possibility, almost as though you could take flight into that twinkling sky. Now he felt nothing except the woods, invisible in the night, but cinched tight all around the town. The town had stayed the same, even shrunk, but the trees had grown.

Gil came to the path at the end of Spring Street. A wooden sign arched overhead. The lettering, once gilt, was barely readable: Amvets Memorial Field, 1951. Ahead loomed the high shadow of the announcing booth, the baser shadow of the concession stand, and the chain-link perimeter fence, glinting here and there with starlight. Gil climbed it, and dropped down to the cold wet grass on the other side.

He made his way to home plate, rubbed it with the toe of his city shoe: a tasseled loafer, actually. Tasseled loafers had been on a list recommended by Cincinnati. The crushed-stone base paths seemed luminous to Gil, a hollow diamond in the darkness. He walked to first, or where first would be had the bags been in place, slowly; rounded it, stumbling just a little, and continued on to second and third, even slower now, barely dragging one foot in front of the other by the time he reached home. There was no internal soundtrack of cheering and yelling, or any of that shit: he'd seen all those stupid movies. All he heard was his own breath, sibilant between his lips, rasping in his throat.

"No appealing," he said aloud, and stamped on the plate, dead center: safe. Then, picking up his pace, he crossed to the home-team dugout, a simple cement-block bunker with a flat roof, and sat on the concrete bench. He stared out at the pitching mound, a pale, negligible hump.

Later, feeling the cold, he pulled his suit jacket around him and curled up on the bench, facing the dugout wall, hands between his knees. He closed his eyes, or they closed themselves; he fell asleep, or he passed out.

Richard Renard left St. Jeanne d'Arc Hospital the morning of the deciding game of the Series. Didn't sign himself out or consult anyone: simply waited until after rounds and rose from his bed on the ward. He put on some clothes from his locker, then sat on the bed and rested for a while. After that, not wanting to risk being spotted on the elevator, he took the stairs to ground level, resting on every landing, and a few times in between.

He found his car in the parking lot out back, unlocked it, got in, rested. Then he drove a hundred and fifty miles to the ballpark. Game time was 1:00 P.M. The dashboard clock read

12:57 when he arrived. He rested for three minutes, then tried to leave the car. That involved twisting his torso, raising the door handle, climbing out. The twisting and raising went fine, but not the climbing. He had never before realized the role legs played in getting out of a car. He'd never had to: all his life, he'd had powerful legs. Now they couldn't even lift him off the car seat.

Richard Renard sat in his car outside the ballpark. He rolled down the window, he had the strength for that, and listened to the sounds of the game: cheering, shouting, crack of bat on ball, thump of ball in mitt; a thump slightly deeper in tone indicating when his son was on the mound, or so he imagined. He thought of honking the horn for help, but at first couldn't bring himself to do it. By the time he'd convinced himself otherwise, the physical capability was gone. The ball game and its thumping, cracking sounds began to distance themselves from him, slipping farther and farther away.

Gil was thirsty. His arm ached. Those were distractions he had to ignore. Two more distractions were the crowd, on its feet and roaring, and the runners on second and third, dancing off the bags. Tunnel vision, his father said: a pitcher needs tunnel vision. Gil peered down the tunnel at Bouchard, the Yankee cleanup hitter poised at the plate, big as a man. Bottom of the ninth, two out, two on, and up one to nothing, on Gil's home run in the top of the inning.

First pitch a ball way outside, almost getting by Boucicaut. Boucicaut came out for a talk.

"Maybe we should walk him," Gil said.

"Fuck that," said Boucicaut. "If you want to put him on, at least hit him in the head."

Boucicaut spat right through his mask and returned to his position. He called for the curve. Gil, wincing even before the pain, threw it in the dirt. The runner on third came halfway down the line. Boucicaut bluffed him back.

Boucicaut crouched, gave the sign. Fastball. Bouchard watched it go by. It looked good to Gil. "Ball three," said the umpire.

Three and oh. Bouchard would be taking all the way, right? Boucicaut signaled another fastball. Gil wound up and threw, a medium-speed fastball, right down the pipe; and realized as he let go that Bouchard wasn't taking.

Bouchard uncoiled and got it all, a low screamer right at Claymore between second and third. The ball hit him in the chest, making him cry out and knocking him down, then fell motionless on the base path beside him. Claymore, on his back and in tears, picked it up and brushed the leg of the base runner from second as he raced by. The second-base ump stabbed his fist in the air. Game over: the last out of the championship season.

They jumped up and down. They hugged each other and shouted their heads off. They all got trophies and a handshake from a man in a seersucker suit, and Gil got a special one for being MVP: a brass-plated baseball mounted on a hardwood stand. No one left the field for half an hour or so. That's when they found Gil's father's body, cold and gray, slumped in the front seat of his old Chevy on Spring Street.

Gil, wearing his stand-up red-and-black tie and the shirt and suit so recently unwrapped from dry-cleaner's plastic, awoke on the dugout bench, shivering. It was still night, but the moon had risen; frost silvered the grass all the way to the outfield fence. Stiff with cold, Gil rose and puked in the corner of the dugout. Nothing but liquid, foul and bitter: what his stomach had done to all the beer and shots. He hadn't eaten since . . . he tried to remember when and couldn't.

Gil climbed the fence, not so easily this time, and got back in his car. He drove back to Main, heater on full blast, and turned up Hill, following it to the northern edge of town where the cemetery separated the last dwelling from the woods. Like many reps with snowy territories, Gil carried a folding shovel in his trunk. He took it now and entered the cemetery.

The town might have been smaller, but the cemetery, like the woods, had grown. The gravestone of Renard, R. G., which had been in the farthest row, with nothing but empty field between it and the trees, now had other stones all around it. Familiar town names: Pease, Laporte, Spofford, Cleary, Bouchard. Gil read them in the moonlight. It took him some time to locate Renard, R. G.

The lawyer who'd executed the will had sold the Chevy to pay for the stone: marble-faced and round-topped, a little nicer than some of those around it, but not very big. There was room for no more than the carved name and the dates of birth and death, bracketing an interval that might have represented the average life expectancy in some sub-Saharan country. Gil pushed it over easily.

He unfolded the shovel, snapped the handle in place, started digging. Quickly down through a wet layer, slow through a still-frozen layer beneath that, a little faster through the dry earth below. Gil began to sweat, although his hands and feet were cold. He dug himself down, knee deep, waist deep, down into his father's grave, his moonlit breaths rising urgently in the night. After a while, the eastern sky turned milky, as though a celestial eyelid were opening, but Gil, up to shoulder level in darkness, didn't notice. He bore down with the shovel, tossed out earth, bore down, tossed out, bore down, tossed out, in rhythm, just like hammering at the anvil. It was almost enjoyable, certainly better than any work he'd had since those days at the forge. Should have been a grave digger, he thought, but was considering the possibility that grave digging too was controlled by men like Garrity and O'Meara, when the shovel struck something hard. He looked down, realizing only then that it was day-break and he had to hurry, and saw a cleared section of pine board, the varnish dulled and grimy. Gil cleared a bigger section, then raised the shovel high and plunged the blade down with all his strength, splitting the wood at his feet. He paused, his nostrils anticipating the arrival of some putrescent smell, but none came.

Gil struck a few more times, smashing a small hole. Then he knelt, snapped off a few jagged pieces—pine, but thin and pocked with knots—and peered inside. He saw the buttoned-up buttons of a white shirt, a white shirt decaying and full of holes; a scattering of little bones, palm and finger bones, resting on a rep tie, also eaten away; and, lying among the bones, a brass-plated baseball mounted on a hardwood stand, perfectly preserved. Gil stuck his hand inside and took the trophy. A few of the little bones came with it, one somehow slipping under the cuff of his shirt, sliding coldly up his forearm.

Gil let out a sound then, not loud, but totally uncontrolled by his larynx, vocal cords, brain. He shook his arm frantically, launching the bone into the brightening sky and out of sight. With the trophy in the other hand, he tried to scramble out of the hole, but lost his balance and tumbled back down the side, landing on the coffin. He made the sound again, perhaps more loudly this time, and then, without knowing how, he was up on ground level, clawing on all fours through the dirt, crawling at an unsustainable pace. He fell forward, and lay panting, his face on the icy grass. Gray light spread softly around him. He puked again, but nothing came out.

Gil got up, looked around, saw no one. Beyond the cemetery and down Hill Street, the town was still in shadow. He returned to the grave, filled it in, tipped up the stone, walked it back in position. Then, trophy in hand, his trophy, he turned to go. At that moment, something flashed orange in the woods, and he heard the crack of a rifle. Gil ran, ran as hard as he could, dodging gravestones, ran toward the road, cold in the small of his back, waiting for that cracking sound again, for the hot ball tearing through him. But there wasn't a second shot. Gil slowed, glanced back.

A man stepped out of the woods. He had a rifle in one

hand, and a doe over the opposite shoulder. Even from where Gil stood, the animal appeared to be under the limit; besides, it wasn't hunting season. Gil understood at once: it was his hometown, after all. The man looked around, scanning the cemetery and beyond. Gil dropped behind a gravestone, a big one with a cross on top.

The poacher moved quickly through the cemetery, heading not toward Hill Street, but to a pickup Gil hadn't noticed before in the darkness, parked behind a shed at the end of a dirt track. A big man, powerfully built, but grossly overweight. He had shoulder-length hair, an untrimmed black beard, and like many fat people didn't appear to feel the cold: he wore jeans and a T-shirt. Blood stained his bare arms. Gil crouched behind the gravestone, and would have remained there, but as the man came closer, as close as his path was going to bring him, about twenty yards away, it struck Gil that there was something familiar about that rapid, bowlegged stride. He stood up.

"Co?"

At the sound of Gil's voice, the poacher dropped the deer, wheeled, raised the gun, all in one quick motion, impossibly quick for such a huge man. That proved it.

"Who the fuck are you?" said the poacher, gun muzzle pointed at the middle of Gil's chest.

Boucicaut, without a doubt. Gil had never been as happy to see someone in his life.

12

By God," said Boucicaut, flinging a handful of deer intestines out the door of his one-room trailer, "some car you got there, Gilly." The 325i sat in Boucicaut's muddy yard beside the pickup, a rusted and doorless oven, bald tires, a stained mattress, windblown scraps, garbage. Gil, drinking coffee at the grimy-topped card table by the sink, remembered yards like that from his childhood, but the Boucicauts' hadn't been one of them.

"Thanks," Gil said, but he knew the car was ruined for him now. It meant payments he could no longer make and that pissy smell inside; his mind shrank from the thought. "So what are you doing these days?" he asked. The coffee was trembling in his cup, as though the earth were unsteady, far below. He put it down.

"Running for Congress," Boucicaut said.

Gil, not sure he had heard right, stared at him.

"Joke, man," sad Boucicaut. "What'd you think I'd be doing?"

That was easy, and Gil blurted it out: "Catching for the Sox."

Boucicaut laughed a barking laugh, then said, "I don't get you."

"That's what I always thought," Gil said. "That you'd end up in the big leagues."

"Then you were living in a dream world." Boucicaut gave Gil a long look. The expression in his eyes changed. "That's a sharp suit, Gilly. To go with the wheels."

A cheap suit, compared to what was out there in the world of suits, and stained with coffee besides. Gil said nothing.

"How does it feel?"

"How does what feel?"

"Raking in the big bucks."

"I wouldn't know."

"Don't appear that way to me," Boucicaut said. He had the deer laid out on newspaper on the vinyl floor and was gutting, skinning, and butchering it, all with a monstrously oversized and ill-made hunter, probably from China. Gil watched Boucicaut hack away for a minute or two, his oily black hair hanging over his face in two wings, then pulled out the thrower and gave it a quarter spin across the room. It stuck in the floor, a foot or two from Boucicaut's hand. Boucicaut didn't even twitch.

"Try that," Gil said.

Boucicaut turned to him and smiled. Both incisors were missing. "You kept it up?"

"Kept what up?" said Gil, and rubbed his tongue over his chipped tooth.

"Throwing."

"Not really."

Boucicaut jerked the thrower out of the floor. "Your old man's?" he said.

Gil nodded.

"What's it worth these days, a blade like this?"

"I'm not sure."

Boucicaut ran the edge lightly across the ball of his thumb. "Jesus." A red line seeped onto the skin, taking the shape of a lipsticked and unsmiling mouth. Boucicaut licked it off and returned to the deer, using Gil's knife. He sliced easily through the white tendon at the back of a hind leg; the long purple hamstring slid free.

How to hamstring a man, thought Gil: dive, roll, come up behind, slice just like that and just there. His father had taught him that with rubber knives, not far from where he now sat, in a trailer too, and with a yard outside and under the same sort of scudding clouded sky; but it had all changed.

"Sure knew how to make 'em, your old man," said Boucicaut. He pushed himself up with a grunt, his stomach hanging over his belt, and opened the fridge. "Switch to beer?"

It was eight in the morning, Gil had a headache and still hadn't eaten, but he said yes to Boucicaut. And thought, yes, wouldn't it be nice if Boucicaut took over, took charge, took care of him, the way the catcher does the thinking for the pitcher.

Boucicaut took out four Labatt's Fifties and handed him two, leaving a red smear on the fridge door. "Some watch you're wearing, Gilly," he said, Gil's sleeve sliding up as he reached for the bottles.

"No one calls me that anymore."

"No?"

"No."

Boucicaut knelt over the deer. He stuck his hand in the rib cage, twisted, ripped out the heart. Then he whistled. A big black mongrel appeared in the doorway and Boucicaut tossed it to him. The dog caught it in the air and ran off. Boucicaut's eyes fastened again on Gil's car.

"No one calls you Gilly?"

"No."

"What do they call you? Mr. Renard?"

"Some do."

"Some do." Boucicaut shook his head. "You made it, didn't you, old pal? Went out into the big bad world and made good."

Gil didn't want to think about how he'd done. For the second time, he asked: "What are you up to these days?"

"This and that," said Boucicaut.

"Looks like you're making out all right," Gil said.

Boucicaut stopped whatever he was doing inside the deer carcass, the thrower out of sight. He gave Gil a look, the same combative look, Gil supposed, that he used to see through the bars of the catcher's mask when the game was on the line. But now it had a menacing effect he didn't remember; maybe it was just the black beard. "Is that meant to be funny?" Boucicaut said.

"You've got a truck. You've got this place."

Something snapped inside the carcass. "The truck's a rusted-out piece of shit with two hundred thousand miles on it. And this pigsty isn't even mine. Belongs to my old lady."

Gil couldn't stop his gaze from sliding toward the bed against the back wall, empty and unmade.

"Don't get a hard-on, Gilly. She won't be back till August."

"Gil."

Boucicaut tilted a beer to his lips, swallowed half of it. "Ask me why, Gil."

"Why what?"

"Why she won't be back till August."

"Why?"

" 'Cause she's in the pen."

Gil didn't say anything.

"Ask what for."

"Just tell me, Co."

"No one calls me that either."

"What do they call you?"

"Len." Boucicaut finished his first bottle, set it on the table, coming close to Gil. Gil heard him breathing, the heavy breathing of a fat, middle-aged man, not a big-league catcher. That didn't make sense. "It's my name, right?" said Boucicaut.

"Right."

"Did you know that Boucicaut was a knight in the Crusades?"

"No."

"A real one, not like Robin Hood. A college chick told me that."

"You went to college?"

"That's a good one. This was a college chick I picked up in a bar." Boucicaut started on the second bottle. "You haven't finished asking me."

"Asking what?"

"What they got my old lady for."

"Speeding?" Gil, his first beer drained too, was feeling lightheaded.

"Another joke. You're out-jokin' me, old pal."

"I give up, then."

"Sellin' her tail."

"They locked her up for that?"

"She was workin' the ski places. Not a bad idea—that's where the money is. Hurt their image, though, so they went after her. Image is the whole fuckin' deal with those assholes."

"Sorry."

"Don't be sorry for me. I miss the money is all."

The mongrel returned to the door. Boucicaut threw out another red organ.

They emptied their second beers, had a few more. Boucicaut finished with the deer, bagged the meat, put it in the fridge; then kicked the remains outside, rolled up the newspaper, stuffed it in the woodstove. "What day is it?" he said, wiping the thrower on his jeans and handing it to Gil.

For a moment, Gil wasn't sure. Was that what it meant to be unemployed, you lost track of time? Then he pictured his schedule, laid out in boxes, now demolished. "Thursday," he said.

"Thursday," Boucicaut said. "Sale on ammo, down at Sicotte's. Think I'll run down." He stepped outside, crossed the yard, stopped by the 325i. "Wouldn't mind a little test drive."

"Want me to drive you there, you mean?"

"More like drive myself. Unless you don't trust me.

Gil went outside, gave him the keys. He'd trusted Boucicaut since he was five years old. "Be right back," Boucicaut said. He opened the car door, saw the trophy lying on the passenger seat. "What's that?"

"Nothing," Gil said. "My kid's." He reached inside, took it out.

"You've got a kid?"

"Yeah."

"Me too. A couple."

"In school?"

"If it's really Thursday."

"They must have left early."

Boucicaut looked puzzled.

"For school," Gil explained. "They were gone when we got here."

"They don't live here, for Christ's sake. They're with their ma."

"In jail?"

Boucicaut's forehead knotted. "Not her, man. Down in Portland. This was before."

He climbed into the car, wheeled it around as though he'd been driving it for years, and sped off, spewing mud. His whoop of pleasure hung in the air, or else Gil imagined it.

Gil went back inside, closed the door. It was cold. He lit the stove, had another beer, looked around. He found nothing interesting—unless guns and ammo were interesting; plenty of guns, plenty of ammo—until, on the floor at the back of the only closet, he came across two baseball gloves, both buried in dust balls. One was a fielder's glove, the other a catcher's mitt. A black Rawlings. Gil recognized it. He put it on, pounded his fist in it a few times; then he took it off, sniffed inside, and set it on the table beside the trophy.

He lay down on the bed, got a hard-on. Boucicaut's old lady was a whore. That meant she'd sleep with him if he paid. He toyed with the idea of sleeping with Boucicaut's old lady, decided he wouldn't do it. But what if she walked in the door that very minute? He watched the door for a while. Then he closed his eyes.

When he opened them the trailer was cold and full of shadows, and the objects he saw—trophy, mitt, beer bottles— had fuzzy edges. He checked his watch: six-thirty. He'd slept all day. Gil rose, opened the door, went outside. No car. Sicotte's, as he recalled, was about fifteen minutes away. The mongrel trotted past, toward the woods.

"Here, boy."

The dog growled and kept going.

Gil took a piss, watching the lane, listening for the sound of an approaching car. He heard no cars, heard nothing at all. The temperature fell, the silence grew, like a living thing. Gil felt the woods all around. He stuffed his hands in the pockets of his suit jacket for warmth, for comfort.

And felt something crumpled up in one of them. He withdrew it, smoothed it out: a long, sealed white envelope, addressed to him. He opened it.

Inside was a legal document he could make no sense of at first. Words and phrases from various parts of the page leapt out at him: "Defendant's DOB," "Probate and Family Court," "Plaintiff"

"Hold it," he said aloud, "just hold it."

The mongrel reappeared, wagging its ragged tail, brushing Gil's leg. Gil kicked it away.

He forced himself to begin at the top, read word by word. Ellen's name was typed in the box labeled Plaintiff. His appeared in the box beneath: Defendant. For a moment he thought he was the good guy; the plaintiff was a complainer, right? Then he read on:

THE COURT HAS ISSUED THE FOLLOWING ORDERS TO THE DEFENDANT (only items checked shall apply):

There followed nine numbered lines, preceded by little boxes. X's appeared in two of them:

YOU ARE ORDERED NOT TO ABUSE THE PLAINTIFF by harming or attempting to harm the plaintiff physically, or by placing the plaintiff in fear of imminent serious physical harm, or by using force, threats, or duress.

YOU ARE ORDERED NOT TO CONTACT THE PLAINTIFF or any child(ren) listed below, either in person, by telephone, in writing, or otherwise, and to stay at least 100 yards away from them, unless you receive written permission from the Court to do otherwise.

CHILD(REN): Richard G. Renard II.

Gil's first thought was a crazy one: someone had slipped into the trailer while he slept and stuck the envelope in his pocket. Then came a dim recollection, dim not because of a long passage of time, but because it was such a cool bland memory in a hot sea of them: red-faced Bridgid in tears, Garrity's pink and snappable leg, shaking Figgy's Judas hand. A cool bland memory of a man in a windbreaker rising from a chair in the office waiting room, polite and smiling. "Mr. Renard?" Then the long white envelope. And: "Have a nice day."

A cool bland process server. Ellen had hit him when he was down. Every muscle in his body went tense, frozen between need for action and ignorance of what that action might be. Gil stood in the mud outside Boucicaut's trailer, with the pressure building and building inside, until he thought he might just die there, and it would be a good thing; and then he remembered the thrower, strapped to his leg.

The next moment he had it in his hand, a work of art, but also an ugly little bugger, as Mr. Hale had said. Gil flung it at a tree across the yard, ten yards away, perhaps farther. The knife missed the trunk completely, flashing into the woods and out of sight.

Gil went after it, found it lying on a wet pile of leaves, returned to the tree he had missed. A red maple; he could tell by the few dead leaves that had held onto its branches all winter. Gil inscribed a circle at chest height, the size of the deer heart Boucicaut had cut out, or a little bigger. He measured fifteen paces across the yard, hefted the knife. Perfectly balanced to rotate around its midpoint, maximum effective distance for a one-and-a-half-turn, handle-to-point throw forty-two to forty-eight feet, taking into account the extent of the sticking range. Front foot forward, leg flexed, elbow bent, wrist locked, knife behind the head.

Gil let go, careful to keep his wrist still until the follow-through, careful to aim high, allowing for gravity. The knife spun through the air one and a half times and stuck in the trunk, two or three inches to the right of the circle, blade pointing up at a forty-five-degree angle. Gil retrieved it and tried again, monitoring the movements of his arm more closely this time.

Stick: on the outside of the circle, blade pointing down at about thirty degrees.

And again: Dead center, blade at a right angle.

And once more: Dead center, blade at a right angle.

For Ellen: Same.

And Tim: Same.

And Figgy: Same.

And Bridgid: Same.

And the busybody old lady in the Harvard cap: Same.

And who else?

Bobby Rayburn: Missed.

Bobby Rayburn: Missed.

Gil cried out, alone in the clearing, night falling around him, no words, just a noise tearing up from his chest, through his throat, out his mouth.

Bobby Rayburn, who had humiliated him in front of his kid, face it, face it, face it: Bull's-eye.

Bobby Rayburn: Bull's-eye.

Bobby Rayburn, Bobby Rayburn, Bobby Rayburn: harder, harder, harder: same, same, same.

It was springtime. Sap ran down the trunk of the red maple like blood.

13

Boucicaut came back in a good mood, bursting into the trailer with Gil's car keys in one hand and a pint of something in the other. It was raining hard now, pounding on the flat roof, and Gil hadn't heard him drive up. He slipped off the catcher's mitt and set it on the table.

"Nice wheels, old buddy," said Boucicaut, flipping him the keys. He glanced around. "You didn't light the stove?" Boucicaut knelt, opened the blackened stove door, tossed in sticks of wood and scraps of paper, struck a match. "Don't tell me you're turning into a city boy." Flames shot up inside the stove.

"I wasn't cold," Gil said.

"Tough guy, I forgot," said Boucicaut. "Good thing."

"Good thing?"

" 'Cause we'll be spending time outside tonight. If you can lend me a hand, that is."

"Doing what?"

"Nothing much." Boucicaut took a hit from the pint bottle, passed it to Gil.

Canadian. Gil didn't like Canadian. He drank some anyway. Sour and harsh, compared to Mr. Hale's Scotch, but it felt good going down. He realized that he was indeed cold, and had some more.

"Know your muffler was gone?" asked Boucicaut.

Gil nodded.

"Not to worry. It's all fixed."

"It's all fixed?" said Gil; he didn't have the money for new mufflers.

"And there was a little bumper problem. That's fixed too."

"What do I owe you?" asked Gil. Right words but wrong sound: he was instantly aware of the dismay in his tone, of failing to sound successful.

"All taken care of."

"I can't let you do that."

"Do what?" said Boucicaut. "Didn't cost a cent."

"How's that?"

"Friend of mine's got a lot of spare parts and a welding torch." Boucicaut kicked the wood-stove door closed with the toe of his boot.

What kind of friend had mufflers for a 325i hanging around? Gil was wondering whether to ask or just let it slide, when Boucicaut noticed the baseball gloves on the table. "Where'd you find those?"

"In the closet," said Gil. He waited for Boucicaut to ask what he'd been doing in the closet.

But Boucicaut did not. He just took another drink from the bottle, and handed it to Gil.

Gil finished the bottle. It went to his head, hot, harsh, challenging. "What did you want me to help you with?"

"No big deal," said Boucicaut. He went to the table, picked

up the trophy, turned it in his hand. "You like practical jokes, right?"

"Depends."

They took Gil's car, Gil driving, Boucicaut navigating. The scraping sound was gone, the car again riding as quietly as it had the day he'd driven it off the lot. They drove west, out of town, into the storm.

"What are you sniffing at?" Boucicaut said.

"Nothing. Where are we going?"

"Ski country, said Boucicaut. He had another pint. They passed it back and forth. "I bet you're a skier, Gilly. Successful guy like you."

"No."

"Golf? Tennis?"

"No."

"Thought all you corporate dudes were into shit like that."

Gil felt a strong urge to confess that he wasn't a corporate dude, that he didn't even have a job, that he was done: to spill everything to Boucicaut. He overcame it. "Too busy," he said.

Boucicaut laughed and clapped him on the shoulder, hard. "Too busy makin' money, right? Son of a bitch. How much're you worth, anyway?"

"Give me a fucking break." Gil realized he had shouted the words.

There was a silence. Then Boucicaut said, "Easy, old buddy."

They climbed out of the rain and into falling snow, up in the highlands where winter lingered. Ahead lay the light of the access road, and beyond it the mountain, the top a shadow in the night, the bottom lit like a pearl for night skiing. It was all new to Gil, not just the development: even the shape of the mountain had changed.

"Hang a right," said Boucicaut.

Gil turned onto a road barely wide enough for two cars to pass. It mounted a rise, swung into thick woods, and then began climbing steeply up and out of sight, around the side of the mountain. The tires whined in the mix of mud and snow. Gil stopped the car.

"We'll never get up that."

"Sure we will," said Boucicaut. "Just pop the trunk."

"What for?"

"So I can get the chains."

"I don't have chains."

Boucicaut laughed and got out. Gil popped the trunk. In the rearview mirror he watched Boucicaut, reddened by the taillights, pulling out a set of chains. Gil felt questions stirring in his mind, raising their heads like sea worms in the sand, only to be flattened by a calming wave: Boucicaut was taking charge.

Boucicaut got back in the car, slamming the door on a swirling funnel of snow. "Let's go."

Gil drove up the side of the mountain, the chains digging in like teeth. After a few condo clusters came the chalets, at first close together and big, later farther apart and enormous, almost all of them shining an outside light or two, but dark within.

"This is where the New Yorkers stay," said Boucicaut. "Jews. They never come up this time of year, no matter how much snow's left. Cut the lights."

Gil braked, switched off the lights.

"Did I say stop?" Boucicaut said.

"You want me to drive with no lights?"

"Why not?"

"I can't see a thing."

"You have turned into a city boy, old buddy."

Gil drove, very slow. He saw nothing but black snowflakes striking the windshield, their edges green from the instrument lights. But Boucicaut, silently, with little movements of his hand, showed him the way. Gil hunched over the wheel, peering into the darkness. Boucicaut sat back, tipping the bottle up to his mouth once or twice. The chains crunched unhurriedly through the snow.

A yellow light glimmered in the distance. Boucicaut put the bottle down. The light grew bigger and brighter: a lantern light, mounted on a post. "Close enough," said Boucicaut.

Gil stopped in the middle of the road. From his pocket, Boucicaut fished out a key ring loaded with twenty or thirty keys. Flipping through them, he felt Gil's gaze. "Screwed every maid in the valley," he said. "For fun and profit." He selected a key and slid it off the ring. "Just pop the trunk again and sit tight." Boucicaut got out, walked toward the light. For a minute or two his silhouette moved behind a curtain of black snowflakes. Then the light went out, and he was gone.

The wind rose, made aggressive noises in the trees and around the car. Gil ran the motor to keep warm. After a while, he switched on the radio, pressed AM, hit SEEK. He caught a few bars of different songs he didn't know, rap, lite, country, rock. Then, faint, crackling, distorted: ". . . two on, two out, top of the sixth, with the score . . ."

Gil set the station, jacked up the volume. The game faded away, like windblown voices. Another station ballooned across the frequency, playing some stupid oldie. Gil slapped the dashboard, hard enough to make his palm tingle. That felt good, so he did it again, a little harder. The game returned for an instant, almost lost in I'm-gonna-love-you-all-night-long bullshit: ". . . and he rings him up—Rayburn didn't like that call one bit. He's . . ." And it was gone again. Gil's hand was raised to strike the dash once more, when a bear-sized shadow loomed in front of the car.

Not a bear, although there were probably bear still in these woods, but Boucicaut, carrying a big box, or a stack of smaller boxes. Gil slid down the window. "You have to play it so fuckin' loud?" said Boucicaut. "I could hear you all the way up to the house."

Gil shut off the radio. Boucicaut moved around to the trunk. The rear end sagged for a moment. Then he was at the window again. "Don't go away," he said.

"Where would I go?" said Gil. "I'm lost."

Boucicaut laughed. Gil started laughing too, a laugh that gathered momentum and took on a life of its own. He clamped it off.

"Got that bottle?" said Boucicaut.

Gil found it on the floor. Boucicaut took a hit, then Gil, then Boucicaut again. "Save me some, old buddy," said Boucicaut, walking off in the darkness.

Gil switched on the radio, pressed SEEK. SEEK couldn't find the ball game. He swallowed some more Canadian, then punched in the FANLINE on his autodialer. The number rang and rang.

"Fucking answer," he shouted down the line.

But there was no answer. He counted fifty rings and hung up.

Boucicaut came back, made the rear end sag again, snapped the trunk shut, got in the car. "Vamoose," he said.

"Where?"

Boucicaut had the bottle in his hand. "Back down, for Christ's sake."

"The joke's over?"

"What joke?"

"The practical joke."

Boucicaut smiled, his remaining teeth green in the panel light. "Yeah, it's over."

Gil drove down the mountain, back into the rain, lights out most of the way. Boucicaut emptied the bottle, chucked it out the window. "Bang and Olufsen any good?" he said, as they came to the stop sign at the access road.

"Top of the line."

"Hey," said Boucicaut, "we make a good team." He got out and took off the chains.

Gil thought: Yes. I know that. He ran his tongue along the edge of his chipped tooth.

At the bottom of the mountain, Boucicaut pointed west, away from town. Gil followed almost-forgotten back roads for ten or fifteen minutes, turned down a long, unpaved lane, parked in front of an old farmhouse. Boucicaut went in without knocking. He came back with a man even fatter than he was, shirtless despite the cold. They emptied the trunk, carrying everything inside.

Boucicaut came back alone. "Nice work," he said, shoving something into Gil's shirt pocket.

"What's this?"

"Your share," said Boucicaut. "Not too rich to turn down a hundred bucks, are you?"

Gil wasn't.

"And something else," said Boucicaut when they were back on the road. "I thought of you as soon as I saw it, old buddy." He reached into his jacket, flicked on the interior light, held something up for Gil to see: a baseball, in a clear crystal box. A yellowed, autographed baseball, but Gil couldn't take his eyes off the road long enough to read the name.

"Who is it?" he asked.

"The Babe," said Boucicaut. "Who else?"

"That must be worth a lot of money."

"It's yours."

Gil wanted to say something like, "I couldn't do that," but he was too choked up. Boucicaut set the ball down on the edge of Gil's seat. It rolled against his thigh and rested there.

Miles went by, with rain pelting down, Boucicaut leaning back, eyes closed, Gil feeling the ball against his leg, thinking, we're a team. They were almost in town when Boucicaut opened his eyes and said: "Ever see *American Blade* magazine?"

"Sure."

"Came across a copy today. Some of your dad's knives were listed in the back."

"I know."

"Guy was asking four grand for one of them."

"They're collector's items."

"That's where they all went—to collectors?"

"Most of them."

"How many've you got?"

"You've seen it."

"Just the one? How did that happen?"

"It happened."

Gil drove back through town, into the woods, up the lane that led to Boucicaut's trailer. The wind died down; all at once the windshield wipers were squeaking on dry glass.

They parked, got out of the car, Gil taking the ball. "Wait a sec," Boucicaut said. He went into the trailer alone. The outside lights flashed on, illuminating the yard. When Boucicaut came back he had the baseball gloves in his hand. "Feelin' loose?" he said.

For a moment, Gil couldn't speak. A thrill went through him, shooting down his spine, along his arms and legs, up the back of his neck, into his face.

"Thought we'd play a little catch," said Boucicaut. "How's the old arm?"

"Best it's ever been."

Boucicaut laughed, donned the mitt, motioned for the ball. "We're going to use this?"

"What it's for, ain't it?" replied Boucicaut. Gil handed him the ball. Boucicaut put it in the fielder's glove and handed it back. Then he walked to the edge of the yard, turned, got down in his crouch. His legs must have been very strong, Gil thought, because he did it quite easily, despite all that weight.

"Let's see what you got," Boucicaut said, pounding his mitt.

The thrill washed through Gil again. He rubbed the ball in his hands, felt the softness of the old, oiled cowhide, saw the signature in the yellow glow of the outside light: Babe Ruth. He slid his left hand into the glove, gripped the ball across the seams with his right.

"Give me a sign," he said.

Boucicaut smiled a thin smile and held his index finger along the inside of his thigh. Gil toed an imaginary rubber, went into his windup. It all came back, the slow and easy pivot, left leg coming up, arm sweeping back, nice and loose. He even remembered to point the ball for an instant straight at center field; it felt tiny, his hand huge. He himself felt huge, light, full of possibility. And then he was bringing it all up and forward, bending his back, bearing down, closing his shoulder, snapping his wrist like a whip: perfection. He let go and followed through, left leg whipping around, knuckles almost in the mud. The ball flew in high and blazing.

But too high? And blazing perhaps only for Boucicaut, who got his mitt up oh so slowly, barely managing to tip it. The ball sailed up out of the yellow dome of light and into the woods, crashing softly out of sight.

"Ball one," said Boucicaut, laughing. Gil didn't join in. Ball one, maybe, but catchable. He kept the thought to himself.

They got flashlights from the trailer, poked beams of light between the tree trunks.

"Know any of these collectors?" asked Boucicaut, kicking at a soggy mound of leaves.

"What collectors?"

"Knife collectors."

"A few."

"How many knives have they got, guys like that?"

"Of my old man's? I know one who's got twenty at least. And hundreds of knives all together—Randalls, Scagels, Morseths."

"Hundreds? At four grand apiece?"

"They're not all worth that."

"But some?"

"Some."

"They must keep them at the bank or something, right?"

"Not the ones I know," said Gil, thinking of Mr. Hale, with his velvet-lined drawers; and his safe, behind the photograph of Mrs. Hale and her fencing team.

They searched the woods for twenty minutes or so. No ball.

Boucicaut whistled. The black mongrel bounded out of the shadows. "Find the ball, Nig," said Boucicaut.

But Nig couldn't find it either.

"Goddamn it," said Gil. Nig stiffened.

"It was probably a fake," Boucicaut said. "Let's get something to drink."

A good idea. Gil's elbow was starting to hurt. "We'll find it in the morning," he said.

"Sure, Gilly."

14

Bobby Rayburn said: "Whenever I get headache pain, I just knock it out of the park with extra-strength Moprin."

"Fantastic, Bobby," came a voice from the other side of the bright lights, "DeNiro couldn't have done it any better. And I worked with him when he was in his prime. Personally. So on this one let's just try holding the product up the weensiest bit higher. Right about thereabouts. Absolument perfecto. Ready, everybody?"

"Rolling."

"Speed."

"Take nine."

"Anytime you want, Bobby."

Bobby said: "Whenever I get headache pain, I just knock it out of the park with new extra-strength Moprin."

"Oscar time, folks. That's a keeper if I ever . . . *new*? He said new? So? Where the hell doesn't it say new? Stronger that way if you want my hum—"

Whispers.

"All right, everybody. Bobby. The account folks here say we've got to lose the *new* for some reason, FDA blah blah blah, although personally I like it better and think they should be grateful for your creativity, end of bracket, so this time let's try it sans new, and with the product up nice and high where the art director likes it."

"Sans new?" said Bobby.

"They don't want you to say new," said Wald, also invisible behind the lights.

"I said new?"

"Thank you so much, Mr. Wald. I'll handle this. Everything's okay, Bobby. Better than okay. I loved it. We all loved it. But this time let's just stick to what's on that tedious old screen."

"Can he see it from there?"

"Can you see the screen, Bobby?"

"Yes."

"What a question, with his eyesight. In hindsight. All right, now. In fact, it's a gas. Ready, everybody?"

"Rolling."

"Speed."

"Take ten."

Bobby said: "Whenever I get headache pain; I just knock it out of the tarp with extra-strength Moprin.

Silence.

"Tarp?"

"They do that shit for a living?" said Bobby when it was over, and he and Wald were on the plane.

"A good living," said Wald.

"I hate it," Bobby said. He hated the way they treated him like an idiot, hated New York, hated planes. He liked only that it was an off-day. Still learning: today he had learned that off-days were good when you were batting .147 at the beginning of June.

"How do you feel about the four hundred grand?" asked Wald.

"Is that what I'm getting?"

"Less my percentage."

Bobby shrugged. "Easiest money I ever made."

"Is it?" said Wald.

The flight attendant appeared. "More champagne, Mr. Wald?"

Wald had more champagne. Bobby had a Coke: no booze until he shook the slump.

"What did you mean by that?" said Bobby.

"By what?"

"When you said, 'is it?' "

"Just making conversation, Bobby."

The plane landed. They hadn't even reached the end of the covered ramp before Wald's phone buzzed. He took it out of his pocket, said, "Yes," listened, said, "I'll get back to you," clicked off.

"Interesting," he said.

Bobby looked beyond the gate for Val. She was supposed to meet him.

"That was Jewel Stern," Wald said.

"Who?"

"Radio reporter. You met her down in spring training."

Bobby tried to remember.

"In her forties. Attractive. She wants to do a piece on you for the *New York Times Magazine.*"

Bobby spotted Val, hurrying in with a ponytailed man. "You're telling her to forget it, right?"

"Might not hurt to meet her," Wald said.

"Why, for Christ's sake?"

"The Sunday magazine. A lot of important people read it."

"So what?"

Val was coming forward, a big smile on her face.

Wald shrugged. "Baseball's not forever, Bobby."

"What does that mean?"

Val threw her arms around him. "I'm so glad you're back, Bobby." He'd only been gone for the day. "I want you to meet Philip." The ponytailed man stepped forward. "Philip's got the most exciting ideas."

"About what?" Bobby said, shaking hands.

Philip opened his mouth to explain, but Val beat him to it: "The kitchen, Bobby."

"What kitchen?"

"Our new kitchen, of course. Philip has a whole new approach. He's an architect, Bobby. Famous."

"What's wrong with it the way it is?" Not that Bobby liked the kitchen, particularly, but he knew the fault must be his. How could it be otherwise with its terra-cotta floor, granite countertops, stained-glass windows from a church in some town he'd vaguely heard of?

A kid moved toward them, pencil and paper in hand. "Why don't we talk about it over dinner?" Val said.

"That sounds perfect," said Philip. "How about Fellini's?"

"Have you ever been hypnotized?" the sports psychologist asked Bobby.

"No."

"It can be very useful in imaging therapy."

"Therapy?" said Bobby.

"Imaging training," said the sports psychologist. "A kind of workout. No abracadabra, no Bela Lugosi business. Nothing but science, applied to the mind."

"What do I do?"

"I just want you to relax, deeply. Deeply, deeply, deeply." The sports psychologist's voice deepened and softened with each repetition of the word. "Release the tension from the core of every muscle, from the marrow of every bone, from the nucleus of every brain cell." Long pause. "If you feel inclined, turn your gaze to the painting on the wall."

"With the cows?"

"And the farmhouse. Perhaps you'd like to watch the glow of the hearth fire, just visible through that window beside the deep-crimson shutter."

Pause, perhaps long, perhaps not.

"Bobby?"

"Yes."

"Can you hear me?"

"Yes."

"I'd like you to lie down on the couch now. Yes. Like that, on your back. Comfy?"

"Yes."

"Can you still see the farmhouse?"

"Yes."

"And the glow of the fire?"

"Yes."

"I want you to relax, Bobby, to deeply, deeply relax. Releasing tension. Relaxing." Pause. "How is your rib cage, Bobby?"

"Fine."

"No pain?"

"No."

"No discomfort?"

"No."

"Good. I want you to relax all the muscles around the rib cage, Bobby, releasing tension from all around the area where it used to hurt. Relax, relax, relax. Let go, let go, let go."

Bobby sighed.

"Now, Bobby, now that you're so deeply relaxed, do you think you could tell me what it is you're afraid of?"

Pause.

"Or worried about?"

Pause.

"Or concerned about?"

"Something happening to Sean. I'm afraid of something happening to Sean."

"Who is Sean?"

"My son."

"Is he sick?"

"No—"

"Is—"

"—not to my knowledge."

"Is there anything wrong with him?"

"No."

"I see." Long pause. "What I really meant to ask was what are you afraid of in baseball?"

"Nothing."

"Are you afraid of getting hit with the ball?"

"No."

"Are you afraid you're not going to be able to perform as well as you have in the past?"

Long pause.

"Are you afraid that you will have difficulty shutting out the distractions of off-field aspects of your life?"

"No."

"Are you worried, or concerned, that in any way your new contract will make it harder—not hard, simply harder—to achieve what you've achieved in past seasons?"

"Yes."

Pause.

"Bobby?"

"Yes."

"Are you still looking at the glow of the fire in the window by the crimson-colored shutter of the little farmhouse?"

"Yes."

"I want you to picture something, Bobby, an object, to see this object so strongly that everything else—the glow of the fire, the crimson shutter—vanishes. Everything else vanishes, Bobby. Do you understand?"

"I understand."

"Good. Now I'm going to tell you what it is I want you to see. Are you ready?"

"Yes."

"The object is a baseball, Bobby. A perfect white baseball with perfectly even red-stitched seams. Can you see it, Bobby?"

"Yes."

"See it and only it?"

"Like a coffee table book."

"I'm sorry?"

"As clear as those pictures in a coffee table book."

"Very good. What is the ball doing, Bobby?"

"Starting to spin." Pause. "It's a slider. Outside corner. Maybe low." Pause. "Maybe not."

"Could you hit it?"

"Don't know."

"I want you to hit it, Bobby. I want you to see that slider all the way, and do all the things you have to do to hit it. I want you to hit it on the sweet spot of the bat, and then I want you to feel the feeling of doing it."

Long pause.

"Did you see the ball all the way, Bobby?"

"Yes."

"Did you feel the feeling of hitting it on the sweet spot of the bat?"

"Yes."

"Did you feel the feeling in every muscle, in every bone, deep in your brain?"

"Yes."

"Very good. You will remember that feeling, in every muscle, in every bone, deep in your brain. You will remember that feeling, and you will remember that sharp image of that perfectly white baseball with its perfectly even red-stitched seams. Let us just be here in silence, building those memories."

Silence.

"Bobby, I want you to get up now, to sit in the chair. Good. I'm going to count backwards from five, and when I reach zero our session will be over. Do you understand?"

"Yes."

"Five, four, three, two, one, zero."

"Philip has a vision," Val said. They were at Fellini's, one of those restaurants making a statement that Bobby didn't understand. "Tell him about it, Philip."

Philip leaned over the table. "It's really a shared vision," he began. "Mine and Valerie's. Your wife has a good eye, Mr. Rayburn."

"She does?"

"Certainly. When it comes to design."

Food came, strange-tasting and not enough. Philip described his vision, a large vision that lasted through dessert. Bobby had stopped paying attention long before that. He didn't want to hear about sculptured spaces and recessed cans. He wanted to hurry through the rest of the off-day, get to tomorrow, get to the ballpark, get to the plate, hit. He was going to hit: his hands, his wrists, his whole body had the feeling it always had when he was on a roll.

The bill arrived. Philip, drawing on his napkin, made no move to pick it up, so Bobby did. Under the table, Val's foot pressed against his. "Well, Bobby," she said, "what do you think?"

"Talk to Wald," Bobby said, rising.

"Wait," said Val. "We haven't even discussed the pool enclosure."

"Got to go," said Bobby.

He went home, leaving Val and Philip with their coffee.

Val's mother was reclining in front of the forty-five-inch screen, her fingers in a bowl of popcorn.

"Where's Sean?"

"Gone to bed, dear," she said, her eyes on the young Marlon Brando.

Bobby went into Sean's room. It was dark, except the space-station control panel, glowing in the corner. Bob went to the bed, gazed down.

Sean was fast asleep. In the light from the space station, Bobby could see that he didn't look at all like the other Sean, the bald, hollow-faced chemo kid from the hospital. His Sean was almost as big, but he was not yet six, and the other Sean had probably been at least ten. His Sean had thick blond hair, a broad face, broad forehead, well-knit frame. His Sean wasn't dying. He was sleeping peacefully, recharging the batteries, his hands lying relaxed on the covers. His Sean had nothing in common with the other Sean. The other Sean wasn't even around anymore, for Christ's sake. Still, it was bad luck, two Seans, and no amount of rationalizing could change that.

Bobby went over to the space station. Did Sean like it? Bobby didn't know: he'd been on a road trip almost the whole time since they'd moved in. He sat at the console. There was a message on the screen: "Captain Sean: Invasion of the Arcturian Web requires heroic action. Awaiting instructions."

Bobby pressed a button. A menu appeared on the screen. "Choices. 1. Abandon planet. 2. Activate Weapon X. 3. Send negotiator bearing intergalactic white flag of peace."

Bobby rubbed his rib cage. No pain at all, and he felt loose, as loose as he'd felt on the first day of spring training. Point one four seven. Just a stupid joke. In a month, two weeks even, no one would remember. No heroic action required: he just had to get up there and do what he did.

But a hero is what he had been to the other Sean. *Hit a home run for me,* and *you're my hero,* and all that shit. Was hitting home runs on request heroic? It was luck, pure, blind, and simple. And what was luck? The residue of something—preparation?—according to some old baseball saying he'd heard from some coach along the way. Still, he could have handled the other Sean situation, the chemo Sean situation, differently, could have said that the grand slam in the opener had been for a little boy he'd met on a hospital visit in spring training. Or, better, let the facts slip out through that DCR guy, whatever his name was. Or Wald—Wald would have known the best way. A good idea—he was still learning to play the game—but too late.

Bobby selected 3. "Send negotiator bearing intergalactic white flag of peace."

The screen went blank. A new message popped up. "Alien invasion successful. You are now a prisoner of the Arcturian Web. Awaiting instructions."

The next day—the first hot day of the year, with the sun shining and the breeze blowing out—Bobby was on the field before anyone else. He ran for a while, feeling loose and strong, stretched, ran some more, broke a sweat. In BP the ball was a perfect white sphere with perfectly even red-stitched seams, and he punished it, sending six drives in a row over the wall in left, the last two over the lights as well. Punished it and felt good.

In the clubhouse Burrows handed him a printout, showing his lifetime stats against Pinero, the opposing pitcher. He was hitting .471, twenty-four for fifty-one, with eight doubles, a triple, and six home runs.

"Just remember what I think of stats," Burrows said.

"What's that?"

"Half the time they're bullshit."

"And the rest of the time?"

"They're bullshit the other way."

Bobby smiled. He was starting to like Burrows.

At his stall, Bobby pressed PLAY, listened to a few tunes,

then put on his game shirt with number forty-one, not even seeing the digits today, for the first time not bothered by it at all. Then he took the field and went oh for four, lowering his average to .138. The Sox fell to last. Primo hit for the cycle.

Bobby got home after midnight, driving with a beer in his hand, and then another. So what? He wasn't some salesman on the road late after an office party, or some other—he couldn't think what; he was Bobby Rayburn, he was under pressure, and he had to relax, had to let go, let go, let go.

Val was in the kitchen with the ponytailed guy, drinking white wine.

"Can I see you?" Bobby said.

Val followed him into the hall.

"What the fuck's he doing here?"

"Planning, Bobby. The kitchen. You know all about it. And I'd prefer you didn't talk to me so rudely."

He gave her a push, not hard. She fell against the wall, her eyes opening wide in surprise. He'd never laid a hand on her. Then she started to cry, or would have, if Philip hadn't stuck his head around the corner.

"One little point of clarification, Valerie, if you don't mind."

"Some other time, Slugger," Bobby said. "Nighty-night."

Meaning that Philip should leave. But he just stood there and said, "Sleep well." So Bobby went upstairs by himself: he didn't want to do any more pushing.

He took the phone out on the balcony, called Wald. Wald answered after four or five rings, his voice grainy with sleep.

"Missed the game, Bobby. How'd it go?"

"I'll pay what he wants," Bobby said. A ship slid across the dark sea, far away. He could distinguish every light showing: there wasn't anything wrong with his eyes.

"Sorry, Bobby, I don't get you."

"Primo. My number."

"You're talking about the fifty grand?"

"Right."

"You'll pay it?"

"That's what I just said." Why not? He was spending twice that or maybe more to fix a kitchen that didn't need fixing.

"You're the boss," Wald said.

"I want you to do it now."

"Now? It's—"

"I know what time it is."

"I'm not sure I can reach—"

"Try."

"Whatever you say."

Bobby stayed on the balcony watching the ship sail out of sight. The phone buzzed.

"Yes?"

"No."

"What do you mean?"

"I mean I offered them fifty and they turned it down."

"Who is they?"

"His people."

"Did they talk to him?"

"They said they did."

Another ship appeared, smaller than the first, but every light on it just as clear to him. "Offer them more."

"How much more?"

"Offer them a hundred. Isn't that what they wanted in the first place?"

"That was then."

"So?"

"So nothing. A hundred grand's still a lot of money, Bobby, that's all."

"We can always bag the goddamned kitchen."

Wald was quiet for a moment. "I don't know, Bobby. I kind of like Philip's vision."

15

Is Primo something else this year or what?" said Jewel Stern.

"Sure is," said Norm. "If the pitching comes through—"

"And if Rayburn can shake this terrible, terrible—"

"Then who knows what might happen? Let's see what's happening in Fanworld. Gil on the car phone. What's up, Gil?"

"Hello?"

"You're on, Gil. Go ahead."

"Jewel?"

"Hi, Gil. What's on your mind?"

"And better be brief, Gil. We're getting some breakup on the line."

"Jewel?"

"Yes, Gil."

"I heard what you said about Primo, that's all."

"And?"

"And it won't last. He's a hot dog. Hot dogs always fold in the end."

"Is that right, Gil? I could name you five or six so-called hot dogs in baseball right now who are going straight to the Hall of Fame."

"Then there's something wrong with the Hall of Fame."

"Tell 'em, Gilly!"

"Sounds like Gil's got a like-minded buddy in the car with him, Jewel."

"A like-minded buddy in a very good mood, Norm, perhaps artificially induced. Let's go to Ruben in Malden. What's up, Ruben?"

Way to go, Gil, thought Bobby Rayburn, parking in front of the terminal, maybe a little late. Was Primo going to fold? Was some fan, possibly drunken, onto something? Probably not: the woman was right about the Hall of Fame. Jewel. Was she the reporter who wanted to interview him? For some important magazine, Wald had said. The only important magazine Bobby knew was *SI*. He'd been on the cover three times.

Coach Cole was already outside the terminal, a white-haired, leather-skinned old guy blowing a big pink gum bubble. Coach Cole: played fifteen years in the minors, coached college for twenty more after that, including Bobby's four years, now lived in a one-bedroom condo a few feet from a sand trap on a third-rate golf course near Tucson. Never made it, not even close. But he understood hitting; more important, understood the way Bobby hit.

"Fuckin' ugly town," said Coach Cole, getting in.

Bobby handed him a check for two grand, to cover the tickets and a few hours' work. Coach Cole rolled it up tightly and stuck it behind his ear. In all those years he'd never made head coach, not even in junior college—maybe, Bobby now realized, because he was always doing things like that.

"How you been?" Bobby said.

"Fuckin' slice is killing me. And I get up six times every

night to piss. Other than that, no complaints." Coach Cole cracked his gum.

They drove out to a college in the suburbs. A kid in sweats was waiting inside a batting cage enclosed with netting on all sides, behind the practice field.

"All warmed up?" Bobby said.

"Yes, sir."

Bobby went inside with his bat, took his stance at the plate. The kid, behind a notched-out protective screen, reached into a basket of balls. Coach Cole stood outside, blowing pink bubbles.

The kid zipped one in. Bobby got a piece of it.

"Ease into it," Coach Cole said to the kid. "I'm no scout or nothin'." And in a lower voice, that only Bobby could hear, added: "And you're no bonus baby." How Coach Cole could tell after only one pitch, Bobby didn't know.

The kid started pitching, and Bobby started whacking, buzzing drives all over the narrow cage, rippling the netting, making it bulge and quiver from the disturbance within.

"Little more," Coach Cole told the kid.

The kid threw harder. Bobby hit harder.

"Now some cheese," said Coach Cole.

The kid, sweating now, began to air it out. No movement on his ball, but good velocity, and the netting made a lousy background. Still, Bobby hit every pitch on the screws, the kid ducking out of the open notch to safety behind the screen the instant he let go.

"Turn 'em over," said Coach Cole.

The kid threw his breaking stuff. Not much of a slider, but a sharp curve. Bobby hammered them both.

"Mix it up," said Coach Cole.

The kid mixed it up.

Bobby hammered.

"Change speeds."

The kid changed speeds.

Bobby hammered.

They took a break, drank water, went back in, did it all again. Sweat was dripping off the kid's chin now, dripping off Bobby too. The kid had thrown a hundred pitches by now, maybe more. A bulldog, Bobby realized, who must have been thinking that, despite what Coach Cole had said about not being a scout, this was his chance. Too bad he didn't have it.

The kid started to lose a few inches, a foot, two feet, from his fastball. He also got a little slower ducking behind the screen. One ball shot past his ear so close it ruffled his hair, like a blow-dryer. The kid checked the clock on a nearby steeple after that. Coach Cole made two quick clicking sounds in his mouth, the kind that tell a horse to get going. The kid reached into the basket for another ball. Bobby kept hammering.

Finally one pinged the kid on the shoulder. Or upper arm; Bobby didn't really see. But a glancing hit, not head-on. The kid grabbed his arm anyway, as though it were something precious, like Nolan Ryan's. Bobby waggled his bat, waiting.

" 'Kay," Coach Cole said. "I've seen enough."

Bobby walked over to the kid, handed him fifty bucks, although he'd said forty on the phone. "You all right?"

The kid nodded, but kept rubbing his arm. He seemed about to say something. Then he didn't. Then he did. "I'm supposed to start on Saturday."

Meaning I hope I haven't pitched my goddamn arm out. Maybe the kid wasn't a bulldog after all. "Go get 'em," Bobby said.

Bobby and Coach Cole drove off. "Kid's got a future," Coach Cole said.

"That's not what you said before."

"As a batting-practice pitcher. Smart, obedient, good-natured. Not many kids like that around anymore. Kids are the biggest assholes in the world these days. Everything's upside down."

"And the sweethearts are old guys like you?"

"Bull's-eye," said Coach Cole, blowing another bubble. "And as for you, you just wasted two G's. Plus whatever you gave the kid."

"Why is that?"

"Because there's nothing wrong with you. Stance, preparation, swing—all perfect. Never looked better, and I checked tapes going right back to college."

"Then how come I'm batting whatever the fuck it is I'm batting?"

"Can't be seein' it, that's all. You might think you are, but you're not. So either you need your eyes checked—"

"I did that already."

"—or there's something on your mind. Blockin' you, if you get what I mean. In which case you don't need me. And you still wasted two G's." There was a silence. Then he added, "Plus whatever you paid the kid."

Bobby drove back to the airport. Coach Cole got out of the car, paused. "I've seen a lot of guys go through slumps," he said. "I mean a lot. And you know what the truth is?"

"What?"

"The truth is slumps are like zits. No matter what you do, they go away all by themselves, when they're good and ready. Nothing changes that, not even the big bucks." He closed the door and walked into the terminal.

A skycap knocked on the window before Bobby could pull away. Bobby slid it down an inch. The skycap lowered his mouth to the opening. "Hey, Bobby, how's it goin'?"

Bobby grunted.

"How about an autograph? For my kid."

Bobby nodded.

The skycap passed him a baggage tag. Bobby signed it, gave it back. "Wee-oo," said the skycap.

Bobby spent the rest of the afternoon just driving, bothered by nobody, trying to think about nothing, then headed for the ballpark. The phone buzzed as he was turning into the players' lot.

"No go," said Wald.

"What do you mean?"

"I mean they turned you down. Us down."

"They turned down a hundred grand?"

"Yup."

"But that's what they wanted before."

"I know."

"They're breaking their word."

"So what are we going to do? Sue Primo?"

"It's not funny."

"I know that too."

"Maybe you're giving them the idea there's something funny about this."

"Now, Bobby—"

"Maybe that's why we're getting nowhere."

"That's not true, Bobby. I've been doing my very—"

"There're other agents out there, you know."

"I'm aware of that."

"Then get it done. I want you to take this seriously."

"I am taking it—"

"As seriously as you took that Moprin bullshit, for example. Is that too much to ask? I want that fucking number." Boyle, pulling up alongside in his Lamborghini, was staring at him.

"How much am I authorized to offer?" Wald asked.

"Whatever it takes," said Bobby, lowering his voice.

"Okay," said Wald, "but there's something you should understand."

"What's that?"

"He doesn't have to do it at all."

"Why not?" Bobby's voice rose again.

"Because it's his number, Bobby, that's why."

"It's my number. Goddamn it, Chaz, whose side are you

on? I was wearing it up in the show before he ever got off his stinking island—"

"But that was with another team, Bobby. On this team he—"

"—and he's a banjo-hitting little shithead and I'm—" Bobby stopped, lowered his voice again. "I want my number, that's all. Eleven."

"I'll do my best, Bobby. Call you after the game."

Bobby went into the locker room. The first person he saw was Primo, diddling his Nintendo. Relax, he told himself. Release the tension from the core of every muscle, from the marrow of every bone, from the nucleus of every brain cell. Let go, let go, let go.

"The object is a baseball."

"Excuse me?" said Stook, the equipment manager, coming over.

"I didn't say anything," Bobby said.

Stook nodded. "Got that order," he said, and handed Bobby a package.

Bobby glanced around, saw that no one was watching, opened the package. Inside was a plain white T-shirt, size XXL. Plain except for the number eleven, printed in red on the back.

"That do it?" Stook said.

"Thanks." Bobby gave him a C-note.

Stook winked and went off. With his back to his stall, Bobby put on the T-shirt, then his sleeves, then his warmup shirt. No number of any kind on the warm-up shirt. Just the secret number underneath. He felt good.

Not long after, Bobby was on the field, where the setting sun was splashing purple and gold all over the sky. Bobby gazed at the colors; maybe that kind of thing would help him relax. Lanz, shagging flies a few yards away, said: "Checking out the blonde?"

"What blonde?"

"In section thirty-three. With her tits hanging over the rail. She likes you."

"How do you know that?" Bobby, looking at Lanz. Lanz had circles under his eyes. His average wasn't much better than Bobby's, and Burrows had dropped him down to six. Bobby was still batting third.

" 'Cause she told me last night. She wanted your number."

"My number?"

"Your phone number."

"You didn't give it to her, did you?"

"I don't even know it."

Bobby backpedaled a few steps and pulled down a soft liner.

Bobby was murderous again in BP, pounding drive after drive, feeling better and better. On the way into the clubhouse, he said to Lanz, "What's her name?"

Lanz thought. "It'll come to me."

First time up, Bobby heard some boos. He'd been wondering when that would start. "Playin' for forty thousand drunks," said the catcher, a veteran Bobby had known for years. "I hate these Saturday-night games."

"If you sniff real hard you can smell the urinals," said the ump. "Let's go."

Bobby dug in. He knew the pitcher too, a marginal player who had spent most of last year in Triple A and was only up now because of injuries on the staff. He had a fastball that sank a little and a curve that sometimes broke sharply and sometimes stayed up; and that was it.

Bobby guessed curve on the first pitch, and got it. He picked up the topspin immediately, knew almost at the same time that it was going to hang, then swung, not from the heels, but under control, feeling that pull down the left leg and diagonally around the left side of his torso, the pull that always indicated proper form. And popped out to the second baseman.

More boos the next time. Again the curve on the first pitch, again hanging, and again Bobby was waiting for it. This time he watched it all the way, spinning down, seeing it with that coffee table book clarity. *The object is a baseball.*

"Steeee," said the ump.

Now he'll try the fastball, Bobby thought. And it came, backspinning, up in the zone. Bobby took his rip, again smooth, controlled, perfectly coordinated. But this time, even as he swung, he was aware of something strange: something obtrusive, a shadow, a fog, that hadn't been there on the pitch before.

"Two," said the ump.

A fog? A shadow? Or was it simply a matter of blanking out when the pitch was on its way? Bobby picked up the next one right out of the pitcher's hand, the fastball again, this time a better one, dropping an inch or two at the end. He saw it perfectly.

The ump rang him up.

"Jesus Christ," said the catcher. "I really can smell the fuckin' piss. This is gross."

A fog? A shadow? A blanking out? Yes, *but only when he swung.* If he just watched it and didn't swing he saw it perfectly. Bobby, hands on his knees in center field, remembered Coach Cole: *Can't be seein' it, that's all. You might think you are, but you're not. So either you need your eyes checked or there's something on your mind. Blockin' you, if you get what I mean.*

Blocked. But only if he swung. Could it be true? In the bleachers a man screamed, "Rayburn, you fuckin' thief" Bobby couldn't wait to bat again.

He came up in the seventh. Tie game, two out, no one on. New pitcher: a rookie Bobby had never seen. A rookie with heat. He threw Bobby four blazing pitches, none of them close. Bobby watched them all the way: coffee table. But that didn't prove anything, he thought, taking his lead off first. He stole second on the next pitch. Washington flied out, and Bobby walked back into the dugout, thinking: blocked, but only if I swing? Could it be true?

He batted in the ninth, down by a run, with Primo on second, Zamora on first, nobody out. They gave him the bunt sign. Bobby was a number-three hitter. He hadn't seen a bunt sign in years. He stepped out, looked down to third, got the bunt sign again. Bobby stared down at the third-base coach, watched him go through it one more time. Were they paying him whatever the hell number of millions it was to bunt?

"Why don't you be more obvious about it?" said the catcher. The third baseman moved in toward the edge of the grass.

Bobby stepped back in. Never got the bunt sign, but he'd always been a good bunter. He could handle the bat.

The pitch. Fastball, high and tight, hardest pitch to bunt. Bobby pivoted with the bat head up, saw the ball coffee table clear not halfway to the plate but all the way, and laid down a beauty, deadening it just right. The ball bumped and rolled lazily down the third-base line. There was nothing the third baseman could do but watch it roll foul, which it did, by an inch. The third baseman picked it up, and everyone went back a base, Primo to second, Zamora to first, Bobby to the plate.

They gave him the bunt sign again. In came another fastball high and tight, but this time a little too high, a little too tight. Bobby laid off.

"Steee," said the ump.

Bobby gave him a look. The ump looked right back; that's the way they were now, bitter assholes, every one.

Two strikes. They took off the bunt sign. The next pitch was a split-finger inside. Bobby watched it. Coffee table. Ball one. Then two more balls, both curves in the dirt, both coffee table. Full count.

Bobby had no idea what the next pitch would be. Nobody

out: could be anything. Pitcher in the stretch. The pitch. Fast-ball, but with a little something funky on it. In the zone. Coffee table. Bobby went for it, and as he did the fog, the shadow, came from nowhere, or rather from right behind his eyes, and he missed the ball completely.

"Steee-ryyyy."

Blocked, except for bunting. It was like cutting off his balls.

Washington walked. Sanchez flied out, not advancing the runners. Lanz K'd. Game over.

After, in the locker room, a little guy with glasses came up to Bobby. "Bobby?"

"Who the fuck—" And then Bobby recognized him—the community-relations guy. "What is it?"

"Call for you."

"Did you screen it?"

"It's Mr. Wald," said the DCR, handing him a phone.

"Bobby?"

"Yeah?"

"Tough game."

"Yeah."

"Listen."

"I'm listening."

"It's no go."

"What do you mean?"

"Primo."

"I know that. What do you mean?"

"No go. At any price."

"There's no such fucking thing. You told me yourself"

"I'm just the messenger."

Bobby clicked off. He showered and dressed. Blocked: and he knew why.

Primo was still in front of his stall, wrapped in a towel, beer can on the rug beside him, playing Nintendo. Bobby walked over. Primo kept his eyes on the screen.

"I think we should talk," Bobby said. "No agents. No bull-shit."

"Talk," said Primo, not looking up.

"Not here."

Primo avoided a falling anvil and shot the head off an attacker who looked half man, half tulip. "You know Cleats?" he said.

"No."

Primo told him how to get there.

Bobby went out to the players' lot. The blonde whose name Lanz couldn't remember spoke through the fence.

"Hi, Bobby," she said.

"Gotta run," he said. But he gave her a smile.

Bobby arrived at Cleats before Primo. There was a lineup. He was recognized right away and shown to the only empty table, in an alcove under the crossed bats of Aaron and Mays. There was one other table in the alcove. Two men sat at it, drinking beer and shots of some pale gold liquid that might have been tequila. They were both big, one in good shape, wearing a suit, the other fat and black-bearded, wearing a black-and-red-checked lumberman's jacket. The clean-shaven one glanced at Bobby. His eyes glazed over; Bobby couldn't tell if the man recognized him or not.

"What can I do for you, Bobby?" said the waitress.

Primo walked in, his Jheri-curled hair silvered in the rays of the big-screen TV.

16

Here's a riddle," Boucicaut said, walking into the trailer.

"I don't like riddles," Gil told him.

"You'll like this one," Boucicaut replied. "What's the best thing about living in ski country?"

Gil thought.

"Give up?"

Gil nodded.

"No one thinks twice if you're wearing a ski mask," Boucicaut said, holding up two of them. "Get it?"

Gil didn't answer—his mouth had suddenly gone dry. He got it, all right.

Boucicaut smiled. "Red or black?"

Gil shrugged, not wanting to commit himself out loud. Boucicaut tossed him the red one, tried on the black himself "How do I look?" he asked.

Not safe.

Boucicaut was still smiling. With his face obscured, those misshapen teeth could have belonged to some other species.

It was all implicit after that. They left the 325i parked behind the trailer, took Boucicaut's pickup instead, never discussing the reason why, but both knowing it. Both thinking silently together—like a longtime battery, like the battery they'd been. *The catcher is the father, the son is the pitcher.* Gil was beginning to understand what it meant. Everything felt right.

A sunny afternoon, sprouting green leaves on the trees, mud everywhere else. Boucicaut took the first shift at the wheel. They were a good team and Gil was feeling right, but letting Boucicaut drive was a mistake. Boucicaut still drove like a kid. Flashing blue lights, and they were pulled over, not quite beyond the limits of the town.

The cop walked up to the driver's-side door. Boucicaut tucked his bottle under the seat and rolled down the window, but did nothing about the ski mask on his head. He'd had it on since morning, maybe as a joke, maybe to prove the truth of his riddle.

The cop glanced in the window. He had red hair, graying at the sides, wore glasses. "Cold, Len?" he said.

Boucicaut was silent.

"Or just feeling shy?"

"That's a funny one," said Boucicaut.

"So's doing sixty in a forty zone. And those brake lights are a laugh riot." The cop hunched down a little so he could get a look at Gil. He took his look, straightened, said, "Told you about those brake lights last month, and the month before."

"Still waiting on that part," Boucicaut said.

"Where's it coming from? China?"

"China," said Boucicaut. "Another funny."

"Here's two more." The cop wrote him up, twice, and drove off. The squad car wasn't out of sight before Boucicaut tore off the ski mask, tore up the tickets, threw them out the window.

"What an asshole," Boucicaut said, his voice rising. He pounded the steering wheel once with the flat of his hand, sending a tremor through the cab. "Was he always an asshole like that?"

"Who?"

"Claymore, for Christ's sake."

"That was Claymore?"

"The little cunt. He's doin' good. Not as good as you, but good."

Boucicaut felt under the seat for his bottle. They changed places. After a few miles, Gil said: "It's not right."

"Don't be a jerk," said Boucicaut.

Gil realized that Boucicaut thought he was talking about what they were about to do. But that wasn't it. Gil had been thinking about Claymore. It wasn't that Claymore was a cop, while Boucicaut was whatever he was: it was the way Claymore had talked to him. Claymore was just a supporting player. Boucicaut was a star.

Something had gone wrong.

Gil had no intention of stopping at Cleats. It just happened, the way things seemed to be just happening now that he'd hooked up with Boucicaut. Hadn't planned to stop at Cleats, hadn't planned to stop anywhere. He'd meant to drive straight through the city, to put on the red ski mask, to get it over, like a cold call that had to be made. But at the first sight of skyscraper lights on the horizon, Boucicaut had straightened in his seat and said, "Sure could use something wet right about now."

And Gil had replied, "I know a place." It had just happened.

They parked outside Cleats. "When was the last time you were here?" Gil asked.

"Never been here."

"In the city, I meant."

"Never been in the city," said Boucicaut.

"You're joking."

Boucicaut rested a heavy hand on Gil's shoulder. "What's the joke?"

They walked into the bar just as Lanz was striking out on the big-screen TV. Then came a shot of handshaking players. Game over. "He sucks this year," Gil said.

"Who?" said Boucicaut, looking around, his eyes bright.

The bar was packed, and all the tables taken, except for the two in the alcove. Gil didn't like the alcove because you couldn't see the TV. "Sox Wrap" came next, followed by "Baseball Tonight" and "SportsCenter." He sat down anyway, pointing out the crossed bats of Aaron and Mays.

"I'm thirsty," Boucicaut said.

They ordered two drafts and two shots of Cuervo Gold. Leon noticed Gil and brought the drinks himself.

"How you doin', Gil?"

Used his name. Out of the corner of his eye, Gil saw that Boucicaut was watching, was impressed. "Not bad, Leon," Gil said. "How about you?" Expecting, if anything, a little more chitchat, followed by Leon's exit. But instead Leon let him down.

"Since you're asking," he said, setting the drinks on the table, "you recall that knife you sold me?"

"Knife?"

"The Iwo Jima one."

"Oh, yeah," Gil said, half remembering.

"What's the warranty on it?"

Gil didn't know, didn't care. He was no longer in the knife business, and what was more, Leon knew that. Boucicaut, on the other hand, did not. Gil swallowed his annoyance, put on a professional face. "Something wrong, Leon?" he said.

"Blade broke off."

"There isn't a knife on the market that's covered against

abusive treatment," Gil told him. "What were you doing with it?"

"Cutting a bagel in half."

Boucicaut let loose a burst of laughter, spraying beer across the table. A few droplets arced onto Leon's white apron. Leon frowned.

"Bring it in sometime," Gil said. "I'll see what I can do."

"I'll have it here tomorrow," Leon said. He went off.

"Another satisfied customer," said Boucicaut.

"Just part of doing business." Gil's mouth was dry again. He reached for his beer. "Let's get going," he said.

"What's the rush?" said Boucicaut. "I like it here."

"It's almost eleven."

"Relax, businessman. The night is young."

They had another round.

"You like this shit?" said Boucicaut.

"What shit?"

"Tequila."

"No one's forcing it down your throat."

"Hey. No offense, old pal. It does the job."

And another round after that. They drank at the same pace. Gil began to feel right again.

"Know any girls?" Boucicaut said.

"Some."

"How about two, for starters?"

Gil thought right away of Lenore and her sister. A crazy image sprang up in his mind, an image of the four of them in bed together—Lenore, her sister, Boucicaut, himself. He was trying to remember the sister's name—almost had it, just needed a few more seconds—when Bobby Rayburn walked in and sat at the next table.

Gil's bodily rhythms and flows—pulse, respiration, perspiration, adrenaline—all sped up, and in his mind the bedroom image vanished at once. In its place rose another: Boucicaut's red maple, dripping sap from the wound the thrower had made. Gil turned away from Bobby Rayburn, looked at Boucicaut. Boucicaut, wiping froth off his mustache with the back of his hand, didn't appear to have noticed Rayburn at all, or if he had noticed, had no idea who he was.

Gil, still not looking at Rayburn, picked up his shot glass and emptied it in one swallow. He heard a waitress say, "What can I do for you, Bobby?" glimpsed Leon rubbing his hands in the background, and another man walking past him into the alcove. A copper-skinned man with shining hair whom Gil didn't recognize at first, out of uniform, and then did: Primo.

Gil heard Rayburn say, "Hey, my man, buy you a drink?"

"No buying here, Bobby," said Leon, coming forward.

"Huh?" said Primo.

"I mean your money's no good here. What'll it be, gentlemen?"

"Heineken," said Rayburn.

"Coke," said Primo, sitting down.

Gil felt a kick under the table, turned to Boucicaut. "You gone deaf or something?"

"What?"

"I said you're right. It's time to get goin'. Drink up."

Gil couldn't quite make sense out of what Boucicaut was saying. His gaze swung back to the other table. The waitress rushed over with the drinks, a platter of baby back ribs, a bowl of Leon's special sauce. Gil felt another kick.

"So get the bill from your colored friend over there," Boucicaut said.

Gil checked his watch, thought: Christ. He gestured at Leon. Leon, hovering over the other table, looked right through him. All at once, a sour cactus taste rose up Gil's throat and he felt sick. He pushed himself to his feet.

"Where you goin'?"

Gil hurried out of the alcove, past the bar, into the bathroom.

On the TV screen over the urinals, Bobby Rayburn was standing bare-chested in front of his locker, fenced in by handheld microphones. Gil started puking right then, finished in and on a toilet in one of the stalls. Then he pictured a cactus growing in his gut and did it all again, bent double at the waist, hands clutching knees, tie decorated with sour bits from inside him.

Gil took deep breaths, straightened. He felt lightheaded for a few seconds, then steadied. He loosened his tie, carefully pulled it over his head, dropped it behind the toilet. Another fucking tie. He started cleaning himself with toilet paper: the lapels of his jacket, the cuffs of his pants, his shoe tops. He was almost finished when footsteps sounded on the bathroom tiles.

A man said: "It's getting late."

A second man said: "So?"

The first man said: "So let's not dick around. Just tell me what you want."

Gil thought he recognized the voice. He put his eye to the crack between the stall door and the frame, and saw Bobby Rayburn standing with his back to one of the sinks. The man he was talking to was out of sight, but Gil could see his reflection in the mirror; it was Primo. Above their heads, Rayburn's image continued to field questions on the TV screen.

Primo said, "I want nothing."

"What's that supposed to mean?" said Rayburn.

"Nothing. *Nada.*"

"You wanted something before."

"Before?"

"In spring training."

"What you talking about?"

"A hundred grand. It wasn't that long ago, amigo."

Primo's image stiffened in the mirror. "Watch the way you talk to me."

"What way?" said Rayburn, looking puzzled.

"Like that." Primo noticed something about his reflection he didn't like, patted his hair.

Rayburn sighed. "Let's start over, my man."

Primo's image stiffened again, but he said nothing. The seed of another sour cactus ball sprouted in Gil's stomach. He took a deep but silent breath to make it go away, to drown it in clean air. The cactus ball stopped growing, but didn't go away. Gil peered through the crack.

"Maybe," said Bobby Rayburn, "you just don't understand the way things work here."

"How is that?" said Primo. "I've been here for five years. You just came."

"I don't mean this team," Rayburn said. "I'm talking about the whole country. It's different than down where you come from."

Gil, in the stall a few feet away, knew only that something was being negotiated, and that Rayburn knew nothing about negotiation. He took another deep breath.

"Different?" Primo said.

Rayburn smiled, as though they were getting somewhere at last. "Up here there's a kind of pecking order. Someone like me, coming to a new team, things get worked out, that's all."

"Worked out?"

"Sure. We can think up something if we try."

Primo's eyes were hooded. "I already know what I think."

"Yeah," said Rayburn, "but we got to be flexible, right? It's a long season."

"Not so long."

"Hundred and sixty-two games isn't long?"

"Not for us. We play winter ball when this is over."

Rayburn had an idea. Gil could almost see it forming in his mind. "What kind of uniforms have you got down there?"

Primo frowned. "Uniforms."

"Nice?"

"Just uniforms."

"What color?"

"Green and white. What difference——"

"And what's on the back of yours?"

Primo paused. *"Once."*

"Onsay?" said Rayburn.

"Like this." Primo held up his index fingers, side by side. "So forget it." Held those fingers close to Rayburn, almost in his face. Rayburn didn't like that. He closed his fist around Primo's index fingers and squeezed.

"Name your price, you little greaseball," he said.

Primo tried to pull away, but couldn't.

"No price," Primo said.

With the back of his free hand, Rayburn smacked Primo's face. Not particularly hard, thought Gil, but then saw blood dripping from Primo's nose.

"The price," Rayburn said. "It's my fucking number."

"No price," Primo repeated, glaring up at Rayburn; puzzling Gil, because he didn't seem afraid. "The pecking order has changed."

"Meaning what?"

"Meaning check the averages in the morning."

Rayburn blushed. Then he straightened his back and took another swing, this one much harder than the first. It knocked Primo against the wall, half into the sink, and made more blood flow. Rayburn, fist cocked, took a step toward him. The next instant, Primo was halfway across the room, crouching, a blade in his hand. He'd done it so quickly that Gil hadn't seen where the blade—a stiletto, pearl-handled, double-edged; exactly the kind of knife Gil would have expected him to have, if he hadn't been a ball player—had come from. He only saw Rayburn, backing away; Primo, half smiling now; and that blade. The sight of the blade excited Gil, killed the cactus in his stomach, made him feel good. He bent down, reached under his pant leg for the thrower.

The bathroom door opened. Boucicaut came in. Primo glanced back at him over his shoulder; the knife disappeared. Boucicaut moved to the urinals, unzipped. Primo, the half smile still on his face, backed out the door. Bobby Rayburn said, "Shit," not loudly. Boucicaut, pissing, looked sideways at him. Rayburn walked out.

Boucicaut shook off, zipped up. Gil stepped out of the stall. Boucicaut saw him in the mirror. "There you are," he said. "Ready to boogaloo?"

There were a few red drops on the mirror. Above them, on "Sox Wrap," Bobby Rayburn laid down a bunt that started sweet and rolled just foul.

17

Have you done this kind of thing before?" asked Gil.

"For Christ's sake—you were with me," said Boucicaut.

They stood side by a side at a rest stop just south of the bridge, pissing. No cars went by. There was nothing to hear but the sibilance of their piss in the tall grass, and the tide flowing through the canal, also a liquid sound, but deeper, and infinitely more powerful. It was late, dark, quiet. Above, the stars were bright and beyond count. How could whatever you did down here mean anything at all, one way or the other? The boys who held the whip hand knew that from birth.

"I meant with people inside," Gil said.

"Lots of times," Boucicaut told him.

"Lots?"

"Some."

"And what's it like?"

"Like?"

"What happens?"

"Nothing happens. They sleep like babies. The whole country's doped to the eyeballs every night." Again Gil felt Boucicaut's heavy hand on his shoulder. It reassured him. "This is going to be cake," Boucicaut said.

Gil turned onto the Mid-Cape. Boucicaut spread his tool belt across his lap, stuck the tools through the loops: crowbar, flat bar, three different screwdrivers, glass cutter, pencil flash. Gil thought right away of Boucicaut on one knee by the dugout, strapping on his catcher's gear. "Tools of ignorance" was the phrase sportswriters used for catcher's equipment when they were trying to be funny, but Gil had never known why: catchers were smart. Boucicaut had been more than a rock; he'd done the thinking for all of them. Boucicaut with dust streaks like war paint on his face, Boucicaut spitting through the bars of his mask, Boucicaut doing the thinking: *If you want to put him on, at least hit him in the head.* Gil smiled to himself. He felt right, there in the quiet cab of the pickup, with Boucicaut beside him. He opened his mouth to say something that began with the word *remember,* but Boucicaut spoke first.

"Cake," he said, "as long as you can fence 'em."

"No problem."

Still thinking: yes, Boucicaut was smart. Bobby Rayburn, Gil thought abruptly, was not. Not as smart as Primo, certainly. Gil pictured Primo's flashy blade. "You like the number eleven?" he asked.

"Huh?" said Boucicaut, folding the tool belt and laying it on his knee.

"Rayburn's old number," Gil replied.

"Don't know what you're talking about, Gilly."

Gil took the exit, turned onto the shore road. They drove through the darkened village, past the stone church, where a light shone in the tower, stopped in the deserted parking lot of the seafood restaurant, no longer boarded up. They got out,

Boucicaut strapping on the tool belt, Gil slinging an empty backpack over one arm.

"I'll take the keys," Boucicaut said.

Gil gave them to him.

They walked to the road with the PRIVATE sign posted at the entrance. Not far ahead a TV screen glowed blue through the windows of the guardhouse. Gil and Boucicaut ducked into the scrub beside the road. Moving as one, thought Gil. A team. They passed the guardhouse in silence—through the trees, Gil saw a head in the window, silhouetted in blue light— and cut back onto the road.

"Cake," Boucicaut said. After that there was silence again, past the golf course, sand traps like patches of leftover snow in the night, past the houses at the base of the bluff, just big shadows spreading back into invisibility from their front-door lights. Silence: except for the creaking of the leather tool belt, the jingling of the keys in Boucicaut's pocket, and the gurgle of his bottle, once or twice.

On top of the bluff, Mr. Hale's house stood completely dark. They put on the ski masks, but at the same time Gil had an exciting thought: *They're still in Florida. The house is empty.* Relief washed through him like a drug. He glanced at Boucicaut, saw nothing but the brightness in his eyes. Cake. Side by side, they started up the driveway. A light flashed on over the garage before they'd gone ten feet.

Gil froze. He got ready for anything—a dog, gunfire, sirens. There was none of that. Boucicaut, not breaking stride and not even trying to keep his voice down, said, "If you're afraid of a bullshit sensor, this ain't for you." Gil hurried after him, feeling blood rising in his cheeks.

They left the driveway, circled to the back of the house. The light went off. For a few moments, Gil could see nothing. He felt the slick grass under his feet, heard the ocean breaking on the rocks below. Then his eyes adjusted and he could sea the gazebo where Mrs. Hale had sat painting, now blocking a gazebo-shaped patch of stars. On the other side, the house remained dark and quiet, and again Gil thought: Florida; again felt a wave of relief, although not so powerful this time.

Boucicaut was already shining his flash on the door that led to the walk-out basement. The narrow beam traced the perimeter of the storm door, screen already clipped in place for the summer. In seconds, it was unclipped and leaning against the stone foundation wall. Boucicaut reached inside, unlocked the storm door, pulled it open. The inner door was more substantial, solid wood except for two small glass panes near the top. Boucicaut took a suction cup from his pocket, pressed it to the glass, then scored along the sides of the pane with his cutter. The sound sent an unpleasant vibration down Gil's spine.

Boucicaut tugged at the suction cup. The pane came free with a faint cracking sound, like an ice cube splitting in a highball glass. Boucicaut twisted off the suction cup, then spun the windowpane away like a frisbee. It sparkled a few times with reflected starlight, then vanished, far over the sea. A wonderful sight. Boucicaut had had a great arm, had it still.

Gil, turning back toward the door, realized he was a little drunk. Probably a good thing: his reflexes were always sharper when he'd had a few drinks. "Everything all right?" he whispered.

"Shut up," said Boucicaut, his arm hooked through the opening. Something clicked. Boucicaut grunted. The door opened.

They went in, Boucicaut first, panning the darkness with the beam of his flash. Gil caught glimpses of a wheelbarrow, a bicycle with a straw basket, an easel bearing a partly finished painting of a red-and-white-banded lighthouse. The cone of light found an open inner door and went still. They moved toward it; and in the quiet house the creaking of the tool belt and the jingle of the keys sounded clear and precise in Gil's ear, as though piped through a high-end digital system. Then the furnace clicked on, and their sounds were muffled by its hum.

They went through the door and into a carpeted corridor. There were several doors off it, all closed but one. Boucicaut poked his beam through the open doorway as they passed. Gil saw lacy black panties, hardly more than a G-string, hanging on a shower-curtain rod. He couldn't imagine Mrs. Hale in underwear like that; then he remembered the maid.

At the end of the corridor stairs rose up into gloom. Gil avoided the middle of the treads, thinking they would make less noise if he hugged one side, but he saw that Boucicaut didn't bother. Gil realized that he was afraid and Boucicaut was not. That was the difference between them. Boucicaut moved as though it were broad daylight, and this his house. Boucicaut was a rock. Following him up the stairs, Gil felt his eyes grow misty. A phrase hit him at that moment: *Fear strikes out.* He knew its origin—Jimmy Piersall, of course; and all at once, he found himself remembering the first time his father had taken him to a ball game, and how they had all booed some player, how he had stood on his seat so he could see, hands cupped to his mouth, laughing and booing with the rest.

At the top of the stairs, Boucicaut's light gleamed on the marble floor, and Gil knew where he was. He pointed down the corridor. They walked along it, details from oil paintings glistening and disappearing under the glow of Boucicaut's light: another lighthouse, this one pure white; a humpback whale spouting red; a harpooner in brass-buckled shoes tumbling overboard. As they came to the library door, the furnace shut off. The next moment the sole of Boucicaut's sneaker squeaked on the marble, the sound so distinct that Gil wasn't sure that he had really heard what came right after: a woman's moan, somewhere in the house, somewhere close by.

He clutched the back of Boucicaut's jacket, stopping him, then put his face close to Boucicaut's ear, so close he could smell ear wax, right through the wool of the ski mask, and whispered, "What was that?"

"What was what?" Boucicaut replied, not whispering, not even lowering his voice much. Gil smelled the booze on his breath.

"I thought I heard—" Gil stopped himself, thinking he'd heard it again.

"Don't think," Boucicaut said, and pushed open the library door.

The library was warm and smelled of smoke. There was another smell too, that made Gil think of Lenore. Boucicaut's light skimmed the heavy furniture—the wingback chairs, the floral settees, the couch overlooking the sea view, its back to the room—and settled first on the built-in cabinets, then on the photograph of the young Mrs. Hale in her fencing outfit. He was there in a moment, taking down the photograph, spinning the dial back and forth, without result.

"Let's do the knives first," he said.

"Shh," said Gil.

Boucicaut laughed softly to himself.

They moved to the cabinets, tried the drawers. Locked. Boucicaut handed Gil the flash. Gil shone it on the drawer where he'd seen the old Randall bowies, steadied the beam on the oval brass keyhole. Boucicaut drew the flat bar from his tool belt, swung his arm back, and drove the claw end at the keyhole. There was a sound like a tree falling, and the flat bar sank halfway into the drawer, taking the brass keyhole and jagged oval of splintered wood with it. Steel gleamed through the hole. Yes, Gil thought. Cake. He twisted slightly to remove the backpack, then stopped. He'd seen something. The twitch of a shadow, near the couch that faced the sea. He swung the beam across the room, at first seeing nothing. Then a figure ran through the cone of light and disappeared, a bare foot trailing a momentary glow like a comet's tail.

"Co!"

But Boucicaut was already moving. There was a crash in the darkness, then a cry—a woman's cry; and a grunt—Boucicaut's. Gil trained the light on a dark, shifting mass on the floor, and in the unsteady beam saw a naked, dark-skinned woman struggling to get out from under Boucicaut. The maid. Gil thought of the panties on the shower-curtain rail, thought he should have been prepared for something like this. Why was he always one step behind?

"Well, well," said Boucicaut, looking down at the woman. Her eyes were wide, her skin stretched so tight with tension across her face that it must have hurt.

"Please," she said. A high, carrying sound that vibrated unpleasantly in Gil's inner ear. Boucicaut didn't like it either. He put a hand over her mouth, pushed himself up to a sitting position, straddling her.

"Well, well," he said again. With his free hand, he reached down, took her nipple between thumb and forefinger, and gave it a twist, as though it were a dial on some machine.

The woman whimpered. "No more noise," said Boucicaut, and did something to her breast that made furrows pop out on her smooth forehead. Then he reached down, underneath himself, toward her crotch.

"What the hell are you doing?" Gil said.

"Just having a little fun," Boucicaut replied. He took his hand from her mouth, fumbled with the buckle of the tool belt, then with his pants.

"Stop," Gil said.

"You just get busy on that drawer," Boucicaut said, "and shut the fuck up." He pulled his pants down to the knees, exposing his buttocks, pale and enormous.

Then the door banged open and the lights flashed on. Mr. Hale stood in the doorway, wearing a velvet robe, his hair sticking up in white spikes. He blinked once or twice.

"Esmeralda," he said: "Have you got some explanation for this?"

"Oh, sir," she said, and started to wail.

"Jesus Christ," said Boucicaut, backhanding the side of her face.

"Now, just one minute," said Mr. Hale, stepping forward.

That was a mistake. Without getting up, Boucicaut grabbed the tool belt and swung it at him. Something hard caught Mr. Hale on the point of the chin, carving a deep red notch. He went white, fell back against the doorjamb. The maid wailed again and Boucicaut hit her again, much harder this time. He rose, his pants falling around his ankles and over the maid's hips, revealing Boucicaut's sagging belly and an erection beneath it, surprisingly unimposing. He looked at Gil.

"We're gonna need tape or something."

Gil wanted to say, "What for?" but he knew he couldn't let Mr. Hale hear his voice. He shrugged.

"Don't go numb on me, old pal," Boucicaut said. He gave the maid a little kick. "We need tape, wire, something like that."

She stared up at him, trembling and silent. Boucicaut turned to Mr. Hale. "Did you hear me, you old asshole?"

Mr. Hale's mouth moved, but no sound came out.

"C'mere," Boucicaut said.

Mr. Hale walked toward him, blood dripping off his chin, onto his velvet robe. He now bore only a distant resemblance to the Mr. Hale Gil knew. This Mr. Hale could have been the other's father, very old, fragile. When Mr. Hale got within punching distance, Boucicaut said, "Fuck the tape then, if no one's going to cooperate," and hit him in the face. Mr. Hale fell backwards, his eyes rolling up, then lay still.

"For God's sake," Gil said, and was trying to think of a way to calm things down when a movement on the other side of the room caught his eye. A woman was rising stealthily from the couch that faced the window, wrapping her naked body in something filmy. Not a woman like Esmeralda: she was gray-haired and tiny. The context was all wrong, and a few moments passed before Gil realized it was Mrs. Hale. In those few moments, she had plucked the basket-hilt rapier off the wall and advanced on Boucicaut. Standing behind him, Gil said: "Co!"

Boucicaut wheeled around, saw Mrs. Hale coming, a tiny figure, mottled and half naked, one of her empty breasts exposed; but sword arm out straight, knees bent, legs apart, in perfect fencing form, like a stunt man in a Technicolor swashbuckler. Boucicaut laughed out loud, and was still laughing as he stooped to pull up his pants. But they were twisted now, and his posture—still straddling the maid—awkward. Boucicaut lost his balance, fell on his hands and knees. Mrs. Hale strode forward and drove the blade down through the top of his massive shoulder, down into his upper body, longitudinally; her lead foot stamping lightly with the thrust.

An instant later, Mrs. Hale lay face down on the floor with a red seepage in her gray hair and Gil close by, dented flashlight in his hand. Boucicaut, on his knees, the rapier sticking out of his body, looked up at him. "A fuckin' dyke," he said. "Whyn't you tell me?"

"I didn't know," Gil said. And he still hadn't understood until Boucicaut spoke. Boucicaut had brains, while he was always a step behind.

"Don't just stand there," Boucicaut said. "Pull it out."

"I'm not sure that's the right thing. We should go to the hospital."

"You're out-jokin' me again, old pal. Not the time."

Gil dropped the flashlight, slipped his hand into the basket handle. "Get ready for a gusher," Boucicaut said, his eyes still bright.

Gil pulled. The blade slid free without resistance. There was no gusher, hardly any blood at all, no more than from a shaving cut.

"Well, well," said Boucicaut. "She missed me." He got his

feet beneath him. Gil held out his hand. Boucicaut ignored it, gathered himself, rose. A little blood flowed out then, but not much.

"Need a hand with the pants though," Boucicaut said. That's when they realized that the maid was gone.

Gil ran from the library, into the front hall. "Kill her," Boucicaut called behind him.

The front door was open. Gil ran out. The sensors had triggered the lights and he could see the maid running, not very fast, across the lawn. Gil tackled her before she reached the road. She went down hard, the breath knocked from her in a little grunt. Gil slung her over his shoulder and carried her up to the garage.

There were three cars inside—Volvo wagon, Mercedes sedan, Saab convertible—and a golf cart. Gil opened the door of the Mercedes, popped the trunk, dumped the woman inside, banged it shut. The keys to the golf cart were in the ignition. Gil drove it out of the garage, up the lawn to the front door. Boucicaut stepped out.

"Get her?" he said.

"Yeah."

"Do what I said?"

Gil nodded.

Boucicaut handed him the backpack, about one-quarter full. "Emptied out that one drawer," he said. "They valuable?"

"Should be."

"Sure as fuck hope so," Boucicaut said, and climbed onto the cart.

Gil drove across the lawn, onto the road, down the hill, past the other houses, past the golf course, stopped when he saw the blue light from the guardhouse.

"You up to walking?" he said.

"Why not?"

They walked, into the woods, beyond the guardhouse, back onto the road, all the way to the restaurant parking lot. Boucicaut had a little trouble climbing up to the passenger seat. Gil gave him a push, then took the wheel. "Got the keys?" he said.

"In my pocket."

"Give them to me."

Boucicaut tried, but for some reason couldn't get his hand in his pocket. Gil reached in, couldn't help feel the quivering in the huge thigh.

"Sure as fuck hope so," Boucicaut said again.

They drove in silence, until Gil saw a blue road sign with a white *H* and flashed the directional signal. Boucicaut reached for the wheel, held it straight until they'd passed the turn. "For a successful guy, Gilly, you can be pretty dumb."

Clouds had rolled in, hiding the stars. No traffic. Gil drove past the rest stop, over the bridge. They were silent again. Now and then, Gil glanced at Boucicaut. At first Boucicaut's eyes were open. Then they were closed.

"You asleep?" Gil said.

"Nope."

Then silence again, until Gil couldn't stand it any longer, and spoke once more. "Remember that season?" he said.

"What season?"

"What season. When we won the state. The championship season."

"So?"

"You ever think about it?"

"Think what?"

"I don't know. That things could have been different."

Gil waited for an answer. None came. He glanced over Boucicaut's eyes were closed again.

"You sleeping?"

No answer.

Gil pulled to the side of the road. Boucicaut fell against him. Gil twisted free, opened Boucicaut's jacket, unbuttoned his shirt, examined the shoulder. Only a little blood, now sticky.

"No blood, Co," he said. "You're going to be all right."

Boucicaut opened his eyes. "That's good," he said. Then came a gurgling sound, and blood, shiny green in the dashboard light, poured from his mouth.

"Oh, God," Gil said, fighting to get free, fighting to get his hands on the wheel, to get to that hospital. But Boucicaut's heavy arms were around him and he couldn't move. He'd been in that embrace before, more than once but long ago, halfway between the plate and the mound, pitcher and catcher in victory. He put his arms around Boucicaut now, their masked heads touching, side by side.

"The catcher is the father," Gil said aloud.

Boucicaut's blood ran onto Gil's jacket and down his back.

"Hang on, Co. I'll get you there."

But there was no answer, just the warm wet flow.

Gil began to cry. "Oh, Co, you were the greatest. You could have played in the bigs."

Then Boucicaut spoke his last words. His voice was soft and thick, but right in Gil's ear. "You're an asshole, Gilly, you know that? It was Little League. We were twelve years old."

18

Bobby Rayburn, sitting at the space console in Sean's room, was still a prisoner of the Arcturian Web. He'd done everything: offered to trade the uranium planet Bluton for his freedom, revealed the secret hidden at the core of the Cloud Nebula in Orion, read the software manual from cover to cover. "When dealing with the Arcturian Web," it said under Troubleshooting, "remember that the first error is never fatal. If caught, use creative thinking. (Press F4 for complete creative-thinking menu.)"

Bobby tapped at the keys. Outside it was morning; inside, with Sean's heavy curtains drawn, dark as night. After ten or fifteen minutes of frustration, his hands grew still, his mind began to wander. *The first error is never fatal.* What was the first error? That was easy: losing his number. Wald's fault. And the second error? He could identify it as well: the second error was getting mixed up with Chemo Sean. That was the community-relations guy's fault. Fatal? Or correctable, through creative thinking? Bobby pressed F4 and scrolled through the headings of the creative-thinking menu: Analogies, Making Connections, Brainstorming Trees, Beginning at the End, Redefining the Problem. He clicked on Redefining the Problem, clicked again on the subcategory Naming and Renaming, read what came up on the screen. Then he closed the files, saved the game, and went down the hall to the entertainment center.

Sean, in pajamas, was watching cartoons on the big screen, an enormous teddy bear beside him. Bobby put it on the floor and sat down.

"Hi, Sean."

"Hi."

"How's it goin'?"

"Good."

"What're you watching?"

"Bullwinkle."

"I've been thinking about something."

"He's a moose."

"What?"

"Bullwinkle. Rocky's the squirrel."

"Did you ever notice how many—"

"With the goggles. 'Cause he's a flying squirrel."

"Would you shut up for a minute?"

Sean turned to him for the first time; his lower lip quivered, but he stuck out his jaw at the same time.

"Sorry. I just meant pay attention. Okay?"

Sean nodded.

"I was wondering something, that's all."

Sean didn't respond. He watched Bullwinkle step onto a diving board.

"Do you want to know what it is?"

"What?"

"I've been wondering if you ever noticed how many Seans there are."

"No." Sean rubbed the teddy bear's head with his foot.

"I mean what a popular name it is. All the other kids around named Sean."

"I don't know any Seans."

"A dime a dozen. Take my word for it. You'll see when you get older."

"I know Corey. And Tyler."

"I said take my word for it."

Sean nodded. "Got a game today?"

"Yeah. The thing is—"

"Can I come?"

"Not today. What I'm saying is that maybe your mother and I made a—"

"Is it on TV?"

"What are you talking about?"

"The game."

"Hell, I don't know. Aren't they all? The point is, Sean's a lousy name."

Sean's lower lip quivered again, but a little less this time. And his jaw stuck out more.

"I don't mean lousy. I just mean . . . dime a dozen. Like I said before."

"Dime a dozen?"

"All over the place. Not like Bradley."

"Bradley?"

"Your middle name. Didn't you know that?"

"I know my name."

"There you go, then."

"I don't like it."

"What don't you like?"

"Bradley."

"Bradley's a fine name. It's Grandpa's name."

"I don't like it."

"Would Grandpa want to hear you say that?"

"And Mommy doesn't like it either."

"Don't make up stories."

"I'm not. She told me."

"But it was her idea, for Christ's sake."

"She told me."

On the screen, Bullwinkle sprang off the diving board and saw that the pool was empty. Freeze frame. Commercial. "You could be Brad for short."

"I don't like it."

"Why the hell not? Brad's a cool name."

"I like Sean."

"Well, I don't. So think about it." Bobby rose and headed for the door. The commercial ended. Bullwinkle resumed his fall. His antlers caught in the cords of Boris Badanov's descending parachute and he wafted safely down.

On the way to the ballpark, Bobby tried to picture a perfect white baseball with red-stitched seams, tried to feel the feeling of hitting it on the sweet spot of the bat. As hard as he tried, all he could visualize was a blurred, generic baseball, not even that, more the idea of a baseball; and he could feel nothing at all. He gave up. At that moment, another image rose in his mind, complete to the finest detail: the painted farmhouse on the hypnotist's wall, with the glow of the hearth fire just visible through the window with the deep-crimson shutters.

"Goddamn it," he said aloud. "I'm not centered." The back of his hand began to tingle, where he'd hit Primo.

Bobby parked in the players' lot, got out of the car, put on the headphones, pressed PLAY. The music was just a jumble of unconnected noise. He pressed STOP.

"See you a minute, Bobby?" said Burrows as Bobby entered the clubhouse.

They went into Burrows's office. Burrows sat at his desk, a metal one with nothing on it, and lit a cigarette. Bobby took a card-table chair on the other side.

"How's the rib cage, big guy?"

"Fine. Jesus."

"Hey. Gotta ask. Valuable commodity."

"What's up?"

"Not much," said Burrows. He gazed into the distance, although there was no distance in the windowless room. "Thinkin' about restin' you today, is all."

"Forget it. I'm not tired."

Burrows took a deep drag on his cigarette, let the smoke drift slowly from his nostrils. His eyes grew dreamy, just for a moment.

"There's tired and there's tired," he said.

"What's that supposed to mean?"

"It means I got to take care of my players. That's what managing's all about nowadays. Protecting the investment. It's a long season. Don't need to tell you that, Bobby."

"The rib cage is fine," Bobby said. "Never was anything wrong with it. And I'm not tired, in any meaning of the word."

"You're a tiger, Bobby. That's one of the reasons you're . . . what you are. Why we're so doggone glad to have you here. But sometimes even tigers got to rest." He dropped the cigarette on the floor and ground it under his heel. "Just for the day, big guy. Take some of the pressure off."

"I'm not feeling any pressure."

" 'Course not." Burrows rose. "Just for today, then."

And who's going to start in my place? That was the question in Bobby's mind, but he didn't ask it.

He dressed: the number-eleven T-shirt first, then sleeves, jock, sanitaries, stirrups, pants, cleats, warm-up jersey—and walked down the tunnel to the dugout. The lineup was already taped to the wall. *Rayburn* was at the bottom, with the rest of the reserves. Someone named Simkins was playing center field and batting seventh. The name meant nothing to Bobby. He scanned the field, found the newcomer in the batting cage, recognized him after some thought: the kid from spring training, the phenom with the all-arm swing and the too-quick feet, who hadn't even made it to the final cut. Now he was back. Bobby watched him rattle three balls off the center-field fence, then rocket a few more onto the street. In a few months the kid had turned into Ted Williams.

When Bobby's turn came, he didn't think about picturing baseballs or feeling feelings. He just swung as hard as he could, and the ball started taking off all over the yard. The most vicious drive of all tore past Primo's head in shallow left. Primo didn't flinch, didn't move at all, just stood there relaxed and arrogant, like a matador. Bobby went into the dugout, part way down the tunnel, then swung his bat as hard as he could at the cement wall. It splintered in his hands. He felt a little better.

The feeling lasted until the fourth inning. Bobby sat in the dugout beside Boyle, chewing gum. The Yankees on a sunny Saturday afternoon. S.R.O. Zero-zero. Then, with two out and nobody on, the kid jerked one down the line in left, fair by five or six feet, and gone. He ran quickly around the bases, head down, keeping the smile off his face. The crowd rose, the way crowds do for someone's first big-league home run.

"Why do they do that?" Bobby said.

"Why do they do anything?" said Boyle, spitting a thin jet of tobacco juice between his feet.

That helped, but not enough. The cleansed feeling that had come from smashing the bat kept slipping away. Then, in the top of the fifth, the kid made a good, not great, over-the-shoulder catch in the triangle to save a run, and got another standing O as he ran off. The cleansed feeling vanished completely, replaced by an internal stew of bottled-up energy, adrenaline, aggression. On the outside Bobby was perfectly still. The tension between the two states was unbearable, made him want to smash again, and shout, and tear onto the field.

In the ninth the bullpen broke down, and they fell behind, three to one. Simkins led off the bottom of the inning, went to a full count, and walked on a close pitch. Where was that, ump? thought Bobby, or perhaps he'd said it aloud: Boyle's eyes shifted his way for a moment. Lanz struck out and Zamora flied to right. The aisles clogged with fans trying to beat the traffic. Then Primo doubled off the wall in right center. They held the kid at third.

"Bobby?"

Bobby looked up. Burrows was standing in front of him.

"Could use a little bingle," Burrows said.

"You're putting me in?"

"Why not?"

Bobby went to the bat rack, looked for the one he'd used in BP before remembering, and picked out a new one. He walked slowly onto the field. Lots of noise. He shut it out, slipped the donut onto the bat, swung easy until he felt loose, knocked the donut off, moved to the plate. The catcher went out to talk to the pitcher. Bobby took a few more swings.

"My feet are killin' me," the ump called out to the mound. The catcher returned, crouched behind the plate. Bobby stepped in, took his stance. He thought about the pitcher: good fastball, better slider, pissy little change—and looked for the slider on the first pitch. He didn't put himself through picturing anything, or feeling anything, or any other bullshit. He just got ready to do what he'd been doing all his life: hitting a baseball.

And there it was, slider, not a good one, up and over the plate; the kind of pitch he'd punished so many times. Bobby leaned into it and got it all, or almost all. Or maybe just a piece. Just a goddamned piece. The ball soared into the sky, seemed to hang motionless, then looped and began the long drop back down, down into the second-baseman's glove. Bobby's first thought was of Bullwinkle.

Bobby hadn't taken a step. He was still in the batter's box when Primo trotted down the third-base line, on his way to the dugout, eyes on the ground, but with a little smile turning up the corners of his mouth. He slowed down, allowing Simkins, loping across the infield, to catch up, and whacked him on the butt as they went by.

Bobby stood in the batter's box, not wanting to move. Where was there to go? Then he felt eyes gazing at him from all directions. That broke the spell. He hurried into the dugout. Everyone else was already in the clubhouse. Bobby stopped by the water cooler and smashed it to bits. The act had lost its cleansing power. This time it didn't make him feel better at all, not even for a minute. In the clubhouse, he tore off his shirt with the hideous 41 on the back and ripped it apart. Stook saw him do it, didn't say a word.

Bobby stayed in the shower until the media was gone. He dressed, gulped down a beer, and went out. Wald was waiting.

"Did you forget?" he said.

"Forget what?"

"That interview for the *Times Magazine*."

"Did I say yes?"

"Don't you remember?"

Bobby didn't remember. "Cancel it," he said.

"How can I do that?"

"With a phone call, the way you do everything."

"But she'll be at the house by now, Bobby."

"At my house?"

"That was the arrangement. She wants to see it."

"Why?"

"It's a profile piece, Bobby. Just the thing to get you in front of a wider world."

"What wider world?"

"The one beyond baseball, Bobby, like I told you before. The world that's still going to be out there after all this is over."

Bobby looked down at Wald. "I want to be traded," he said.

"That's a joke, right?"

Bobby grabbed a handful of Wald's silk shirt. "Get me traded," he said.

"Let go."

Bobby didn't let go. "Trade me," he said, backing Wald against the clubhouse door.

"Have you gone nuts? I'm the agent, not the owner."

"Anywhere will do," Bobby said. "As long as . . ."

"As what?"

"You know what." Bobby released him.

Wald nodded. He knew. Eleven.

19

Bent over a legal pad in the windowless office she shared with Bernie and Norm, Jewel Stern worked on the list of questions she would put to Bobby Rayburn. She parceled them out in subgroups: "$," "Lifestyle and Family," "The Game," "Misc." "The Game" was further subdivided into "Mind" and "Body." Thirty-seven questions, so far. Jewel reviewed them at random:

Who do you respect most in the game?

What's given you the most satisfaction in your career?

If you could change anything, what would it be?

How does being on the road so much affect your family life?

Who's your wife's favorite player?

Do you miss California?

Do you feel under any special pressure because of the big contract?

Jewel hated every one. She had the feeling they were all

the same question anyway, except perhaps the last, and she'd already asked him that in spring training, to no effect. Still, dumb questions didn't always lead to dumb answers. Maybe Bobby would open up on his own, bubbling forth eye-popping quotes, exploding with inside stuff. Maybe, for example, when she asked him about his family life, he'd blurt something about all the girls he screwed on the road. Maybe she'd get lucky.

Jewel swept that hope aside. Hoping to get lucky was a step toward mediocrity, and mediocrity wasn't what Jewel wanted. If she was fated to sit one day in some nursing home for husbandless, childless biddies, she wanted at least to be able to dazzle them with what she'd had instead. The Rayburn profile was her chance to rise to another level. Jewel squeezed the pencil tightly in her hand, as though physical intensity might somehow give birth to a good idea.

"The answer's yes," the editor at the *New York Times Magazine* had said of her proposal, and Jewel had been so thrilled she hadn't paid much attention to what had come next: "But we still feel it needs a stronger hook."

"Don't worry," she'd said. "I know it'll come out of the material."

But now she was a week from deadline, and worried. In her proposal the hook had been the question of money and pressure, weak in their eyes and now proven impotent. She knew that the *Times Magazine* liked to do profiles of sports figures, in the desperate hunt for the possibly extinct male reader, but why green-light hers if they didn't like the hook? Jewel couldn't help but wonder what would have happened to her proposal if she'd been a man. Were they favoring her to make some kind of statement, or was she still, after a generation of court cases and locker-room scenes, a novelty? Or was it just possible they realized she knew the game?

None of those questions arose at the station. They knew she knew the game; she also had the voice. They paid her well. She slept in nice hotels, ate in nice restaurants, lived in the buzz of a hectic schedule. The question that arose at the station was in her own mind, and attacked from another direction: Had she gone to journalism school, now more than twenty years ago, to spend the rest of her life covering a boys' game? If asked what Janie was up to—Jewel was her *nom de guerre,* suggested by her first agent, the one who had discovered her, as he liked to put it, at that dinky three-thousand-watt station in Hartford—her mother would say, "She's in the media," and if pressed add, "working in radio," and only if cornered admit: "baseball analyst."

Jewel doodled a baseball bat wearing a bow tie and an angry face. Her mind drifted back to the image of career biddies in the nursing home. In some track-jumping way, that prompted a new question, one she liked, and wrote down: *What kind of ball player do you think*—she checked her notes for the name—*Sean will be?*

Bernie stuck his head in the room. He had an ink smudge on the tip of his nose. "When's the Rayburn interview?"

"After the game."

"Maybe I got something for you."

"What?"

"Or it might be nothing."

"That's all the foreplay I need, Bernie. What is it?"

"Know Cleats?"

She knew Cleats.

"Where were they sitting?" Jewel asked, raising her voice over the howling dirt bikes on TV.

"Right there," replied Leon. "Primo had a Coke, Rayburn had a beer."

"What kind of beer?"

"Heineken. He didn't finish it."

Jewel walked into the alcove, glanced at the crossed bats of Aaron and Mays. Aaron's bat looked authentic, but Mays had used an Adirondack 302 for most of his career, and this was a Louisville Slugger. Leon came up behind her, wiping his hands on his apron.

"And then what happened?" she said.

"What makes you think anything happened?"

"We have our sources."

"Tanya?"

"Who's she?"

"One of the waitresses."

"Can't answer that," Jewel said.

Because the tip had been anonymous. But Leon, as she hoped, inferred a zealous concern with protecting confidentiality, and nodded with approval. "They went to the can." He pointed it out.

"Together?" Jewel moved toward it. Leon followed.

"Yeah. Sort of."

"Sort of?"

"Primo went in first, I guess. But Rayburn was right behind him."

"Chasing him, you mean?"

"Nothing like that. This is a classy place."

Jewel stood outside the men's-room door. The sign read: DUDES. "And then?"

"They were in there for a while."

"What's *a while?*"

Leon shrugged. "Five minutes."

"Did you hear anything?"

"I'm not an eavesdropper."

"Of course not. But you did see them come out."

"I was right there," Leon said, indicating the beer taps behind the bar, about twenty feet away. "I keep a low profile, that's my style, but I don't miss much."

"Despite your aversion to eavesdropping," Jewel said, trying to remember how much money she had in her purse.

"Excuse me?"

"Nothing," she said. "And then?"

"And then?"

"Did it look like they'd been fighting?"

"Who told you that?"

"Sources. Didn't I mention that already?"

There was a pause. Jewel could almost see Leon fishing through his thoughts, just beneath the surface of his eyes. She waited. "Was it one of those news tips?" he asked. Subtler than most.

She smiled. "News tips?"

"You know. Fifty bucks for the best news tip of the week."

"We don't do that," Jewel said. "I wish I could offer you an inducement but it's against station policy."

"Oh."

Silence. Jewel resisted the impulse to glance at her watch. "But I can reimburse for reasonable expenses," she said.

"Expenses?"

"Like travel."

Leon blinked. Subtle, perhaps, but not in her league.

"Suppose we took a little trip, for example."

"Where to?" said Leon.

"How about Federico's?"

"But that's just down the block."

"It meets the definition," Jewel said.

Five minutes later, they were sitting at a tiny wrought-iron table at Federico's. Drinks came: a latte with double cream and cinnamon for Jewel, a split of Cordon Rouge for Leon. Jewel took out a twenty, laid it on the table, safely under her hand. "So," she resumed, "it looked like they'd been fighting."

Eyes on the twenty, Leon said, "What about the return trip?"

"Now you're getting into the spirit."

Leon laughed.

Jewel laughed with him, took out another twenty, slid it on top of the first. "Let's have it," she said.

He stopped laughing. "It's like you say. Looked like they'd been fighting."

"How so?"

"Primo's nose was bleeding."

"He came out first?"

"And left in a hurry."

"What about Rayburn?"

"Not a mark on him. What would you expect, a little guy like Primo going up against him?"

"I don't know," Jewel said. "What else happened?"

"Nothing else. Rayburn signed a couple of autographs and split."

"No idea what it was about?"

Leon shook his head.

"What did they act like?"

"I'm sorry?"

"Their mood. Expression on their faces."

"On the way out of the can, you mean?"

"Sure. On the way out of the can."

"That's a funny thing."

"Funny?"

"Now that you mention it. Primo was the loser, right? But he went out smiling."

"And?"

"Rayburn looked grim."

Jewel thought about that. Leon finished his champagne.

"Trip over?" he said.

Jewel checked her watch. Game time. Unable to think of anything else, she started to hand him the money. He almost had his fingers on it when she paused. "Did anyone actually see what happened in there?"

"I told you. They were in the can."

"Alone?"

"Alone?"

Jewel withdrew the money. "Or was anyone else in there?"

Leon sat back. "Come to think of it."

"Who?"

"A guy."

"You know him?"

Leon licked his lips. "This feels like a detour."

"Detour?"

"On our trip."

"Jesus Christ. Do you know him or not?" She could see in his eyes that he did.

Leon raised thumb and index finger to his mouth, zipped it shut. Jewel wanted to smack him. She took out another twenty instead.

He shook his head. "This is one of those side trips that's worth the whole voyage," he said.

She showed him another twenty.

"How about one more?" he said.

"Fuck off," she told him.

He grinned. "Gil," he said.

"That's it? Gil? That's worth the trip?"

"He's sort of a regular."

"What's his last name if he's sort of a regular?"

"Don't go in for a lot of last names here."

"Where do I find him, then? What does he do? Where does he work? Et cetera."

"He works for that knife company."

"What knife company?"

"Or he used to."

"What knife company?"

Leon stared down his empty champagne flute for a moment or two, then brightened. "It's on the Survivor."

"What are you talking about?"

"I'll show you."

They returned to Cleats. Leon ducked behind the bar, came up with a knife. It had a red-and-white-checked handle, and a blade that ended in a long, jagged point because the underside of the tip was broken off. He handed it to her.

Jewel put on her reading glasses. "R. G. Renard?" she said.

"Right. It's all coming back to me now."

"What is?"

"Renard is the company. But it's his last name too."

Jewel handed over the money.

"How about a bonus?" Leon said.

"You'll get a turkey at Christmas," Jewel told him.

Jewel, driving late to the ballpark, called R. G. Renard and asked for Gil.

"No longer with us," said a woman with some sort of attitude, Jewel didn't know what or why.

"Can you tell me how to reach him?"

"No."

Jewel waited for elaboration. None came. "It's important," she said.

Silence. Jewel heard a phone buzz at the R. G. Renard office, then another. She had maybe five seconds, and nothing to go on but the woman's seeming antipathy toward Gil Renard. "He owes me money," she said.

"Oh?"

"Yes."

"A lot?"

"You could say that."

Half a minute later, Jewel had Gil Renard's address and phone number. She dialed it, listened to a few rings, and then, "I'm sorry, the number you have dialed is no longer in service."

She checked the time—two-seventeen—switched on the radio: "top of the third, one out, nobody—" The ballpark was ten or fifteen minutes away, Gil Renard's address in the northern suburbs at least half an hour farther than that, maybe more. She knew she should go to the ballpark—how could she interview Rayburn in the evening without having watched him play in the afternoon?—but she drove north instead.

The radio was tuned to the game, but Jewel wasn't really listening. Questions for Bobby Rayburn, half formed, unsatisfactory, rose and fell in her mind. She was parking in front of the worn three-decker in a working-class district off the ring road before she realized he wasn't playing.

Jewel mounted the steps to the open porch. There were five buzzers. She pressed number four, Renard. She waited ten or fifteen seconds and pressed it again, listening this time for a buzzing sound inside and hearing none. She tried it again, and once more. Then, on the chance that the buzzer wasn't working, she knocked, first lightly, then harder.

No response.

Jewel stepped back from the door, looked around. A few plastic garbage bags stood in one corner of the porch, next to a cardboard box marked IWO JIMA: THE SURVIVOR, NEW FROM R. G. RENARD FINE KNIVES. She looked in the box. There was nothing inside but an empty bottle of Jose Cuervo Gold and five or six yellow neckties. She picked one out, saw nothing wrong with it.

Jewel walked around the house. There was an alley at the back with a squat apartment building on the other side, its bricks sooty from the pollution of decades. Parked outside the back door of the three-decker was a rusted-out pickup with Maine plates. Jewel went a little closer. A big bearded man sat in the passenger seat, head against the window, eyes closed.

"Excuse me," Jewel said.

He didn't respond. Was there any point in waking him, any chance he lived in the building, or knew someone who did? Jewel tapped on the glass.

Still no reaction. "Excuse me," she said again, a little louder, and tapped a little louder too. The sounds she made had no effect on the bearded man, but they did mask a crunch in the gravel behind her. Jewel was just starting to turn when something hard and heavy struck the back of her head. The blow rang changes through her senses, making her taste bile, feel sick, see nothing but cloud, black and quivering around the edges.

Jewel got up on her hands and knees in time to see the pickup round a corner at the end of the alley and disappear.

20

Bobby Rayburn put one arm around his wife and gave her a squeeze. Val turned to him, gazed up into his eyes, and smiled her brightest smile.

"Very nice," said the photographer from the *New York Times Magazine,* changing lenses. He had a faint accent, the *R* in *very* more liquid than an English *R* and slightly rolling.

"All done?" said Val.

"Your part is," the photographer replied. "Thanks so much."

Val slipped out of Bobby's grasp, her smile fading fast. Bobby walked down toward the pool. Wald was sitting at the edge, talking on the phone, his suit pants rolled up, his bare feet, pale and hairy, dangling in the water.

"This is pissing me off," Bobby said.

"Almost done," the photographer called. "Perhaps one or two more with the *piscine* just a little in the background?"

"Pissing me off big time," Bobby said.

Wald lowered the phone. "No one knows where the hell she is."

"I'm splitting."

"Ten more minutes, Bobby."

"Why should I?"

"It's important."

"To them, maybe. Not to me."

Wald took off his sunglasses. "I'm going to tell you some thing crucial right now, big guy."

"Crucial?"

"The world—our world, Bobby—sits on four pillars. The owners, the agents, the players, the media. It's just like this house. If one of the pillars is shaky the whole thing comes crashing down."

"What are you getting at?"

"Simply this: you've got to learn how to use the media."

"Mr. Wald, is it?" said the photographer. "If you would be kind enough to clear the shot?"

Wald got out of the way. The photographer took a few more pictures. "Perhaps with the *chemise* removed? On the diving board?"

"What's he talking about?"

"I think he wants you to take your shirt off," Wald said.

"Forget it."

Val, on her way up to the house, stopped and turned. "Come all over shy?"

Wald laughed.

The photographer smiled a puzzled smile. "It's up to you, of course," he said.

Bobby thought: I'm in the best shape of my life. And: It might be good for a GM or owner somewhere to see that. Use the media. But sticking it to Val was reason enough. He took off his shirt, stepped onto the diving board. Val crossed the patio, disappeared through the French doors, closed them hard enough for the sound to carry down to the pool.

"If you would maybe sit on the end of the board," said the photographer.

Bobby sat.

"And be looking directly in the lens."

Bobby looked. The lens was a big indigo eye. He could see his reflection in it, tiny but very clear. There was nothing wrong with the eyes that did the seeing, nothing wrong with the reflected body they saw.

"Relax," said the photographer.

That annoyed Bobby. "I am relaxed," he said.

"Of course." Click. "Very nice." Click click. "All finished. Thank you so much." The photographer started packing up.

Bobby felt the evening sun on his bare back. He closed his eyes. A minute or two later the photographer said good-bye, and Bobby, eyes still closed, nodded. Was he relaxed? No. He knew that. Out on the end of the diving board, he tried to relax, to the marrow of every bone, to the nucleus of every cell. Not easy, with his ninth-inning at bat replaying itself in his mind. He didn't watch it, but it was there, looping around over and over. Bobby told himself: I've still got the eyes, the body, the hands, good as ever. A gift, like Einstein's brain. He'd tried everything, gotten nowhere. The solution was obvious: he had to play on a team where number eleven was available. All his problems, even the fiasco of his stupid, broken promise to Chemo Sean and the lost four-leaf clover, stemmed from not wearing it.

"I meant it," Bobby said. "About trading me."

No answer.

He opened his eyes. Wald had gone too. Bobby stood up, took off the rest of his clothes, dove into the water. It was warm. He floated, gazing up at the purpling sky, quieting his mind. He could almost have fallen asleep like that, except for an awakening tension in his groin, caused simply by the warm water and his nakedness, but sparking desire for a woman. He thought at once of the scraps of paper jammed in his glove compartment, scribbled in girlish hands with names and phone numbers. Easy to dial the numbers, easy to meet somewhere; the problem was he couldn't picture the faces that went with the names. A bar, then? That sports bar, Cleats, for example. Almost as easy.

A hand touched his shoulder.

Bobby jerked his head out of the water, twisted around. A woman knelt by the side of the pool, her arm still outstretched.

"Didn't mean to frighten," she said, "but you didn't hear me."

"My ears were underwater," Bobby said. "And you didn't frighten me."

The woman almost smiled. She seemed familiar, but he couldn't place her. No chance that he'd slept with her, though, so nothing embarrassing was about to happen: she was older than the women who hung around ball players, her dark hair streaked with gray along the sides. But not unattractive, despite her pallor and a nasty scrape along one side of her jaw.

"Sorry I'm so late," she said. She glanced up at the house. "Your wife told me to just walk down."

"Late?"

"Jewel Stern. For the *Times* interview. I was . . . unavoidably detained."

Bobby had forgotten he was pissed off. He slipped back into the mood. "I'm on my way out," he said.

"I don't need long."

Bobby shook his head.

"Fifteen or twenty minutes." No pleading in her tone, he noticed, a little surprised; just announcing the fact.

"I've got other commitments." Bobby swam to the ladder, started pulling himself out. He was halfway up when he remembered he wasn't wearing a suit. He turned to see if she was watching.

She was. "Catch," she said, and tossed him a towel.

Bobby caught it, wrapped it around his waist, climbed out.

"Funny how no one ever goes into a fielding slump," she said.

On the top step, Bobby paused. "What do you mean by that?"

"Just an observation."

Bobby started up the slate path that led to the house. She drew alongside after he'd gone a few steps.

"Beautiful," she said.

"What's beautiful?"

"The flowers. I didn't take you for a gardener, Bobby."

"I'm not." He hadn't even been aware of the flowers bordering the path. Who took care of them? He hadn't noticed anyone working on the grounds. Now he saw that the flower beds needed weeding, and the lawn needed mowing. He would have to speak to Wald.

The woman went up the patio steps ahead of him. She had a nice body. Use the media, he thought. Then he realized he'd forgotten her name.

"Why don't we start with the tour?" she said. "We can talk after."

"Tour?"

"Of the house. Didn't Wald mention that?"

"You don't seem to be hearing me," Bobby said. "I'm on my way out."

"I hear you," she said.

They went into the kitchen. There were drop cloths on the appliances, wires dangling through holes in the ceiling, pink-and-green marble tiles forming the beginning of a checkerboard pattern at one end of the plywood subfloor.

"What's this?"

"She's remodeling. Valerie, if you're going to mention her in the article."

"Not Val," the reporter said. "She already covered that."

Again, she seemed to be on the verge of smiling. "But how can there be an article with no interview?"

"Not my problem," said Bobby. "Can you find your way out?"

"Of course," the woman said. She reached into her shoulder bag. "Your wife asked me to give you this." She handed Bobby a note.

He unfolded it and read: *Gone to dinner w/Chaz. Sean's eaten. He's in his room. V.*

Bobby looked up. The woman was watching him. He thought of the girlish handwriting on the scraps of paper in the glove compartment. This woman's handwriting wouldn't be anything like that. Without a word he turned and went upstairs.

Sean was at the space console, the crusts of a peanut-butter and jelly sandwich on a plate beside him. "You have thirty minutes, eighteen seconds," came a deep voice from the computer. "Then your entire planet will be sprayed with the gas Sorgon B, and all oxygen-based life will be vaporized." In an on-screen window, a video previewed the catastrophe.

Not looking up, Sean said, "What's oxygen?"

"The stuff you breathe. Is the baby-sitter here?"

"I don't know."

"Is she coming?"

Sean, tapping at the keys, didn't answer. He paused, waiting for a response from the computer.

"Negative," said the deep voice.

Bobby returned to the kitchen. The woman was sitting on the bottom rung of a stepladder. She had known the whole time, of course, known he wasn't going anywhere. He was forming a stinging remark when he saw that her face was even paler than before.

"I'd like some aspirin, please," she said.

Bobby searched three or four of the seven bathrooms, without success. Then he remembered that the Moprin people had sent him a case. He found it in the basement, brought her a package. She was where he had left her, motionless on the bottom rung of the ladder.

He handed her the package. She removed the bottle, fumbled with the plastic seal around the top. She couldn't get it off. He took it from her, ripped the seal, popped off the top, pierced the foil, drew out the cotton. Her gaze was on his hands the whole time; another one of those women who noticed hands. He waited for her to say something about them, but she did not. Instead, she took the bottle—her fingers felt cold—shook out two pills, and asked for a glass of water.

Bobby found a glass in a box in the pantry, turned on the tap. No water came out.

"Christ."

"Never mind," the reporter said. She put the pills in her mouth and swallowed them. A little color returned to her face almost at once. He could still get rid of her, invent some other excuse; but he was no longer pissed off.

She glanced around the room. "What sort of house did you have in California?"

"Nicer than this."

The reporter looked surprised.

Bobby hadn't considered his answer; it had just popped out. Was this part of the interview? He began to see ways it could be used to make him look like a spoiled asshole. "Not fancier," he explained. "Nicer."

"In what way?" She took a legal pad and a mini tape recorder from her bag. "Mind if this is on?" Bobby did mind— that was one of the things he hated about reporters—but before he could say anything, she added, "Just so I don't misquote you," and he said nothing. "Nicer in what way?" she asked.

"In every way," he said, wondering for a moment what this had to do with baseball. But now that he was started on this subject, he found that he wanted to finish the thought. "See those tiles?" he said, pointing to the unfinished pink-and-green checkerboard. "They're from Italy. You wouldn't believe how much they cost."

"How much?"

Bobby couldn't remember. Perhaps he hadn't been told. He just knew no one would believe their cost.

"Probably worth every penny," the reporter said. "They look like something out of Tiepolo."

"I don't know what *town* in Italy."

The reporter smiled. "I'm ready for that tour now," she said.

Bobby had forgotten about the tour. He began to get pissed off again.

"You need me," she said.

"Why is that?" Bobby asked, thinking of Wald's four pillars.

"Because I did a lot of baby-sitting in high school."

Bobby looked at her: an older woman, yes, but good-looking. And smart. He smiled too. "Where do you want to start?"

"Wherever you want," she said. She rose. A nice body, but not very strong-looking. And was it his imagination, or did she sway just a little as she stood up?

"Are you all right?" he asked, surprising himself. He couldn't remember ever expressing, or feeling, concern for a reporter.

"Never better," she said.

What the hell was her name? Jewel? That couldn't be right. They started downstairs. Bobby led her from room to room. She said: "What did you pay for this place?"

Bobby remembered standing by the pool, remembered Wald bullying the real-estate agent, but he couldn't remember the price.

"Off the record," the reporter said

"You'll have to ask Wald."

She took out her pad, made a note. They were in one of

the bathrooms. It had a black-marble floor, matching Jacuzzi, mirrored walls.

"Tell me about Wald," she said.

"He's smart," Bobby replied, conscious of her many reflections on the walls. It was a big bathroom and she was small, but he felt surrounded by her. For a moment or two it was unpleasant. Then not.

"Can you give me an example?"

"He's got it all worked out. Mentally."

"How so?"

"The whole game. It's like a house with four pillars. Knock one down and everything collapses."

"What are the pillars?"

Bobby counted them off on his fingers. "Owners, agents, players, media."

Her head tilted slightly, as though she were lining up a target; the movement was reflected simultaneously in mirrored distances. "Didn't he forget something?"

"What?"

"Or maybe it's not a pillar, but more the ground the others stand on.

"What's that?" asked Bobby.

"The fans," she replied.

They went into Sean's room. "This is Sean. Sean, say hi to . . ."

"Jewel Stern," the reporter said immediately, not giving him time to squirm, or showing the slightest embarrassment. Not bad looking, smart, and tough as well.

"Hi," said Sean, eyes on the screen, fingers on the mouse.

"Negative," said the computer voice.

Jewel stepped up to the console, glanced at the screen. "Caught in the Arcturian Web?" she said.

"Yeah."

"How long till they spray the Sorgon B?"

"Five minutes."

"Did you try Alt F4?"

"No."

"Try it."

Sean pressed Alt F4. Bobby moved closer. A new menu flashed on the screen.

"Click on Trade Goods," Jewel said.

Sean clicked on Trade Goods.

"Two minutes, thirty seconds," said the computer voice.

"Click on Tobacco."

Sean clicked on Tobacco. A message appeared on the screen: "Offer Arcturians Earth's entire tobacco supply in perpetuity and at no cost? Y/N?"

"Y," said Jewel.

Sean pressed the Y key. New message: "Offer accepted by Arcturian Grand Council. Web withdrawn to Galaxy 41-B in the Crab Nebula. Earth saved."

The computer played a trumpet fanfare. "Congratulations, Captain Sean," said the computer voice. "The Federation hereby authorizes me to promote you to commodore, effective immediately."

"Hey," said Sean, turning to Jewel. "Thanks."

"Don't mention it, Commodore."

"How did you know?" Bobby said.

"That's all they ever want," Jewel answered. "They're completely addicted."

Sean went to bed a few minutes later. He asked to say good night to the nice lady. Bobby showed her into his room.

"Sweet dreams," she said.

"I don't have dreams."

"Be polite," Bobby said.

"That's all right," said Jewel. "If he doesn't have dreams, he doesn't have them."

Sean nodded. He gave her a long look, one Bobby didn't

recall seeing from him before. "Do you like Bradley?" he asked her.

"Bradley who?"

"It's my middle name. Instead of Sean. Daddy likes it better."

Bobby felt Jewel's gaze on him. He shrugged, as if at some childish fantasy.

"I'm sure your father wants you to be called whatever you want."

"Even if it's bad luck?"

Bobby saw Jewel tilt her head again at that measuring angle, but all she said was, "Sleep well."

They sat in the entertainment center, Jewel with the legal pad on her knee, the tape recorder on the couch between them. Much more than fifteen minutes had passed. She'd asked him a lot of questions he'd been asked before, but for some reason Bobby wasn't bored yet.

"A beer, or something?" he said.

"No, thanks."

"Wine?"

"Not for me."

She flipped through the pages of the legal pad, sighed. "What kind of ball player do you think Sean will be?"

That was a new one. He looked at her. She was waiting, her head tilted again. Bobby imagined he was seeing deep inside her, to some essence beyond the fact of her being a woman. That had never happened to him before either.

"No idea," he said. "But I wouldn't want him to be a ball player."

"Why not?"

"I just wouldn't."

"Do you think you're just saying that because of the slump?"

Bobby's guard was down. He almost said yes, almost told

the truth, because it was the truth, although he hadn't known it until she'd spoken. But he got a grip on himself and said: "I'm not in a slump."

"You're a lifetime .316 hitter, Bobby, and as of today you're batting .153."

"They're just not falling in, that's all."

There was a long pause. Bobby could hear the tape recorder whirring. "Do you feel any pressure because of the big contract?"

"How many times do I have to answer that? No."

"Never again. I promise." She scanned her notes. "What about your new teammates?"

"What about them?"

"Getting along okay?"

"Sure."

"No problems?"

"What do you mean?"

"Sometimes there are problems when a big star comes to a new team. You know that. Especially if . . ."

"If what?"

"If he gets off to a rocky start."

Bobby rose, crossed the room to the wet bar, got a beer from the small refrigerator beneath it. "There are no problems," he said.

"Not with any of the players?"

"Correct."

She opened her mouth as though to say more, stopped herself. They sat in silence, broken only by the whirring of the recorder. He still wasn't bored.

All at once, she began to pale again. She took a deep breath. "You've been generous with your time, Bobby." She rose, again slightly unsteady. "Just one more thing."

"What's that?"

"Have you ever heard of someone called Gil Renard?"

Bobby thought. "I'm bad with names," he said.

She laughed, seemed to lose her balance, reached out, touched his forearm. "Don't I know," she said.

"Is he in the minors?" Bobby asked.

"No."

"Why do you ask?"

"It doesn't matter." Jewel put the legal pad and the tape recorder in her bag.

"That it?" said Bobby.

"I might have a follow-up or two when I pull everything together."

"Just call." *I said that?* he thought, and felt a strange thrill that was almost of danger.

She tilted her head again. "Thanks, Bobby." Then she was gone. Her touch lingered on his forearm.

Jewel walked toward the parking area in front of the four-car garage. She had a sharp pain in her head and a deep, dull one in her jaw, throbbing in some infernal harmony. She got in her car, parked next to Bobby's jeep, closed the door, rolled down the window, breathed in the cool night air, hoping for clarity, or simply the strength to drive home. Pull everything together? She didn't know where to begin.

Jewel was about to turn the key when a car swept into the circular drive and stopped on the other side of Bobby's jeep. She sat motionless. The night was quiet, and what breeze there was blew her way. She heard Wald speak, low but clear: "And now the asshole wants to be traded."

Then came Val's voice: "For Christ's sake, where to?"

"It's a pipe dream," Wald said. "No one would touch him. That contract makes him a leper."

"So what's going to happen?" Val said.

"Who knows?"

"Can't you do better than that?"

Wald's voice rose. "You're complaining?"

"Shh. I'm not. It's just that I'd like to know what's going to happen. Is that so awful?"

Wald snorted. "This one's up to him."

"I don't understand."

"He's going to have to start hitting. It's as simple as that."

"And if he doesn't?"

"He's through."

"But he's only thirty-one."

"Thirty-two in a few weeks. Almost geriatric in this game, even though he's still seventeen in real life."

"You don't need to tell me that," Val said.

21

Should have been a grave digger.

Another black night, moonless and starry, but now the air was warm, and alive with soft breezes. Surrounded once more by the old town names, written in stone—Pease, Laporte, Spofford, Cleary, Bouchard—Gil toppled the marker that read Renard, R. G., and dug again his father's grave. This time the once-turned, unfrozen soil had lost its resistance. The earth felt weightless, and Gil very strong, stronger than he could ever remember. He was a big man, he reminded himself, bigger than Bobby Rayburn, as he had discovered when they stood so close at the ballpark; and much bigger than Primo. He pictured the knife flashing into Primo's hand in the men's room at Cleats, and his insides stirred with a feeling he hadn't known since the last time he had faced some dangerous hitter: butterflies.

In what seemed like moments, Gil was down in the earth to shoulder level. The shovel blade struck the pine box. Recalling the jagged holes he had made in the wood, Gil knelt and cleared the rest of the dirt by hand. Then he climbed out of the pit and walked to the shed at the end of the dirt track crossing the cemetery. The pickup was parked behind it. Gil opened the door, reached inside, bent his knees, and hoisted Boucicaut's body onto his shoulders.

A heavy and unbalanceable load: Gil carried Boucicaut half the distance, dragged him the rest of the way by his belt, bumping him over rocks and tree roots. Gil knew he couldn't hurt Boucicaut anymore but still was crying by the time he got him to the grave. Boucicaut: a knight in the Crusades, according to some college girl; a real one, not like Robin Hood. He smoothed Boucicaut's hair a little, plucked a twig from his beard. Bent over the body, Gil was conscious of the stars above, the vast black spaces between them, the infinite blackness beyond. He knew he should say something, eulogize Boucicaut in some way.

"Len Boucicaut," he said. "Catcher."

Then he rolled him into the hole. Boucicaut landed with a heavy thump, facedown.

Beside the shovel lay Gil's MVP trophy, the brass-plated baseball on the hardwood stand. Gil picked it up. He had brought it with the intention of placing it in Boucicaut's arms. Boucicaut was the MVP, always had been, always would be. It was the right thing to do, but how was it feasible, now that Boucicaut had landed facedown like that? He could climb down into the pit, wrestle the body into position; that was one way. Gil stood at the edge, picturing himself doing it. But he didn't do it. In the end, he shoveled the earth back in, working faster and faster, hurling and flinging the last clods of it, then tilted his father's headstone back in place, and hurried off, shovel in one hand, trophy in the other.

Gil drove to the trailer in the woods. The 325i was still parked in the junk-strewn yard, but that wasn't what first caught his eye. What first caught his eye was the light glowing in the trailer.

He got out of the pickup and closed the door softly. Had they left a light on? Possible, but still he moved as quietly as he could toward the trailer. Now he heard voices, realized as he drew closer that they were TV voices. Could they have left the TV on too?

Gil found a window where the plastic curtains were only half drawn, knelt, and peered over the sill. He saw no one except the figures on the TV screen. Black-and-white figures in some old movie: a man in a tuxedo breathed smoke from his nose and asked a woman in a strapless gown to dance. She breathed smoke from her nose and said her feet were tired.

Then Gil felt something hard in the small of his back, and a real woman said: "Hands way up.

He didn't move.

"This is a twelve-gauge, peeping boy, and my finger's wrapped around the trigger."

Gil considered the thrower on his leg, tried and failed to imagine reaching it before she could pull the trigger; and raised his hands.

"Now, kneeling down just like that, turn around so I can see your pretty face."

Gil started to turn. She prodded him with the gun muzzle. "Did I say anything about lowering them?"

Gil raised his hands higher, twisted around, still on his knees. He looked up at the woman. She had painted eyebrows, frosted hair, upside-down Cupid's-bow lips.

"How to keep men the way you are right now," she said. "That's the problem."

"You're making a mistake," Gil said. "I was only returning the truck."

She didn't turn to look. "What were you doing with it?"

No smooth lie came to mind. But he did remember something: *She's in the pen.* "Returning it, like I said," Gil told her. "I didn't expect to see anyone here, that's all. You weren't supposed to be back till August."

A guess, but not a wild one: her eyes wavered, and so did the gun. At that moment, the mongrel came bounding out of the darkness.

"Hey, Nig," Gil said, and held out his hand. Nig sniffed it, then sniffed it some more.

"Who are you?" she said.

"A friend of Co's."

The gun came up again. "No one calls him that."

"I always did."

"What's your name?"

"Onsay." A thrill shot through him.

"He never mentioned you."

Gil shrugged. Nig kept sniffing him, wagging his tail.

"He likes you," the woman said. "And Nig don't like nobody except Len."

Gil said nothing. He knew what the sniffing was about.

"Where is he?" the woman said.

"In the city."

"What's he doing there?"

Gil paused. He was starting to feel clever. It was a nice feeling. Clever people could have the whip hand, even on their knees looking up a gun barrel. He gave his clever answer: "I don't like to say."

"Son of a bitch," said the woman. "He just can't keep his zipper up, can he? And don't tell me he couldn't wait. You don't know what I've done for that prick."

Gil didn't reply. He didn't know what she'd done for Boucicaut, suspected there was a lot he wouldn't understand about a relationship where a whore demanded sexual fidelity from her man.

"When's he coming back?" she said.

"Whenever I get down there and bring him back."

The woman lowered the gun. There were still tough questions she could have asked, but she fed him an easy one instead. "Is that your car?" She pointed the muzzle at the 325i.

He nodded.

"Nice car," she said. The expression in her eyes changed. "You can get up."

Gil rose. She backed away, but only a little: living with Boucicaut, she must have gotten used to size in a man. Gil thought of another clever line. "I won't bite," he said.

"No?"

They looked at each other.

"What did you say your name was, again?"

"Onsay." The thrill again, just as strong.

"What kind of a name is that?"

"It's my lucky name," Gil said. "What's yours?"

"Claudine," she said. "But it's not lucky."

"Maybe that'll change," Gil said, astonished by his sudden glibness, as though he were someone else, a tuxedo-wearing star from the thirties; a real player. And then it hit him: I can be someone else—I'm already on the way.

"Want to come inside?" she said. "I guess I owe you a drink, anyway."

Gil went inside. Claudine laid the gun on the kitchen table. They sat down. On TV, tuxedo man was dancing with another woman; the sore-footed one looked on from the sidelines through narrowed eyes.

"Beer?" said Claudine. "Or there's usually some Canadian."

"Beer." He never wanted to taste Canadian again.

She opened two beers. "What do you do?" she asked.

"I'm into a lot of things right now."

Not much of an answer, not the kind that would do for someone like Garrity, or O'Meara, but it did for her. She nodded and said, "You've got a phone in your car, eh?"

"You peeked," he said.

She giggled. This was supreme, to have the right words at hand with a woman; and he was cold sober.

"Who's the peeper now?" he said.

Claudine gave him a long look. The nightgown she was wearing slipped a little off her shoulder. "Did Len say much about me?"

"Some."

There was a silence. Gil heard the beating of heavy wings above; probably an owl.

Then Claudine spoke. "I could give you a special rate."

"I've never paid for it," he said.

"That'll make it all the more exciting."

It did.

Wonderfully more exciting. It was nothing like that last time with Lenore. This went on forever, and she came with loud cries, and there was no bitching and whining after. They lay together on the bed in the back of the trailer.

Claudine said: "What's that hard thing?"

Gil laughed: "You still don't know?" What ease!

"Not that," she said: "I mean on your leg."

"Nothing," Gil said. He rolled on top of her and buried himself in her soft, wet space in a single surge. Then he moved like a madman. She didn't cry out this time, but that was because she was even more turned on; he could tell.

"How was that?" he said after.

"Great."

"Better than Co?"

Pause. "No one calls him that."

"I always did. I told you already. Something wrong with that?"

"No," she said. She gave him a little squeeze. "Nothing wrong."

Soon she rolled over. Gil closed his eyes. He listened for the beating wings of the owl, but it didn't come. He slept.

Gil had a dream. He was a crusader, riding a red Schwinn across a barren plain. He came to a headless body lying on the ground. It wore a magnificent shirt of spun gold. He stripped it off as a gift for the king. The king's domed palace opened for him, and he was about to gaze upon the king's face when something cold and hard pressed against his forehead.

Gil opened his eyes. The woman, Claudine, now fully dressed, stood over him, holding the shotgun to his head.

"You killed him, you son of a bitch," she said.

"What are you talking about?" Gil tried to sit up. She pressed the muzzle against his skull, keeping him down.

"I'm talking about the blood all over the goddamn truck, Mr. Gil Renard."

"That's not my name," said Gil, realizing he no longer felt the thrower around his leg.

"Then it's not your fancy car out there either, is it? The one with 'Gil Renard' on the registration."

Gil said nothing. A single lamp shone in the trailer, on the kitchen table. He spotted the thrower beside it, in its sheath.

"Maybe you stole it," Claudine said. "Maybe the two of you stole it and then something went wrong, eh?"

Now she was the one with the power of words, and Gil had lost it. His racing mind offered up nothing better than the rules of the successful commission salesman. Take the offensive.

"I didn't kill him," he said.

"Then where is he? And whose blood's all over the truck?"

Gil had no answer.

"I'm calling the cops," she said. She backed away toward the wall phone, holding the gun on him. Sinews twitched in her forearm. At that moment, something rough and wet rubbed against the sole of Gil's foot.

Nig. Nig was licking his foot. The dog smelled Boucicaut all over him.

Gil had an idea.

"It's deer blood," he said.

Claudine paused, her hand on the phone. A gratifying pause. He was coming into himself at last.

"Deer blood?"

"He shot a deer yesterday. I was driving, on that old logging road north of the bypass. He just leaned out of the window and pow."

"And then you put it in the cab?"

"To keep it out of sight. Not exactly hunting season, Claudine."

That sounded like the Boucicaut she knew: he could see it in her eyes. But the gun was still pointed at him. "You said he was in the city."

Gil tried to look sheepish. "That wasn't quite true."

"But he's with somebody, right?"

Gil nodded.

"Close by?"

He nodded again.

"Show me."

"Aw," Gil said. "I don't want to do that."

Her hand shifted back to the phone. "Then I'll have the cops track him down." The gun barrel, heavy for her, dipped toward the floor.

"You win," Gil said. He got off the bed, reached down to pick his shirt off the floor.

Claudine laughed a mean laugh. "Don't want them to take a gander at that bag of knives in the truck, do you?"

Gil looked puzzled. "Why not? I'm a collector."

She thought. Gil knew what she was thinking: knife collector, 325i, it fit. There were lots of things that didn't fit, though, and Gil could see she wasn't finished with them. She started to frown. At that moment, Gil heard the heavy wings beating overhead again, going the other way this time. Nig, at the foot of the bed, heard them too. Whether the sound reminded him of some nocturnal fright in his past, whether he was reacting to something else, or nothing at all, Nig suddenly began to howl.

A loud and startling intrusion that filled the trailer with bestial noise. Claudine jumped. Gil jumped too—right across the room and full force against her legs. She fell, lost her grip on the gun. Gil got his arms around her, started to shift his weight on top. Then Nig landed on him, and sank his teeth into the back of his thigh. Claudine squirmed away.

She ran across the room and out the door. Gil scrambled up. Nig bit him again, the other leg this time. Gil took the thrower off the kitchen table and sank it to the hilt in Nig's head.

Then he was out the door too, bloody thrower in hand. Claudine was halfway across the yard, already past the pickup and the 325i. She had no keys, he realized. He ran after her, gaining at first. In seconds he was close enough to hear the high-pitched noise she made at the beginning of every breath. But then they were in the woods, where the ground was rough, and she had shoes on and he did not. He ran as hard as he could, but stopped gaining. Her frosted hair flashed on through the trees. There were trails in the woods, trails she probably knew and could probably find, even in the darkness. She was going to lose him. Without thinking of the proper form, without calculating distance or rotation, Gil drew back the thrower and let go.

How much time passed? Half a second? Three-quarters? It seemed much longer to Gil. Then he heard her say, "Oh," and she crumpled and fell.

Gil hurried to the spot, bent down, and saw that he had been perfect. He rose and leaned against a tree to catch his breath. His hand encountered gouges in the bark. He looked, and discovered the deer-heart-sized circle he had carved, and the deep marks of his practice session.

"Yes," he said.

He carried Claudine back to the pickup, laid her on the front seat. He put Nig in there too. If it was blood they wanted, let them find a confusion of it. Of course he knew who they would look for first. Boucicaut, even in death, a rock for him.

Gil went inside, showered and dressed, retrieved the bag of knives; then climbed into his car and drove away. He was coming into his own.

The custodian of the cemetery called the police station next morning.

"Been some digging again," he said.

"What kind of digging?" asked Claymore.

"Just digging. No vandalism or nothin'. Everything put back, like. But digging, all the same."

"Probably just some kids," said Claymore.

"Maybe, but why would kids dig up the same place twice?"

"What do you mean, the same place?"

"The same grave, like."

"Whose grave?"

"Renard, R. G."

"I'll be right over," said Claymore.

22

"Coming up on the All-Star break now, Bernie."

"Sure was fast, Norm."

"Faster for some than for others."

"Slow going for the old town team, is that what you're trying to say?"

"You got it."

"Good a time as any then, Norm—what's your mid-season assessment?"

"In two words, Bernie? De pressing. They're dead last and going nowhere."

"What the heck happened, Norm?"

"More what didn't happen."

"Like?"

"Like Rayburn, Bernie. It starts and maybe ends right there. Wasn't Rayburn supposed to be the missing piece of the puzzle, the big bat in the middle of the lineup that was going to put them over the top?"

"Don't look at me, Norm. Who warned everybody he wasn't the Messiah? Taking nothing away from his great career, of course, but he's been stuck in this woeful slump so long now, it's maybe getting to be time we asked ourselves if *slump* is still the right word."

"The implication being?"

"Just that all good things got to end. All things must pass, right? George Harrison."

"Not my favorite Beatle."

"Who was?"

"Ringo."

"Me too. Where were we, Norm?"

"Bobby Rayburn."

"Right. He's no kid anymore, is he? Lose a little off your bat speed, it gets around the league pretty quick."

"Trade rumors are already percolating."

"So I hear, from reliable sources. But it may already be too late for them to get anything for him. It's like the stock market—by the time John Q. Public gets wind of something, the insiders have already discounted it."

"Except they don't spit tobacco juice on Wall Street, Bernie."

"Might be an improvement if they did. Let's go to the phones. Who's out there? Gil? Gil on line three. Go ahead, Gil."

Dead air.

"Gil?"

Dead air.

"Looks like we lost Gil. Let's go to—"

"Hello?"

"That you, Gil?"

"Am I on?"

"You're on, Gil. What's up?"

"Trade rumors?"

"Say what?"

"There are trade rumors about Rayburn?"

"Just speculation at this point, Gil."

"What kind of rumors?"

"The usual kind—unconfirmed. What's your point?"

"You said reliable sources."

"I may have."

"Like who?"

"Like people close to some of the principals. I can't get more specific than that, Gil, without violating a confidence. I'm sure you understand."

"Bernie here, Gil. I take it from your tone you don't think trading Rayburn would be such a good idea."

Dead air.

"Gil? You still there?"

"It would be a disaster."

"Isn't that putting it a little strong, Gil?"

"Not strong enough. Not nearly. Bobby Rayburn's the best thing to happen to this team in years, and all they've done is screwed him up and down."

"Who's they?"

"Everybody. Look how they mishandled the rib thing. And they didn't exactly welcome him to the team, make him feel at home, did they?"

"That's a new one on me. You hear anything like that, Norm, not welcoming him to the team?"

"Never. Can you give us an example maybe, Gil?"

"I could."

"Well?"

Dead air.

"Gil? You still there?"

"I'm still here. But what's the use?"

"What's the use of what? I don't get you, Gil."

"Just get this, Bernie. I'm sick and tired of you taking shots at him all the time. When's it going to stop?"

"Right now. Let's go to Chuckie in Malden. What's shakin'?"

Jewel Stern walked into the control room, pressed the talk-back button when Norm went to commercial. "What was that guy's name?"

Bernie, sitting opposite Norm in the studio, pressed his button. "Gil."

"A regular, would you say?" said Norm, emptying packets of sugar into his coffee.

"Not quite," Bernie said.

"Gil who?" said Jewel.

"No last names here," said Norm. "You know that."

"Just like in porn movies," Bernie added.

Fred, at the controls, raised his hand. "Coming to you in three, two, one." He stabbed his index finger at the glass.

"That's a pretty thought," said Jewel. "Think I'll take a shower."

And Norm and Bernie were both laughing as they came out of commercial.

"We're back."

"Ain't sports a gas?"

"Wee-ooo. Let's get right to the phones."

Gil saw he was doing eighty-five, eased off the pedal. Assholes, Bernie and Norm, but they were right about one thing: the team was going nowhere. Driving south, remembering from time to time to ease off the pedal, Gil listened to fans from all over the region searching for the reason why, listened to Norm and Bernie, the supposed experts, searching for the reason why. None of them had a clue.

Only he knew.

Ninety. He eased off

Only he knew. Gil had a thought, so powerful, so exciting that he broke into a sweat. It dampened his shirt, trickled down the undersides of his arms, moistened the leather-covered steering wheel beneath the palms of his hands. He was in a position, a unique position, to help the team. To actually help the team: to help them win games, to turn the season around, go all the way: almost like a real player. They needed him. Gil began to shake. He shook; it was no figure of speech. He had never before physically felt the force of an idea, felt it taking hold of his body like this. In his mind, a short and logical chain of events uncoiled into the near future.

On the South Shore, a block or two from the school where the Little League tryouts had been held, Gil found the ball field. A low chain-link fence ran parallel to the street, down the right-field line. He parked, got out, leaned on the fence rail.

An orange-shirted team was playing a green-shirted team, orange shirts at bat. Gil checked the electric scoreboard in center field: HOME 15, VISITORS 17, bottom of the fifth. Three and one on the batter, two outs. Gil looked down toward the infield, not far away. Runners on first and third, one of them with a long ponytail dangling from under an oversized batting helmet. A girl, he realized, but not immediately.

The pitcher wound up, threw. The ball arced slowly toward the plate. The batter, a fat boy with a stiff-legged stance, swung at it, even more slowly. He wasn't even looking at the ball but hit it anyway, or it hit the bat, making a dull metallic twang: a soft fly to right.

Directly to the right fielder, standing about ten yards from Gil. He didn't have to move a step. But for some reason he did move, in fact charged in wildly, as though the ball were going to fall in front of him and a diving catch was called for. At the last second he recognized his mistake and leaped, stabbing his gloved hand as high as he could. He missed the ball by an inch or so; it went over his head, landed behind him, bounced a few times, and rolled the rest of the way to the outfield fence.

The right fielder made a little moaning sound and chased after it. He picked it up at the base of the wall, turned, and threw. The shortstop, a tiny kid who ran well, knew enough to come out to take the cutoff, waving his sticklike arms. But the right fielder's throw, a feeble, sidearmed effort, went nowhere near him. All the runners, even the fat boy, scored. HOME 18, VISITORS 17. The orange players jumped up and down.

The green center fielder, who hadn't backed up the play, hadn't even budged the whole time, glared through his thick glasses at the right fielder. "You geek, Richie," he yelled. "You just lost us the game."

The right fielder hung his head.

Richie.

The first thing Gil wanted to do was hop over the fence and smack the center fielder's face. The second was smack Richie's.

Gil did neither. He stood by the chain-link fence, gazing at Richie, thinking of what he should say.

"That's okay, Richie, everybody boots one from time to time." But boot them like that? And then throw like that?

Or: "Get your head up—they're still playing."

Or: "Don't snivel, you little bastard."

Before he could say anything, the next batter hit a little pop-up that the pitcher—another girl, Gil saw—caught easily, and the inning was over. The green team ran in. Furiously wiping his eyes with the back of his hand, Richie ran in too.

Gil hopped the fence. In foul ground, he walked toward the infield. The grass was soft and springy under his feet. Memories that he didn't have time for arose instantly in the back of his mind, waiting for his attention. The orange team took the field, began throwing balls around. If only one got loose and rolled to him, he'd show them what throwing was about. He pictured himself flinging a bullet over the centerfield fence, over the church across the street, over the trees behind it, gone. But no balls got loose and rolled to him.

There was a small set of bleachers along each baseline; three or four rows of benches, perhaps a dozen spectators in all. Gil sat in the bottom row on the first-base side, as close to the plate as he could get.

The umpire was a white-haired man who might have played third base long ago: bandy legs, Popeye forearms, leather skin. "Top of the sixth," he said, pulling on his mask. "Last ups."

The pitcher led off for the green team. She had a relaxed stance and a smooth, compact swing. She lined the first pitch up the middle for a clean single, and took second when the center fielder hesitated, sliding in under the throw. A man on the bench above Gil's said, "All right, Crystal."

"Ain't over yet," said another man. "Anything can happen, especially in the minors."

"We just moved here," said the first man. "Too late for the draft. Or Crystal would have been in the majors."

The second man said nothing.

The first man spoke again: "According to that Pellegrini guy."

The second man said nothing.

"He was real upset about it," the first man said. "Called me personally."

The second man remained silent. The first man gave up.

The next batter was the tiny shortstop. He walked on four pitches.

Gil turned to the second man. "Where are we in the order?"

The first man answered for him. "My daughter Crystal bats cleanup."

The number-six hitter nubbed one down to first. The first baseman picked it up and stepped on the bag. The tiny kid and Crystal scooted over to second and third. One out, tying and go-ahead runners in scoring position.

The number-seven hitter surprised everyone by laying a bunt down the first-baseline. But as he ran out of the box, the ball bounced up and hit him in the thigh. The umpire called him out.

"What the hell is that?" said Crystal's father.

"The rule," replied Gil without turning.

Two out. The number-eight hitter stepped up—the center fielder with the thick glasses—and Richie came out of the third-base dugout and into the on-deck circle. At almost the same moment, the gate in the fence on that side opened, and Ellen and Tim walked in.

The first pitch was on its way. "Come on, Brendan," called the second man. Brendan took a cut, but after the ball was already in the catcher's mitt.

"Jesus," said Crystal's father, not quite under his breath.

"Come on, Brendan," called Brendan's father, louder this time.

Brendan watched the second pitch all the way, bat at rest on his shoulder.

"Strike two," said the ump.

"Game over," said Crystal's father, making even less attempt this time to keep his voice down.

On the other side, Ellen had caught Richie's eye and was waving to him, a big smile on her face. Richie didn't wave back. Good boy, Gil thought. At that moment she saw Gil. Her eyes widened. She turned quickly to Tim.

The pitcher wound up, lobbed it in. Very slow, a little inside. Again, Brendan didn't move. The ball glanced off his forearm. He screamed and fell down, writhing. After five or ten seconds, he realized he wasn't hurt and took his free pass to first.

Two outs, bases loaded, game on the line. Richie stepped in.

Gil was on his feet now, but silent. Behind him Crystal's father said, "Maybe he'll get hit too. It's our only chance."

Richie took a few practice cuts. Horrible ones. Gil heard

Ellen calling, "You can do it, Richie." Gil shot a glance at the third-base side. Tim had disappeared.

The first pitch: a meatball, right down the middle. For a moment, Gil thought that Richie was going to let it go by; nothing wrong with that, taking the first pitch in a situation like this. But at the last moment, Richie swung, and missed by a foot.

Crystal's father said, "Christ almighty."

The second pitch was over Richie's head. He swung at that too, coming a little closer this time.

"Strike two," said the ump.

Behind him, Gil heard the two fathers gathering their things. He checked the third-base side. Ellen was watching him. Their eyes met. There was an expression in hers he had never seen before: a negative expression, but not her hostile one, with which he was familiar. This was fear. The sight pleased him. She looked away.

The next pitch bounced two feet in front of the plate. Richie started to swing, then held back. From the other side, a voice called, "He went, ump."

"Ball one," said the ump.

The pitcher bounced another one in the same place. Richie didn't even twitch this time.

"Ball two," said the ump.

"Time," called the orange coach, stepping onto the field. The pitcher walked off the mound, met him at the third-baseline. The coach knelt down and said something. The pitcher replied, a long reply, accompanied by finger-pointing at several of his own players. The coach cut him off, raising his voice a little, loud enough for Gil to hear, or think he heard: "Just get the damned thing over. No way he's going to hit it."

"Play ball," said the ump.

The pitcher returned to the mound. Richie took another

horrible practice swing. Then the pitch, way inside. Richie went down.

"That hit him, didn't it?" said Crystal's father.

"Sure looked like it," said Brendan's father.

But Gil knew it hadn't. If it had, Richie would be crying. The ump raised both fists. Full count.

"What the hell's wrong with you, ump?" yelled Crystal's father.

Richie got up, straightened his batting helmet, took his wretched stance. Both teams were on their feet now, screaming this and that. Gil heard Ellen above the din: "You can do it, Richie. You can do it."

He thought: *Be a hero, boy.* He saw himself up there, powerful, coiled, murderous: driving one over that fence, over that church, over those trees. Grand slam. *Be a hero, boy.*

The pitch. Aimed, not thrown: the fattest one yet, somewhat inside. But not as far inside as the one before. Richie went down again. The ump punched the air with his right fist. "Strike three."

The orange team mobbed their pitcher.

Richie lay in the dirt.

Crystal's father said, "What did I tell you? What did I fucking tell you?"

Gil wheeled around and smashed him in the face.

He took a swing at Brendan's father's face too, but he was farther away, and the blow struck his shoulder.

"What the hell?" said Brendan's father.

"No one calls my boy a geek," Gil said.

"But I didn't call him anything, you—"

Brendan's father, getting his first good look at Gil, fell silent.

Gil vaulted the fence. How quickly he was moving now, like a giant on a puny planet! In no time, he was at home plate. The ump was bent over Richie, talking quietly. Gil grabbed him from behind, straightened him up, twisted him around, whipped off his mask, and hurled it over the stands.

In a giant's voice, he said: "That was a ball, you cheating prick."

"Get the hell away from me," the ump said, and gave Gil a push.

A mistake. The ump was strong, but not as big as Gil, and much older. With a giant's roar, Gil charged into him, drove him all the way to the backstop. The ump lost his breath in one barking grunt, and slid down.

Then Gil had Richie in his arms, and was striding down the right-field line, toward his car. He was aware of orange and green, of people shouting, and running around, and staring; aware, but barely.

Richie looked up at him. He had Ellen's eyes, and Ellen's new expression in them: fear.

"Please," he said.

"Please, Dad," Gil corrected.

Richie bit his lip.

"Please, Dad," Gil repeated.

Richie started to cry.

"Haven't you been wimpy enough for one day?" Gil asked. "Say *please, Dad.*" Richie cried, but he wouldn't say it.

Then someone jumped on Gil's back. Someone light: Ellen, of course. Gil tried to shake her off, but she wouldn't shake off, clung desperately. He held onto Richie with one hand, grabbed at Ellen with the other. Richie wriggled free, fell to the ground.

"Run, Richie," Ellen cried.

Richie ran.

Gil turned to go after him. At that moment, he heard a siren in the distance. He let go of Ellen.

"Why did you do it to me, Ellen?"

"Because you're out of control."

"I don't mean the cops. I mean taking Richie away."

"That's what I meant too," Ellen said. "And I didn't do it. You did it to yourself."

Gil didn't hit her. What was the point? He'd known for a long time that she didn't understand him. "You're so *small*," he said. "All of you." Then he hopped the fence, jumped into the 325i, drove away.

After a few blocks, he passed a squad car, siren blaring, blue lights flashing, going the other way. Behind the squad car came Tim in the minivan. He saw Gil and started honking frantically. But the cops must have thought he was merely getting into the spirit of the chase; they kept going. Gil laughed.

Just after dawn the next morning, Gil knocked on door 3A of a suburban condo. He kept knocking for a minute or so; then the door opened and Figgy, wrapped in a towel, sleep in his eyes, peered out.

"Gil?"

"Right, old colleague. May I come in?"

"Gee, it's pretty early, Gil, and—"

But he was already in.

Gil looked Figgy over. "I didn't know Bridgid could cook."

"I'm sorry?"

"Spare tire's inflating, Figster."

Figgy pulled the towel higher. "You've come for the fifty bucks, is that it, Gil?"

Gil laughed. "What's fifty bucks between old colleagues? Didn't I already tell you that? What I've got in mind is a proposition of a different kind. One I think you'll like, Figster, especially if you're still stoked on the 325i."

"You want to sell the car?"

"Bingo."

Figgy licked his lips. "How much?"

"Five G's. This is a one-time offer. The book is ten-six."

"I haven't got five G's."

Gil moved past him, toward the rear of the apartment.

"Where are you going?"

"Bridgid's got five G's. She's a regular little squirrel with money, everyone knows that."

Gil went into the bedroom, Figgy hurriedly following. A shaft of sunshine poked through the slightly parted curtains, fell across the bed, spotlighting Bridgid, asleep under a sheet that covered her to the waist.

"Hey," said Gil. "I never knew Bridgid had such nice tits."

Her eyes snapped open. "Oh, my God," she said, tugging at the sheet.

"It's all right, Bridg," said Figgy, coming into the room. "Gil wants to sell the car, that's all."

"What the hell are you talking about?"

"His car. The 325i. He's giving us a deal. Five G's. The book is ten-six."

Gil sat on the bed. He smiled at Bridgid. "One-time offer," he said.

Bridgid opened her mouth, closed it, opened it again. "But we've already got two cars."

"Mine's a piece of shit, Bridg," said Figgy. "You know that."

She looked at Gil, at Figgy, at Gı

Gil smiled at her again. "Strictly business, Bridg, old girl. No personalities."

She nodded, glanced again at Figgy, got no help from him, and said: "I'm sure we appreciate the offer, Gil. We'll have to think it over seriously, of course, think it over and let you know."

"That's right," said Figgy. "Think it over and let you know."

Gil kept the smile on his face, but it was work. "A one-time offer means a limited-time offer. I thought that was understood."

"Let's be businesslike," Bridgid said. "I don't see how you can expect—"

Gil grabbed the sheet and yanked it off her. Her body trembled. That made it all the more attractive. "You're a lucky man, Figgy," Gil said.

Figgy stiffened, as though he was about to do something; but that was it.

Gil took in the sight for as long as he wanted. Then he rose. "Let's get going."

They drove to Bridgid's bank in the 325i—Figgy at the wheel, Bridgid in front, Gil in back. "Rides like a dream, doesn't it?" Gil said. The pissy smell was almost undetectable.

With five grand in cash and his knapsack of knives, Gil took a cab to the airport. He unstrapped the thrower and put it in the knapsack as well. Inside the terminal, he paid cash for a ticket, checked the knapsack, passed through security, and boarded the plane. He took a coach seat, a tight squeeze for a man his size, and he didn't like flying to begin with, but there was no choice. His team was playing on the coast. They needed him.

23

Jewel Stern parked in front of the peeling three-decker. The green garbage bags were no longer on the porch. She was about to buzz number four, Renard, when she saw that the front door was open an inch or two. She went in.

On either side were the doors to one and two; ahead, the stairs. She climbed them. At the next landing, she found number three on her left and a dim corridor on her right. She followed it, past a closed and numberless door—the bathroom; she could hear the toilet running—to number four at the end. Like the front door, it too was slightly ajar. She pushed it open a little more so she could see inside.

The room was small and without belongings: no clothes, no papers, no bedding. Deserted, abandoned, tenantless: except for the man in jeans and a T-shirt, standing at the window, his back to the door. Jewel cleared her throat.

He wheeled around. A slightly built man with wire-rim

glasses, freckles, and red hair, graying at the sides, thinning on top.

"Mr. Renard?" she said. "I didn't mean to frighten you." Remembering Bobby Rayburn in the pool, she wondered whether she had advanced beyond merely making men emotionally uncomfortable, as her mother would have it, to some ultimate disjunctive phase of physically terrifying them.

Like Bobby, the red-haired man said, "You didn't scare me."

"Of course not," Jewel said.

His eyes, narrow to begin with, narrowed some more. "Who are you?"

"Someone looking for Gil Renard. Have I found him?"

"You didn't answer my question."

"Nor you mine."

"The difference is," said the red-haired man, unfolding a badge, "I'm a cop."

Jewel crossed the room and read it. The red-haired man was a sergeant in some town up north she'd never heard of His name was Claymore.

"Has there been a crime?" she said.

Sergeant Claymore stuck out his jaw. She could picture him as a kid: scrawny red-haired scrapper. "I'm still waiting," he said.

"Jewel Stern," she said. "I'm a reporter." She handed him her press card.

He examined it carefully. "What kind of reporter?"

"Sports," she said. "Baseball, particularly."

He gave it back. "And what are you doing here?"

"Working on a story."

"What story?" he asked, and before she could settle on just the right evasive answer, his eyebrows, bushy and rust-colored, went up and he said, "Don't tell me he still plays ball?"

"Who?" said Jewel.

"Gil Renard. Isn't that who you said you're looking for?"

She nodded. "But I didn't know he was a ball player." Her assumptions about the encounter in the men's room at Cleats began to change shape in her mind.

"I don't know as he still is," said Sergeant Claymore.

"But he was?"

"I guess you could say that."

"At what level?"

"What would you mean by that?"

"The majors? Triple A? Double A?"

Claymore smiled a shy, small-town smile. "Oh, nothing like that, to the best of my knowledge."

"College? High school? Legion?"

He laughed, embarrassed. "We played Little League together, is all."

"I see," said Jewel, although she didn't, not at all. The puzzle of what had happened at Cleats, barely begun, fell apart completely.

"Getting back to the story you were working on," he said.

A scrapper. Well, she could scrap too. "I don't have to tell you."

He surprised her. "That's true. Constitutionally, although I'm no expert. But on top of that I'm out of my jurisdiction. And it's my day off. So you don't have to tell me a thing."

"You're friends, is that it?"

"Who?"

"You and Gil Renard."

"What makes you say that?"

She shrugged. "Little League."

"We're not friends. Never were."

"Then there has been a crime," Jewel said.

He gave her a long look. "Yes."

"What kind of crime?" Jewel said. Sergeant Claymore stuck out his jaw again. "You don't have to tell me, of course," she added. "Constitutionally."

He smiled, and was still smiling when he answered, "The crime of murder. Double murder."

"And Gil Renard did it?"

"I'm a long way from knowing that."

"But you suspect him?"

"*Suspect* is too strong a word. It's just that . . ." He paused. Whatever thought he was pursuing went unspoken.

"That what?" Jewel said.

He sighed. "The victims were stabbed, for one thing."

"And Gil Renard sells knives."

"Did, until he was fired. But it's much more than selling knives. His father was a well-known blade maker back home, a real artist. Gil's been around knives his whole life."

"And?"

"And what?"

"And what else have you got?"

Sergeant Claymore's face colored slightly. "You seem to be asking all the questions."

"Let's not stop," she said. "We're getting along so well." His face colored some more; then he shook off his annoyance, almost visibly, and pressed on, like a tourist coping with a foreign culture. "What else I've got is something a little weird. One of the victims was buried in Gil's father's grave. Right on top of the coffin."

"I don't get it."

"Neither do I. He was a local guy, a thief and brawler named Len Boucicaut."

"Like the crusader."

"Excuse me?"

"Nothing. Who was the other victim?"

"His girlfriend. A prostitute, just out of jail."

"Did Gil Renard know them?"

"I couldn't say about the woman, but he knew Boucicaut. Long ago, that was. Gil left town and never came back." He hesitated. "As far as I know."

"What does that mean?"

"Probably nothing. I stopped Boucicaut for speeding a while back. Not unusual. He had a passenger. Didn't make much of an impression at the time, but when Boucicaut's body turned up where it did, I got to thinking."

"That the passenger was Gil Renard."

"That it might have been," Claymore corrected. "Until I can establish that Gil did come back, that they'd been together, it's just a stack of guesses."

Jewel nodded. A fly buzzed around Claymore's head and darted off. "Did you recover the knife?" she said.

"That's another problem," Claymore replied. "Not just that we don't have the knife, but it looks like two different weapons were used, and one might not have been a knife at all—the wound's too deep."

Claymore sat on the bed, took off his glasses, rubbed his eyes. A scrapper, but tired. So what? So was she. So was everyone she knew, except the ball players: they got all the sleep they wanted, like babies.

"What about motive?" Jewel said. "Were they enemies?"

"As kids? Far from it. In fact—"

"Boucicaut was on the team too."

"How did you know that?"

I know boys and their games, Jewel thought, but she didn't say it. "Were you the star, Sergeant?"

"They were the stars, the two of them. Gil was the pitcher, Boucicaut was the catcher. They took us all the way to the regionals."

"That means you won the state."

"We won the state." Claymore looked inward for a moment, and seemed about to say something more, but did not.

The fly returned, buzzed Jewel. She swatted at it, missed. It was hot in Gil Renard's old room, and airless. No motive, no connection; she was getting nowhere. "This man you saw in Boucicaut's car—"

"Truck," he said.

Connection. "A red pickup?"

"That's right. How—"

"Was he a big man?"

"Yes."

"Round face? Long black hair? Black beard?"

Sergeant Claymore got off the bed.

"Is that Gil?" she asked.

"Not Gil," he told her. "Boucicaut. Where did you see him?"

Jewel went to the window, pointed down into the alley. "Right there." She told him what had happened. Even as she spoke, he was inching toward the door. "Where are you going?" she said.

"No more guessing. I'll put him on the computer right away." Almost across the threshold, he turned, came back, shook her hand. "Thanks," he said. Then his eyes narrowed, just the slightest bit this time. "The story you're working on," he said, "any murder in it?"

"Oh, no," Jewel said. "Nothing like that."

Sergeant Claymore left. Jewel stayed for a few minutes, opened every drawer, peered under the bed, saw nothing. She left Gil Renard's room, went back down the corridor. At the base of the stairs leading to the top floor, she heard something from above. It sounded like a woman crying.

Jewel felt the personality of the house around her. She got out as fast as she could.

24

On the flight west, Jewel Stern, in business class, telephoned the *Times Magazine* editor in New York and got a one-week extension on the Rayburn piece. After that, she took out her laptop and her notes and tried to find a beginning.

Why wouldn't Bobby Rayburn, one of the brightest stars in the major leagues over the past decade, she wrote, *want his only son to be a ball player too?* She read the sentence over and hit DELETE.

In a world where 35 is geriatric, middle-aged doubt comes early. Jewel deleted that too.

The hands are what you notice first. DELETE.

Sometimes even All-American boys get the blues. Jewel read that over a few times and went on to the next sentence. *If the phrase "All-American boy" still has any meaning at this late date, it surely applies to Bobby Rayburn, probably the best center fielder in baseball for the past decade.*

The hands are what you . . .

Jewel worked straight through, eating nothing, drinking nothing, not letting her eye be caught by the man in silver-filigree cowboy boots across the aisle, who didn't stop trying to catch it until the movie began. She had fifteen-hundred words by shutoff time for all electronic devices.

At the back of economy, Gil Renard slept the whole way.

Gil took a taxi to the stadium, bought a bleacher ticket, was in his seat in the first row behind the center-field fence with two beers and a box of popcorn in time for the first pitch; knapsack at his feet, thrower strapped to his leg. He couldn't tell what the first pitch was from that distance; all he could see was Primo slapping at it, and the ball looping over the second baseman and hopping over the grass. Under the lights, the ball looked too white, white as rabbit fur, and the grass too green; as though someone had messed with the tint control. Maybe it was jet lag. Gil rubbed his eyes, took a big swallow of beer, gazed again at the field. Nothing had changed.

Primo stole second on the next pitch; he had such a big jump the catcher didn't bother to throw down. Then Zamora flied to right; not deep, but Primo tagged and went to third anyway, surprising the right fielder and just beating the throw.

"That fucking Primo," said a fan behind Gil. "What's he smokin' this year?"

"Whatever it is, give me some," said another.

They laughed.

Washington batted third. Gil leaned forward, checked the scoreboard. He swung around. "Where's Rayburn?"

"Not playin'."

Gil squinted toward the distant third-base dugout, thought he saw Rayburn sitting deep in the shadows, chin resting in his hands.

Washington struck out, and so did Odell, ending the inning. When the Sox took the field, Simkins, the kid, was in center.

Gil stopped watching the game. He just watched Simkins' back. Simkins wore number thirty-three. Not a number Gil himself would have chosen: Christ's age when he died. Maybe Simkins thought he was too good to worry about things like that.

Simkins, you asshole. The words grew louder and louder in Gil's mind until he had to shout them out: "Simkins, you asshole."

Simkins didn't react.

"Simkins, you asshole."

No reaction from Simkins, but Gil felt eyes on his own back. He shut up, finished his beers. He had to stay cool. And sober. Easier to do if the tint was normal. After a while, he went to the beer counter. Only two more, he told himself. On the way back, he spotted a C-type battery lying on the ramp and pocketed it. When he returned to his seat he gave the beers to the men behind him.

"Hey, thanks, man. We'll get the next round."

"Not necessary," said Gil, feeling strong, purposeful. He stared at Simkins. Stay cool. Stay sober. Just for tonight.

Gil got his chance in the top of the sixth. One out, bases loaded, and the batter popped one up in foul ground, far back of third, possibly out of play. Primo sprinted after it from short, crossed the foul line and dove fully outstretched, almost at the base of the stands. He caught the ball, and just as he did, just as all eyes were on him, Gil rose, as others were rising, and threw the C-type battery as hard as he could at Simkins.

The battery spun flashing under the lights and caught Simkins in the back of the head, an inch or two below the band of his cap. His hand flew to the spot; as though he'd been stung by a wasp. Then he looked and saw—and Gil saw too—a blood smear on the palm. Slowly Simkins turned his head, and slowly scanned the bleacher seats, his eyes wide. Gil tilted the popcorn box up to his face.

The next batter—the very next batter! on the very next pitch!—hit an easy fly ball to center field that Simkins dropped. Three runs scored, and that was the ball game, barring the kind of miracle comeback the Sox hadn't pulled off yet this season.

I'm a player, Gil thought. *I'm a player in the game.*

When it was over, Gil waited with other fans outside the players' entrance. To a girl wearing a Sox jacket and a lot of makeup, he said: "Know what hotel they stay at?"

"Palacio," she said, and cracked her gum.

Gil took a cab. He didn't like taking cabs. He missed the 325i, with its WNSOX vanity plate, its moon roof, its . . . companionship. Was that the word? He remembered the way he'd had his best ideas in that car. *Without wheels you're dead.*

Outside, the city stretched from horizon to horizon in grids, lit like the glowing mother board of a giant computer. It disoriented him, like the rabbit-fur ball and the too-green grass. He realized he was holding his breath, let it out, inhaled, exhaled, deep, slow. He saw the driver glance at him in the rearview mirror; and felt the weight of the thrower on his leg.

The lobby of the Palacio had a waterfall, sparkling lights, soft couches. Gil sat on one with a view of the front doors, reception, the elevator bank. After a while, a waiter appeared: "Something to drink, sir?"

Stay sober. But he heard himself reply: "Got any tequila?" Maybe it was the *sir* that did it.

"Any special brand, sir?"

"Cuervo Gold."

The drink came on a silver tray, with a bowl of quartered limes and crusted salt lining the rim of the glass. Gil sipped it slowly, not like a commission rep on the road, but like a CEO unwinding after a hard day. He watched the front doors. Gil was halfway through his second glass when the team arrived. Odell, Zamora, Boyle, Washington, Lanz, Sanchez, Simkins, Primo; all of them, thought Gil, except Rayburn. They were quiet, surly, grim. Some of them headed toward the bar, the others, including Primo, to the elevators. Young women materialized. They fell in step with the players, were absorbed without fuss into the group, like dancers executing a well-rehearsed routine.

Primo was second-last to board the middle elevator. Gil was last. He wedged himself into the only space left, in front of the control buttons.

"Floors, anybody?" he said; thrilled by his composure, his creativity.

"Sixteen," said someone, and "nine," someone else, and right behind him, "fourteen," with a faint Hispanic accent: Primo. Gil pressed the buttons.

At fourteen, Primo got off, alone. "Another Nintendo party tonight?" someone called from the elevator. Boyle, perhaps; Gil thought he recognized the voice from interviews.

Primo stiffened but said nothing, and started down the hall.

"What's that all about?" asked a woman.

"He's married," Boyle explained.

"Ain't we all?" said another man. Lanz.

The woman laughed. They all laughed. Gil stepped through the closing doors.

Primo was standing at a door near the end of the hall, sticking his key card in its slot. He went in. Gil walked down the hall, paused outside the door. He put his ear to it, heard nothing.

Gil stood motionless outside Primo's room, considering various strategies. He still hadn't picked one, when his right hand made a fist and poised itself for knocking, as though it were making the decisions now. At that moment, Gil heard footsteps on the other side of the door.

He backed away, so quickly he staggered, then wheeled and headed toward the end of the hall, forcing himself to slow down, weary CEO on the way to his room. But even as he did, he knew that he shouldn't have moved at all, should have reached for the thrower, done it there and then. Or didn't he have the guts? Was that it?

Gil heard the door open, heard Primo going the other way. He risked a glance, and saw him stepping into an elevator, wearing a terry-cloth robe and flip-flops. His mind tore through images from his past, looking for the answer to the question: Did he have the guts?

The health club was on the lowest subfloor, three stops below the lobby. Looking through the glass door, Gil saw a man sitting behind a desk stacked with towels, a lone swimmer in the pool beyond him, and in the background an unoccupied exercise room. As he watched, the swimmer climbed out, toweled off, put on a terry-cloth robe like Primo's and approached the desk. She dropped her towel in a basket; the man handed her a key card. She came out, passing Gil without a glance.

The water in the pool grew still. The pool man glanced at the sole key card remaining on his desk, checked his watch, yawned; then rose and entered a door behind him marked STAFF. Gil stepped inside.

He walked the length of the bright blue pool; too bright, too blue, and the reflected ceiling lights on its surface too dazzling. He was suddenly dizzy, and almost lost his balance, just walking. *Forget it,* he thought. *You're in no shape to do this.* But the same mind that could think that could also counter it: *Haven't got the guts?* and *Are you a player, or are you not a player?* Gil kept going.

Beyond the pool, he followed an arrow to the men's locker room. First came the lockers, then the urinals, then the showers, then the sauna; finally the steam room, red light glowing on the control panel outside. There was a small round window in the door, like a porthole. Gil looked through.

The steam room was small and not very steamy. There was a dim recessed light in the ceiling, a nozzle for the steam in one corner, and a double row of tile benches on three sides. Primo lay prone on the top row at the back, wearing nothing but a gold chain. His head was turned toward the door, but his eyes were closed. The cross on the end of the chain rested on the tile near his chin; one of those crosses bearing a twisted figure of Jesus.

This was perfect. No need for all those moves he'd practiced long ago with his father: hitting the ground, rolling, springing up from behind with a slash-slash at the back of the knees. Primo was laid out like a lamb for the slaughter. Gil raised his pant leg and pulled the thrower from its sheath. This was perfect; but he just stood there, watching. Then the control panel clicked, and steam began hissing from the nozzle in the corner. Gil opened the door and went in.

Into the heat and the noise. Not hissing, much louder than hissing; the steam roared from the nozzle like a violent storm. That was perfect too; no way that Primo could hear him. He fixed his eyes on one of those sinewy, copper-colored legs; just one, the near one, the right one: he would do no unnecessary damage. He would be a pro. Steam billowed around him as he moved closer, and sweat seeped into his clothes. Cut deep, but clean—the surgeons would probably have him fixed well enough for golf by next spring. He had plenty of money, was set for life; it was a slightly premature retirement, that was all. He raised the knife.

Primo opened one eye.

Slash: at the back of that coppery right leg, just above the knee.

But the coppery leg was no longer there. The blade cracked against the tiles, sending a jolt up Gil's arm, down his spine. And Primo was no longer prone on the bench: he was behind Gil, almost at the door already. Gil had never seen a man move like that. He lunged across the room, knife out, aimed low, at the back of those legs. But Primo lived in a fast-forward world—they all did, goddamn them—and before Gil could react, or even realize what was happening, he had whirled around and kicked Gil hard, inside the elbow. Everything went wrong at an unreal speed. The knife flew out of Gil's hand. Primo caught it, caught it by the handle, right out of the air, and slashed Gil across the chest, opening him up from nipple to nipple. Gil fell to the tile floor, shrank toward the benches.

Something hard and lumpy pressed into his back. The knapsack. He reached over his shoulder, struggled with the flap, got his hand inside. Primo stepped toward him, sweat running down his body, sinewy muscles popping in his chest, face all jaw and cheekbones, eyes burning. And Gil, fumbling over his shoulder to free a knife from its sheath, knew that he was no match for this man. This man was harder, tougher, quicker, blessed.

Primo came forward, crouched, Gil's father's blade out in front. Gil slid a knife free and threw; a wild throw, jerky and aimed nowhere. But lucky. It caught Primo high up one leg, sticking at a funny angle in the inner thigh. Not deep; it couldn't be deep, because at least six inches of blade were showing.

Primo stopped, looked down, then yanked the knife out in fury. He held it high over his head, an enormous bowie, twelve inches at least, and advanced on Gil. Gil cowered on the steam-room floor. Something warm and sticky sprayed him in the face, blinding him. He waited to die.

But nothing happened. He wiped at his eyes, looked up. Primo had stopped again, was again looking down. Blood—too bright, too red—was gushing from the hole in his thigh, and arcing onto Gil. Primo frowned. Then he sat down, hard. Down there on the floor, his eyes met Gil's.

"Get Stook," he said.

He gazed expectantly at Gil. Then the expectant look faded

from his eyes and was replaced by nothing. He sank back and didn't move again.

Gil rose. He gathered up the knives, put them in the knapsack, stepped over Primo. A cloud of red mist followed him out the door.

25

Bobby Rayburn sat very still on a stool in the visitor's clubhouse. He checked the urge to move because he knew that any movement he made would lead to breaking things, and he didn't want to do that with the press around. He glared at the back of Burrows' head, bobbing over a microphone. Maybe he wouldn't have gotten a hit—maybe he would never hit again—but he would never have dropped that fly ball. From long ago came a memory of kids' teams he'd played on—how the subs would roll in the dirt and slide on the grass, just to get their uniforms dirty too. The memory maddened him: they were subs, and he was who he was. In his spotless road uniform, he glared again, uselessly, at the back of Burrows' head. Maybe he would never hit again.

A few stools away sat Primo, shirt off and sweaty, surrounded by Spanish-speaking reporters, some from Mexico or God knows where; it was always like that when they played on the coast. Stook stood behind him, massaging his shoulders.

"Just a little sore," Bobby heard Stook say, "from when you made that catch."

"Be on the highlights, for sure," said someone else.

"Take a sauna when you get back," Stook said.

"Don't like saunas," Primo said.

"A steam, then," Stook replied. "It doesn't matter."

Enough of that, Bobby thought; enough of watching Primo get treated like a superstar instead of the slap hitter he was. He began unbuttoning his shirt, a little roughly perhaps. The last button snapped off and flew across the room. A woman coming through the door picked it up and handed it to him.

"Jewel," he said.

She nodded. "Got it in one," she said. "I thought you were supposed to be bad with names.

Bobby didn't like that. "What do you want?"

"I mentioned I might have a few follow-up questions, and you said—"

Just call. "I know what I said. But I didn't expect to see you out here."

"I'm a reporter, Bobby. Whither thou goest I shall go."

Bobby felt a smile coming, despite how angry and pent-up he was. He took a close look at her face, and in it caught a glimpse, no more than that, of the world beyond baseball. Many people said there was such a world—Wald said so all the time—but it had never penetrated. A world beyond baseball, and this woman had a foot in it. "Let's have 'em," he said.

"Let's have what?"

"Your questions."

She glanced around. Primo said something in Spanish and the reporters laughed. "Why don't we go somewhere?" Jewel said. "I'll buy you a drink."

Because I don't socialize with reporters. That was the answer that popped up first in his mind, and the right one. But aloud Bobby said: "Why not?"

"No reason I know," Jewel replied. "Got your ID?"

Bobby laughed. A minute or two before, he'd been ready to demolish the clubhouse, and now he was laughing. He stopped when he noticed Primo looking at him.

Jewel had a convertible. She wheeled up to the entrance at the players' lot.

"Nice," said Bobby, walking through the gate.

"Hertz."

He got in.

"You disappoint me," she said.

"How's that?"

"I expected you to leap over the door, not open it."

"I've already been to high school," Bobby said.

She shot him a quick glance. "Not me," Jewel said. "I'm still making up for it." She stepped on the gas, hard enough to make the tires squeal, just a little.

"You didn't go to high school?"

"Not what you mean by high school."

"And what do you think that is?"

Jewel didn't answer right away. She swung onto a ramp and accelerated onto a freeway. The night was warm and Jewel drove fast, her eyes on the road, her hands in proper ten-minutes-to-two position on the steering wheel, but relaxed. He noticed her hands: small, but strong-looking, the nails unpainted. Workmanlike, he thought; yet for some reason he had to force himself to take his eyes off them.

That's when she said: "Val."

"Val?"

"Valerie. Sorry. That's what you mean by high school, isn't it, Bobby?"

"I didn't go to high school with Val."

"Girls like her, then," Jewel said. "And the whole scene that goes with it."

"Isn't it the same all over?"

"At my high school, boychick, if you didn't win a prize at the science fair, you were a nobody."

"Did you win a prize?" Bobby asked, making a mental note to ask Wald exactly what *boychick* meant.

"I did," Jewel said. "But not in science."

"In what?"

"Poetry. There was a prize every year for the best poem."

"What was it?"

Jewel was silent for a moment. *"The Oxford Book of English Verse."*

"I meant the poem."

Jewel, topping eighty miles an hour, turned and gave him a look. "Some other time," she said. She flashed her brights at a Ferrari, forcing it over and breezing by.

"Where are we going?" Bobby asked.

"A place I know."

"Where?"

"Right," she said. "You lived here. I forgot."

"I should never have left," Bobby said. The words were out before he could stop them. She didn't look at him or anything, but she heard: he could tell by her hands.

She took him to an old lodge on a saddle peak in the mountains. It had a view of the Valley on one side and the ocean, dark and endless, on the other.

"Makes you think of Raymond Chandler, doesn't it?" said Jewel, as the valet took the car and they started up a piney path.

Bobby, who'd suddenly been wondering what it would be like to play in Japan, said: "What do you mean?"

"You know. *Farewell, My Lovely.*"

"I thought that was Robert Mitchum."

Jewel burst out laughing and took his hand. "I'm thirsty." After a few steps, she let go. Her touch lingered on his palm.

They sat in high-backed wicker chairs on a terrace overlooking the treetops, and beyond them and far down, the sea.

Nearby a pig turned on a spit over a wood fire, reflecting the flames on its glazed skin. A miniature flame bloomed from a candle on the table between them. The air, cooler in the mountains, smelled of eucalyptus.

A waiter in ruffled white shirt and string tie appeared.

"Champagne all right with you, Bobby?" Jewel said.

He nodded, although beer was what he wanted. She ordered, pronouncing the French brand name in a way that sounded French. "Aren't you taking a chance," he said to her, when the waiter had gone, "ordering champagne?"

"Why?"

"What if I start spraying it all over the place?"

Jewel laughed. "I'm sure there's more to you than baseball, Bobby." Bobby didn't know about that. Perhaps she read his mind, because she added: "The very fact that we're having this conversation proves it."

The waiter returned, popped the cork, poured. Jewel raised her glass. "Here's to singles up the middle."

"I don't want to talk about baseball," Bobby said.

Jewel laughed again: "I wasn't." Bobby didn't get that at all. She stopped laughing and asked, "What do you want to talk about?"

You, thought Bobby, but he didn't say it. This wasn't some hotel-lobby bimbo he was going to end up in bed with. This was a . . . what? He really didn't know.

Jewel took a sip of her drink, more than a sip. "How did you get together with Wald?" she asked.

"Is that one of the questions?"

"Yes."

Bobby shrugged. "He was a brother."

"Brother?"

"Fraternity brother. I didn't know him well back then—he was a year or two ahead. And a bit of a . . ."

"Nerd?"

"I was going to say *dweeb.* That's not for publication."

"Of course not. Funny how the dweebs of yesteryear become the movers and shakers of today."

Bobby frowned. "Chaz isn't a mover and shaker. He's my agent."

"Do you know how many other clients he has?"

Bobby shrugged. "Boyle, for one."

"Primo?"

"No." Bobby put down his glass.

So did Jewel. "I've done some research. Charles Wald has twenty-three clients in baseball alone, sixteen in the majors as of Opening Day. Doesn't that make him a mover and shaker?"

"He's just an agent," Bobby said, but then he remembered the four pillars, and wasn't sure.

"He probably makes more money than you do, Bobby."

Bobby was appalled. He picked up his glass and drained it; then saw that she was looking at him in that measuring way again, her head slightly tilted.

"Why do you want to be traded, Bobby?"

Jewel watched Bobby's face as he dealt with that one. First came surprise, then anger, then wariness.

"Who says I want to be traded?" he asked.

Jewel refilled their glasses. This was too easy. Not that Bobby was stupid; it was just that she was a woman and he, in many ways, still a boy, as Wald had said. That was the appeal, of course; maybe the appeal of the whole game. The realization that this was a mismatch made her feel bad, in passing. "Word gets around," she told him, and pressed on. "Does your wanting to be traded have anything to do with Primo?"

"I don't know what you're talking about."

And on: "Is it because he's having a career year and you're in this horrible slump?"

Bobby negated that suggestion with a sweeping gesture of

his arm; his glass crashed on the flagstones. He raised his voice. "I'm not in a slump. They're just not falling in."

The sudden violence didn't frighten her; it confirmed that she was on the right track. She nodded and said, "Sometimes it must feel like you're never going to hit again."

Jewel expected another demonstration of annoyance, frustration, rage: more raising of the voice, more shattering glass, something. But there was nothing. And then in the candlelight, she saw his eyes fill with tears: the doubly reflected flame trembled, wobbled; but there was no overflow.

She wasn't ready for that. "Excuse me." She went inside to the bathroom, splashed cold water on her face; a hard face, she saw in the mirror, with Janie way underneath. She also saw a new gray hair, which she plucked. When she returned, Bobby was drinking a beer and his eyes were dry. He tried to make them opaque as she came near. Jewel didn't want that, didn't feel like pressing him anymore. She could fill in the gaps without him.

"Ready?" she said.

He nodded. She paid. They went to the car. On a whim, she took the bottle of champagne, still half full, with her. On a whim: that was what she told herself.

Jewel drove along the narrow mountain road that led to the head of the nearest canyon. She no longer drove fast; there was no traffic, the night was quiet, Bobby silent. A baseball-sized rock fell out of the darkness into the cone of her headlights, bouncing on the pavement, and back into the night. She slowed down even more; that was the only reason she spotted the lookout around the next bend. Without thinking, she pulled off the road, continued between two tall rocks like gateposts, and parked on the edge of a black abyss. Without thinking: that was what she told herself.

In the distance lay the coast highway, traffic crawling along it like glow-worms. Then came a white fringe of surf, and beyond that the sea. Jewel felt Bobby's eyes on her.

"Black as night," she said,
"My heart,
Black as coal
Black as the ace of spades
Black as the blackest cliché,
Heart of my heartest heart,
Come give me a love."

There was a silence. Then Bobby said: "What's that?"

"The beginning of my poem," Jewel replied. "The prize-winning poem."

"You're scaring me," Bobby said.

Jewel laughed. "There's nothing to be scared of," she said, although she was trembling when she said it. Then she put her arm around him and kissed him on the mouth. He kissed her back, but tentative, almost shy. That surprised her.

And it surprised her when he said: "Are you making up for high school?"

"You're very smart, for a ball player," Jewel said. She kissed him again. She felt the strength of his body, the night all around, soft and warm, the abyss so close; everything conspiring with the mood she was in. "Take off your clothes," she said.

He did.

His body was beautiful, as beautiful as the most beautiful cliché. She must have known that already, of course, having seen him many times in locker rooms, but she hadn't let it register: that was the rule.

She put her lips to his chest, then started slowly down; going down on him, as so many women, or girls, did every season. She didn't want to be one of them—did they have sex as infrequently as she, once in the last year, not at all in the two years before that?—but she wanted to go down on him anyway. She was close to coming already, and that wasn't like her either.

Bobby stopped her. He drew her head up, level with his.

The look in his eyes was complex; she would parse it later. Her own eyes, she supposed, were wide black holes of lust.

"You too," he said.

"Me too, what?"

"Your clothes."

"No."

"Yes."

He helped her. She didn't resist.

"Not bad, for an old lady," he said.

"There's an endorsement."

"Here's another."

Then they were in the back seat; starry sky, soft night, abyss. And Jewel was having sex unlike any she had known; or so she thought. She fell under the illusion—did it have to be an illusion?—that something had clicked into place, and her whole life suddenly made sense. She came and came.

After, when they were dressed and sitting in their proper places in the front of the Hertz convertible, Bobby surprised her once more: "Will I see you again?"

A surprise, and a nice one, but she didn't want to think about all the problems—how could they see each other, as long as they did what they did? Also, she didn't want moony talk: she wanted to stay in this mood. She swigged from the bottle, then shook it and sprayed champagne into the night. "Here's to singles up the middle and doubles in the gap, to round-trippers and grand slams."

"Double entendre, right?" said Bobby.

"As double as it gets," said Jewel, thinking it might not be a mismatch after all. She hurled the bottle over the edge.

26

4:15 A.M., but Bobby Rayburn didn't feel at all tired as he opened the door to his room at the Palacio. He felt light and quick and cheerful. It didn't last. A man was sitting at the desk, wearing a dark suit and a dark tie, a half-eaten Reese's Peanut Butter Cup in one hairy hand.

"Mr. Rayburn?" he said. "I'm Detective—" Bobby missed the name—"of the LAPD. Mind telling me where you've been?"

Bobby tried to remember if the Sox had a curfew. Had Wald mentioned something about that? He couldn't recall. But sending a cop to enforce it was way out of line.

"Yeah," Bobby said. "I do mind. And what gives you the right to come in here without my permission?"

With his free hand, the detective removed an envelope from his jacket pocket. "This warrant, signed by an honest-to-goodness judge." He held it out, but Bobby made no move to take it. The detective popped the rest of the Reese's Cup into his mouth, licked his fingers, and rose. He was short and round, with a day-old beard and purple bruises under his eyes. "I'll give you a lift to the station," he said.

"The station?"

"We can talk better there."

"That doesn't even make sense," Bobby said.

The detective blinked. "Why not?"

"Are you stupid or something? The whole point of curfew is to make sure the players get a good night's sleep, right? So here I am, ready to go to bed. And now you want me to go someplace else. Why don't you just clear our of here, tell Burrows I've been a bad boy, and let them fine me whatever the hell they want to fine me?"

The detective sat back down. He was silent for a few moments. "Mr. Rayburn?"

"What is it?"

"Did you take a steam bath tonight, by any chance?"

Bobby was getting angry. "What now? No steam baths after the game? Are you going to ask me if I said my prayers too?"

The detective blinked again. "Let's start over."

"Fine."

"When was the last time you saw Primo?"

"That asshole? Who the hell knows?" Then Bobby remembered he did know: in the clubhouse, after the game. And he also remembered Stook telling Primo to take a steam bath for his shoulder or something. He changed his tone a little. "In the clubhouse, I guess," he said. "Why?"

"The why of it brings us back to my first question, Mr. Rayburn."

"What was that?"

"First question: where have you been?"

"Oh, yeah," said Bobby. "And it's still none of your business."

The detective rose again. "Let's get going," he said. "Where?"

"To the station, like I said before."

"Why? Has something happened?"

"Something's happened," said the detective, "if you think Primo getting himself knifed counts as something happening."

"Oh, my God," said Bobby. "Is he going to be all right?"

The detective shook his head.

"What does that mean?" Bobby said.

"Means he's dead, Mr. Rayburn."

Bobby sat down on the edge of the bed. "I don't understand."

"What don't you understand?"

"Any of it. Why you're asking me."

"Why I'm asking you what?" said the detective.

"Where I've been."

"Simple," said the detective. "We heard there was some bad blood between the two of you. That you got into a fight in a bar back East, for example."

"Who told you that?"

The detective smiled, revealing a double row of misshapen teeth. "I think we'll be able to answer all your questions much better at the station."

Bobby didn't like that smile at all. "I went out for a few drinks," he said.

"Where?"

"I don't know the name of the place. Somewhere up the coast."

"Anyone who can corroborate that?"

Bobby nodded.

"And who would that be?"

"I was with a reporter."

"Name of?"

Bobby told him.

The detective brightened. "I saw her on ESPN the other

day," he said. "She's very good." He gave Bobby a look. "Any idea where I could reach her?"

"Now?"

"Oh, yes. Now."

"She's staying at a hotel."

"This one?"

Bobby shook his head. "At the airport." He named it.

"Mind if I use your phone?" the detective asked.

Bobby didn't reply. The detective used it anyway. He dialed, said hello, asked a few questions, mostly listened. After, he turned to Bobby. "Checks out," he said. "For now. Hope I didn't disturb you." He moved to the door, then stopped. "Say, Bobby, think you'd have time to give me an autograph? My kid's a big fan."

Bobby signed his name on the search-warrant envelope.

"Gee," said the detective, showing his horrible teeth. "Thanks a million."

The team met that afternoon in a conference room at the hotel. Everyone was there—the players, the coaches, Burrows, Thorpe the GM, Mr. Hakimora the owner, lawyers for the team, lawyers from the league.

The GM spoke. "In the face of this . . . terrible situation, the league has given us permission to postpone tonight's game. We can make it up as part of a double-header when we're back in September. Or we can go ahead and play. The only stipulation is that we notify them by three-thirty. That gives us"—he checked his watch— "just over half an hour." He looked around the room. "No pressure, boys. It's up to you."

"I no play," Zamora said.

"That's fine, Pablo," Thorpe said. "You don't have to. But we're discussing whether the game itself should be played or not."

Thorpe looked around the room again. The lawyers, the owner, the coaches, were all sitting up straight. The players slouched, heavy and silent. "Anybody got an opinion?" Thorpe said.

No one did. There were several phones in the room, all lights blinking. Outside the floor-to-ceiling window, a seagull glided by, then rose out of sight. Bobby put up his hand.

"Yes, Bobby."

Everyone looked at him. "I think we should play," he said. Zamora made an unpleasant sound, deep in his throat.

"Why is that, Bobby?" asked Thorpe.

Bobby thought. He knew he had a reason, but he had spoken before really knowing what it was. He turned to Zamora. Zamora's eyes were red and angry. Bobby held up his hand. "Not because Primo would have wanted us to, or anything like that," he said. "I hate that kind of bullshit. It's what's wrong with . . . everything." Washington grunted. "But the thing is," Bobby went on, "it's what we do. You know? Play ball. So as long as it's what we do, we should do it. And there's nothing to stop us from, like, playing the rest of this season with him in mind if we want, maybe turning things around a little bit."

Then came another silence. Bobby looked down at his shoes. He shouldn't have said a word—he was new to the team, he hadn't contributed, and he'd punched Primo in the face. He was trying to think of some way to apologize when Odell rose.

Odell was the player rep. "Anybody else?" he said, with a slight catch in his throat. There was no one else. "Then let's vote," he said. "Players only."

Lawyers, owner, GM, manager, coaches, left the room. Lanz closed the door behind them. "All in favor of playing tonight?" Odell asked.

They all raised their hands, except the Latins. Zamora's eyes were redder now, but not as angry. "We play for him?" he said.

Odell nodded.

Zamora raised his hand. The other Latins raised theirs.

"One minute," said Washington, rising. He was the biggest man on the team, and a minister at his church in a one-stoplight town down South.

They all stood up, held hands in a circle, bowed their heads. Bobby had Simkins' hand on one side, Zamora's on the other. He didn't know any prayers. He just thought: *I hated you, Primo, but I never wanted this.* He thought it over and over, until Washington said, "Amen."

Odell turned to Lanz. "Okay," he said. "Let in the suits."

They all started laughing. They were still laughing when the suits came in, surprise on their faces.

There were a lot of cops at the ballpark—mounted ones in the parking lot, shotgun-carrying ones outside the clubhouse door, rental ones at the foot of every section in the stands. But, warming up, Bobby didn't really notice. What he noticed was how light the ball felt as he played long toss with Lanz. With no effort at all, he was throwing ropes, two hundred feet, two-fifty, more. And that wasn't all: the field itself seemed to have shrunk, down to Little League size. When he took BP, the ball kept rocketing into the seats, jumping off his bat time after time, as though made of some new material. None of that object-is-a-baseball shit, with its perfect red stitches, or relaxing to the nucleus of every cell, or staring at a glowing fire in some painting, or whatever the hell that was, or fog, a shadow, a blanking-out whenever he swung: the ball came in and he banged it out. Simple.

But it was only BP.

When Bobby went into the dugout it was unoccupied, except for Burrows, taping the lineup card to the wall. Bobby didn't need to go any closer than the top step to see that he wasn't starting. His heart sank. There was nothing to say, of course. That was part of the game.

But Bobby spoke anyway. Just one word; he couldn't stop himself: "Coach."

Burrows turned, looked at him. Bobby looked back. Then Burrows peeled the lineup card off the wall and walked down the runway to the clubhouse. When he returned, Bobby was batting third.

Their shirts arrived just before game time. A small number eleven, circled in black, had been sewn on the right sleeve of every one. Bobby stared at his five or ten seconds before putting it on.

Zamora led off, striking out on three pitches without taking the bat off his shoulder. Lanz tapped out to the first baseman. Bobby stepped in, unaware of who was pitching, unaware of how they were playing him, unaware of whether it was day or night.

The first pitch. Coffee table. It was going to be a ball, a couple inches outside. But Bobby swung anyway: he couldn't bear to wait. He didn't feel the contact at all, just saw the ball zoom off into the sky, hang there, like that seagull outside the conference-room window at the hotel, and arc slowly down into the right-field stands.

And as Bobby circled the bases, he knew that what had happened, what was happening, had nothing to do with lost shamrocks, or Chemo Sean, or even number eleven. It was all about what he had learned last night: there was a world beyond baseball, probably many of them, in fact. He didn't need this. He didn't need the game. He was free. The third-base coach swatted his butt as he rounded the bag.

In the fourth, Bobby hit another dinger, also solo, this one to left. In the fifth, he saved two runs with a diving catch, landing right on his ribs and feeling nothing. He struck out in the seventh, frozen on a three-and-two change-up, then drove in Zamora with the winning run in the ninth, doubling up the gap in left center. In the dugout, Zamora high-fived him with both hands, hard.

After, Bobby stayed in the shower for a long time, letting water pound his back, hot as he could stand. When he got out, reporters, players, coaches, were all gone. There was no one left but Stook.

"Nice game, big guy."

"Thanks."

"How's that rib cage?"

"Good as yours, Stook."

"Good as mine? Then you're in trouble, boy."

Bobby walked out into the corridor. A girl was waiting. No, a woman: Jewel. He went to her. She took a step back. There wasn't the slightest sign on her face that last night had happened at all. He realized he had a lot to learn about her.

"Hi," he said.

"Just give me a straight answer," she told him. "I'm looking right at you and I'll know the truth anyway. Did you have anything to do with it?"

"Sure," he said. Her look, already hard, hardened some more. "I didn't see anything wrong with it. But we all voted, so don't blame me totally."

Jewel's eyes grew puzzled.

"Maybe it looks bad to outsiders, but it's what we do." Bobby sighed. "That probably doesn't make much sense to you, and I really can't ex—"

Jewel moved forward, put a finger over his lips. She was smiling now. He didn't understand her at all.

"I'm thirsty again," she said.

"Thirsty?"

"Parched."

Didn't understand, but at least there was a glimmer. "I've got my ID," he said.

27

What else can we say, Bernie?"

"I don't know, Norm. It's a tragic, tragic situation."

"A tragedy, in the true meaning of the word. What does it say, and this is the question that keeps coming back to me, what does it say about the kind of world we're living in these days, Bernie?"

"Nothing good, Norm. But I suppose we're going to have to wait till all the facts are in before we can really make a judgment. In all fairness."

"Right you are, Bernie. It's all still very murky at this point in time. There was a report on CNN a few minutes ago that the authorities are looking into a Mexican connection, that there may be some relationship to the troubles they've been having, since Primo's wife's family—"

"A lovely, lovely lady—"

"—is involved in politics down there. Her brother, or her brother-in-law, having some job with the ruling party, whose name escapes me at the moment. Fred, have you got that name? P— something. Fred's getting it. In any case, we'll just have to wait and see."

"Just a tragic—"

"—tragic—"

"—situation. I don't know what more we can say."

"I think we've said what needs to be said."

"Me too. And we've still got a few minutes to the top of the hour . . ."

"Think we should go to the phones?"

"Why not? Here's Gil on the line right now. Gil?"

"Hi, guys.

"Where you calling from, Gil? Sounds like Siberia or somewhere."

"No place special."

"What's on your mind?"

"Lots of things."

"It's a lousy line, like I said, Gil. Make it quick."

"This . . . thing."

"You're talking about the Primo tragedy?"

"I was wondering."

"Wondering what?"

"If they'll give Rayburn back his old number now."

"Not sure I'm following you, Gil."

"Onsay."

"Excuse me?"

"Eleven. What he used to wear his whole career. Not that stupid forty-one."

Pause.

"That's kind of a strange question, Gil."

Dead air.

Days later in an airport bar, Gil caught the highlights of the first post-Primo game on "This Week in Baseball." When Rayburn knocked the first one out of the park, he pounded the table in triumph, as though he had done it himself. And, in a way, he had done it himself, hadn't he? He was a player. A player in the game.

He pounded the table when Rayburn hit the second shot, but not as hard. He'd opened his wound the first time, felt blood seeping into the bandages he'd wrapped around himself. Gil didn't mind the wound much: the wound was what made it self-defense. He hadn't meant for things to play out the way they had, but, left with no choice, he'd taken care of business. That was what it meant to be a pro. Leaving his glass of Cuervo Gold untouched—he was losing his taste for it—Gil drained one last beer, and felt no pain.

No physical pain. Emotional: that was different. There the painful part was that although he was a player, no one knew. Perhaps *pain* was too strong a word. *Confusion*, that was more like it. He would have to sort things out. Looking up at a monitor, he saw the flight he was waiting for flashing on the arrivals list and went downstairs to the baggage carousels.

Standing outside the glass wall, a camera crew nearby, Gil watched the team coming down an escalator, watched closely. They looked tired and subdued; but not unhappy. He understood. On one hand was the Primo thing, on the other the fact that they'd closed out the west-coast swing by reeling off six straight, climbing out of the cellar.

And Bobby Rayburn was on fire. Sixteen for twenty-one in the last six games, with seven homers and fifteen RBI's. He'd had a good month last week, "This Week in Baseball" had just said, and Gil's heart had leapt at the words. It leapt again as he spotted Rayburn walking toward the carousel, a bounce in his step.

"All right, Bobby Rayburn," he said, under his breath. Had other fans been there to greet the team, he might have shouted it, but there were no other fans; the team had won six straight in July, not October. But they were on the way. Gil knew it. He was in a position to know.

Bobby came through the door, carrying his bags. Ordinary luggage, Gil noticed with disappointment: Bobby could have done better than that. A reporter asked him a question, stuck a microphone in his face. Gil heard Bobby say: "We'll just have to go on, that's all."

The reporter said: "About your own play; you really seem to have turned things around." And stuck the microphone in his face again.

Bobby said: "That's the way the game is sometimes." And pushed by.

He walked right past Gil, not two feet away. Gil felt a huge smile spreading across his face, but Bobby passed without looking at him. He left behind the scent of that coconut shampoo he used in the ads, and Gil made a note to get some.

Fishing pole in his hand, knapsack on his back, hair freshly washed and smelling of coconut, Gil walked along an endless beach that was sometimes sandy, sometimes shingle. The sea was glassy blue; a red sail cut across it toward the eastern horizon. On the other side of the beach rose big houses, separated from each other and the water by broad lawns, tall hedges, well-trimmed bushes. Gil stopped when he thought he'd come to the right one.

Unlike Bobby's luggage, the house looked the part. Tall, sprawling, shining, it had chimneys, arches, balconies, decks, a terrace, and a pool, gleaming under the clear sky. Two lines of cedars marked the borders of the property from the house all the way down to the beach. Some dead branches needed clipping and the lawn needed mowing, but otherwise this was the model of life perfected. Still and peaceful: Gil gazed and gazed, losing track of time.

Then a movement caught his eye. By the pool a leg—bare, a woman's leg—straightened, stretching up into the air. Red-painted toenails sparkled in the sunshine; Gil could see the color all the way from the beach. He walked along the shore to the nearest line of cedars and ducked behind the first one.

From that angle, he could see her better. She lay on her back on a chaise, wearing a baseball cap, oversized sunglasses, and a skimpy bathing suit, or perhaps none at all; Gil couldn't tell. He began making his way up toward the pool, moving from tree to tree, silent, like a woodsman back home. Once he disturbed a crow. It took off, and spiraled cawing into the blue. The woman turned her head to watch it. He recognized her from the shots they always took of players' wives in the stands: Valerie Rayburn. He crept closer, close enough to see that she wore bikini bottoms but no top, and stopping only when his next step would have brought him into the open. He crouched behind a cedar branch, with nothing in mind.

Somewhere nearby a radio played, quiet but very clear. Gil couldn't see the speakers, but he heard the sound:

". . . just missing, inside. Boyle walks around the back of the mound. He wanted that call. Two and two. Infield still at double-play depth. Boyle steps on the rubber . . ."

Valerie Rayburn raised her other leg, stretched, sighed. A long, well-toned leg of the kind *SI* liked to feature in the swimsuit issue. And Val was that kind of woman. Gil couldn't take his eyes off her, and not only for erotic reasons. This was no Lenore, or Boucicaut's woman, he couldn't remember her name. This woman was fine. He didn't even get aroused, at first.

French doors swung open at the back of the house. A man in a suit came out, carrying an enormous inflated great white shark. Val saw him, made no attempt to cover up. The man crossed the terrace, walked onto the pool deck. Gil didn't recognize him.

"Sean napping?" he said.

"She put him down ten minutes ago."

"Where is she?"

"I gave her the afternoon off."

The man smiled. He put the shark down, went to Val, and lightly brushed the underside of one of her breasts with the back of his hand.

"Mmm," she said.

He knelt beside her.

". . . down by three, Zamora'll lead it off. The little guy's oh for two this afternoon with a sac fly in the . . ."

Gil looked around again for the source of the sound, without success. Was he imagining it?

Soon Val and the man were naked, except for their sunglasses, squirming on a towel by the side of the pool, skins glistening. "Oh, Chaz," Val said. Gil parted the branches for a better view.

Chaz was a balding man with a paunch and a cock that looked average size or smaller. Why would someone like her want to fuck someone like him, especially when she was married to Bobby Rayburn? Gil didn't get it at all. But Val said, "Oh, Chaz," again, and wrapped her elegant legs around his flabby back.

". . . and the crowd comes to life as Rayburn steps up. Bases loaded, two out, Rayburn representing the winning run. He singled up the middle in the first, doubled into the gap in right center in the fourth, hit the solo round-tripper that brought them within three in the sixth. Normally a fast worker, Mardossian is taking a lot of time out there. Looks in for the sign and here's the pitch. Strike one, over the inside corner. That's the call Boyle hasn't been getting all day. Hard to call 'em from up here, of course, but . . ."

Val got her legs up on Chaz's shoulders. Sweat dripped off his chin. "Oh, Chaz, I—" Gil thought she was going to say, "I love you," but she didn't finish the sentence.

Chaz grunted and pounded harder.

". . . and the pitch. Swing and a miss. A curve ball and a beauty. Dropped right off the table. Oh and two. Mardossian steps on the rubber . . ."

Val pounded back.

"... here it comes. Rayburn swings. And there's a long drive, deep to left, a looooong drive, deeeeeep to left, it is going, it is going. See. You. Later. Grand slam, a grandslam ding-dong-dinger for Bobby Rayburn ..."

"I don't believe it," said Chaz, going still.

That's when Gil knew the game was real.

"You didn't come, did you?" Val said.

"No, I didn't come." And Chaz started moving again, but Gil could see that the mood had changed. "Can't you turn that thing off?"

"The controls are in the kitchen. Come on, Chaz, I'm so hot. Don't leave me here."

Chaz reached down between them.

"Oh, Chaz, I'm coming."

"Me too."

And they did, but the mood had changed.

"... touch 'em all, Bobby Rayburn ..."

Chaz and Val rolled into the pool, drifted apart. He paddled around for a while. She got out, wrapped herself in a towel, and went up to the house. A few minutes later, he got out too, dried himself, put on his suit, knotted his tie—red and black, much like the stand-up tie Gil had lost somewhere along the way—and followed, leaving the blown-up shark by the side of the pool.

"... believe we've got Jewel Stern down on the field. Can you hear me, Jewel?"

"Loud and clear. I'm standing with Bobby Rayburn, and, Bobby, I think everyone's asking themselves—"

The radio went off.

It was quiet. Gil sat behind the cedar tree. He thought he heard a car start up, drive away. The sun, lower now, glared huge on the sea, much smaller on the pool. A breeze sprang up, rustling the cedars to life and cooling his skin; like Val and Chaz, he had sweated too, had heated up too, but not just from the voyeur part: he'd had an idea.

At first, his idea seemed full of possibility. In minutes, he began to have doubts. He lacked information: about Chaz, Val, and Bobby, and their various relationships. The idea began unraveling in his mind.

And then, as he had in the steam bath, he got lucky. The French doors at the back of the house opened again, and out came a boy in shorts. A boy younger than Richie, Gil saw as he came closer, but sturdily built, and graceful. He rose, and crouched behind the cedar.

The boy spotted the inflatable great white shark at once and went toward it. A gust of wind came off the ocean, bent the cedars, snapped Gil's pant legs, and blew the shark into the pool, just as the boy was reaching for it. The shark floated in the water, a foot or so from the side of the pool. The boy knelt at the edge, stretched out his arm, got a hand on the shark's dorsal fin. The shark slid away under the boy's weight; and then he was in the water.

The boy went under right away. Gil straightened, stayed behind the tree. The boy came up, but under the shark. One of his hands splashed the surface wildly. There was no other sound. Then he went down again. Gil, still holding the fishing pole, stepped out from behind the tree and moved toward the pool. He looked down, saw the thrashing boy a few feet under, eyes and mouth open wide, bubbles streaming up. Gil dropped the pole, shook off the knapsack, took off his shoes, hesitated over the thrower, leaving it on; then dove into the water. It was the right thing to do, from every angle he could think of.

He got his arms around the boy, still thrashing but weaker now, and kicked up to the surface. Gil flipped the boy onto the pool deck, climbed out. He heard a scream from the direction of the house, but didn't look up.

The boy had landed on his back. Gil knelt, turned him over.

Water flowed out of his mouth, then a little mucus, then nothing. He made a sound, half sob, half cough, sucked in air, and started to wail.

A woman cried, "Oh, God." Now Gil looked up, saw Val, wearing a pretty dress, running down from the house. She grabbed the boy in her arms, yelling, "Is he going to die? Is he going to die?" over and over.

"He's breathing, isn't he?" Gil said, but she didn't hear him.

After a while, quite soon, in fact, the boy stopped wailing, put his arms around her, said, "Mama." Then it was her turn to wail:

"It's all my fault."

For cheating on your husband? Gil thought.

"I didn't get that fence built."

She rocked the boy back and forth, back and forth. His wet body dampened her dress, making it transparent. Gil could see her nipples, tiny now, compared to what they'd been before.

"Well, no harm done," Gil said.

Val stopped rocking, looked at him, seeing him for the first time. The boy looked at him too.

"Lucky thing I happened to be fishing off your spot here," Gil said. "Never have heard him hollering otherwise."

The boy kept looking at him.

"But he seems like a tough kid," Gil said. "Probably would have done okay on his own.

"Tough kid?" said Val, bursting into tears again. "He's just a baby."

"You saved his life," said the doctor, about fifteen minutes later. The boy sat in a chair by the pool now, wrapped in a blanket and sipping a Coke. "Nice job, Mr.—"

"Onis," said Gil, right off the bat. "My friends call me Curly." So much like Onsay, and he remembered Curly Onis's meager line from the *Baseball Encyclopedia:* and like Curly, he'd taken just one cut in the bigs.

The doctor smiled. "Your hair looks pretty straight to me, Mr. Onis."

"It was different when I was a kid," Gil said.

The doctor left. Val came forward, held out her hand. "Oh, Mr. Onis, how can I ever thank you?"

"That's all right," Gil said.

She didn't let go of his hand. "I'm Valerie, by the way. Valerie Rayburn."

"Nice to meet you."

"Sean, this is Mr. Onis."

The boy's eyes came up, fastened on him.

"Lookin' good, Sean," Gil said.

"Thanks to you, Mr. Onis," said Val. "Thanks to you."

Gil sat down, took off his socks, wrung them out, put them back on, and then his shoes. He rose, picked up the knapsack and the fishing pole.

"You're not going?" said Val.

He looked at her.

"Oh, don't go. We've got to give—I'm sure my husband will want to thank you personally. He should be home any minute."

"You've already thanked me, Mrs. Rayburn." He got a kick out of saying the name like that, casually, in conversation.

"But not nearly enough, Mr. Onis. There must be something we can . . . what do you do for a living, if you don't mind my asking?"

Gil glanced around. "Funny you should bring that up," he said, "since I happened by chance to notice you could do with a little work around here. I'm a landscaper by trade."

She clapped her hands. Actually clapped them. "Bobby and I—that's my husband, Bobby Rayburn—" He registered nothing at the name. "—we were just talking about that. Consider the job yours."

"That's very nice, Mrs. Rayburn. But I really couldn't."

"But you have to. I couldn't live with myself if you didn't."

Gil shook his head. "It's asking too much, Mrs. Rayburn. See, I live a ways away. It would mean you putting me up somewhere at the beginning, at least while I got things in order."

"That's not asking too much. There's that apartment over the garage, right, Sean? Just sits empty."

"It's full of spiders," Sean said.

"We'll have it cleaned, of course," Val said. "There. It's settled."

"Thank you, Mrs. Rayburn, but I really—"

"And call me Val. Valerie."

Gil shook his head a few more times, said he really couldn't a few more times, and then they went up to the house. Val said: "I need a drink," and poured an Absolut on the rocks for herself.

"And for you, Mr. Onis?"

"If I'm calling you Valerie, you better call me Curly."

"Curly."

"I'll have a glass of milk," Gil said.

Val was on her second Absolut when Bobby came in. She took a step toward him, stopped, started crying. The story came out in a jumble. The moment he had the gist of it, Bobby blew past her, took Sean in his arms.

"I knew something like this was going to happen," he said.

"Because of the fence?" said Val. "It's all my fault."

"I didn't say *this*, I said something like this."

"What do you mean, Bobby?"

He didn't answer right away. Then he said: "It's the luckiest day of our lives, that's all." He closed his eyes and gave Sean another squeeze.

"Stop it, Daddy," said Sean.

Bobby let him go, approached Gil. Gil stood up. Yes, he was just as tall as Bobby, and just as powerfully built, if not more: Bobby seemed a little smaller out of uniform. Bobby held out his hand. "I'm forever grateful to you, Mr.—"

"Onis." They shook hands. Gil resisted the urge to squeeze hard. "My friends call me Curly."

"Whatever I can do for you, just name it."

"As a matter of fact," said Valerie, and she explained her plan. Bobby nodded his assent right away. Gil said he really couldn't a few more times. They had a drink together, Bobby a beer, Val another Absolut, more milk for Gil. Then Bobby took him out to the garage and showed him his apartment.

"This do, Curly?"

"Do? Better than that." And it was: twice the size of any home he'd ever had, and far more luxurious. He didn't see a cobweb. "But I really—"

Bobby held up his hand. "I couldn't have it any other way." He paused, and for a moment Gil imagined the unimaginable: that Bobby was about to cry. Then he said: "It's a miracle."

Gil didn't know what to say to that. He laid down the fishing pole and knapsack.

"Maybe you can show Sean a little about fishing," Bobby said. "Haven't had much time for him lately."

"What is it you do, Mr. Rayburn, if you don't mind my asking?"

Bobby laughed. "I'm a ball player."

"Baseball?"

"With the Sox."

Gil nodded. "Sorry," he said. "Don't follow it much."

"Nothing to be sorry about," said Bobby. "There're lots of worlds outside baseball."

28

Fred, the engineer, played the tape for Jewel:

Hi, guys.

Where you calling from, Gil? Sounds like Siberia or some-where.

No place special.

What's on your mind?

Lots of things.

It's a lousy line, like I said, Gil. Make it quick.

This . . . thing.

You're talking about the Primo tragedy?

I was wondering.

Wondering what?

If they'll give Rayburn back his old number now.

Not sure I'm following you, Gil.

Onsay.

Excuse me?

Eleven. What he used to wear his whole career. Not that stupid forty-one.

That's kind of a strange question, Gil.

"Play that last part again," Jewel said.

Onsay.

Excuse me?

Eleven. What he used to—

"That's enough," Jewel said.

Fred stopped the tape, said something Jewel didn't catch because his mouth was full.

"He's a regular, isn't he?" she asked.

"I don't know," Fred replied. "I never listen to any of them."

"I want to hear all his calls."

"All his calls?"

"We tape everything, don't we?"

"Sure. But how are you going to find this guy's calls? It'd be like looking for a needle in a haystack."

"I hate that expression," Jewel said.

She spent the rest of the day in her office, fast-forwarding through cassettes. She found Gil a few times:

I've been waiting a long time.

What kind of numbers is he going to put up in the bandbox, and with that sweet swing of his?

I heard what you said about Primo. It won't last. He's a hot dog. Hot dogs always fold in the end.

Just get this, Bernie. I'm sick and tired of you taking shots at him all the time. When's it going to stop?

I know what disillusion means.

After that, Jewel called the *Times* editor and asked for another extension.

"Having problems?" he said.

"It's not that. The story keeps changing on me." She wished immediately she'd put it another way.

"It happens. You'd still be entitled to a kill fee, if that's what's worrying you," said the editor.

"It's a developing story, that's all I meant."

"Developing in what way? I thought it was just your basic jock puff piece."

"Did you?" said Jewel. "There's the Primo murder, for starters."

"Who's Primo?"

"Don't you read your own damn paper?"

"Not the sports."

"I'm impressed." She hung up on him. Five minutes later, she was trying without success to think of some nonhumiliating way to make amends.

She called Sergeant Claymore in his little town up north.

"Anything new?" she said.

"Yes and no."

"I hate that expression."

"Sorry," said Claymore. "Renard's disappeared without a trace, if that's what you want to know, but now it looks like he may have only been a witness to the Boucicaut killing. Which turns out to be self-defense, in any case. Two guys in ski masks broke into a house on the Cape a while back, and one of them got stabbed with a sword. A rapier, which we've got now. The medical examiner says it fits Boucicaut's wound."

"And the other guy was Gil Renard?"

"We don't know, because of the ski masks. But it all fits— turns out it was the day before the break-in when I stopped them for speeding, and Boucicaut was wearing his."

"Wearing his what?"

"Ski mask."

"How did he explain that?"

Claymore laughed an embarrassed laugh. "He didn't, really."

Jewel was silent.

"That probably sounds a little strange to an outsider. Me not asking him, I mean."

"Nothing sounds strange to me anymore, Sergeant Claymore. I'm immune. Are you still looking for him?"

"Sure. He's a suspect in this break-in now, as well as in the murder of Boucicaut's old lady."

"Then I suggest you try to find out if he flew to Los Angeles around the time of the Primo murder."

"Why?"

"Because your first instinct was right. This is all about baseball."

Jewel sat in front of her terminal, typed some copy, printed it, found Bernie, said, "Read this."

Bernie read: "JOC-Radio is putting together a panel drawn from our regular callers for a new weekly feature called 'Between Brewskis.' Participation will involve a nominal payment, but much more than that, a chance to shoot off your mouth on a regular basis. Would the following callers please get in touch on the station's office phone during business hours: Manny from Allston, Donnie from Saugus, Ken from Brighton, Vin from the Back Bay, and Gil, who's usually on his car phone."

Bernie looked up. "Great idea. But you left out Randy from Milton. And they'll never let you call it 'Between Brewskis.'"

"For Christ's sake, Bernie. It's a ruse. We'll get the cops to put a trap on the line, and when this guy Gil calls we'll have him."

"Have him for what?"

Jewel explained. Later she explained it again to the station manager, and once more to some cop from the Primo investigation. The cop said, "I've heard your station. He's not the only nut you've got calling." Jewel had him speak to Claymore. Then he said, "Still don't see what this has to do with Primo, but if they're looking for him up north, why not?"

After he left, the station manager said, "Let's go with it, Jewel."

"Go with what?"

" 'Between Brewskis.' For real. But with just one change."

"What's that?"

"I think we can do without that nominal payment."

Gil awoke before dawn, took the money left from the sale of the 325i, and went by cab to the nearest town. By noon he had bought a truck with two hundred and forty thousand miles on the odometer, a lawn mower, a rake, a spade, hedge clippers. He picked up a can of paint, stenciled Onis Landscaping on the side, and drove back.

Gil unloaded the lawn mower, rolled it around the house, and started mowing. First he cut along the borders of Bobby's property, down one line of cedars, along the beach, up the other row, outlining a rectangle in the grass. Then he followed the inside of the swathe he'd cut, overlapping one wheel width to make sure he left no tufts showing. He wanted to do a good job for Bobby. The sun was hot, the lawn huge, but Gil didn't even stop for a drink. Like grave digging, not a bad job.

Someone tapped him on the shoulder.

He wheeled around. Chaz.

Chaz spoke. Gil put a hand to his ear. Chaz reached down and shut off the machine. Gil didn't like that.

"My name's Wald," he said, not offering his hand. "I manage things around here."

"Onis," said Gil. "My friends call me Curly."

Wald made a short slashing gesture with the side of his hand. "Nice about the boy and everything. But I do all the hiring. No particular objection to hiring you, but it's got to be done in the proper way."

"What's proper, Mr. Wald?"

"Three recent references, the name of your bank, your landlord if any, and your authorization to run a credit check." He glanced around. "You'll be paid for the work you've done already, and there'll be something for the business yesterday as well."

"Are you asking me to leave?"

"Telling. Until you complete the application process, that is. Then, if I hire you, you'll be welcomed right back. The place needs a lot of work."

Gil stared at him, stared, that is, into his sunglasses.

"Your name's Chaz?"

"Mr. Wald."

"And you manage things."

"Didn't I just say that?"

"Then I should probably tell you something, just so you're in possession of the facts."

"Shoot."

"I was fishing off your beach yesterday."

"I know that. Perfectly legal in this state."

"The thing is, I was out here twice. The second time was when I heard the boy." Something flickered behind Wald's dark lenses. "The first time was a bit earlier. That's when I saw you doing some managing on Mrs. Rayburn."

There was a silence. Gil examined his reflection in Wald's glasses: a big guy in a sweaty T-shirt, with a big smile on his face. The big guy moved his lips. "Nice meeting you," he said. "But the grass is growing under my feet." Gil cranked up the mower and pushed off toward the beach, not looking back. By the time he made the turn, Wald was gone.

The whip hand, even over an operator like Wald! He'd come into his own at last. How? It had something to do with Curly Onis, something to do with getting back his trophy, something to do with strapping the thrower on his leg. But Gil finished mowing the whole lawn without really figuring it out. All he knew was that he was finally on the move, and moving fast.

Gil was raking when Sean appeared. He was carrying a baseball and two gloves.

"Hi, Curly."

"Hi."

"We're friends, so I can call you Curly."

"Right."

"Play catch?"

"Sure."

Sean put on the smaller glove, handed Gil the adult-sized one. Gil examined it: a Rawlings Gold Glove, soft and oiled, with "Rayburn ll" branded on the strap. One of Bobby's old gloves. Gil slipped it on: a perfect fit.

Gil took the ball. "Here you go," he said, backing up a step or two and lobbing a gentle toss. Gentle, but a bit off line. Gil was all set to say, "Sorry, bad throw," when the boy reached out and snatched the ball out of the air, as though he couldn't wait for it to get there.

"Move back, Curly," he said.

Gil backed up a little more. Sean wound up and threw. Gil had no time to get his glove up; the ball hit him in the chest, hard enough to hurt, especially since he wasn't quite healed yet. The boy looked up at him, puzzled. "Daddy catches those," he said.

"I wasn't ready," Gil said. He lobbed another underhand toss. Sean caught it easily.

"Overhand," the boy said, moving farther away before he threw it back, harder than the first one. Threw it on a line, chest-high, perfect. The ball smacked into Bobby's glove. Gil tossed it back, still gentle, but overhand.

"Harder next time," said Sean. And he zinged Gil another. Was it his imagination, or did the ball have some movement on it? Gil threw back harder, much harder. Sean caught it as effortlessly as he had the others.

"A grounder."

Gil threw him a grounder. The boy got his butt down, got his glove in the grass, scooped it up, whipped it back.

"Another one."

Gil tried one on his backhand this time, but Sean got to it so quickly he didn't have to go to the backhand. Down. Scoop. Throw, on the money.

Gil tried another to the backhand, but the ball got away from him a little, bouncing across the new-cut grass so far to Sean's right that it was unplayable. Except that Sean took one step, so swift, and dove, fully outstretched through the air, eyes on the ball the whole time, fierce eyes, and the ball disappeared in the pocket of his toy glove just as he hit the ground. An instant later, he was up on his knees and throwing, throwing from his knees: another rope, right at Gil's chest.

He had soft hands.

He had a gun for an arm.

He had textbook form for every move he made.

Goddamn you, Richie. It wasn't fair.

"Another diver," Sean said. "Throw me another diver."

But Gil didn't want to throw him another diver. He didn't want to play at all anymore. "Got to get back to work," he said.

"Just one more."

The boy pounded his fist in the pocket of his glove. Was there a baseball gene that a few had and most did not? It wasn't fair. Well, Gil had that gene, didn't he? It was Ellen who had screwed things up. He thought of her and hurled the ball at Sean as hard as he could, a throw that would have killed Richie, or that fucking Jason Pellegrini, or any of the others. But Sean caught it, showing no consternation, no surprise, nothing.

"Thanks, Curly," he said. "For playing with me." And he ran off. He was fast too.

Gil had knocked off for the day and was lying on his bed, naked except for the thrower, when the phone rang. He answered. It was Val.

"You did a great job on the lawn."

"Thanks."

"And Sean had such a good time playing ball with you."
Gil said nothing.

"Would you like to go to the game tonight?"

"Game?"

"Bobby's game. Sean's never been to a night game and he
really wants to go. The problem is the architect's coming
tonight and I've got to be here. I can drive you there though,
and Bobby can drive you back."

"Sounds like fun."

"Wonderful."

At the ballpark, Val double-parked in front of an unmarked
door. They got out, Val, Gil, Sean. She knocked at the door.
An old man in a red blazer opened it; Gil remembered him
right away—his veiny red face was the same, but his personality had changed. He was all smiles.

"Hey, big guy," he said to Sean, "now the game's in the
bag."

"This is Mr. Onis," Val said.

"How do you do, sir?" said the man in the blazer, pumping
Gil's hand.

Val went off. The door closed. The man in the blazer made
sure it was locked, then led them up a corridor.

"Want some popcorn or something?" the man said to Sean.

"I want to see Socko."

Socko the mascot was a red, pear-shaped creature, with
yellow clodhopper feet and a grinning yellow face. Gil hated
mascots.

"Sure thing," said the man in the blazer, knocking on the
next door they came to.

"What is it?" came a voice.

"Visitors," replied the old man. "Are you decent?"

"Decent as the next guy.

The old man opened the door. They entered a little dressing

room. Socko sat on a chair, wearing everything but his yellow head. He was in his early twenties, with long hair and several rings in each ear.

"Hi, Sean. How's it going?"

"Can I put on the head?"

"Sure," said Socko, giving it to him.

Sean put on the yellow head, looked in the mirror. "Oooo oooo," he said in a scary voice.

Socko raised his enormous yellow hands; each with three fingers, like a cartoon character's. "Don't hurt me."

"Oooo oooo," said Sean.

Everyone laughed. Gil joined in.

Sean took off the head. "It's hot in there."

"No kidding," said Socko. "I take water breaks every three innings." Bottles of mineral water sat on the dressing table.

They went to their seats, in a glass-faced box high over first base. A waiter in a bow tie hurried to them. Sean ordered a hot dog, a pretzel, popcorn, and a Coke.

"Anything for you, sir?"

"Milk, if you've got it."

"Whole, two percent, or skim?"

"Whole," said Gil.

The game began. Bobby doubled down the right-field line in the first inning, driving in two runs. Socko danced on the first-base dugout. There was a lot of noise in the box. "See what your daddy did?" said a man with a highball glass.

"RBI's forty-nine and fifty," said Sean.

Everyone laughed. Gil joined in.

In the third inning, a woman appeared, knelt in the aisle beside Sean.

"Heard you were here," she said. "Any more trouble from the Arcturians?"

"Nope," said Sean. "This is Mr. Curly Onis. That's what his friends call him. He mows the lawn."

The woman looked at Gil. She seemed familiar, but he couldn't place her.

"Curly lives over the garage," Sean added.

"Nice to meet you," she said, offering her hand. "Jewel Stern."

At that moment, the moment he learned who she was, Gil also placed her, standing by Boucicaut's pickup in the alley behind the three-decker. A shudder went through him; her hand was still in his, but there was nothing he could do about it.

She let go, but tilted her head slightly, as though drawing a bead on something. "Enjoy the game," she said. She tousled Sean's hair, and then she was gone.

The Sox won nine-zip. Bobby Rayburn went two for three with two doubles, three RBI's, and a base on balls. After, the old man in the red blazer took them down to the clubhouse. It was a fan's dream come true.

"Hey, there," said Washington, spotting Sean. Soon he had the boy on his lap, was making a quarter disappear in his belly button and come out his ear. They were all there, Boyle, Lanz, Zamora, Odell, Simkins; loose and noisy, grabbing food from the buffet, drinks from the cooler: a fan's dream come true.

Why do you think you're winning, assholes? Gil stood by the door and didn't say a word. He just watched.

Bobby drove the Jeep, Gil sat in the passenger seat, Sean, in back, fell asleep right away. Bobby yawned. "Have a good time?" he said.

"You were sitting on the fastball both times, weren't you?" Gil replied.

"Sure, with Zamora on. He's a threat to go anytime." After a minute or two, Bobby added, "I thought you didn't know anything about baseball."

Safe from observation in the darkness, Gil felt himself

redden with pride. How much prouder he would have felt to have heard those words from Bobby in some earlier time, even a month ago! But now everything was complicated by what he'd done for the team, by, yes, the sacrifice he'd made. And suddenly he understood, in sharpest possible focus, what he had done, and his role on the team. He'd given himself up, laid one down to advance the runner, sacrificed himself. The sacrifice: a subtlety of baseball that came with a stingy reward—it didn't count against your average, that was all.

"I just said I didn't follow it," Gil replied. "I played at one time."

There was a silence, the meaning of which Gil knew immediately: Bobby was waiting for Gil to place himself on the ladder.

"Drafted out of high school, as a matter of fact," Gil said.

"What organization?"

"The Padres," said Gil, because they were far away.

"Yeah? Were they around back then?"

Back then? What was that supposed to mean? He was only three years older than Bobby, and looked younger, if anything, didn't he? Gil remained silent until he couldn't stand it anymore. "Had a cup of coffee, as they say."

Bobby nodded, as though he'd heard it many times.

"Hurt my arm."

"You pitched?"

"Some."

Bobby yawned again. "Val says you did a nice job on the lawn. Worked things out with Wald yet?"

"What things?"

Bobby shrugged. "I don't know. Salary? Duties?"

"There won't be a problem," Gil said.

More silence. Gil's mind drifted back to the sacrifice he'd made in the steam bath of the Palacio Hotel. Bobby switched on the radio.

"Before we go to Jewel for the postgame, you've got an announcement for us, Norm."

"Right, Bernie. JOC-Radio is putting together a panel drawn from our regular callers for a new weekly feature called 'Between Brewskis.'"

" 'Between Brewskis'?"

"That's what it says here. This'll give some lucky listeners what they've always wanted—the chance to shoot off their mouths on a regular basis."

"Just like us."

"Or even more trenchant."

"Trenchant?"

"Something to do with bad breath. So listen up—would the following callers please get in touch on the JOC business number during office hours: Manny from Allston, Donnie from Saugus, Ken from Brighton, Vin from the Back Bay, and Gil, who's usually on his car phone."

Gil jumped at the sound of his name. He checked Bobby out of the corner of his eye. Bobby was yawning again and didn't seem to have noticed anything. How could he have missed it?

"So what have you got for us, Jewel?"

"Just another dominating performance by this team, Bernie. They've got it all going now—pitching, hitting, defense. Turned things around completely, as though the horrible events out West were some sort of wake-up call. They could have fallen apart instead, written this season off, and everyone would have understood, but for some reason they didn't."

"What could that reason be, Jewel?"

"I've given that a lot of thought, Norm, and I just can't tell you. Part of it has to do with Bobby Rayburn, of course. I've never seen a hitter stay this hot this long. He simply picked up this team after Primo's death and carried them on his back."

"But he was in a slump all year, Jewel. How did he get himself out of it?"

"How do you get out of slumps, is that the question? If I knew the answer to that, Bernie, I'd—"

"—own the team, right?"

"I was going to say I'd start my own religion."

Bobby laughed. Gil looked at him. He was leaning forward, face rapt. A glory hound, Gil realized. Rayburn was a glory hound: after all the years and years of hearing himself praised, he still couldn't get enough. The problem was that this time the glory didn't belong to Bobby—it belonged to him. Gil almost blurted the whole thing, right then.

"Let's go to the phones. Here's—"

Bobby switched it off. He was smiling to himself, as though thinking about something pleasant, maybe those two doubles.

Casually, like someone making conversation, Gil said: "How did you get yourself out of the slump, Bobby?"

"Who the hell knows?"

I do. "There must be some explanation."

"Oh, I've got an explanation, all right, but it doesn't make much sense."

"Try me."

"I stopped caring."

"I don't get it."

"I said it didn't make sense."

"You stopped caring?"

"About the game, how we did, how I did, everything. Especially that, how I did."

"You think that's how you got out of it—you stopped caring?"

"Until a better explanation comes along."

"You stopped caring."

"Right."

"But how could you do a thing like that? You've got a chance to make the Hall of Fame."

Bobby burst out laughing, as though Gil had surprised him with a witty observation. "Let's just say I found religion." He chuckled a few more times, then stopped abruptly. "I thought you didn't follow the game."

"Everyone knows about the Hall of Fame," Gil said.

Bobby looked as though he was about to say more, but at that moment a Porsche whizzed by in the night, going the other way, and he said, "What's Wald doing out here?"

"Managing things," Gil said.

"Excuse me?"

"That's what he told me he did—managed things."

They drove in silence the rest of the way, Bobby glancing at him once or twice.

Bobby carried Sean into the house. Val met them at the door.

"That was a quick game," she said, taking the boy and starting up the stairs.

"Just a second," Bobby said. "What was Wald doing here? He's supposed to be in New York."

"Chaz? What makes you think he was here?"

"I saw his car."

"That was Philip. He drives one just like it."

"Philip?"

"The architect, Bobby." She went up the stairs.

When she was out of sight, Gil said: "Car of choice, for a certain type of guy."

Bobby turned to him, then laughed. He'd been witty again. "How about a nightcap?" Bobby said. "And don't say milk. I'm having a beer."

"Beer'll be fine," Gil said. "But what I'd really like is tequila. Cuervo Gold, if you've got it."

They sat by the pool: Bobby and Gil, with a sixpack of Heineken and a bottle of Cuervo Gold. Soft, starry, silent: a beautiful night.

"You married, Curly, or anything like that?" Bobby asked, cracking his second beer.

"Nothing like that," Gil replied, thinking of Richie. *See you, Richie.* He was getting that cactus feeling inside again, but he refilled his glass anyway.

Bobby stretched out on a chaise, sighed, feeling good.

"Got a nice place here, Bobby," Gil said.

"Not bad."

Gil raised his glass to his mouth, found it was empty, took a hit from the bottle.

"You're a lucky man," he said.

"Lucky?"

"Sure."

"I've worked pretty hard, Curly."

"Taking BP? Shagging flies? Lying in the whirlpool?" *Easy, boy,* Gil thought.

But Bobby laughed again. "You've got a sense of humor, Curly." He opened another beer, drank, closed his eyes. Gil watched him, and drank from the bottle, feeling the cactus growing inside him, watching. For a moment, he thought Bobby had fallen asleep. Then, without opening his eyes, Bobby spoke: "What kind of a pitcher were you, Curly?"

"First pick, every goddamn time."

Bobby's eyes opened. "I missed that."

"I was good," Gil said.

Bobby nodded.

"Fucking good."

"I'm sure you were."

"I still am. My arm's stronger than ever, now that the soreness is all gone."

"Yeah?" said Bobby, and closed his eyes again.

Gil took another hit from the bottle. He remembered how hard he'd thrown to Boucicaut in the woods, too hard even for Boucicaut to catch. And he had a wonderful idea, the kind of idea he never used to have, the kind of idea that accompanied this delayed coming into his own. Simple, daring: he would show Bobby Rayburn, just show him. It was perfect.

"Tell you something," Gil said.

"What's that, Curly?"

He took another drink. "Open your eyes."

Bobby opened his eyes.

Gil looked right into them. "I don't think you can hit me," he said.

Gil felt a thrill when he said that. It reminded him of legends he had learned, of songs he had heard, of Steve McQueen movies. It was the kind of simple, daring statement that made America great.

But Bobby didn't get it, because he said, "Why would I want to hit you? You saved my kid's life."

His obtuseness maddened Gil, but he kept it inside. "I meant hit my pitching."

Bobby laughed out loud; Gil realized he must have been witty again. Bobby quickly stifled the laugh, putting his hand over his mouth, like a girl.

Gil's own hand was moving down his leg. He stopped it. "What's so funny?" he said.

"Nothing. Sorry. I'm used to guys challenging me, in bars and stuff, but no one ever challenged me to hit off them."

"That's what I'm doing," Gil said.

Bobby shrugged. "Okay, if you really want to, someday."

Gil rose. "Not someday. Now."

"Now?"

"Why not?"

"It's night, for one thing."

"So turn on the floods."

"And I don't even know what equipment I've got out here."

"Sounds to me like you're looking for excuses," Gil said.

Bobby drained his bottle, tossed it away. He rose too. "Sounds to me like you're calling me chicken."

They stared at each other. Yes, Gil thought: I've found the man inside, gotten to him, and he's like any other guy.

"Batter up," Gil said.

He went to the apartment over the garage to get Bobby's old glove, which he'd put under the bed. When he returned the floodlights were shining behind the house, and Bobby was standing on the lawn below the terrace, a bat in one hand, a bucket of balls in the other. They were at the foot of the slope; from there the lawn stretched flat to the beach.

Bobby handed him the bucket, motioned him toward the beach. "Pace off sixty feet," he said. "If any get by me, they'll just roll up the hill."

Gil paced off sixty feet, thinking: if any get by you. He turned, took a ball from the basket, toed an imaginary rubber. Bobby took his stance over an imaginary plate. The floods were on, but it wasn't like playing under big-league lights. The lawn was dark and shadowy. An advantage, Gil thought, that would compensate for his rustiness.

"All set?" Gil said.

"You've got the ball, Slugger."

Gil rotated the ball in his hand, got his grip, went into his windup. Smooth and strong, everything just right, the way his father had taught him. If only Boucicaut were catching. Hip turn, high leg kick, back bent, step, drive—and he whipped that four-seamer in exactly where he wanted it, high and tight.

At first, because of the way Bobby just stood there, Gil thought he was going to let it go by. Then, at the last instant, after the last instant, Bobby swung. So fast. Then came a crack like the trunk of an oak splitting, then a sizzling sound, then a long silence. And finally a distant splash, in the sea. Gil never saw the ball.

He looked at Bobby. Bobby was in his stance over the imaginary plate, silent, waiting, bat cocked. Gil picked up another ball. He remembered some of the great pitches he had thrown, fastballs over the outside corner, curves that made batters bail out before ducking over the plate, that wonderful knuckler he'd fed Pease with the game on the line. And with all that to back him up, he went into his windup, smoother and stronger now, if anything, and threw another fastball, a blazing fastball, surely the hardest he had ever thrown, this one low and outside—but too low and too outside to be a strike. And again, despite having seen what he'd just seen, Gil was sure Bobby was going to let it go by, possibly didn't even see it. And again, when it was too late, Bobby swung. And again, that terrifying crack, that sizzle, then the long silence, even longer this time, and the splash, even fainter.

He looked in at the batter. The batter was in his stance, bat cocked, absolutely still. Gil reached into the bucket, tried his curve, pulled the shade, broke off the sharpest curve he'd ever thrown, starting it right at Bobby's head. Crack. Sizzle. Silence. Splash.

Bobby, back in his stance, spoke. "That one had a little wiggle on it." he said.

The remark infuriated Gil. He dipped into the bucket, went into his motion—a big strong guy made all the stronger by his fury, and the Cuervo Gold—and threw the ball with all the force in his body straight at Bobby's head. Bobby leaned back a little, somehow swinging at the same time. Crack, and a sizzle that came much closer, an inch or two from Gil's ear; Gil felt his ear redden just from the sound.

Bobby was back in his stance before the splash, expressionless.

Gil, breathing hard although he'd only thrown four pitches, looked in the bucket. "No balls left," he said.

Bobby lowered his bat, came forward. "That was kind of fun," he said, extending his hand.

Gil ignored it. "Get more."

"There are no more. No hard feelings, huh, Curly? I'm a pro.

It would be like us having a lawn-mower race or something, I wouldn't stand a chance." He put his hand on Gil's shoulder.

Gil shook free. "You're saying I don't stand a chance?"

"C'mon, Curly. It's over. Shake hands."

Gil shook, but kept his hand limp. Limp, like three limp generations: his father, him, Richie; versus Rayburn's father, Rayburn, Sean.

"What was your father like?" Gil just blurted it.

"My old man?" said Bobby in surprise. "He's a high-school guidance counselor in San Jose."

"That doesn't make any sense."

"Nothing makes much sense at this hour, Curly. Let's get some sleep."

"I'm not tired."

Bobby laughed. "You sound just like Sean."

"I'm not at all like Sean. I'm like Richie."

"Who's Richie?"

"Nobody."

"C'mon, Curly. It's late, and tomorrow's a day game." Bobby put his arm around him. They walked up the slope toward the terrace. "Kind of fun though," Bobby said. "Listening for the splash. Lanz'll get a kick out of it."

Gil felt nothing but the thrower on his leg.

29

All the Sterns were poor sleepers, and Jewel was the worst. She left the ballpark at eleven-thirty, was home in bed by midnight, and then just lay there, eyes wide open. She thought about Bobby, and Sean, and Val, and Bobby again. She got up, had a glass of water and two Tylenol, in case the pressure behind her eyes blew up into a headache, and, while she was at it, swallowed a Vitamin E, in case some cell in one of her breasts was planning to mutate later that night. Then she went back to bed, rolled over, closed her eyes, and stayed awake.

Mr. Curly Onis. The name rang a bell, of course, but so distant. In her work she met a lot of people, heard a lot of names. Jewel had a good memory. She searched it now. The media rep in Chicago? The head grounds keeper in Oakland? That lawyer who worked with the umpires' union? All had names with C's and O's in them, but none was Curly Onis. Maybe the name didn't ring a bell at all, maybe it was a case of déjà vu. She found her eyes were open, closed them, rolled over.

Or maybe he was a ball player somewhere, a minor-leaguer. There were a lot of wonderful ball-player names— hadn't someone written a song composed of nothing but? Sure: "Van Lingle Mungo," by Dave Frishberg. Sometimes, when she couldn't sleep, she opened the *Baseball Encyclopedia*, which lay on the floor by her bed, and leafed through it, just reading the names.

Sometimes, when she couldn't sleep.

Jewel snapped on the light, grabbed the encyclopedia, whipped through the pages. And there he was, on page 1226 right above Edward Joseph Onslow, lifetime B.A. .232: Manuel Dominguez "Curly" Onis. One big-league at bat, a single, for the 1935 Brooklyn Dodgers. Batted 1.000. Jewel thought right away of John Paciorek, her favorite example of this kind of thing, and recalled the shtick she and Bernie had done about European movies. Curly Onis' case was even purer.

But having thought that, she didn't know what to think next. She switched off the light, lay down, monitored her systems. They were all humming away at mid-morning speed. She got up, went back to the bathroom, drank another glass of water, swallowed another Vitamin E. Jewel had a phone in her bathroom, dating from a long-ago decision to live a little. She stared at it for a while. Then she picked it up and dialed Bobby Rayburn's home number.

One ring and a microsecond of the next. Then Bobby said: "Hello?"

His voice was thick and sleepy, and very near. The sound did something to her.

"It's me," she said.

"Oh." Pause. "It's kind of late." In the background, Jewel heard Val—she hoped it was Val—say, "Who is it?" She hoped it was Val? Good God.

"I know the time," Jewel said, "so obviously it's important. I just looked up Curly Onis in the *Baseball Encyclopedia*."

"He's there?"

"On page twelve twenty-six."

"Christ, he's really deteriorated."

"What?"

"He told me he was up for a cup of coffee, but I didn't believe him. Lots of guys say that."

In the background, Val said, "What's going on?"

"I'm not following you, Bobby," Jewel said.

"Having a cup of coffee. It means playing briefly in the show."

"I know what having a cup of coffee means, Bobby. I've been covering this stupid game since before you put on your very first jock strap. And don't forget to wear it." That last part just popped out; she couldn't help it. Think it, say it— like, see the ball, hit the ball—she was a natural, at running her mouth.

Bobby laughed. In the background, but louder now, and more insistent, Val said, "Who is it? Who's calling at this hour?" And more, but muffled as he smothered the receiver in his hand.

Then he said, "What was his record? With the Padres, right?"

"The Padres?" said Jewel. "Curly Onis played for the Dodgers in nineteen thirty-five. The Brooklyn Dodgers, Bobby."

"This is his son, then?" said Bobby. "I don't get it."

"I don't think—" Jewel began, and then came the soft but stress-inducing pulse of her call-waiting. "Hold on." She hit *flash.* "What is it?"

"Fred."

"What?"

"I'm at work."

"And?"

"You wouldn't believe this 'Between Brewskis' thing. Guess how many calls we've had so far."

"I don't give a shit. Was one of them Gil Renard?"

"Three hundred and seventeen," said Fred, giving her the information anyway. "And one was Gil. He didn't leave a last name."

"What did he say?"

"I can play it. Hang on." Jewel hung on. She heard a high-pitched whir, then: "This is Gil. Tell them thanks, but I stopped caring." Click.

"That's it?"

"Yup."

"When did he call?"

"About three-quarters of an hour ago. But I just got the slip. Things are backed up here tonight. Like I said, three hundred and—"

"Shut up. Did they trace it?"

"That's why I'm calling at this hour," Fred replied, offended, "if you'll give me half a chance."

"And?"

"This is the strange part. It might be a hoax or something."

"Why?"

"Because it came from a phone at Bobby Rayburn's house." Jewel hit *flash*. "Bobby?"

"Still here. Listen, can we continue this another—"

"Lock your door."

"What?"

"Call the cops. Don't go near a window."

"What are you talking about?"

"Gil Renard is in your house."

"Who's he?"

"Curly Onis. He killed Primo."

"Why would he do that?"

"That fight you had with Primo. Gil Renard was there."

"Fight?"

"Stop it, Bobby. You've got to be smart now. Don't go near him. I'm on my way."

"But what about Sean?"

"What about him?"

"He's in his bedroom."

Jewel had no immediate solution to that, and it had to be immediate, because the next instant she heard the phone drop to the floor of Bobby's bedroom.

"Bobby?" she said. "Bobby?"

She heard Val: "What's going on?"

And Bobby: "Get in the bathroom and lock the door."

"Why? What's happening?"

"Just do it."

Then there was silence, except for Val's whimpers. Call-waiting flashed again. Jewel switched lines.

"I got tired of holding," Fred said.

"Did you call the cops?"

"Sure. What do you take me for?"

She switched him off again. Now, at Bobby's house, there was nothing to hear at all, not even whimpering.

Bobby went into his walk-in closet, ripped out the long wooden clothes rail. Then he moved down the hall, crouched, on the balls of his feet, almost running. He entered the playroom, lit by the glow from the space-station console, and stopped at Sean's closed door. Not a sound came from the other side. That had to be because Sean was tired from the long day, and deep in sleep. Bobby threw open the door, snapped on the lights.

The bed was empty.

And neatly made.

Bobby's heartbeat rose in two stages, as he absorbed those facts. Something lay on the pillow. An empty bottle. He picked it up. Jose Cuervo Gold, but not quite empty. There was a rolled-up note inside. Bobby upended the bottle, tried to shake it out. It wouldn't come. He smashed the bottle on the floor, fumbled for the note in the broken glass.

Dear #11:
You've got a lot to learn about gratitude. Gone fishin'.

The Fan

P.S. Val and Chaz, sittin' in a tree.

Bobby ran outside, down to the beach. The moon had risen and he could see quite well. No one was fishing. "Sean," he called. "Sean." There was no answer.

Bobby ran around the house to the garage. The landscaping truck was gone. He went up to the apartment. The door was open. There was nothing inside but the fishing pole.

He went back into the house, back to Sean's room. It was all real: empty bed, neatly made, and shards of glass all over the floor. On the way back to the master suite, he saw the message on the space-console screen: "Nice job, Vice-Admiral Sean! Save game (Y/N)?"

He rapped on the bathroom door.

"Bobby?"

"Open up."

Val opened the door, then stood trembling, arms crossed over her breasts. He handed her the note. She read it, looked up, and said: "What did you expect, after all those years you've been screwing around?"

A moment passed before he understood what she was talking about. "I couldn't care less," he said.

"Clearly."

"About you and Wald, I mean. Do what you like. The point is he's taken Sean."

"Curly has?" She looked down at the note. "But we couldn't have been more grateful," she said. "We gave him a job."

"It has nothing to do with that."

"Then what?"

"I knew this was going to happen," Bobby said. "I just knew it."

"What have you done?" she said.

He reached out to touch her shoulder. She flinched away.

Bobby went into the bedroom and saw the phone, lying on the floor. He picked it up. "Jewel?"

"Let's have it."

"He's taken Sean."

"Goddamn it."

"I knew something bad was going to happen to him," Bobby said. "I've known since day one."

"Grow up," Jewel said, and then came a click and a dial tone. Bobby saw blue lights flashing through the trees. He hurried outside.

Hanging up on people left and right, thought Jewel as she threw on some clothes: wielding the phone like a goddamn club, in mid-season form. She took the elevator down to the underground garage, got into her car, and started driving north. She came to the exit that would lead her to Bobby's, and kept going.

The needle quivered at ninety, crept higher. Jewel sat on the edge of her seat and clutched the wheel, hanging on more than controlling the car, but she didn't slow down. There was little traffic; she examined every car she passed. What model was she looking for? She didn't know. She eased off the pedal to call Bobby for the information, and got a busy signal.

After that she tried Claymore. It took her some time to bully his home number out of the night man at his station. Claymore answered, not as quickly as Bobby had, but just as throatily. This time it did nothing for her.

"Jewel Stern," she said. "Gil Renard's on the loose. You'd better get out to that cemetery."

"How do you know he's going there?"

"That's where he does his burying, isn't it?"

He gave her directions.

It was still night when Jewel drove into the little town, found the cemetery, stopped the car. She stepped out, into what she thought at first was complete silence. Then she heard a breeze in the tree tops, an animal scurring on dried leaves, a mosquito's tiny whine. It bit her on the neck.

Jewel walked into the cemetery. Moonlight illuminated the names on the tombstones, all non-ethnic, unless French counted as ethnic. She hadn't been in a cemetery since her father's funeral, a horrible convocation of nosy parkers, almost all of them answering to ethnic names at one time or other in their lives, almost all of them calling her Janie.

Tombstones: Pease, Laporte, Spofford, Cleary, Bouchard. Renard, R. G. A sudden light dazzled her eyes.

"That you?" said a voice. Claymore.

They sat behind the tombstone of Renard, R. G. Claymore shut off his torch. Jewel's night vision, what was left of it, returned. A mosquito whined in her ear. She slapped at it.

" They're not bad this year," Claymore said. "Pollution's maybe getting to them at last, thank God."

Jewel glanced at her watch. "He should have been here by now."

"Maybe he's not coming," Claymore said. "He could be anywhere. People get around these days. Two years ago we busted a guy from Djibouti. I'd never heard of it."

"They don't play ball in Djibouti."

"Pardon?"

"Nothing." She turned to him. He pushed his glasses higher

on his nose. In his other hand, she noticed, he held a gun. "You played ball with him."

"That's right."

She checked her watch again. "What kind of a player was he?"

"The star. I told you. Him and Boucicaut. They were the biggest kids in town back then, and they could both hit a ton. And Gil had a cannon for an arm."

"And what position did you play, Sergeant Claymore?"

"Shortstop."

"Batting first, right?" She could picture him, a speedy little red-haired kid with freckles.

"Ninth, actually," said Claymore. "I could never hit much. Astigmatism in both eyes. And I was too slow to lead off anyway."

"This was Little League?"

Claymore nodded.

"How far did he go?"

"Go?"

"In baseball."

"That was it, to my knowledge. The high school had already dropped it a year or two before. This was after they closed the mill. We had baseball again for a while during the Reagan years, but now it's gone."

"But you still have Little League?"

"Haven't had new uniforms in five years, but, yeah, we've still got Little League."

They went silent. Jewel slapped at a few more mosquitos, checked her watch. "Something's wrong."

"It's a big world," Claymore said.

She was starting not to like him. If he mentioned Djibouti again, there was a danger she would let it show.

He cleared his throat. "Tell me," he began, "how is it that you, you know, a woman, got so interested in base—"

Jewel held up her hand. "Where's the field?"

"Field?"

"The Little League field."

"Amvets."

"Is that where they've always played?"

"Always?"

"You. Gil. Boucicaut. Is that where you played?"

"Yes," he said. "No need to shout at me."

She was already on her feet. "Let's go."

"I don't—"

She grabbed him by the collar and pulled him up.

"What are you doing?" Sean said.

"Digging for worms," Gil replied, standing knee-deep in the hole he'd dug under home plate. "Need worms for fishing."

"Found any yet?" asked the boy, kneeling by the hole and peering in.

"No." Gil could have done it right then, lifted the spade and just done it, but the hole wasn't deep enough, and he didn't want to linger after it was over. Just because it was logical and right didn't mean it would be easy. He went over the logic: how he'd sacrificed so much—his career, Richie, Primo—that the world was tilting crazily and the balance had to be restored. Plus, Bobby had to be taught a lesson about team play. And what had become of the hop on his fastball? All very clear. But that didn't make it easy.

"The mosquitos are biting me," Sean said.

Gil hit a soft layer, began tossing up rapid spadefuls. "Smack 'em," he said.

Sean smacked his cheek. "Look at the blood, Curly." He held out his hand. Gil, now up to his waist, looked. There was a streak of blood on the boy's cheek too. Gil almost puked.

"Can't you stop interrupting?" he said.

The boy backed away a little. Five more spadefuls, Gil decided. One, two, three, fo—

"When's my daddy meeting us?"

Gil paused, looked at his watch. Dirt covered the face. "Soon," he said.

"And my mommy?"

"She's not coming. Your mother's a whore."

The boy started crying.

"What are you crying about? You don't even know what it means."

"I do. Like on MTV." He cried harder. The sound was unbearable. It was hard to think of him as a potential big-league star when he was carrying on like that. "I want to go home."

"Soon, soon." Four, five. Gil stopped digging. "Here's a big fat one," he said. "Have a look."

The boy didn't move. "I don't want to go fishing. I want to go home." He glanced around. "It's night," he said.

"Best time for fishing, I told you," Gil said, and grabbed his arm.

"What are you doing to me, Curly?"

"Showing you the big fat worm." With his free hand, Gil got a good grip on the spade handle, started to raise it.

A light flashed on near the first-base dugout, blinding him. He had to drop the spade to shield his eyes.

A man said: "Let the boy go, Gil."

Gil tightened his grip. "Claymore? Is that you?"

"Let him go, Gil. I'm aimed right at you."

Gil tried to see beyond the glare. He picked out one shadow, maybe two. "Did I ever thank you for that play you made at short?"

"I don't know what you're talking about, Gil. Let him go."

"A lucky play, but still." He raised his right foot, found a toehold halfway up the inside of the hole, in easy reach.

"We can reminisce later, Gil. Let him go."

"Why would I want to reminisce with you?" Gil said. "We both know you couldn't carry my jock."

"Never said I could, Gil. I was a big fan of yours. Just let him go."

Gil let go. Had Claymore really been a fan? He hadn't known. Perhaps there'd been others. Too late.

Sean stood still, by the edge of the hole.

"Come here, son. I'm a policeman. I won't hurt you."

Sean didn't move.

Somewhere behind the light a woman said, "Sean."

"Mommy?" He took a step toward the light, then another. The beam wavered off Gil and onto the boy. Gil whipped out the thrower and hurled it at the glaring disc.

The beam changed directions wildly, trying different points of the compass, finally coming to rest pointing straight up at the stars. Pupils dilated, Gil couldn't see a thing. He felt for the surface of the ground, started clawing out of the hole.

Jewel crouched over Sergeant Claymore, saw a knife stuck deep in his throat, and no life in his eyes. She ran onto the field, grabbed Sean, swung him around, and took off the other way, carrying him in her arms.

She ran, out through the gate Claymore had unlocked in the chain-link fence, onto a path, silvered in the moonlight. As she passed under the arched Amvets sign that led to the road, she heard him coming.

Jewel went right past her parked car. She didn't trust herself to get them both in and start it in time. She fled down a street lined with dark houses, the boy in her arms. Footsteps pounded closer.

"Put me down," Sean said. "I'm fast."

But Jewel wouldn't put him down. She came to a crossroads, saw the main drag, and a blue light shining a block and a half away. Now she heard nothing but her own panting breath, did nothing but try to go faster. The blue light: POLICE. Jewel banged open the door.

The night man, dozing at his desk, jerked his head up in surprise.

Jewel slammed the door and rammed the bolt home. Rising, the night man wiped drool off his chin.

"Even Mommy runs better than that," Sean said. But he was in no hurry to be put down.

30

Gil awoke from a forge dream, drenched in sweat. He looked out the front window of the bus, saw the towers of the city in the distance, and a bright blue sky that hurt his eyes. He went back to the bathroom, splashed water on his face, took stock.

He had the clothes he wore, $217.83, an old Kwikpik lottery ticket he didn't remember buying, and the thrower, on his leg. He'd lost the knapsack full of knives in the darkness. It didn't matter. He was all set.

Inside the bus station, Gil bought a cup of coffee and had the clerk check his lottery ticket. The clerk ran it through the machine. "Won a free ticket," he said. "Want to stick with the same number?"

"Forget it," Gil told him, and walked out.

He followed downtown streets he'd known for years. They seemed unfamiliar. Not new—there was none of the excitement of being in a new place—just strange. He passed Cleats.

A sign in the window read: CLOSED TILL FURTHER NOTICE. SPACE FOR RENT. And suddenly Gil knew what was different. For the first time, the city's impermanence was laid bare to his eyes. It would all soon be gone.

Gil went into a bar near the ballpark. An old bar, dark and grim. Even now, not long before game time, it was almost empty. Gil was hungry. He had a steak sandwich and a slice of deep-dish apple pie. But he drank nothing, not even the water that came with the meal. He had lost his thirst.

The TV over the bar played soundlessly. Gil watched highlights from an old World Series that he remembered well. But the colors were off, the haircuts ridiculous: almost like a satire of the game. The plays had lost their meaning. Would the games they played now be like that in twenty years—so bleached and blurred, compared to his memories?

A truck commercial appeared on the screen, followed by a beer commercial. After that came a reporter, standing in front of the arched Amvets sign at the old ball field; the path under the arch was now barred by a strip of yellow police tape. Then a still picture of Bobby Rayburn appeared, followed by one of Sean, cutting a birthday cake. After that came footage of a body being loaded into an ambulance, and of Jewel Stern ducking into a squad car and driving off; and then his own picture—his company ID photo—with the words "Gilbert Marcel Renard" in big letters underneath. Gil ate the last bite of deep-dish apple pie, paid his bill, adding a ten-dollar tip—the biggest, as a percentage, he had ever given—and left.

The game had already started by the time Gil reached the ballpark. He wore sunglasses and a Sox cap, carried a clipboard, a large cardboard box taped securely shut, and a ballpoint behind his ear. There were cops at the ticket windows and at every gate, and a sniper on the roof of the press box. A man with a radio to his ear hurried by.

"Some doubt about whether Rayburn would play today, Bernie."

"He's out there in center field, Norm. And I've never seen security this tight at . . ."

The sound faded. Gil walked around the corner to the unmarked door and knocked.

"Who is it?" called a voice.

"Package for Socko," Gil replied.

The door opened. The old red-faced man in the red blazer peered out.

"Urgent," said Gil. "It's a new foot."

The old man reached for the cardboard box.

"He's got to sign for it," Gil said.

"I can sign."

"No way. I almost got canned doing that once."

"But he's on the field."

"I'll wait. He'll be taking his break at the end of the third inning, won't he?"

The old man squinted. "You know him?"

"Sure. He gets all his stuff from us."

"Thought you looked familiar," the old man said, and he stepped aside to let Gil pass.

The old man closed the door, made sure it was locked, then led Gil down the corridor. As they came to the door of Socko's dressing room, Gil said, "I'll just wait in here."

"Don't you want to watch while you're waiting?"

"Baseball's not my game," Gil said.

The old man continued down the hall. Gil went into the dressing room, closed the door, laid the package on the dressing table beside the bottles of mineral water. He heard a distant roar. Socko's dressing room shook all around him.

Time passed. There were a few more roars, more shaking, then quiet. Gil stood against the wall by the door.

It opened. Socko hurried in, tore off his yellow head, made for the dressing table. He grabbed a bottle of mineral water and drank greedily, head tilted up, face bathed in sweat. He had just noticed the package when Gil stepped forward and cut his throat.

Everything took much longer than Gil had imagined: stripping off the Socko costume; getting the body to stay hidden under the dressing table, with no hands or feet slipping out; putting on the costume. Once inside the costume, he strapped the sheath around his right wrist, stuck the thrower inside, and donned the huge three-fingered hand. Then he pulled on the grinning yellow head and went out, almost stumbling over his clodhopper feet.

The old man in the blazer was coming down the corridor. "What's the matter?" said the old man. "It don't fit?"

"Fits fine," Gil said, his voice muffled by the mask.

"Where's the delivery guy?"

"Gone," Gil said, pointing a cartoon hand toward the exit.

"I'll just make sure it's locked," the old man said, and he kept going.

Gil walked to the end of the corridor, turned up a ramp, and suddenly emerged into blazing daylight, standing in the aisle behind the box seats that fronted the home dugout. It was all perfect, perfect as the first time he'd ever seen it: the red dirt, the green grass, the white lines, the tiny cloud of powder rising from the back of the mound, where the pitcher had just dropped the rosin bag. And the uniformed players, dazzling, like perfect knights. Gil felt dizzy.

"Hey, there's Socko. Wave to Socko, honey."

Gil moved down the steps toward the dugout.

"I waved, Ma. Why didn't Socko wave back?"

"I don't know."

"He's working to rule," said someone else.

And a beery voice from high in the stands called, "Hey, Socko, sit on this."

Of course, it wasn't perfect, he had to remember that. It was all fake, the players the most fake of all. Gil climbed onto the dugout, as he had seen Socko do many times. "Hey, Socko, do the jerk."

Gil scanned the faces—just once, he wouldn't do that again—and tried to prance around.

"Socko looks like he's in the bag," someone said. Laughter spread from row to row.

It was hot inside the costume. The sheath on Gil's arm was slick with sweat. On the field, Zamora stepped up to the plate, and Lanz came out of the dugout, right under Gil's clodhopper feet, and moved into the on-deck circle.

Up in the press box, someone said, "Fax for you, Jewel." A sheet of paper wafted down beside her notebook. It was from the editor at the *Times Magazine.*

> In awe of your adventures last night. You've single-handedly raised the status of all us ink-stained wretches. Unfortunately, this really takes Rayburn out of the magazine-profile category and puts him on the front page. Let's try again on something else, shall we? Kill fee follows.

Jewel balled it up and tossed it back over her shoulder. "What's that?" said Norm.

"The end of my journalism career."

"Huh?" said Norm. "What do you call this?"

"Hell if I know," said Jewel.

Far below, Zamora singled off the third-baseman's glove, and Lanz moved toward the plate.

"Hey, Socko, you're stinkin' up the joint."

Gil, breathless in the yellow mask, saw Zamora safe at first, heard the voices. He realized he was supposed to celebrate the base hit. Pumping his three-fingered hands in the air, he tried prancing again, but tripped over his clodhopper feet and fell hard on the dugout roof, face down, yellow head hanging over the edge. Laughter rose around him, rolled through the stands.

"Son of a bitch earns his money," someone said.

Bobby Rayburn came out of the dugout, the top of his batting helmet a foot from Gil's eyes. Gil froze, right there on the dugout roof, his heart pounding on the cement. Boyle, sitting on the bench, saw his yellow head hanging there and said, "Get the fuck out of here."

Gil drew back, rolled over, sat up, took a few deep breaths. He gazed out at the field and all its shining colors, and the players, so dazzling. He gazed at Bobby Rayburn in the on-deck circle, swinging that swing, full of grace. Gil rose and walked—no prancing, but walking with dignity—to the home—plate end of the dugout roof

Lanz laid a surprise bunt down the first-baseline and beat it by a step. Rayburn knocked the lead donut off his bat, knocked the dirt off his spikes, and stepped toward the plate. The fans rose and cheered. The dugout roof trembled with the sound. And even down inside, the voices of his teammates called out, "All right, Bobby." Bobby kept his head down and stepped into the batter's box. I've made you a hero, Gil thought. He slipped out of the cartoon hands and dropped down off the dugout roof, onto the field. Even through the clodhopper feet, the grass felt special, like the ideal of grass. It made everything that was about to happen right, like a ceremony.

In the press box, Norm said, "What's with Socko?"

And a VP of something or other said, "That fucker. If he goes up there and plants a kiss on Rayburn, he's fired. He's been warned a thousand times about this kind of bullshit."

Down on the field, Socko kept going. He drew even with the umpire, about twenty feet behind him, turned, and took a step toward the plate.

Jewel rose. "Bobby?" she said. Then she saw Socko's yellow hands, lying in the grass. She leaned out the open window of the press box, leaned as far as she could. "Bobby," she called at the top of her lungs. "Bobby."

Crouched behind the plate, neither the umpire nor the catcher saw Socko. Bobby, digging in, didn't see him either. Socko broke into a clumsy run. Jewel saw something shine bright in his hand.

"Bobby."

Down on the field, Bobby's head shifted. He saw Socko coming, started to turn toward him. The umpire started to turn too, started to raise his hand. Socko, still running forward, drew back his throwing arm.

What happened next was clear only on the slo-mo replay. Socko threw a knife, which spun half a rotation and flew point-first at Bobby's chest. At almost the same instant, Bobby stuck out his bat, as though he were trying to bunt a high, inside pitch. The blade sank deep into the center of the barrel, slightly below the sweet spot.

Then there was a gunshot crack from the press-box roof, and another from much closer. Socko fell, and cops rushed out of the stands.

Gil didn't want to think about the implications of what he'd just seen. He wanted to lie in that perfect grass, safe from all the noise and yelling, safe inside the mascot skin. But too soon the yellow head came off, came off with a sweaty popping sound, and as it did his mouth filled with blood. The first thing he saw was Bobby Rayburn looking down at him.

Gil spoke.

"I can't hear you," Bobby said.

Gil cleared his throat—it took all of his remaining strength—and tried again. "You're a bum," he said.

31

"Well, Norm, what can you say?"

"About a season like that, Bernie? I wouldn't know where to begin."

"Why not start with the Series?"

"Unbelievable. In case you've been on some other planet, folks, this team—"

"—dead last on the Fourth of July—"

"—has just swept the World Series in four games, with last night's—"

"—this morning's—"

"—right, the bags under my eyes have bags—this morning's four-to-three ten-inning classic out on the coast."

"And Bobby Rayburn—"

"—two-run double in the eighth ties it, solo home run in the tenth brings that long-sought championship home. And that catch he made in the bottom of the tenth, highway rob—"

"Whoa, Norm. What I was trying to bring up was Rayburn's bombshell announcement in the winning locker room.

"The retirement thing? Do you believe that?"

"He seemed pretty serious,"

"After a season like that? I'm from Missouri."

"We're trying to get some comment from him, of course. He's said to be traveling right now and unreachable."

"But I'm sure our own Jewel Stern will have the inside dope."

"When she gets back from her brief vacation."

"Brief vacation?"

"Didn't Fred tell you? She called in late last night, early this morning, whatever. But, hey—don't you think she's earned it?"

"If anyone has. Whew. Don't need that espresso to get the blood going today, Bernie. The phone lines are lit up like Christmas trees. How about we take some calls? Here's Sal on the car phone. What's shakin', Sal?"